The Legend of Paks

The Legend of Paks

Earth and Shadow

David C. Smith

Rev. date: 03/03/2015

To order additional copies of this book, contact:
Xlibris
1-888-795-4274
www.Xlibris.com
Orders@Xlibris.com
702554

Prologue

The world known as Paks is controlled by humans, but it was not always that way. In ancient times Paks was a much different place. The world was abounding with magic and wonder. Three magical races, the Ignati, the Aerii and the Tellurians: known as the Magi, ruled over the land. The air was crisper, the sky was brighter; blue with the slightest hint of yellow, and the sounds of nature were heard no matter if you were walking through the dense foliage of the Shroud Forest or the vast sands of the Southern Desert. The blackness of night was illuminated by Paks' moons, the Three Guardians, known as Vala, Tula and Sola; raining a reddish hue across the land. This was known as the Emerald Ages. This was the age of the Magi.

The Three Magi used the flow of natural energy through Paks to control and use magic. By drawing that natural energy into their bodies they could manipulate it and expel it in any way they deemed fit. Each of the Magi was able to manipulate this energy in to a specific form. The Aerii, the Masters of the Sky, created wind through this energy, granting them incredible power. Using this power, an Aerious could topple houses, castles and mountains. The power of wind could crush, raze and slice through any object. They rode giant Eagles into battle like horses, summoning their powers from far above the heads of their enemies. Similar in form to a human, they were beautiful examples of why the Emerald Ages where such a wondrous time. Their hair mirrored the light blue hue of the Paksian sky and their movements were reminiscent of the Verturian Flatland Deer, an animal whose grace was unmatched by all other Paksian creatures. Like the eagles they rode, their bodies were light and sleek, a trait advantageous to a sky-bound warrior.

Able to produce fire, the Ignati were the most powerful of the three. Their physical features were as sharp and striking as the power they produced. Jet black hair was contrasted by the deep red of their eyes, changed over centuries of flaming energy flowing through their bodies. Burning anything in their path, there were none that could stand against them. Said to have been created in the beginning by the Almighty; Ignati were immortal beings. Their one weakness lay in their inability to have children. Some say this made them stronger, but I believe the bond of family can only strengthen one's heart.

Not every Magi was considered a shining example of peace. The Tellurians were the only grotesque impurity on the gem that was the Emerald Ages. Their power was simple, but strong. Instead of changing the natural energy into a different form, they focused it and sent it straight back to where it came from; nature. They controlled nature itself, from the great Everwood Trees down to the bare soil of Paks itself. Even their bodies looked as if they crawled from the deepest regions of Paks' earth. Though they were human in shape, a Tellurian's skin was like deep brown scales and as rough as the bark of the Holicone trees. At birth, a Tellurian was given the ability to transform into another living creature, be it a bird, a fish or a wild dog. There was one Tellurian that was given an even more amazing transformation ability. The Tellurians took the birth of this Magi as a sign from the Almighty that it was finally time for them to rise from the soil and take control. The next thirty-five years were known as the Magi Wars.

For decades the monstrous Tellurians crusaded across the land shouting their prophet's name with zealous fury. From a young age, this Tellurian absorbed this religious fanaticism and thus saw himself as a god. This child deity was perfectly aware of his power over his people and he cultivated that power in order to fulfill his prophecy. He threw his people headlong into the fire and wind that stood in his way.

In order to stop the tireless onslaught of the Tellurians, the Ignati and Aerii banded together. The Tellurians' numbers were great, and even the combined deadliness of fire and wind could barely cut through the armor created by the Tellurians' religious fervor. Each side was ground to dust over the bloody decades to such a point that it was unclear if there would be a single soul left.

We humans, who at this time were just simple creatures eking out a meager existence on Paks, were caught in the middle of this deadly feud. Unable to feel the flow of natural energy, we were bound to an un-magical world and thus ignored by the more powerful Magi. What we lacked in magic, we made up for with ingenuity and a desire to stay alive. In order to protect ourselves from the hurricane of magical energy flowing through Paks during those times, we created a weapon. This weapon had such a power that it could stand against the strongest of the Magi.

Before we could use this weapon against the Tellurians, the war came to a sudden end. It was said that both sides fought till the final two souls remained, and with their last ounce of strength they both fell. No Magi has been seen in the land of Paks since. We were free to build our empire. The Emerald Ages were over. The natural energy that flowed through Paks was still there, but there was no one left to feel it. The air wasn't as crisp, the bright sky faded and the sounds of nature were so faint that you had to stand perfectly still just to hear the chirp of a cricket. It seemed that the natural world of Paks went into a deep slumber; waiting for the time when the Magi would come again.

-Excerpt from "*Chronicles of the Emerald Ages*", by Alexander Pierson,
1st Chief Historian of the Valorian Historical Society.

The world known as Paks is controlled by humans; but there are some that believe it is time for a change.

1

Bishop Kaiser was running. From what he was unsure, but he was running. Like a frightened prey running from the wild predator, Bishop stumbled as he sprinted through the foggy trees. Fresh blood dripped from the cut above his left eye and sweat poured down his face, spreading the blood and preventing the wound from closing.

The forest floor was riddled with roots from the ancient Gregormores and the mist made it hard to see more than a few feet in front of him. Bishop did not know what was chasing him, but after what he had just witnessed, he knew the only thing he could do was run. Fighting back was not an option. It was as if the forest itself was coming after him. There were no footsteps following him, no panting breaths behind him, but he knew they were there. Tirelessly in pursuit, the predator was not letting this prey get out of its sight.

Bishop did not know how much longer he could keep up this suicidal pace, but he knew what the alternative was. The mist began to clear and he briefly felt a slight breeze touch his face. As quickly as Bishop was running, he quickly came to a stop. He watched as debris from under his feet tumbled over the edge of the cliff in front of him. Even with the danger behind him, Bishop did not think leaping from a cliff was a reasonable escape from the pain that was sure to ensue when his enemy found him. Or maybe it was.

Knowing that it was all over, Bishop brushed off his coat and turned to face his attackers. Even in the face of death, the Supreme Regis must not show fear. The blood from his eye had begun to stain the collar of his uniform, and his sweat had soaked through his outer coat. His coat was so torn and bloodied from the chase that he removed it, throwing it over the edge.

What good was it now? he thought.

He closed his eyes and breathed, trying to calm himself, but it was no use. One cannot truly be calm with the knowledge that they are about to die. He drew his sword and waited. The sword was more for show. There was no part of him anymore that believed that he could fight back and survive. It frightened him that he had completely lost the courage to fight.

The forest was quiet. Not a single sound could be heard as Bishop intently waited, but he knew they were out there. Suddenly, there was a rustle, and out of the mist sprang a wolf. Its silvery gray fur was rigid with anger as it came sliding to a halt in front of Bishop. As if examining his prey before the kill, it paced back and forth without averting its piercing gaze from Bishops stoic eyes. It let out a long melodic howl. Such a howl would make any man cower in fear, but at the moment, Bishop had no more reason to fear. He was more at a loss; wondering what the wolf was doing. *Was it alerting the rest of the pack? How many more were there?* Bishop wondered.

What came though did not have fur, nor did it alert its arrival with the sound of footsteps. There was just the slight sound of wing beats and a crow, the color of deep endless black, softly landed on the head of the wolf. Bishop's confusion made his calm outer appearance waver. His forehead, which was just recently dried, began to moisten again with the return of fear. Bishop, though, was royalty and had spent many years learning how to keep a dignified and fearless appearance, even under horrifying circumstances.

Three more wolves came through the fog and stopped just behind the other. The crow turned its head as if to acknowledge the arrival of the wolves. It gave a soft caw and the four wolves coiled in preparation to attack. Then, a bellowing human voice came through the mist, "Not yet, Corvus!"

The sound of a familiar, discernible voice calmed, yet terrified, Bishop. The voice was human, but what came out of the trees was far from it. It walked on two legs surely, but its skin was that of rough brown scales. These scales protruded slightly, almost like feathers, and its frame was slim yet had a powerful look to it. Staring right at Bishop as it talked, the creature spoke with a royal tone and a slight Brivan accent. In fact it sounded remarkably similar to him and it was frightening. "How many times must I tell you Corvus, this one must stay alive... for now," the creature said, staring intently at Bishop.

Bishop's mind was reeling. His face showed nothing but calm, but he was far from it.

"Speechless, Your Highness? I do not blame you," said the creature.

Stuttering slightly, Bishop forced himself to speak. "Who are you? What are you?"

The creature smiled at Bishop's obvious fear and confusion. "I am disappointed. I would think that the Supreme Regis would be a bit more educated. Did you nap through your history lessons? Did your father not tell you any bed time stories?"

The creature turned back to the wolves and the crow. The crow fluttered its wings and lifted off from the head of the wolf. As it hovered there in midair something happened. The crow began to glow ever so slightly, and its shape began to change. It began to grow and its wings lengthened. Its short boney legs became longer and more pronounced. Its feathers shortened and became thicker; hard to the touch. It then fell lightly onto the ground, pushed off from its knees and came to full height. As if it had been cramped in a small space for too long, it shook itself loose. Bishop, astounded, looked back at the first creature.

"Have you finally figured it out, or do I need to show you another example?" the first creature said to Bishop.

Bishop knew what they were, but he couldn't bring himself to say it. He remembered hearing about them in stories and legends. They couldn't possibly be here, in front of him. "You are Tellurians," he said, almost in a whisper.

Smiling with a haunting grin, the first creature laughed slightly and clapped with an obvious ironic undertone. "Bravo, Your Highness. Bravo. I knew that you were not a complete fool."

The rest of the wolves all transformed as well, and now Bishop was surrounded by the devilish looking creatures. The creature that was originally in the form of a crow took a few steps forward.

"Can we not finish this, Master? I smell his fear and it delights me."

The first creature held up a cautious hand. "Not yet, Corvus. I have been waiting for this moment for a long time. I do not want to rush it." It turned back to Bishop; the smile gone from its face. "You have many questions, I can tell. You are probably wondering how we could possibly be here."

"You're all supposed to be gone. Dead after the Magi Wars," Bishop blurted, cutting the creature off.

"That is where you are wrong. You humans, out of fear, made up lies to cover up the truth. We were never dead; just in hiding."

Bishop began to relax slightly. Now knowing who his pursuer was caused his fear to begin to mitigate, but he knew he was still in grave danger. He felt his desire to live rush back into him and he began to look for a way out. "Hiding from what?" he said, trying to stall for time.

The Tellurian, Corvus, angered by the comment, lunged towards Bishop. "Corvus!!" the second creature yelled. "I said calm yourself!"

"But Grand Master," Corvus pleaded angrily.

In an attempt at confidence and to get his foe off guard Bishop smiled. "Grand Master. That is an interesting name. Is that your title? Are you leader for these creatures?"

The Grand Master began to show some annoyance at his overzealous counterpart. He took a few steps towards Bishop, forcing him closer to the cliff. Now about ten yards away, the Grand Master spoke with complete seriousness. "My name is of no importance to you, human; not where you are going. And we were not hiding from someone or something, but rather waiting in secret for a particular moment. It was been centuries, but it will be our time once again."

Attempting to hold his ground and keep his new found confidence Bishop spoke with a royal, heavy tone. "So you are here to kill me? Why wait such a long time for such a minuscule act such as this? You will accomplish nothing from my death."

"Ha!" The Grand Master laughed boisterously. The ground seemed to shake slightly. The rest of the Tellurians also laughed. "We have not waited, in secret, for the past five hundred years just to kill you." The Grand Master walked forward and stood within a step of Bishop. Bishop held his ground as the Grand Master looked down on him from his seven foot frame. He was so close Bishop could feel the heat from his breath as he spoke. "Killing you would accomplish nothing, we know. Do not take us for fools. Another one of you humans will just take your place."

"Whatever you intend to do, you will not succeed. We humans are not as weak as we once were," Bishop asserted.

"I know Your Highness. I am counting on it."

After a short second of contemplation, "You are after the throne," responded Bishop. There was a hint of question in his response. "You intend to supplant me. But how?"

"I have my ways, human. That is of no concern to you, though." As he spoke, the Grand Master lifted a hand and some small sticks rose from the forest floor. He tensed his arm and the outer layers of the sticks exploded away, leaving long sharp needles of wood. "Corvus, would you do the honors?"

Corvus walked forward with a devilish grin. Without averting his eyes from Bishop, Corvus reached out and snatched the needles. Bishop grabbed the hilt of his sword, ready to draw if necessary. Corvus took the needles and licked them, sticking his tongue out like a reptile. He handed the needles back to the Grand Master and took a step back.

"You see, even if we kill you, because of me you will live on," said the Grand Master as he looked at the needles in his hand. Then, without warning, he threw the needles at Bishop with tremendous speed.

Bishop quickly drew his sword and expertly sliced the first two needles in two fluid motions, but the third struck him in the chest. He gasped for air and his eyes widened in shock. He dropped his sword and pulled the needle out. As his vision began to blur he looked up the Grand Master standing there smiling.

Bishop stumbled backwards towards the cliff edge. He tried to summon the strength to stay standing, but his life was quickly draining from him. He stumbled again, but this time his foot caught a rock and he fell backwards. Corvus reached forward to try to stop him, but Bishop fell out over the edge.

To Bishop it felt like he was falling through water, time slowing all around him. A rush of wind blew up from the valley below, rustling his clothing as he fell and the mist swirled around him. The blurred forms of the Tellurians began to disappear from sight as he fell. His mind went blank as he stared up towards the sky. The final thing he saw was Corvus' face peering at him as he fell; a look of fear on the Tellurian's face.

The Grand Master walked up to the edge and looked over at the fog covered valley below. He looked over towards Corvus. "Find him. Confirm that he is dead."

"But Master, There is no way that he is alive," stuttered Corvus; obviously fearing an angry retaliation from his master. "Not even a Magi could survive such a fall."

"Find him!"

Corvus quickly took a few steps and jumped off the cliff, transformed, and flew away into the blackness.

"Sir, there are two humans approaching," said one of the wolf Tellurians. "It seems they were following the Supreme Regis."

The Grand Master stood silently for a few seconds, still looking into the fog. "Let them come. We can use them." He turned back towards the other Tellurians. "Leave. Go and tell the others that it has been done. We head for Valoria."

The Tellurian nodded and all of the creatures transformed back into their wolf forms and ran off into the forest. The Grand Master again turned and continued looking into the shrouded valley below. His eyes suddenly flashed a human-like dark blue as they peered through the mist.

2

One Month Earlier

𝒯rumpets were sounding in the streets of Valoria. The capital city of Briva was full of noise and jubilation. A parade was being thrown for the coronation of the new Supreme Regis. Large, colorful floats carrying dozens of family and friends of the royal family, along with a number of royal servants, rolled down the cobblestone pavement, pulled by majestic Brivan Horses. The street leading up to the palace walls, large enough to have a legion of the Valor Forces march through it, was flooded with people to see the historic moment. Citizens were throwing paper confetti down onto the floats from high windows in the stone buildings along the parade path. Like snow, the confetti clung to people's hair.

Bishop Kaiser rode in the lead float, waving to his crazed Valorians. The coronation ceremony was finished and Bishop was now the Supreme Regis of Paks, so he had to look like a supreme ruler. He stood erect and strong, head held high, with a warm smile that made all Valorian women melt. His full length coat was made from Herousian leather, green with accents of gray, and lined with the dark grey fur of the Short Haired Mountain Fox. A bust of the legendary Hym'Shailan Dragon, part of the Kaiser family crest, was embroidered on the right breast of the coat. Dark blue eyes shone out brightly above a broad white smile and under a sharply cut head of ash blonde hair. The young Lady Kara sat in a throne just beside Bishop. She enjoyed watching her husband absorb the cheers of the crowd.

Soldiers were forced to hold back the crowd as citizens tried to force themselves through in an attempt to get near the new leader. On a lower tier of the float stood Farren Kaiser, Bishop's younger brother; a boy of sixteen. Farren was grinning from ear to ear as he watched the screaming people. He ran up and down the sides of the float waving to every man, woman and child, not able to keep himself still. He looked up at Bishop, who looked down at him and winked.

The float came to a halt at the base of the gate stairs. The stairs were so high that one could not even see the top of the wall surrounding the palace grounds from the base. They were built to force anyone paying homage to the Supreme Regis to walk the hundreds of steps and drop to their knees in exhaustion.

Bishop turned to the crowd and raised his hands to ask for silence. The chaotic sounds of the city instantly hushed, eagerly waiting for the Regis to speak. "I stand before you today not as your Prince, but as your Regis. The untimely death of my father and mother was a travesty not just to my brother and me, but all of Paks." He paused slightly as an image of his parents flashed in his mind. "But we can no longer dwell in the past. The best way to honor them is to carry on with our heads held high and our hearts at true peace."

Every citizen was so engrossed in the speech that there wasn't an eye that blinked or a mouth that took a breath. Bishop again paused, finding it difficult to speak of his late parents. Lady Kara stood and placed her hand on his back, reassuring him. He turned and smiled at his beautiful wife. Taking a deep breath he continued. "My father was a great Regis, and as a person there was none better, but I will assure you that I will do everything in my power to be even greater than he was. My father saw an amazing future for Paks, and now it is my job to see that we achieve it. I leave you now with the salute that my father created." Bishop stood straight and moved his right hand from his left arm, to his forehead and then to his heart. "Strength of arm, strength of mind, strength of heart," he said. Everyone in the crowd saluted as well.

Bishop than turned and ushered Kara back to their thrones. Once Bishop turned, the crowd again erupted in chaos. Farren climbed back to the top of the float and sat next to Bishop and smiled. "They love you brother," Farren said.

"So easily they all forget the past. It's as if father and mother never existed." Bishop continued to look out at the crowd.

Farren's smile faded slightly, but he held a reassuring look. "That's not true brother. They just choose to look to the future rather than be saddened by the past."

Bishop looked down at Farren and cracked a small smile. He put his hand on Farren's head, marring the teenager's wavy blonde locks.

"I do miss them, though," added Farren. "I wish they were here to see us."

"So do I. But they will always be with us, Farren; don't you worry. And, don't forget, we still have each other. Nothing can stop us, as long as we are together."

The two brothers smiled at each other and, for just a moment, they had forgotten about the death of their parents. For a moment, the future did not seem so uncertain and terrifying.

Several servants came running up next to the float with a palanquin, waiting to carry Bishop and his Lady up the stairs to the palace. Bishop looked down and held out a disapproving hand. "We will walk, thank you," he said.

He stepped down from the float and held out a hand to assist Kara. Farren leapt down from the side. Farren turned to start running up the long stairs.

"Pace yourself Farren, it's a long way," warned Bishop.

Farren turned, continuing to back pedal. "Don't worry brother; running is what I do best."

The sun was just peaking above the horizon as the shops of Valoria awakened. In the day time, Valoria was a hub of trade and commerce. Many traders came from all around Briva, as well as the outer sects of Fera and Layalta, to sell their goods in the capital city. Products such as exotic fruits from the Lusai Jungle near Caradice and soft Loci Tiger furs from the north were among the most precious goods being bartered and haggled for. The fruits, only found in the small remote jungle, were delicacies because of their sweet taste and supposed life extending abilities. The white and black spotted furs were worn by only the wealthiest of nobles because the Loci Tigers were extremely difficult to track and kill in the menacing frozen mountains.

Small wooden stands were erected in the crowded streets in front of the stone buildings to display the goods. Colorful cloth awnings covered the stands to not only attract customers but also to protect the goods from the beating sun. The mix of worldly aromas was an attack on the senses. The mix of citrus, cinnamon and other spices was almost disorienting. Anything you could want and desire could be purchased in the bazaar, but at a price.

Many citizens tried to arrive at the shops early, to avoid the largest crowds, but there truly was never a time when the streets were not bustling. Besides, when the crowds began to thicken, the shouts of bartering and the sounds of foreign musical instruments could be heard far across the city, and none could sleep. The eager customers were shoulder to shoulder as they walked to each stand, trying to find the best deals. Confrontations often broke out over prices, or the occasional theft. The thievery was limited, though, and could often be traced back to the same source.

Reme Tepal wandered through the crowd, but showed little interest in the array of goods around him. As he pushed his slender, young frame through the throng, an opening appeared and he tried to squirm his way through it. The crowd closed in and he bumped shoulders, falling to the ground. He looked up to see a plump Dash Hariton standing above him.

"Watch where you are going there pipsqueak," barked Dash.

Reme slowly rose to his feet and dusted himself off. Dash was about Reme's age, but of far different physical proportions. While they were both fairly short, Dash frequented the food carts in the bazaar, giving him a rounder frame. "Sorry fatty. I didn't have enough time to make the long journey around your waist line," countered Reme.

Dash stepped up to Reme and bumped him with his belly. "Sorry, but I do not think I heard you correctly. What did you just call me?"

Stumbling slightly from the bump, Reme regained himself and got into Dash's face. "So, you're fat and dumb, quite the unfortunate combination."

Dash was at a loss and could not find the words to form a comeback to the sharp-tongued Reme.

Their confrontation had begun to draw some attention and a small circle of people had formed around the duo. Not knowing what to say, Dash resorted to being physical, shoving Reme. Shouts began to erupt from the observers cheering each one on as they started to fight. The commotion attracted the attention of a store owner nearby.

"Hey hey hey! Cut it out you two," yelled Frank, as the store owner shoved his way through the crowd to the two boys. He pulled Reme off of Dash to stop the brawl. Reme was still kicking and screaming as Frank lifted him away. "Knock it off. You two are distracting my customers. I am getting sick of your rough housing around here. Do not make me get a patrolman over here again."

"Let go of me old man!" yelled Reme.

Farren, who had been observing from a side alley, snuck into Frank's now vacant stand. The stand had an array of jewelry from necklaces and bracelets studded with precious jewels, to metal rings. Farren snuck into the stand with one specific necklace in mind. He did not waste time browsing through the piles of jewels contemplating his decision; he knew what he wanted.

The necklace was simple, yet elegant. It was not pure gold, or studded with jewels, but just one single red Faryce stone hung from a thin string of horse hair. Farren struggled to reach the necklace, which hung from a hook atop the stand. He jumped, but only managed to jostle it. He began to hoist himself up onto the counter but his foot knocked over a display.

Frank, still holding Reme by the scruff of his shirt, turned to see Farren reaching for the necklace. Farren, realizing he'd been caught quickly reached up and grabbed his prize.

"Farren, you rascal! Get your hands away from my wares or I will cut them off." bellowed Frank. Frank reached into his worker's apron and pulled out a small wooden mallet and threw it at Farren. The mallet smashed into the wooden panel next to Farren's frightened eyes, causing jewelry to come crashing down around him.

Enraged, Frank tossed Reme aside and ran towards Farren, arms raised. "You better run you little thief! Don't you dare try to steal from me again. I will drag you straight back to your brother."

"Run Farren!" belted Reme, as he jumped to his feet. "Let's go big boy," Reme said to Dash.

All three boys made a break for it into the crowd of confused onlookers. Frank tried to give chase but, at his unfit and old age, he quickly gave up. The crowd was too thick and he just didn't have the same stamina he had as a young lad. As he stood, bent over and heaving for breath, Frank watched Farren disappear into the crowd.

Ecstatic and laughing, the three young thieves decided to stop their high-speed getaway. Frank was nowhere to be seen and it did not seem that any patrol guards were called upon. All in all, it was a successful heist. Away from the bazaar, in the morning hours, the city was much more peaceful. The boys had managed to make their way through the throngs of shoppers and into the residential district, where only a handful of citizens were walking the streets.

Out of breath, the hefty Dash pleaded for the others to stop. "Hey, I think we're safe. Let's stop here, I can barely breathe anymore."

Farren and Reme ground to a halt, still laughing. "That was amazing!" yelled Farren. "Did you see the look on Frank's face?"

"I can't believe he's still falling for it. You would think the old man would learn after a while," responded Reme.

Farren walked over to the heaving Dash and patted him on the back. "Look what we're doing to Dash. He can't handle it anymore," said Farren to Reme, with a smile on his face.

"All I'm asking is that we make plans that don't involve running so much. A little more thinking, a little less running," commented Dash, bent over and gasping for air. "Just a thought."

Reme and Farren both laughed at their out-of-shape friend. "If we're running so often, how are you not used to it by now?" asked Reme.

Dash finally caught his breath and stood up. "I wonder that every day."

Reme walked over to Farren and grabbed the necklace from his pocket. He held it up to the light to look at it. "This is perfect. She is going to love it."

"Are you finally going to talk to her then; the girl from the bazaar?" asked Farren. "What was her name again?"

"Valia. Her name was Valia," said Reme, sternly. "And of course I am going to talk to her. Why, you don't think I will?"

Farren looked over at Dash and they smile at their common skepticism.

"I don't care what you guys think," commented Reme, noticing their doubtful looks. "I'm going to do it this time."

Reme put the necklace into his pocket and ran off down the street. He turned around and yelled back. "Wish me luck!"

"I bet you five rin that he backs out again," snickered Dash out of the corner of his mouth.

"No bet. He's never going to do it," said Farren.

They both looked at each other and laughed as they turned and walked off down the street. The streets were beginning to crowd with the returning early morning shoppers from the bazaar. The jubilant voices of the shoppers talking about their new purchases began waking the late sleepers and they started to drag their drowsy selves into the city to get an overdue start on the day.

3

nestled in the center of the bustling capital, the palace grounds seemed out of place. Thousands of royal servants slaved over the vast array of greenery that graced the grounds to make sure they were pristine and worthy of royalty. Thick green grass covered every inch of the beautiful landscape and it was kept so flat it seemed like a tranquil green ocean. Beautiful Shroud Willows dotted the grounds near the few small ponds and towering Everwoods lined the pathway that lead from the front gate to the Palace doors.

Many buildings shared this beautiful garden with the Royal Palace including the stables and the Gallant building. The Gallant building housed, among other things, the smithy used to forge the Gallant's extensive array of weaponry and the large training room used by Valoria's Special Forces, the Gallants. The room was large enough to house a company of soldiers for training and had a vast array of weaponry along the walls and tables.

This early morning, though, the training room was not being used by a Gallant, but rather an exhausted Bishop Kaiser. His tight, sleek sparring uniform was drenched with sweat from hours of sword practice. Ironically, his dueling instructor was nearly passed out with exhaustion while Bishop casually walked over and grabbed a towel to wipe the sweat from his brow.

"You work Andre too hard, dear. Maybe you should take it a little easier on the poor man," called Kara from a couch on the far end of the room. She had been lying on the couch watching the two dueling for hours. Her long, chestnut hair flowed down over her shoulders and stood out against her light pink colored dress. Her voice echoed loudly against the stone walls.

Bishop tossed the drenched towel onto the table and picked up the sheath to his sword. He turned and smiled at his beautiful wife. "Don't take Andre too lightly; he wouldn't like it."

Andre forced out a laugh while gasping for air. "This old man still has a few more fights left in him," replied the aging swordsman. He slowly walked over to his pupil and patted him on the back. "I think I have taught you too well. It will not be long until you will have me beaten in a matter of minutes, I have no doubt. You may even give the Commander a run for his money soon."

As Andre slowly shuffled his way over to the table to remove his training gear, a loud voice echoed through the hall. "Well, there isn't a better teacher in all of Valoria, that is certain," bellowed a voice as a man walked into view. "But I think you may be exaggerating a bit with that last statement, Andre. He still has a ways to go."

"Brother!" said Kara as she jumped up from the couch and ran over to hug her elder sibling.

With a big smile Coal Lucer turned to Bishop. "So, you are using my sister as your personal cheering section these days?"

Bishop walked over to embrace his lifelong friend. Kara put her arm around her husband as if to claim him as her own. "She insisted on being here. She claims to enjoy watching me train, but I think she is just trying to avoid her royal duties," said Bishop.

"Wild accusations I can assure you," countered Kara as she tried to defend herself. "I would much rather be tending to my duties." She could not help but laugh at her obvious guiltiness. Almost having to jump, she kissed her husband on the cheek and then proceeded to cheerfully run out of the room, turning to yell as she left. "Now I have some very important business with a cute young man in the city." She grinned happily and then scampered out of the room.

Coal turned and shot Bishop a confused look.

"She's meeting with Farren," said Bishop, noting his friend's concerned and abashed look.

"Those two are still running around together?"

"I could not separate them if I tried," responded Bishop as we walked back over to the table of weapons. He patted the elderly Andre on the shoulder and nodded to silently inform him he could leave. "And believe me I have tried to."

He grabbed his sword and then spun around to face Coal. "Now, how about a rematch? I am sick of this talk. We have not dueled in ages and I am curious how much worse you have gotten."

Coal paused for a moment and then smiled. "Do you think that prudent? You are already tired from practice. Besides, it is my duty to protect the Supreme Regis, not injure him."

Bishop began to circle Coal like a tiger stalking its prey. "You are already assuming you will win."

"Unless you have been practicing much more than I know, this will end as it always does," spoke Coal, calmly.

Bishop drew his sword and tossed the sheath to the side. The sun rose just high enough to peak through the stained glass windows and glinted off of the steel blade. Coal stood firm, but did not draw his sword. "Still as confident as ever I see," said Bishop. "You won't even turn to face me? It is not nice to insult your Regis like that."

Bishop continued to circle his prey, but Coal did not turn to follow him. When Bishop was behind Coal he jumped forward and swung his sword down on him. In a flash, Coal drew his kidon from the sheath on his lower back and spun around, falling to a knee, blocking the blow.

His halmon, a traditional one-handed long sword, was too large to draw quickly, but the short, defensive kidon was made for quick reactions. Coal pushed up strongly throwing Bishop back. Bishop knew that if he gave Coal the time to draw his long sword that the fight would swing strongly in Coal's favor, so he quickly regained his composure and attacked.

With the kidon, Coal was able to easily block every blow that Bishop threw at him, but its short length made it difficult to start an offensive. He knew he needed to create a brief window to draw his halmon, but Bishop's assault was unyielding.

The high pitched clangs of the duel echoed through the hall, making it seem like an army of swordsman were at battle. Their defensive standoff was beginning to wear on the two fighters. Sweat pouring down their faces, neither faltered. Suddenly, Bishop slipped on the slick surface. Coal took the brief opportunity and punched him in the face, forcing him to a knee. Coal tried to draw his Halmon from his back, but Bishop blindly swung out his sword. Coal quickly blocked with his kidon, but the force of the swing knocked it from his hand. It clattered across the floor and into the wall. He drew his Halmon and then stood watching, as Bishop righted himself.

"You were lucky," said Bishop, wiping the blood from his brow.

"Always be wary of your surroundings. I am certain Andre has taught you that," chastised Coal.

Slightly annoyed by the castigation from his friend, Bishop let out a sigh and lowered his guard. He turned and walked over to pick up his sheath.

Coal was surprised by his friend's lack of enthusiasm. "You are giving up so quickly?"

Sheathing his sword and laying it back onto the table, Bishop responded without turning. "You were right. I am too tired." He began to remove his protective arm guards and chest plate. Coal sheathed his two swords and walked over to Bishop. "Still managing to get in plenty of training I see. Even with many more duties as Regis you have not lost a step."

Bishop turned to face his smiling friend, and could not help but smile back. "I consider keeping my fighting skills honed as important a duty as any other." He walked forward and embraced his friend by grabbing his forearm. "Besides, I can't let you get too far ahead of me just because I am now Regis. You won't win that easily."

"I should hope not," responded Coal.

"So why is it you have come to see me?" asked Bishop. "Surely it is not just to tarnish my pride and chastise me for shirking my duties."

"I have just come to see how you are doing. I have not seen you since the funeral. You looked troubled during the coronation. Have you been holding up? I know that you are under a lot of pressure these days," said Coal.

Bishop wiped the sweat from his face and chest and started to put on a clean shirt. "I appreciate your concern, Coal, but I am doing just fine. Nothing I cannot handle."

"I know you are strong, but I also know how much you loved your parents, Bishop. It is difficult to take on such a weight of responsibility too quickly. It took me quite a while to feel in control again after the war. It is a lot to take in, even for someone as strong as you."

"So, if you understand how I feel, than you also must understand my desire to work through this on my own. Am I correct?"

Coal sighed. "I do understand, yes, but I do not agree. You have friends, Bishop; friends who wish to help you. Let them," urged the Commander.

Bishop stared intensely back at Coal. He finished cleaning himself up and then walked past Coal towards the door, patting him on the shoulder as he left. "Don't you have work to do, Coal," said Bishop, ignoring his heartfelt plea.

Coal could do nothing but let out another heavy sigh. The sun now shown fully through the stained glass windows lining the walls and the room was alive with colorful light. The sounds of the city could not be heard across the expansive palace grounds, but the beautiful song of the tiny yellow Astentine bird filled the morning air. As Bishop left, the bang of the large wooden door crashing shut frightened the small bird and it fluttered away towards the city.

It was early in the afternoon and the city was in full swing, but Farren did not seem concerned with the pandemonium around him. He was off in his own little world. It was surprising that a prince could just sit in the middle of town and nobody would make a fuss. The people of Valoria were used to him. He wasn't a prince, but rather just another delinquent running free throughout the city. Farren wouldn't have it any other way.

The city square was enormous, circled by some of the most popular shops and restaurants. Different from the bazaar, these shops were permanent, housed in buildings built with natural Brivan stone, the same material used throughout the city. It was a cool breezy day, and every window was open to allow the breeze to cleanse the heat from the furnace-like interiors.

Many restaurants set out tables and chairs in front of their shops so people could eat in the sunshine. A duo of small children ran wild through the square, their parents trying to enjoy their meal; ignoring them. This section of the city was mostly frequented by the wealthier Valorians and thus was more civilized.

Not the commotion of the square, the smell of fresh baked bread, or the splashing of water from the fountain could break Farren from his trance. He sat, staring at the ground, oblivious to the chaos of the day. A gentle hand touched him on the shoulder, and he jolted awake.

Kara jumped in surprise. "Farren, you scared me," she laughed. "I didn't mean to startle you."

Farren turned and looked at her smiling face. She had a look of pure innocence; the same look she had always had, even as a child. Even though she may now be the Lady of Briva she was still his childhood friend. They had started to drift apart since her marriage with Bishop and his parent's passing, but they still had a lot of fond memories. In these uncertain times, he needed his old friend again. Looking at that smile erased his anxiousness and he finally smiled back.

"You invited me here because you said you wanted to take me somewhere. Now tell me," said Kara.

Back to his usual self, Farren replied with confidence. "Now calm down there, Kare. No need to be in such a rush." He held out his arm like a gentleman and gave her a wink. "Let us go for a walk."

She laughed and grabbed his arm and they ran off.

Now outside the city, Farren and Kara walked down a dirt path in an open grassy field. They looked out at the bucolic landscape that surrounded the metropolis. Fields of wheat and corn dotted the land and livestock, like Brivan Steer, could be seen grazing in the open pastures. Much of the land, though, was not cultivated, and was taken up by large fields of wildflowers to the west, and the edge of the great Shroud Forest to the north.

Kara was excited to be out of the city and could not help but run ahead. She breathed in the fresh air and smiled. "Ahhh. I love it out here." She ran over to some flowers and smelled. "It has been way too long since I have been outside the walls without a carriage around me or a contingent of soldiers to follow my every move. I forgot how refreshing and freeing it feels."

Farren slowly walked behind, perfectly content with watching Kara enjoy herself. Kara's deep brown hair, usually pulled back in a formal style, fell loosely, blowing in the wind. Despite her youthful personality and charm she was still quite urbane. Skipping through the tall grass, she carried a royal elegance and had such a lively spirit Farren could not help but be intoxicated by it. Even Farren's youthful ebullience was nothing compared to her spirit.

She turned back and yelled to Farren. "So, you haven't told me yet where we are going." Kara waited as Farren traipsed his way up to her. "You know how much I hate secrets. Stop being so cryptic and tell me already."

"So demanding," laughed Farren. "I normally do not bend to such demands but, if you insist, who am I to say no to the Lady of Briva?" Suddenly, he started to sprint off ahead down the path.

"Hey, wait" cried Kara. "Get back here." She ran off after him.

Farren came to the top of a small hill and stopped. Kara came crashing into him, nearly knocking him onto his face.

"Got you" she laughed. She took a second to catch her breath. "What was all that for?"

Farren pointed behind her and she turned to look at the top of the hill. A small river cut through the lea. Only about three feet deep at this spot, the river was a shallow section of the long Tikal River that stretched across Briva. It started high up in the Bardon Mountains to the west and headed southeast, sweeping across the Central Plains and the Shroud and emptied into the Great Southern waters to the southeast of Valoria.

"Do you remember when we were kids and we came here to fish? We escaped the city for the whole day, our parents were furious," said Farren.

Kara stood staring at the river for a few seconds. "And you didn't catch a thing" blurted Kara as she spun around. She ran over and hugged Farren. "I love it Fare. This is so amazing. Of course I remember." She ran up to the water's edge and peered into the crystal clear water. She could see the small fish darting around near the rocky bottom. "Let's catch some fish!"

The river ran swiftly, yet not so fast that one couldn't wade to the other side. There were a few trees growing along the banks and Farren and Kara set up beneath one of them as they cast their lines into the water. The water was so clear that they could see the fish as they nibbled at their bait. The fish were small but numerous. The large fish tended to flock to the deeper portions of the river upstream.

Kara spotted a fish approach her bait and begin to nibble. She leaned forward in anticipation; ready to pull back on her rod when the fish got too greedy. It slowly pecked its way to the bait until finally it sucked in the hook and Kara jumped at the chance. Since the river was so shallow and the fish so small it flew out of the water and onto the bank easily. As it flopped chaotically on the grass Kara tried to subdue it.

She managed to pounce on it and release the hook. Farren shook his head and sighed, wondering how she could always be so spirited.

She tossed the fish onto her small pile of successful catches. Sitting back down, she turned to Farren. "So how many have you caught?" she asked seriously.

He turned to face her serious gaze. After a few seconds Kara could not keep up the charade and burst out laughing. Farren smiled at his presumptuous partner. "Confident are we?" said Farren.

Kara held back her laughter. "I am just trying to bring to attention your obvious lack of fish."

Farren looked down next to him with a blank stare. He had not caught a single fish. "I guess fishing just isn't my thing." Suddenly, a jerk pulled on Farren's rod. They both turned to see a huge fish darting around on the end of his line. About three feet long, it was easily the largest fish they had seen in that part of the river. Surprised by its unfortunate predicament the fish struggled. Farren held fast as his rod bent under the weight. The rods they were using were hand made by Farren and, thus, were not of the finest craftsmanship.

"Come on Farren! You can do it!" cheered Kara, who had jumped to her feet to watch the fight.

As Farren attempted to reel in his large catch his pole snapped and the fish dragged the end of his rod downstream. Stunned at the unpredictable conclusion to the struggle, Farren just stood in disbelief, staring downstream at where the fish made its escape.

There was a long pause as neither one could find words to describe what had just happened. Then Kara broke out laughing, barely able to hold herself up. Farren looked at her and cracked a smile. Kara could not stop herself from laughing, so Farren leaned over and splashed some water at her. She screamed in surprise and splashed back. Water filled the air as they battled back and forth. Eventually, Farren jumped into the river in order to splash Kara with more water. Not wanting to be outdone, she jumped in after him.

Soaked to the bone and out of breath, they stood panting in the knee-deep water. The fish had scattered at the first sign of trouble, but a few dared to venture back now that the commotion had subsided. Farren waded his way to the bank and flopped himself onto the grass. He then pulled Kara up over the bank and they both sprawled out onto the plush, green carpet.

The sun was now starting its descent and the breeze made Kara shiver. She inched her way over to Farren and innocuously curled up next to him. Without saying a thing, they both lay staring at the almost cloudless sky. A small splash could be heard from the river as the fish all returned to their usual routine. There was no reason to speak. The weather was perfect, and neither one of them had a care in the world.

4

oal took the final step of the gate stairs on his way to the palace. The hundreds of stairs were a daunting task, but he had walked them many times and they seemed like just another part of his day. Without a drop of sweat, or a speeding of his breath, he walked to the front gate. The walk to the palace may have been just like any other day, but he was not looking forward to what was to come.

The front gate to the palace grounds was a feat of imagined engineering. The sheer size and weight of the gate would take one-hundred work horses to open, making it nearly impregnable. Standing one hundred feet in height, it was made of solid metal, and had a great Everwood engraved on the front. The Everwood was a symbol for strength, wisdom and eternity; a redoubtable image.

With much abhorrence from Valorian scientists, engineers were brought in from the sect of Fera to assist in the design back when it was built during the reign of Regis Duronante. Fera was one of the four sects of Paks – directly west of Briva– and the least liked during those times. Vertura was to the northwest beyond the Bardon Mountains, and Layalta was on the islands to the far north. The people of Fera, the Davati, were hated by many in Briva, but their scientific intellect was unmatched and necessary in order to finish the build. Through an extensive series of pulleys and immense counterweights, the doors were easily opened by the pull of a single lever by a palace guard.

As Coal approached, the two guards standing at the base of the goliath door saluted his approach. "Good morning, Commander. Give me a moment and I will have the gate opened for you," they said as they placed their fists to their chests. "Commander Coal wishes to enter the palace grounds!" one of the guards shouted up to the top of the wall.

Even in peace time the gate was always closed, as well as the gate to the city walls for most of the day. There were those who were still wary of an invasion from the Creed in Vertura. The War of Paksian Rule -having ended only five years ago- was still fresh in the minds of many, and there was much animosity towards the so called barbarian Creed.

The gate began to slowly open, splitting down the trunk of the giant metallic Everwood. The door opened silently, remarkable for such a large structure. It took several minutes to open, giving Coal unwanted time to muster over his forthcoming meeting. As the door came to a stop, he nodded his acknowledgements to the guards and walked in.

He peered into the vast green landscape of the grounds and for once dreaded the long walk he was going to have to take to the palace. Wheeled vehicles were not allowed on the grounds for fear that they would harm the greenery, and he did not want to bother the guards to find him a horse.

This morning he was to meet with a specific prisoner housed in the palace dungeon. As the suspected assassin of the late Regis Lien Kaiser and the Lady Adina, this prisoner was of the utmost importance. It was thought that there was another assassin involved and Coal was determined to discover the identity of the unnamed killer. Coal knew though that the prisoner was in no mood to talk and there was small chance he would discover anything new.

Bishop approached the palace and the guards at the gate allowed him in. *So many barriers. So much protection, and yet Lien and Adina are dead and these walls did nothing to stop it*, brooded Coal.

The dungeons were housed below the magnificent palace. Stretching hundreds of feet into the ground they were an unseen blemish on the beautiful structure. The two guards stiffened to attention when Coal arrived and they gave him a powerful salute. Coal nodded his acknowledgement and then waved for them to open the thick, iron door. One of the guards banged on the door and whispered the password through to the other side. The door needed to be unlocked from both sides. The builders did not want these criminals to be set loose so close to the royal family. Thankfully, not a single prisoner had escaped since the dungeons construction.

The guard on the outside of the gate flipped a large deadlock and then faint sounds of unlocking bolts and turning cranks penetrated through the door. The gate began to rise. The door slowly raised and Coal quickly rushed into the darkness. The guard on the inside was surprised by Coal's quick entry and barely had enough time to hold up a salute. He tried to follow after them but Coal held up his hand to stop him.

Coal began to venture down the winding stone stairway into the darkness. Cells lined the spiral walkway that led downward. Very few were filled because these dungeons were saved for enemies of Valoria, traitors and murderers. The prison in the city was where petty thieves and crooks were sent for their misdoings.

Torches lit the path and small splashes echoed around the walls as Coal walked through the dampness towards the final cell. He found it unnecessary that the prisoner be kept in the final cell because they were all the same, but the Council found it fitting that such scum be kept as far from civilized society as possible. There was no worse crime than to murder the Regis. He stopped at the dead end and turned to face the rusting bars.

A squalid and gaunt looking man lay on the rocky floor staring at the ceiling. His eyes were open but he did not acknowledge Coal's presence. His hair had grown to shoulder length and the natural waviness had begun to straighten due to the weight of dirt and oil. He seemed oddly content considering his current situation.

"Datro," stated Coal firmly. The man did not move. In fact he did not even blink, and Coal began to get frustrated. "Datro!" he bellowed.

Slowly the man turned his head to look over at Coal. "I heard you the first time, you fool" he grunted. He turned back to stare at the ceiling. "I could hear your heavy breathing and stiff walk the second you entered the dungeon. To what do I owe the honor of the company of the judge himself?"

"Quit the sarcasm Datro. You know why I am here, don't you? We have been dancing around this subject for far too long and I am beginning to lose my patience. Are you finally ready to cooperate?"

Datro began to snicker, and then broke out into an all-out laugh. The laugh echoed upwards through the hallway. "What has changed Coal? What new things have you come to offer me?"

Coal knew that he was bound to get nowhere with the man, but it did not prevent him from getting frustrated with his lack of cooperation. "I offer you a cleaner death. For what you have done, there is no negotiating."

Datro jumped to his feet and ran up to the bars. "Therein lies your problem. I am going to die no matter what I do, so where is the motivation? Why should I help you at all? You are the one that stuck me in this cell. You are the reason I am down here."

"The reason you are down here is because you murdered the Supreme Regis!" screamed Coal, pounding his fist against the bars. Coal calmed his anger, but his eyes were piercing. "Lien Kaiser was a great man, and as a Regis there was none better."

"The man was a fool. His pacifistic ideals brought destruction to Briva." Very few men would be able to face a man such as Coal without fear, but Datro stood firm. He was either inhumanly courageous or knew he had nothing left, and thus no reason to fear. "My research helped protect Briva. I am the reason we still control Paks and not the Creed. But Lien did not see it that way."

"This is a time of peace Datro. There is no need to research weapons of war. That is what Lien believed," explained Coal.

"There will never be peace!" Datro began to lose his calm, sly exterior. He wanted to hit something, but he was surrounded by metal and stone, and he would have done more damage to himself than good. He could not even pace the floor to express his derision because the cell itself was barely large enough to lie down in. He banged his fists against the bars and they shook lightly.

"Why must you be so intransigent Datro? You have nothing to lose now. Try to gain back some honor and tell me who it was you were working with. We know you did not do it alone."

Datro grabbed the bars with one arm and pulled his face up to look at Coal as he spoke. His eyes carried such an evil weight Coal was taken back, and he grinned so maliciously Coal could almost feel himself shiver. "Why do you insist there is another killer? It was not difficult to kill Lien and his wife. The man insisted that his food not be tasted. 'What is there to fear from my own people?' he would say. It was simple enough to create a poison and sneak it into their meal. I only regret that the two boys did not attend the dinner as well."

"I don't know what has happened to you Datro, or what could possibly have warped your mind to such extremes, but I knew the man you once were. You were better than this."

Coal turned to walk out of the dungeon. He knew he would never get the crazed man to talk, but he still felt a sense of failure.

"So, what is going to happen to me now?" questioned Datro.

Coal stopped. Turning to face Datro, he kept his composure. "If you do not cooperate, your sentence will be carried out. You will be hanged for your crimes in front of a crowd of cheering citizens."

Datro smiled at Coal. "When will this festive event occur? When will I receive my due justice?"

Coal boiled with anger. "One week Datro. In one week you will cease to exist and Paks will be better for it."

Coal began to walk away, determined to never have to look at that man's face again unless it was tied to a noose. Datro was beyond saving, and nothing good could ever again come from him, or anything he did. Coal was finished playing his sick game.

"You can't stop him Coal! No one can," yelled Datro.

Coal's walk stuttered slightly, taken by surprise by the comment. He quickly realized though that Datro was playing with him, trying to get into his head, and he refused to give the man the satisfaction. He walked out of sight up the stairs, never looking back to the malicious scientist grinning in his cell.

Back in his cell, Datro lay back down onto the cold damp floor and continued to stare up at the ceiling. He seemed oddly content for a man that had just been told, in one week, he was going to be dead.

$\int$

As the center of political power, the council chamber was a historic sight. Nestled in the heart of the city, the behemoth stone structure sat atop a pyramidal stair. The stairs were not nearly as daunting as those that lead to the palace, but they elevated the chambers above the surrounding buildings.

Even though the building was made from the same stone as many of the state district structures, there was no mistaking it. Circular and bordered completely by enormous stone columns depicting images of the greatest Regises and heroes from history, the structure stood out from the spartan surroundings.

Once atop the stairs, the chamber itself descended into the stone pyramid as if a scoop was taken from the inside. Steep rows of stone benches circled a small stage in the center where the head of the council stood to preside over the meeting. Originally, the stone benches were replaced by lavish chairs to increase the comfort of the councilmen. Meetings tended to last much too long, though, because councilmen occasionally fell asleep, or at the very least, had difficulty keeping their concentration through the prosaic proceedings, so the stone benches were returned and padding was added to the seats.

This morning there were no drowsy councilmen in attendance for the daily congregation. Anton Grey, head of the council, analyzed a stack of papers in front of him to mark the important topics that needed to be discussed in depth with his fellow councilmen.

At the age of fifty-six, Anton had a very youthful and noble air about him. He did his best to keep in shape and slow the inevitable flow of time, and it showed. Only a few years ago Anton even trained with the late Commander Callius Lucer; Coal and Kara's father. Unlike many of the other councilmen, he did not tire from the walk up the council stairs and he found it entertaining to see the panting faces of some as they entered the room. The gray streaks in his dark black hair added to his urbane appearance.

As the final few councilmen stumbled into the chamber, Anton put down his documents and waited for the archaic men to make it to their seat.

"Good morning, gentlemen," Anton stated. The chambers were large but his voice was strong and carried far, so it was not necessary to yell. "I hope you are all well rested. There are plenty of pressing matters to attend to today, as many of you know."

He picked up one particular piece of paper and held it up as he spoke. "Let us start with the problem of crime throughout the city." The councilmen murmured in acknowledgement. "We have always had problems with thefts and minor vandalism but it has begun to escalate."

"It is that Farren, and his band of misfits. They call themselves *The Kaisers*, I believe. The name on its own brings shame to the Regency," bellowed a rather haggard looking councilman. Shouts of agreement echoed throughout the chamber. "They wreak havoc all over the city. I saw them firing stones at some of the guards with sling shots," shouted another. "And they steal from the vendors in the bazaar on a daily basis," barked one from the top of the room.

"Quiet," shouted Anton. "We cannot blame the Prince for the entirety of the problem. Sure he contributes to a large share of the headaches, but he is the Prince."

"Bishop should control him better. It is not becoming of a Prince to act in such a manner," said Councilman Rieven. "He is old enough now that these kinds of activities can no longer be swept aside as childish angst and immaturity." Denuke Rieven was one of the oldest of the councilmen and one of the most respected.

"He is still young. Give him time," commented Anton.

"He does not have the luxury of time, Anton. He is royalty and therefore should act accordingly," shouted another disgruntled councilman.

Anton began to lose his patience and, unlike Denuke, he did not have any qualms about arguing with this councilman. "First and foremost, while in these chambers you will refer to me as Head Council." He began to circle his small stage slowly, looking out at all of the council members as he spoke. "Can you honestly tell me that at your age you were not the same? I seem to remember many of you as young children doing many worse things than what you complain of Farren doing. Yes, he his royalty, but he is also a child." He stopped to look around the room, waiting for a response. "Let the boy be what he is and someday there will be a time when he will change, just like all of us have."

Anton waited to see if there was anyone brave enough to respond. "Now if there are no arguments, I think we should discuss how to solve the problem, rather than what may be causing it."

Having not been disgraced by the Head Council, Denuke spoke up above the hushed chamber. "The solution is simple. We must increase the number of soldiers that patrol the city. These criminals are just petty thieves and miscreants. The sight of more patrolmen will discourage them."

"The number of soldiers in the city is quite high as it is. There have been complaints from citizens that they feel their lives are being infringed upon by these soldiers," responded Anton.

The rest of the council still seemed reluctant to join in the discussion, but they sat in eager attention as Anton and Denuke debated.

"The people do not understand that sometimes you must sacrifice a little to attain security and freedom. Something this generation has forgotten," stated Denuke. He seemed as though he was too frail to be able to stand, but his ancient body stood firmly as he eyed up Anton.

"This is not a time of war Councilman. There is no need for anyone to sacrifice. That is why our generation fought so valiantly is it not? So this generation could live without burden?" said Anton. Denuke showed a slight twitch of a smile, acknowledging Anton's cunning rebuttal.

Councilman Rieven seemed content in his defeat, but a voice sounded from atop the chamber. "Then what do you propose Head Council? Has the Supreme Regis voiced his opinion on the matter?"

Anton and the rest of the council turned to look at where the bold new voice came from.

"Ah. Councilman Balyct, I did not see you up there," said Anton, surprised to hear the young councilman speak.

"I apologize, Head Council. I did not mean to surprise you. I just wanted to know what your solution to the matter was if Councilman Rieven's was unsatisfactory?"

Hayes' expression was calm and confident, but Anton could sense of hint of arrogance from the young councilman. Anton did not tolerate disrespect on any level, especially from an inexperienced youth. "I am not here to come up with all of the answers, Councilman. That is what this council is for. We are here to debate and find the correct solution for the problem."

"Then what is your proposed solution, so we may debate its worth?" responded Hayes confidently.

A hush came over the chamber at the bold response from Hayes. Everyone turned to Anton to wait for his response. In truth Anton was just as astonished, but he showed no sign of it. He was not the Head Council by luck or unworthy appointment. His ability to orate was unmatched and he controlled that council like a General rallied the forces of a great army. He responded without hesitation. "The Regis and I have discussed it and we both agree that more patrolmen are unnecessary. The lack of effort from the patrol already in place is the main source of the problem. All that is needed is stricter enforcement of discipline. Commander Lucer has agreed to assist in the matter."

Anton turned sharply to face the rest of the council. "Now shall we debate? Does anyone have anything more to say in the matter?" he questioned the crowd.

Astonishingly, Hayes seemed unfazed by the firm response. "You intend to use the Gallants to help patrol the streets? That is like using a prized stallion to plow the fields."

Even though Anton was furious at the young councilman for his brash behavior he was impressed by his confidence. That did not mean, though, that Anton intended to let the man make a fool of him. He circled the stage and spoke out to the chamber. "But, if there is no show or race for the prized stallion to take part in, would they not be the most capable horse to plow the fields?" He turned back to Hayes. "Commander Coal has offered to train the patrolmen and instill some discipline in them; that is all. He does not intend to patrol the streets himself."

"Are you implying, Head Council, that Commander Lucer does not have anything more important to do than train mere patrolmen? There is a much greater threat to Briva than just mere street thugs," responded Hayes.

Anton almost laughed at the comment, disappointed that their debate would end on such a ridiculous comment. "What threat do you mean Councilman? We are in a time of peace." Anton smiled as he spoke, hoping the gesture would act as a slap in the face to the young politician. "Do you honestly still hold the paranoid belief that the Creed are still a threat after this many years?"

Anton's smile did, in fact, reach its mark, but it did not crush Hayes' spirit. In fact, it enraged the man, and his calm façade began to waver. He walked out into the aisle and began to walk towards Anton. "The Creed are always a threat. Regis Lien and his son may have convinced the people, but you of all people should know we are never safe."

"Hayes that is enough," shouted Councilman Rieven. The aged Councilman rose from his seat to berate the contentious Hayes.

Hayes turned and glared at Denuke from the corner of his eye. "I'm sorry Councilman, was I out of line? I do believe that the Head Council was the one that advised Regis Lien that the Creed were not a threat twenty five years ago." He turned to look back at Anton, still with an icy glare. "And we all know what happened after that."

Anton began to show his anger and, sensing this, Denuke stepped in again to stop the discussion before it got out of hand. "Councilman Hayes, return to your seat. This discussion is over," he said sternly.

The tension in the council chambers was thick, and one could feel the anger radiating from the two men in the center. Both men refused to be the one to break eye contact. Without looking away, Anton spoke to the chamber. "The council is dismissed."

For a moment the councilmen did not seem to know what to do, but as the first few men began to leave, the chamber emptied quickly. Hayes finally turned and walked out of the chamber past Denuke, who was waiting for one of them to stand down. Denuke and Anton watched as Hayes left the chamber.

"When I woke up this morning, Denuke, I did not think that the council session would end with your voice holding back my rage. I have not felt that riled for many years," said Anton as he watched Hayes disappear from the room. "Do you know anything about him?"

"Not much," said Denuke. "He is young and ambitious; keeps to himself. As far as I know, he has not made any big moves like this."

"He is not a fan of the Creed that is obvious, but the question is why. The Creed have not been brought up in council for a while either. I find it odd that it is happening now. Did something happen to him during the war?"

"I am not certain. As I said, he keeps to himself. He has no friends on the council. He comes in early every day and leaves late. No family to speak of."

As calm as he may have seemed, Anton's heart was racing and he could not get the sight of Hayes' glaring eyes out of his head. The man had an intense malicious aura about him and he could not understand why. Anton had not felt so uneasy in his council chamber for twenty five years. Not since the day the news came that the Creed were attacking.

"We need to keep an eye on that one, Denuke," commented Anton. "I have a feeling this is not the last we will hear from him."

6

It had been almost a month since his inauguration and Supreme Regis Bishop had still not gotten used to his new duties. He sat in his study, thinking about his father and mother, as he so often did. The stress made his mind wander, and he wished his father was there to help him along. He had always taken his father for granted, not knowing the weight that he held on his shoulders. Regis Lien was praised as one of the greatest leaders since the old ages and Bishop found it difficult to follow in such large footsteps.

Bishop was a Kaiser, though, so he never showed his weakness. There were many in the council that were wary of his inexperience, but he gave them no viable reason to make any drastic decisions. Since he was so young, he had to prove himself not only to the council, but also to the citizens, so he worked the best he could. When he needed guidance though, Bishop turned to an old family friend.

Bishop's father had many friends in the council, but none better than Anton Grey. The Head Council and Regis Lien fought to make Briva the center of power of Paks and were responsible for ending the bloody War of Paksian Rule between Briva and Vertura. Diplomacy between the two powerful sects was still tenuous however and, because of this, Anton urged Bishop to try to strengthen the friendship between them; a goal Lien failed to achieve before his death.

"It would be a momentous breakthrough that would make your mark in history and instill some confidence in the council about your abilities," Anton had told him.

Bishop stared at the far window, right into the afternoon sun shining through it. The study was large, so the sunlight barely reached his desk against the far wall. Like many things in the palace, his new study was much too grand for his taste. Bishop felt that it was difficult to think in the large space because his thoughts had so much room to wander and they seldom returned. The door to the room burst open and Bishop was jolted out of his trance.

"Please, come in Coal," said Bishop sarcastically, after his shock wore off. Bishop got up from his desk to meet his friend.

Coal was clad in his formal Forces uniform, seeming as though he had just come from a council of war. Same as the royal dress ware, the uniform was dark green with gray accents. Bishop went to shake his friend's hand, but Coal spoke before he could get there.

"Kaine has informed me that you are refusing their protection on the trip to Coroge. What could you possibly be thinking? There is no telling what could happen on the journey. You need protection," asserted Coal.

While Bishop was the Supreme Regis, in private he and Coal still acted like best friends. In public, Coal's bravado towards Bishop would be considered traitorous and severely punishable.

Bishop smiled at Coal's forcefulness and lowered his hand, realizing Coal was not in the mood for greetings. "And I will have protection, Coal. I am taking a whole troop of Forces soldiers with me. That is more than enough, seeing as though this is a peaceful diplomatic mission." Bishop held his ground against the intimidating Commander. "It would show disrespect to Minor Leo and his generosity if I arrive at Coroge with two Gallants protecting me."

"To death with Leo's generosity," bellowed Coal.

Bishop was unscathed by the heated outburst because he knew his friend, and knew that he tended to act on emotions more often than logic. He sat back down at his desk and responded calmly.

"Coal, I understand you do not like Minor Leo, but do not let that hatred cloud your judgment. I have more than enough protection and your men have more important duties they can be attending to."

"What could…"

"You know I am right Coal," interrupted Bishop. "There is no point in arguing with me. It is decided."

Coal stared at Bishop with an obvious feeling of irritation at Bishop's obduracy. It was clear that he was not going to change his mind, and Coal normally respected that in his lifelong friend, but now it infuriated him. Bishop looked down at his desk and continued to work, silently expressing that the conversation was over. A light knock came to the door and they both turned to see Farren.

"Ah, Farren. Excellent timing," said Bishop. He turned to Coal. "We're done, Commander." Coal bowed to his Regis and marched out of the room. Farren turned to watch Coal leave, clearly frustrated.

"What is wrong with Coal?" questioned Farren.

"You know Coal. He wears his heart on his sleeve."

Farren smiled. "So, what is it brother? One of the palace servants told me that you wanted to see me."

Bishop gestured to Farren to sit down. "I wanted to tell you ahead of time that I will be leaving the city for a few weeks." Bishop got up from his desk and started to pace around the room, reluctant to tell his brother the whole story.

"Where are you going?" asked Farren.

Bishop sighed and hung his head. "I am going to Coroge, to talk with Minor Leo."

"You can't!" blurted Farren without hesitation. He jumped to his feet and pleaded with his brother. "You know how dangerous it is."

Still with his head hung, Bishop turned to look at his brother. He knew how Farren was going to react and so he knew there was little he could tell him to ease his concern. "Regis Minor Leo has agreed to give me passage to Coroge. I am going to negotiate a peace between our two sects. He also wishes to show his condolences for the death of father and mother."

As Bishop predicted, his explanation did little to calm Farren. Farren ran over to his brother and continued to beg. "You cannot trust him, brother. He was the one who started the war."

"This was the one thing that father failed to do before he passed. This was his final goal and he never had a chance to see it through, Farren. I have to do this." His father's face flashed into Bishop's mind and he clenched his fists. He remembered all the nights his father would stay up agonizing over this treaty, wondering what he could do to finally make peace. Farren was too young to remember, too young to realize the importance.

"But..." stammered Farren.

"Do not be a child Farren!" shouted Bishop, interrupting Farren. "You are much too old now to act like this."

Farren stumbled backwards as if Bishop had struck him in the chest. He had not heard his brother raise his voice in anger before, especially to him. Bishop's usually kind eyes were filled with determination and they pierced straight into Farren's fearful heart.

Bishop turned to look out the stained glass windows. "You can't continue to act like a child Farren. You are a Kaiser, so you need to start acting like one." Bishop did not like yelling at his younger brother but his frustration got the better of him.

After a long silence Bishop sighed again and turned back around. "I'm sorry, Farren. I did not mean to yell." He walked up to Farren and put his hand on his head. "You must realize that this peace is important. You know how much father wanted this."

Ever since they were little, Bishop had always been able to ease Farren's emotions with a pat on the head and a big smile, but this time his smile was not the same. There was no joy in it. Farren did remember how much time his father spent toiling over this treaty. He remembered the late nights when he would not come to say good night, or tell them a story. He remembered how he was never around to teach him swordsmanship or help him with his studies. Farren did not want to lose his brother like he did his father.

"I know, brother. You do not have to lecture me about what is important," said Farren. He turned and walked out of the room, Bishop's hand sliding off his head. He slammed the door behind him as he left.

Bishop sighed in frustration. "When will he ever grow up?"

The sun was rising in Valoria and the light began to peak over the city walls. Paks' third moon could still be seen above the horizon but the little light it provided during the night was now dwarfed by the red glow of the sun.

Much to the dismay of many, Bishop was leaving for Coroge this morning. There was no great parade or crowd of cheering citizens for his departure. In fact, after Coal and Farren's reaction to his leaving, he decided it would be best to not inform the citizens of his plans. Even twenty years after the war, hatred of the Creed was still strong and Bishop was unsure how the citizens would react. He was saddened because he was unsure if the citizens would realize the importance of the treaty. They would put their hatred before their logic. How could he expect ordinary citizens to see it his way, if he could not even convince his own brother and best friend?

The council was excited to finally complete the treaty that Lien had begun so long ago, but they were not convinced that the young Bishop had what it took to negotiate with the stubborn Creed.

"Minor Leo is a judicious but stubborn man. He is quite set in his beliefs, but he appeals greatly to logic and that is where you can sway him. Believe me when I tell you, Bishop, Leo wants this treaty as much as we do, but he does not want to be on the losing side of it," Anton told Bishop the previous night. "If you show weakness he will not hesitate to take the upper hand. You must stand strong, and he will respect you for it."

Anton stood at the gate with a small troop of Forces soldiers on horses ready to accompany the Supreme Regis on his mission. Unlike most of the council, Anton had faith in the young Bishop; faith that he was as strong as his father. All he needed was time and a little guidance. Like a military officer, Anton was in full dress and not a wrinkle on his pristine uniform. This was a historic event, even if nobody else was aware.

The faint sounds of hoof beats could be heard coming from the still silent city and Anton and the soldiers became vigilant. Three horses came trotting into view with Bishop, Kara, Farren and Coal atop them. Kara, riding side saddle, sat behind Bishop on his horse, with Farren and Coal riding on either side. As the horses came to a halt, Anton and the soldiers all saluted with an open hand to the heart, a shortened version of the official Brivan salute.

"As you were, men," said Bishop, as he dismounted his horse. He reached up to help Kara down. There was still a slight chill in the air in the early morning, so Kara wore a light jacket overtop her favorite ankle length dress.

Neither Farren nor Coal were excited to be present at the departure but they showed nothing but poise. Bishop walked over to greet Anton with a smile.

"Good morning, Your Highness. I am happy to see you are so excited to start on your journey. This is a momentous occasion. I only wish it was possible for everyone to be here," commented Anton.

"This is how it has to be Anton. But do not worry, the people will soon know what we are doing and they will laud us for it."

As Anton and Bishop spoke Coal dismounted and went to talk to the Forces soldiers. To ease his conscience he needed to reinforce the importance of their duty on this mission. Even though Coal knew that Kaine and Syd would be following the caravan in secret, these soldiers were Bishop's first line of defense and they needed to know that.

Coal approached and the men again saluted and spoke in unison. "Commander!"

Waiving away their formality, Coal spoke bluntly. "The Regis may tell you there is no danger on this mission, but he couldn't be more wrong. You must stay vigilant, and if anything happens to the Regis, there will be strict consequences. He has put you men in a difficult situation, but I will not accept failure."

They all saluted in unison.

Bishop smiled at Coal's censuring of the soldiers. "I see Coal is excited about this in his own way," Bishop said aloud.

Farren was still uncertain about the trip but, knowing that Bishop could not be swayed to change his mind, he could not refuse to see his brother off. He forced a smile at Bishop's attempt to lighten the mood.

"Stop deriding poor Coal, dear. He means only the best," said Kara. She walked over and wrapped her arms around the back of Bishop, burying the side of her head into his back. Bishop looked over to Farren, who was beginning to show his apprehension.

"When I return, Farren, we should go riding together. It has been too long."

Farren smiled at the thought of spending a day with his brother. He knew, even if Bishop meant what he said, there was little chance he would have the time to spend a day with his younger brother. He drew comfort, though, from the fact that Bishop hadn't changed and did not seem about to any time soon.

Bishop pulled Kara's clenching arms away from his chest and turned to face her. "You're going to have to let me go, Kara. The road to Coroge is no place for a lady." He gave her a reassuring smile that told her that he was leaving, but would be back soon. He mounted his horse and the group of soldiers followed suit.

"Good luck, Your Highness. Make your father proud," announced Anton.

Bishop nodded his head and then looked back to his brother. "Watch after Lady Kara, won't you brother? She gets dreadfully bored easily and needs constant attention," he smirked.

Farren walked over and put his arm around the saddening Kara. She smiled at the joke, but her tears overwhelmed the happiness.

Turning his horse around, Bishop motioned to the guards at the gate and the enormous gate doors began to creak open. Slightly larger than the gate doors to the castle, the doors to the city worked on the same counterweight system and had the same engraving of the Everwood in the center.

Not waiting for the doors to open entirely, Bishop galloped out of the opening the moment there was space to do so. Kara huddled closer to Farren and wrapped her arms around him, squeezing his boyish frame. She was nearly the same height as the diminutive Prince and she bent her head to nestle her dark chocolate hair under his chin.

"Do not worry, Kara, Bishop is tough. There is no way he would let some Creed get the best of him. Besides, he would never leave you alone, no matter the circumstances." Coal walked over and pulled Kara away with a reassuring voice.

Anton walked over and put his arm on Farren's shoulder. "You should be proud of him Farren; risking so much to finish what your father started. This is far more important than you can imagine."

Farren did not need someone to tell him the importance of this treaty; he knew. But as he watched his brother ride off towards this goal he could not get the feeling out of his stomach that something wasn't quite right.

Do not make me a liar to Kara, brother, he thought.

As everyone dispersed and returned to the castle, Coal lingered back for a moment. When everyone else was out of view, Kaine and Syd appeared out of a dark alley nearby.

As two of Coal's top captains, Kaine and Syd were among the strongest fighters in all of Briva. Their personalities and looks were so distinct you would find it strange that they had such a brotherly bond. Kaine was lean and spry, with a quick wit and an even quicker sword. Syd, on the other hand, was built like an ox and fought like one too. Kaine was reserved, while Syd was boisterous. Despite their differences, they were the strongest fighting duo in the kingdom and eternally loyal.

"Travel quickly," said Coal to his captains. "You need to keep him within sight, but he cannot know you are there. Once they are safe in Coroge, you will wait for them to depart. The Creed must not feel your presence as well. Do I make myself clear?"

"Of course, Sir. We will be silent stalkers. No harm will come to him, you have our word," said Kaine.

"Good. Now get moving. Bishop is travelling quickly."

The two young Captains saluted and quickly galloped out of gate in pursuit of Bishop and the caravan.

7

After a morning of unruliness and frowned upon activities, Farren was returning to the castle. He was hoping that he could get his concern for Bishop and the mission out of his mind through some escapades in the city with Reme and Dash. While it may have created a temporary mend for his concern, the overarching uneasiness was still there.

Farren walked silently through the palace grounds on his way back to the palace. Whenever Farren spent a day in the city, he liked to walk back to the castle. Of course, as the Prince, he could easily request a carriage or divan to escort him wherever he desired, but he liked to walk amongst the people. He was a citizen of Valoria and nothing more. Besides, his activities were far short of being considered royal, so he did not want anyone around that could easily report his activities back to his brother.

Unlike most people, he enjoyed the long walk through the grounds to the castle. Most people used horses when making the long trek, but Farren was in no hurry. There was a slight breeze, just strong enough to sway the heavy draping branches of the Shroud Willows. It was a peaceful day, with the wind taking the edge off the beating sun hanging in the cloudless sky.

He reached the palace doors, and the guards quickly let him in. While the exterior of the palace spoke of strength and austerity, the interior showed off Valoria's lavish side. The moment one stepped into the main entry they felt insignificant compared to its grandeur. The floor, which seemed to stretch endlessly, was gray marble, polished to such a point that one could see their own reflection. Stone columns lined the side walls, supporting the arched ceiling that spanned the entire length of the room.

The room itself was not excessively wide, but it made up for that in sheer length. The room seemed to come to a point at the end, where a staircase reached up to the second level. The columns not only supported the ceiling but also displayed the carved figures of all previous Supreme Regii, starting with Regis Ethon III, and ending with Regis Lien. Due to Lien's sudden death, Bishop's effigy was not yet under construction.

Again, as Farren made his way through the entry hall he was not awestruck by the immensity or lavishness. He was used to seeing his reflection in the ashen floor and was used to the murals of past battles bearing down on him from the ceiling. The hallways of the palace were less ostentatious, but still held a bright glow. Windows lined every exterior wall; letting waves of natural light brighten the passages. Farren made his way towards the upper floors, where he intended to clean himself up and relax for a time in his room. An older man, around fifty years of age, by the looks of him, wandered towards Farren.

"Captain Mercer, it is nice to see you," smiled Farren at the aging military man.

"Ah, Young Master, it is good to see you as well. I assume you have been keeping out of trouble," responded Captain Mercer with a warm, welcoming smile.

Guy Mercer was the eldest of the Gallant fighters; last of the past generation. He was a scholarly man who was renowned for his mental abilities as much as his physical. He kept a sharp appearance; finely groomed and dressed. His hair was in its final stages of graying and his perfectly kept goatee was much the same. His face began to show signs of wrinkling, but he had the build and stamina of a much younger man. He still had many exciting years ahead of him.

Farren smiled at Guy's friendly sarcasm. "Of course, Guy. You know me well enough to know I avoid trouble at all costs.

"I see you still have that sly tongue of yours. You should be putting that to good use."

"You mean I should be a respectful little Prince and play politics for my older brother?"

"I do not mean to imply anything, Young Master. I only pointed out that you have a sharper mind than you give yourself credit for. Most often that is taken as a compliment."

Farren smirked at the obvious sarcasm. "Is this another one of your precious lessons, Guy? I thought I graduated from your tutorship already."

Guy could not help but laugh at his former student, even though he was being intractable. It reminded him of the days when he tutored Farren as a child. He educated him in the topics of history, politics, mathematics, alchemy and many others, but Farren never seemed too interested in the education process. Even though Farren's focus was, at best, hazy, Guy knew he had a hidden genius. In the end, though, Guy could not get the dispassionate Farren to focus his intellect.

Reminiscing to himself, Guy had a thought. "I am on my way to train, Farren, would you like to join me?"

Baffled by the proposition, Farren was unsure of his response. "Oh, I'm not sure I should."

"Humor an old man won't you, Young Master? What else could you possibly have to do with your precious time?"

Guy ushered Farren along with him before he could decline the offer.

Farren followed Guy into the Gallant building. They made their way into the large training room and Farren spotted a young man standing near the armament table. The room was slightly darkened due to the lack of natural light passing through the large stained glass window on the far wall. Clouds were beginning to role in and glow lights were lit to add some extra light to the room.

Hearing the echo of footsteps off the granite floor, the young man turned. "You are late, Master. I find it a bit hypocritical that I am forced to be early every day and yet you wander in late constantly" He noticed Farren and suddenly knelt to the floor and bowed his head. "I apologize, Prince Farren, I did not see you. It is an honor to meet you, finally."

"Young Master, this is my apprentice, Kaleb," introduced Guy. Kaleb still stayed kneeling, waiting for a command to rise. "The young master does not enjoy royal formalities does he?" joked Guy, looking at Farren for a redundant nod of confirmation.

Kaleb slowly rose to his feet. Like his master, Kaleb was preened to perfection; a true soldier. Unlike his master, though, he was not graying but rather had jet black hair, cut short and sharp. He was young, nineteen years of age, and leanly built from years of hard training.

He did not wear the Gallant issue uniform -dark gray top with green accents and black pants- but rather a simple gray uniform to denote his apprentice status.

"I am sorry for my tardiness, but if you don't mind, Kaleb, I was hoping to train with the young master for a while," requested Guy.

Kaleb seemed slightly disappointed but looked over to Farren and smiled.

"I was hoping to get some practice in, but I cannot complain. Would it be alright if I stayed, Master? I have heard that Kaiser men are formidable fighters. I would be interested to see it in person." Guy nodded and Kaleb removed his training gear and went to the side of the room to sit and observe.

Guy wandered over to the armament table and sifted through the array of weapons as he spoke. "So, Young Master, do you have a weapon of choice?"

Farren had never had any sort of military training. He would have been trained in swordsmanship when he turned sixteen, but his obstinate attitude towards his tutorship made his father give up on him, allowing him to do as he pleased.

"You know that I have had no training. I have no idea what most of these are, Guy" Farren responded as he looked at the table.

"Your brother uses a traditional long sword, or halmon, as did your father." He turned around and looked at Farren briefly before continuing his search. "But you have a smaller frame, so a long sword would be impractical. I might suggest a shorter sword, possibly dual swords." He turned around holding two short swords, each about the length of Farren's arm and with a slight curve of the blade. "Juko are short swords, specially forged to be used as dual offensive weapons, unlike most short swords which are mainly used for defense. They are a nice combination of offense and defense."

Guy handed the swords to Farren, who cautiously took them; confused on quite how to hold them. "I will ignore the implied jape at my height, but short swords?" moaned Farren.

"Some of the strongest fighters in history used short swords. Kaleb uses hand blades. They're even shorter," winked Guy. Farren laughed. "You must play to your strengths and your limitations. Steel is steel, no matter how long or broad it is."

Guy took the swords back from Farren and handed him two wooden equivalents. "These will do fine for now. If you get injured I will not hear the end of it."

Guy grabbed a wooden sword of his own and then walked out to the center of the floor. "Do you intend on training or do you want to quit before you have even begun this time?" jabbed Guy.

Farren grinned and walked out to meet Guy. He took a readying stance, to confirm his willingness. "For the record, Old Master, I did not quit by choice. Your dull rambling bored me into submission," goaded Farren.

Guy quickly swung his sword at Farren, who was able to block but fell to floor, dropping one of his Jukos. Guy helped him up and went to pick up his sword. "The difference between me teaching you now, and teaching you before, is if you do not concentrate now you might get hurt. Like I said earlier, I would never hear the end of it if that happened."

He handed the sword back to Farren and showed him a proper readiness stance. He showed him how to handle the swords and how to parry and defend.

"Footwork is essential. It allows you to make a quick thrust, but also a hasty retreat from that thrust. It is an important aspect for offensive and defensive tactics."

Kaleb watched in amusement as Farren floundered to try to keep up with the arduous demands of the old Captain but could not help but be impressed by his determination.

Guy pushed him through the basics of offensive swordsmanship including, thrusts, cuts and counters. He showed him how to utilize the dual swords to his advantage and how to attack and defend when found weaponless.

"There will always be a time when you are forced to fight without your primary weapon. Maybe your opponent has disarmed you or you were ambushed, but that does not mean you are defeated."

Farren struggled, falling continuously and finding himself out of breath and exhausted, but no matter the abuse he took, no matter how unsuccessful he seemed to be, he could not let himself fail. They continued for hours.

He was riddled with scrapes and bruises, but his ambition was unscathed. He pushed himself to keep up, because he felt an amazing satisfaction from his efforts. He was hunched over, panting, and dripping sweat onto the granite floor.

"You did well, Young Master. I expected nothing less," commented Guy as he placed his sword back on to the table.

Struggling for breath, Farren responded. "Thank you, Sir. That is incredible. I did not realize how exhilarating it could feel." He got to his feet and brushed himself off.

"It makes me wonder how much you would have improved by now if you would have continued your studies. You were such a stubborn pupil."

Farren contemplated silently as he returned his equipment to the table and tried to gain his breath. He remembered vividly the day when his father scolded him about his attitude towards his studies and finally decided to let him do as he pleased. As a foolish child, he was excited about the victory against his father, but now he wondered if he was too hasty.

"It is never too late. I can start my training now," said Farren. "I have little else to do, and when the peace comes there will be plenty of time for you to train me."

Guy was happy to see his old pupil excited about something other than his normal uncouth activities, but frowned knowing there was little he could do. "I am sorry, Young Master. I am no longer the royal tutor, and Commander Lucer would not like it if I spent my time training you, rather than on Gallant matters."

"Then I will speak to him myself. I will convince him to allow you to train me."

"You know as well as I do how stubborn the Commander is. He is unlikely to budge on such a matter."

Farren hung his head, realizing the truth behind Guy's words. "Then I will petition my brother. He surely will allow it." Bishop rarely said no to his little brother and Farren had many tricks up his sleeve to convince him if he did not immediately agree. The thought put a smile on Farren's face. "When he returns, I will talk to him." He began to rush out the door. "Make sure to leave some time in your schedule," he yelled back.

As he left the room Kaleb wandered up to Guy. "Do you think the Regis will say yes?"

"I know his father would have."

"How did you know he would do so well, Master?"

Guy turned and smiled. He began to put on his training armor, and Kaleb followed. "You assume that I knew?"

"Come on, Master, I think I know you well enough by now. You would not have brought him here if you did not believe he had potential."

"He always had potential in anything he did. I was just never able to find a way to unlock it. Like most great men in history, including his father, he just needed a little push. He still has a long way to go, though."

8

With the sun high in the sky the mist was thinned, but visibility was still low. The soldiers of Bishop's caravan marched closely to make sure they did not separate. The vast Shroud Forest was one of the most inhospitable places in all of Paks. Stretching from the northern borders of Valoria, all the way to the edges of the Central Plain, the mist covered forest hid many dangers that could fall upon you so quickly you would never even have time to scream.

The path through the forest was wide but not well-trodden. It was the only path one could take to if they wanted to reach Valoria from the outer sects, unless they came by ship to Herous. Thick grass and thorny bushes grew along its length, making it difficult for the horses to move easily.

Even at the peak of daylight the soldiers were still tense, keeping their eyes locked onto the shadows of the wood. While there were few noises heard above the buzzing of mosquitoes and the screeching of crows, they knew there were many dangers out there and they could strike quickly and silently.

While the mist obscured their vision, it did little to block the heat from the sun. Sweat dripped down the faces of the men, draining them of their precious energy. They would soon rest, staying out of the heat of the day, then continue at dark. It was unwise to rest at night in the Shroud because the monsters that awoke in the dark were far worse than the ones awake in the day. Bishop rode at the center of the caravan, closely surrounded by the guards. He dressed plainly, wearing only a Gallant uniform. Traveling to Coroge he thought it best to dress in military garb to show Briva's strength. He wore no medals or jewelry aside from his ring with the Kaiser family crest; the sign of his royal blood and position as Supreme Regis. The Creed criticized lavishness and believed more in growing one's strength than one's wealth. If he were to ride up to the gates of Coroge dressed in royal attire and followed by an ostentatious parade, he would likely be killed before he reached the walls.

The Supreme Regis sat erect atop his horse, chest out and head held high. He looked the picture of nobility, despite the fact that there was no one around to see him. Even though he showed nothing but poise, he was struggling as much as the men around him. The inner layers of his uniform were drenched with sweat and his collar was dampening from the beads of perspiration flowing down his face.

He wanted nothing more than to slump off his horse and rest motionless on the path, but they had yet to reach their designated rest area and they did not want to stray off schedule in the unrelenting territory. A rustle was heard in the trees off the left side of the path and the guards froze, placing their hands on their swords. A few men did not react immediately, because they were in a daze of exhaustion. Bishop's horse reared back, shocking him back to alertness.

It was a tense moment as the soldiers scanned the tree line looking for movement. A soldier fired an arrow into the trees and a small bird fluttered away into the mist. The men breathed a sigh of relief and relaxed their weapons.

"This is becoming more of a pain than I expected," joked Bishop, trying to lessen the tension of the men and lift their spirits.

The men laughed at the remark, now all fully awake despite their fatigue. The guard Captain pulled a sweat soaked map from his pack and analyzed their position. "The rest point is only a few miles ahead, Your Highness. We should be there within the hour."

"Thank you, Captain. I think we all could use a little rest."

Bishop quietly wiped the sweat from his brow. Even with the constant threat of danger around them and the looming meeting with Minor Leo in a few days, Bishop could think of nothing more than a night of sleep in the arms of his beautiful wife. Knowing this to be impossible, he would be content with a few hours of sleep on hard ground, with a caravan of sweaty men. In his current situation, he clung onto the little things.

Just before the men started to trot towards their long awaited rest, a scream erupted from behind them. In the mist, the soldiers could see nothing and they looked around to check if anyone was missing.

"Are all your men accounted for, Captain?" questioned Bishop.

The caravan's captain, in a panic, darted his eyes around the group. "Where is Forceman Cryne?" bellowed the nervous Captain.

The remaining men scanned for the missing soldier, but they could not find him. Another scream pierced through the mist from the path behind them. This time his screams did not stop.

In the mist it was difficult to see clearly, but a large dark shadow was moving in its depths. The rest of the guards armed themselves. One soldier fired an arrow at the beastly shadow, but it seemed to pass right through it. Suddenly, the man's blood-curdling screams were snuffed and all that could be heard were the sounds of teeth ripping through human flesh.

The soldiers were terrified. They stood armed and ready, but they could not move. Bishop, too, could not believe what he was seeing. His mind was reeling and he wanted to turn and flee.

"Do not fear, men!" yelled Bishop.

It took Bishop all his strength to try to instill courage into the men; something he was quickly losing himself. The creature turned towards the men and slowly emerged from the mist. It stalked its way towards them and the men began to slowly back away. Its sleek black head broke through the Shroud and the men gasped in astonishment. Blood dripped from the dagger-like teeth of the monster, a massive black panther. From the tips of its claws to the top of its sinewy back, it stood almost as tall as the horses the men rode upon. Its coat was a shimmering black, but was caked with blood. The soldiers were shaking, and the horses tried mightily to turn and run.

"It is just one monster! String your arrows and destroy the foul beast!"

The four archers loaded their bows and prepared to fire, but suddenly a pack of wolves sprang from the trees. Three of the archers were tackled from their horses, while the last was violently thrown when his horse reared back to avoid the wild dogs.

The wolves drove their sharp claws into the flesh of the men, pinning them to the ground, not allowing them to retaliate. A few of the men attempted to strike back but they were out-numbered and the mist obscured their vision.

The soldiers shouted and the horses screeched in pain as many of the wolves attacked them as well. A few yelps were heard as the soldiers struck blows to the vicious canines. Bishop fended off the leaping dogs with his sword while trying to calm his terrified horse.

Many of the horses, now rider-less, had escaped into the forest. Most likely they were chased down and devoured by the wolves, but that was of little concern for the soldiers that had been riding them. The men fought for their lives while, at the same time, watching their friends and comrades being brutally slaughtered around them. The mottled fur of the wolves was caked with blood, but little of it was their own.

Strangely, the black panther that had struck the first blow to the men stood motionless where it had first appeared from the mist. It seemed to revel in the carnage that was unfolding in front of it. A creature that size could easily have destroyed one of the guards with a swipe of the paw, but it just stood there, as if content with just watching.

Bishop had finally been thrown from his horse, but was managing to keep himself alive. He kicked away one of the wolves and swung his sword, grazing the creature's silver coat.

Bishop was stained with blood and his neatly trimmed uniform was in tatters. His mind was blank, as he reacted on instinct to defend himself. He was out of breath and barely standing, but little of that mattered. He must stay alive, somehow.

He threw away another wolf as it sprung at his chest, the canine thudded onto the ground, yelping. The panther suddenly sprang into the battle, bounding towards the Supreme Regis. Before Bishop was able to react, the panther had raised its massive paw to strike him down, letting out a roar that pierced so deep into Bishop's chest that he couldn't breathe.

In a frenzy of screams, Farren Kaiser shot out of bed. His body was drenched with sweat and, for seconds after, his screams still echoed from the walls of his bedroom. Farren was grabbing his chest as it heaved, trying to catch his breath. His mind raced.

A nightmare?

9

Commander Lucer was in his private study when a palace guard burst into the room to alert him of the news. *Something has happened to the Supreme Regis.* Coal could not remember the last time he felt so afraid. He dropped what he was doing and sprinted from the room.

For once, he ordered a guard to get him a horse to cross the palace grounds. Time was of the essence. Since the assassination of the previous Supreme Regis, Coal had vowed to never let anything happen to Bishop. Even now he was feeling intense regret.

I never should have let him go!

He only hoped now that Bishop was not too seriously injured.

The streets were eerily empty and quiet. He could hear shouts in the distance, but not a soul walked the cobblestone boulevards. His horse's hoof-beats echoed loudly off the buildings in the deserted streets. Even store owners had abandoned their buildings, some not even bothering to lock the front doors. The shouts began to get louder as Coal neared the city gate. After streaking through the bazaar he could see crowds blocking the streets.

"Clear the way!" he bellowed, not even bothering to slow down his horse.

The crowd was thick across the entire street and the line of people in the rear turned to see the Commander galloping towards them. They scrambled to get out of his way, starting a commotion that quickly created a tunnel for Coal to race through. He reached the gate, where soldiers had walled off the citizens. Coal saluted the patrolmen and they let him pass. A crowd of soldiers, councilmen and palace servants were swarming the injured Regis. Kaine Ducale turned when he heard Coal approach.

"Commander," Kaine saluted.

"What is the situation Captain?" barked Coal, as he hurried past his distraught Captain towards Bishop.

Kaine turned to hurry after him. "He's alive, Sir, but in critical shape. We need to get him to the royal alchemist immediately."

Coal pushed his way past the crowd to the bloodied Bishop. Farren was kneeling at his brother's side. The young Prince had arrived only a few moments before.

Kaine and Syd had tried to assure him that his brother would be okay and there was no reason for concern, but Farren did not speak or respond the entire time. He had arrived in silent shock and had not made a noise since then. His expression was still the same as he stared down at the bloodied form of his older brother.

The Supreme Regis's clothes were in tatters and his body was caked with dried blood and cracked layers of mud. He no longer wore his uniformed coat. His collared under shirt was missing its right arm and was torn extensively. His pants were in much better shape, only showing fraying at the cuffs and a few tears. It was difficult to tell if all of the blood was his own, but it seemed inconceivable that anyone could spill that amount of blood and still be alive. Even with all of his injuries, he seemed almost peaceful in his unconscious state.

Coal turned to Kaine with eyes that could cut through glass. "How did this happen?!" he seethed, shaking with rage.

"Sir, I do not think this is the place to discuss such information," sputtered the Captain; head lowered in dishonor and guilt.

Sweat dripped from Kaine's forehead as he waited for permission to raise his eyes. Coal jerked his head back to look at the limp body of the Supreme Regis. Alchemists had arrived and they began loading his body into a carriage to be taken to the palace. Captain Rayaz was assisting the alchemists as they lifted Bishop up and onto a stretcher. Syd turned to see Coal glaring in his direction. He too lowered his head, eyes sorrowful and repentant.

The crowd, which had been raucous and loud, each citizen fighting to see what had happened to their precious ruler, now hushed as they watched his body being loaded into the horse drawn carriage. Their eyes all widened with concern. Many people raised their heads, looking to the sky for guidance from their god; silently praying for Bishop's safety.

"Escort the Regis' body to the infirmary. Once he is safely in the hands of the royal alchemist I want you to find a quiet place to reflect on what you have allowed to happen here," he said to Kaine, his eyes still transfixed on the bloodied form of the Regis. He turned back to the kneeling Kaine. "Then, I will expect a full report. Spend some time deciding how you will word that, as well. You have very little room for error right now, Captain."

"Yes, sir!" he yelled. He slowly rose to his feet, avoiding eye contact with his Commander. He looked briefly at Coal to salute, then ran over to help the others secure Bishop's body into the carriage.

As the carriage began to make its way towards the castle, the crowd parted silently, like the waters parting to allow the great hull of a ship to pass through. The hushed citizens bowed their heads in homage to their Regis, some even weeping as his body rolled past. After the carriage broke free of the crowds it picked up speed and raced towards the palace. Captain Ducale and Rayaz rode after it on their own horses.

Farren watched silently as his brother was carted off, still having not uttered a word the entire time. Coal walked up behind him and put a hand on his shoulder, a fleeting attempt to ease some of his concern.

"He will be fine, Farren. Dominic Suphik is the best healer there is, and your brother is strong. He won't let something like this kill him."

Coal's words did little to ease Farren's fearful thoughts, but not because his words were ineffective. What Coal did not realize was that Farren was not worried about his brother surviving. He knew how strong his brother was. Coal did not have the slightest clue that Farren had dreamed of this happening only a few days ago and the young Prince could not look at his bloodied brother without thinking that he somehow had something to do with it.

When the Valorian Palace was built after the end of the Emerald Ages, a main focus in its construction was sheer immensity. Every room and hallway was meant to make the visitor feel insignificant when they entered. The ceilings were vaulted to heights taller than most trees of the Shroud and some rooms, including the Main Hall, were so massive you had to strain your eyes to see an object on the other side.

The royal infirmary, though, seemed to have been built from on old closet, or whatever room there was left over after the rest of the construction was complete. It was only meant to heal the royal family, thus did not need to be any larger than needed. It was not a room that one desired to be in.

While it was small, the alchemical equipment it housed was the most advanced in the Kingdom. The art of precise and effective internal surgery was new and the tools were laid out on a sterilized table in the corner. Canisters of alchemical herbs and medicines lined shelves around the perimeter of the room and crude diagrams of human internal systems and processes adorned the walls.

There was clearly little focus on appearance in the room's decor and people often wondered if the dreariness of the room was a detriment to the health of the occupants.

Bishop, though, did not notice, or care, about the austerity of his surroundings as he lay unconscious on his bed. His wounds had been cleaned and stitched and medicated salves were applied to block infection. Even the deep wounds across his chest were successfully closed by the work of Royal Alchemist Dominic Suphik.

Dominic stood above his sleeping patient, observed his recovery and took notes about the operation and its successes. Bishop was doing well. The bleeding had stopped and the trauma to his head was minor, but the Alchemist still worried that his mind may have been damaged. They could only wait and see.

The Lady Kara had arrived as they were bringing Bishop's body into the infirmary and had not left since. Her tears were finally drying and her mood calming. She had heard the news from one of her servants and immediately rushed to her husband's side.

She sat at a small chair at the side of his bed. She wiped the sweat from her hands before clasping back onto Bishop's motionless left hand. While she was no longer crying, her sharp, green eyes were still red from the hours of tears. She had pulled her long hair back in a loose pony tail to keep it out of her face.

The Alchemist's aids had a difficult time ripping her frantic body from Bishop when they first brought him to the infirmary to start the operation. She was a passionate, fiery woman and she would do anything for her beloved husband. But, now it seemed she could do nothing but pray.

It was late into the night now and many glow lights aided the moonlight in illuminating the small room. A handful of aides were finishing cleaning up the room from the operation, trying not to disturb the Regis and his Lady. After watching the carriage drive off with his brother's body, Farren had followed suit and had been in the infirmary the entire time as well. Still confused about the ordeal, Farren had been silent much of the time, speaking only to try to comfort the frantic Kara. He now stood just outside the door, watching his brother and Kara from a distance.

Farren did not want to be too involved in the operation and any questioning because he was in no mood to discuss anything. He just wanted to be alone to contemplate his haunting thoughts, but he also did not want to leave his brother's side.

"You should sleep, Farren. There is nothing you can do at this point," suggested Commander Lucer, as he walked silently up behind Farren.

Farren continued to stare at the two near the bed. Even with all of the other thoughts circulating through his mind, Farren had a sudden touch of envy for his brother. He wondered when he would find a woman who was as truly devoted to him as Kara was to Bishop. Farren shook his head, trying to wake himself from the haze. "Maybe you are right, Coal. Besides, he seems to be in good hands."

Coal smiled, happy to hear Farren not only speak normally, but with a hint of humor. "Go. I will make sure you are informed immediately if anything else arises."

Farren slowly turned, giving Coal an exhausted smile. "Thank you, Coal." He slowly trudged past the Commander and then turned. "Do not let Kara stay much longer either, Coal. I think she might faint from exhaustion if she is not forced to leave soon. We don't have many beds left available in there," he smiled briefly, then walked away down the hall.

A lower level Gallant soldier stopped briefly in the hallway to bow to Farren and then briskly walked his way up to Coal. He saluted rigidly; clearly a little tense in front of the Commander. Everyone knew how serious Coal took his station as Commander and he did not take failure lightly. This soldier had obviously been informed of Coal's earlier outburst.

"Captain Ducale and Rayaz are ready to give their report, Sir," informed the messenger, trying to be brief and to the point. "They await your arrival." The man gave a hidden hand signal, to inform Coal that Kaine and Syd were meeting him in the secret Gallant chambers.

Coal nodded his head to the man, calmly gesturing him to leave. His calm exterior, though, hid his inner concern. The hidden chambers were used only for top secret meetings and discussions of war. The seriousness of these events could possibly be far worse than Coal had originally anticipated.

The sound of Commander Lucer's footsteps echoed loudly across the training room as he walked quickly across the granite floor. He walked down hallway after hallway, not bothering to acknowledge any other soldiers as he passed.

A Gallant trainee jumped out of his chair when Coal rushed into the room. The small library was only regularly used by trainees for study and, therefore, was not highly trafficked. The young soldier saluted smartly.

"Leave soldier," ordered Coal.

He nodded his head, grabbed the books he was reading, and hurriedly left the room.

Coal waited until the young man had left before turning back around to examine the room. It was small by library standards, housing military records from the last centuries of Brivan rule. Valor Forces soldiers used the texts to study for the many exams involved in testing to become Gallant Special Forces.

The ceiling was vaulted, like all buildings in the palace grounds, but the room did not extend far. A scant few desks scattered the floor and many books and scrolls were strewn across them. Coal shook his head in disgust at the disorder, but ignored the blatant lack of discipline for the time being. He would make a point of discovering the culprit later.

He walked towards the back wall, searching the lines of books on the shelf. He stopped at a large green text labeled "The Art of War."

Coal pushed hard against the wall at that point and the shelf nudged forward. He continued to push as the shelf rotated, revealing a dark passage behind. He slid himself through and pushed the shelf back into place. A light glow of light could be seen down the passage.

As Coal entered the hidden meeting room he heard the low sounds of two men talking. When the echoing sounds of his footsteps neared the glow, the sounds hushed.

"Commander?" questioned one of the voices.

"Yes, I am here Captain," responded Coal as he stepped into the widened room.

Captain Ducale and Rayaz were standing at the far end of the room and they saluted when the Commander entered.

The room was small and dark, with only a faint glow from a few glow lights in the corners. A large rectangular table sat in the middle. The walls were cold and bare; made of the stone that comprised the foundation of all buildings on the palace grounds. The room was nestled deep inside the military structure, far from prying eyes and listening ears.

The Commander ushered the two Captains to sit. Coal sat at the head, with Kaine and Syd on either side.

"How is Bishop doing, Sir?" asked Kaine.

"He is recovering well. Dominic assures me he will be quite fine. There were no life threatening injuries. All he needs is rest now."

"That is good news to be sure."

"Good news for whom? You or Bishop?" asked Coal with a serious tone.

"Bishop, of course," defended Kaine.

"It troubles me, Captain, that you wished to deliver your report in this room. Is this situation truly serious enough to validate this kind of secrecy?"

"I do, Sir. When I tell you our report I believe you will agree. I will try to be as concise and direct as possible, Commander," Kaine stated. "I know how much you dislike it when I ramble."

Coal nodded his head

"We were following the caravan as you commanded, at a safe distance. Nothing out of the ordinary had happened and nobody had spotted us. When we entered the Shroud it was difficult to follow them without fear of being detected, so we used the sounds of their voices and hoof beats to determine how far away we were."

"On the second day traveling through the Shroud, we heard screams erupt from the caravan. The men were yelling, but we were unable to distinguish what they were saying. We rushed ahead to try to protect the Regis from whatever was attacking, but by the time we reached them, it was all over. We were further from the caravan than we thought and we arrived too late."

Syd interrupted. "The soldiers were dead, Sir. All of them. Within a matter of minutes, every last one of them was slaughtered."

Coal did not react to the comments. He just sat, contemplating the account that his Captains were retelling him. "Who was it that attacked? Was it a coordinated attack, or just a pack of beasts from the Shroud?" stoically questioned Coal.

"We do not know, Sir. There were no bodies aside from those of the men. Either the men were unable to kill a single opponent, or the attackers quickly removed their dead before fleeing."

Coal sat silently, as if telling Kaine that he had more to say.

Kaine stuttered slightly as his thoughts scrambled to decide what else he should say. Syd again interrupted, sensing his friend's distress.

"The men's wounds were inflicted by claws and teeth. It had to have been animals from the forest, Sir. I don't have a doubt in my mind."

Coal's face twitched, showing a sign of irritation. He turned to Kaine. "Do you agree with your fellow Captain's assessment, Kaine? Or, is there something else you would like to add?"

"I agree with him, Sir. I see no other explanation," Kaine asserted.

Kaine and Syd kept their heads held high, waiting for Coal to make a response. It was quiet in the stone-walled chamber. The only sound that could be heard was the heavy sound of Coal's breathing, which was becoming louder. "So, what you are saying is that a squad of fully trained Forces Soldiers were completely wiped out by a pack of wild animals, without putting up a fight?!" Coal shouted, his anger crescendoing as he spoke.

Coal rose from his seat, pacing the room to try to release some anger. The glow lights seemed to flicker when he released breathes of frustration. "So, what of the Regis? He was still alive, of course," asked Coal. "Did he somehow fight his way through the attack?"

Kaine perked up, thankful for a question he could answer. "We searched the area and could not find his body. We found a trail into the forest, so we decided to follow it. We finally found him on the ground, unconscious."

"And there was still no sign of an enemy?"

"No, Sir. We feared that whatever had attacked them would return, so we took the Regis and fled."

Having calmed himself and regained his composure, Coal returned to his seat. "This disturbs me greatly. I wish we had more answers, but the Shroud conceals everything. I have never heard of such an attack from beasts in the Shroud. Normally, they attack individually or in small groups. This seems too organized and too precise for beasts, but Dominic also agreed that the wounds looked like they were inflicted by animals."

"I wish that we had more answers, Sir. Our first priority was to get Bishop out of there safely"

"As it should have been. At least you were able to do something correctly. If what you say is true, though, then you two are lucky to be alive, as well."

Kaine and Syd sat listening, having no intention of adding any thoughts that might reignite their Commander's retreating anger. "If Bishop had not lived through the attack, you might have been better off not even returning to give your report," quietly added Coal, showing that he still held them responsible and would not forget it.

10

Kara did not enjoy the cramped surroundings of the Royal Infirmary, but she suffered through it. She knew of no other place she wanted to be than next to her dear husband.

The Supreme Regis was healing well, but had not yet awakened. Kara had spent every waking hour at his side, wanting to be there when he finally opened his eyes. She did not realize how much she was actually going to miss him until he left on his mission to Coroge. Now he had returned, but she had not yet had a chance to see his smiling face. It made it worse that she had to look at him every day, but he was not looking back.

There was yet to be a culprit discovered in the attack, even after Commander Lucer's strenuous efforts. He found his Captains' report disturbing and absurd. Coal did not believable that a pack of wild beasts could take out a regiment of Forces soldiers, but there was no evidence to the contrary. Coal had petitioned the Council to allow a search party to set out to investigate the scene of the attack more carefully, but the Council did not think it wise to risk the lives of other men just to satisfy his curiosity.

Coal hated the insufferable men that comprised the council. He found their incessant rambling infuriating. They rarely managed to agree on anything, or get anything done in a timely manner. Even with the guiding voice of Head Council Anton Grey, Coal's inquiry took five days to discuss and even then it was denied. Coal eventually gave up on his search for answers and instead spent his time visiting his friend in the infirmary. When the Regis awakened, he would have his answer.

Dominic Suphik had watched the Regis' condition closely over the past week, along with a handful of his aides. The aides routinely cleaned Bishop and soaked his body in water laden with medicinal herbs to cleanse his body of any contaminants that might hinder his recovery. His wounds were healing nicely and many of the stitches had been removed except the deep cut across his chest, which still needed medicinal salves applied to help heal it.

It was a gorgeous day in the Brivan capitol city and Kara could feel the warmth of the sun through the few small windows in the room. On such a beautiful day, Coal's duties took him away from the palace grounds and Farren was undoubtedly in the city making trouble. Kara, though, was still sitting at Bishop's side.

Over the past days, Kara had made the confined walls of the infirmary her home. To consume her time, she brought books to read. Sometimes she would even read them aloud to Bishop, but only if there was no one else around to hear her. Often, she asked the aides if she could help in the cleansing because it made her feel like she was contributing to her husband's recovery.

The aides were very friendly to the royal lady; making conversation and keeping her spirits high. They brought her food, even though she continuously told them she could get it herself. Unknown to Kara, Coal had ordered the aides to keep his sister happy and well fed; whatever it took. Today Kara read aloud a section from a romantic fiction story that she used to love when she was younger. She knew Bishop would have hated it and she smiled to herself thinking about it. She was in a very cheerful and rebellious mood today.

The Royal Alchemist Dominic walked into the room and Kara quickly quieted, trying to pretend that she wasn't reading out loud to the unconscious Bishop. "Did you know it is theorized that a person still hears the words being spoken around them when they are asleep? They will only remember those words, though, in their dreams," commented the alchemist, giving Lady Kara a wink.

Kara smiled at the middle-aged alchemist. He, along with the aides, had been a major source of comfort during her stay and she enjoyed talking with him.

His grayish white, hair was balding at the top of his head and he had a thick beard that covered much of his face. Kara assumed he was probably in his fifties, but it was possible his lack of personal grooming and uncaring attitude towards his appearance made him seem older than he really was.

Dominic was out of shape and it showed. His stomach protruded from his alchemist's coat and he did little to cover it up. In his younger days, when he traveled throughout Paks, he was a much fitter and handsome man. These days, he cared about nothing more than his experiments and studies.

"Was it you that theorized this, Dominic?" asked Kara slyly, knowing that he liked to boast often of his exploits.

Dominic blushed and smiled. He never did know quite how to handle accolades, especially from a young and beautiful girl such as Kara. Even though the alchemist bragged about his own feats, he did so in jest, so people would find it unnecessary to praise him themselves. He felt awkward when applauded and did not need acclaim in order to continue doing what he loved.

"You flatter me, My Lady. No, it was my old master that theorized it. He did many tests that he believed proved it, but not many others were as certain as he."

As he spoke, Dominic checked Bishop's wounds to assess their status and examined his overall well-being. When he touched the wound on his chest, the Regis's body switched and he started to groan. Kara's eyes widened and she gasped in astonishment. She had been waiting for so long, a part of her thought he would never wake. Dominic turned around and called for aides. Two aides rushed into the room to make sure they were ready when the Regis woke up.

Bishop continued to stir, and then his eyes started to crack open. "Bishop!" cried Kara. She jumped onto him, embracing him as if for the first time. Bishop looked up at her with his half open, dreary eyes, not moving his head.

"Where am I?" he moaned.

Kara was still too overwhelmed to speak, so Dominic responded. "You are in the Royal Infirmary, Your Highness. You are lucky to be alive from the injuries that you sustained."

"Injuries?"

"Do you not remember what happened?" Dominic quickly turned to one of his aides, who scrambled to take notes.

Bishop achingly sat himself up in his bed; a few of the aides assisting in helping him reposition his pillow and head rest. "I remember leaving here and traveling through the Shroud. I was… on my way to Coroge." Bishop struggled to remember what happened.

"Do you remember what happened after that? Do you remember what, or who, attacked you?" pushed the alchemist.

Bishop thought intensely, but shook his head in dismay. "No. It all goes black after that."

Dominic gestured to another aide to fetch some water for the Regis, as the other continued to furiously take notes on Bishop's status.

"Just rest now. It may come back to you in time. You need to recover your strength. I will return in a few hours," reassured Dominic. He turned to walk out of the room. Before he could reach the door, Farren burst in at a full sprint.

"Brother!" Farren rushed over to the bed and grabbed Bishop's hand, startling him. "You're finally awake. The aide in the passage told me you were awake," he shouted.

"Thank the Almighty. I was beginning to worry you were never going to awake," blurted the young Prince.

Kara gasped at the Prince's audacity and openness. "Farren!" she scolded. "Don't tell your brother that." She then blushed slightly, realizing she had thought the same thing.

"Don't worry, my dear. I'm sure he is not the only one that felt that way. I am sorry I worried you," Bishop said with a smile.

"It is alright, Bishop. As long as you are well, that is all that matters. The people will be happy to know you are finally awake. So will Coal," Kara said calmly.

Bishop showed a look of confusion when he heard Coal's name, but covered it up with a smile. The aide finally scampered in with a container of water and poured the Regis a glass. He drank it deeply.

"There has been something I have wanted to ask, Brother," piped up Farren. "Would it be alright if I started sword training? Master Guy has told me his apprentice, Kaleb, would be willing to teach me." The youngster sat anxiously waiting his brother's response.

Bishop sat surprised by the inquiry, mouth agape. "Well, uhhh. If that is what you want, then of course."

"Thank you so much, Brother!" Farren turned and sprinted out of the room. He turned in the doorway and yelled back. "I'm happy you're awake. I will come back later to see how you are doing." He then disappeared around the corner.

Bishop and Kara both let out a sigh of relief to see him leave. Bishop then turned and smiled at his beautiful wife. He took another sip of water and breathed deeply, feeling the cold liquid rejuvenate his body.

"By the way, how long has it been since I was last awake? How long have I been like this?" he asked.

"It has been almost a week since Kaine and Syd brought you back to the city," responded Kara.

Bishop nearly dropped his glass and his gaze turned again from pleasure to shock.

"What's wrong, dear?" begged Kara, seeing his reaction.

"That fool!" Bishop shouted with an intense anger. He ripped off his covers and turned to get out of bed when Kara grabbed his arm.

"What's wrong?" Kara yelled. "You shouldn't be getting up so quickly."

Two aides entered the room when they heard the commotion. Bishop turned to Kara and stared at her with a heated gaze. Kara recoiled in astonishment.

"Let go of me," growled Bishop.

Kara was so alarmed, she instinctively released his wrist. He turned and stormed out of the room, not bothering with the aides who tried feebly to get in his way and force him back into bed. Kara stood dumbstruck at what had just happened. That was not the smiling face she was waiting to see.

JJ

While the city of Valoria was a major hub of trade and commerce in the kingdom, it was still just a small speck in the sea of nature that encompassed Paks. Much of Paks was untraveled and undiscovered, especially the thick trees of the Shroud and the Great Bardon Mountains that separated the three largest sects; Briva, Vertura and Fera.

Once outside the walls of the city, there was nothing but plains, forests and farmland. The farmland supplied much of the produce and grains for the citizens of Valoria, while the more exotic foods were imported from the neighboring sects. The farms also raised cattle and other animals to be butchered and sold in the market.

The Shroud was too dangerous to hunt; so much of the wild game was caught in the less menacing forests to the south. The Wild Southern Boar was found in those forests and its natural spicy flavor made it a favorite in the city taverns. The remaining land around the city was filled by open plains, streams and rocky hills.

The Valor Forces also once used these plains to train; needing the wide open areas to practice battle formations and tactics. The old training grounds were now abandoned and marked as a landmark in memorial to the soldiers lost in the War of Paksian Rule.

Farren sat under the shade of a tree, overlooking the vast training grounds. He could hear the running water of a stream passing near him, and the roar of a small waterfall further downstream that led to the grounds.

Farren wore a tight military training outfit in preparation for his first day of training. The outfit consisted of a grey, tight single suit that formed to his body to allow for complete mobility and a padded vest.

Paks' hot, red sun had just risen above the horizon and had begun beating its heated rays onto the landscape. It was going to be a hot day and there was no wind to subdue the inferno. The regular cheeps from the waking birds were absent; the birds most likely hiding from the heat like the young Prince.

Farren let out a bored sigh as he lay under the shade of the young oak. "Where is he?" he said aloud. "What is the point of me waking up so early if he is late himself?"

After getting the okay from his brother, Farren had quickly rushed to Master Guy, begging for him to start his training. Seeing the eagerness in his old pupil's eyes, Guy was more than happy to oblige.

"Be at the old training grounds at sunrise," instructed the old Gallant. "My apprentice, Kaleb, will be there to start your training."

Farren was slightly disappointed that his old teacher would not be training him himself, but he did not argue with Guy's wisdom. Besides, he was curious to see how strong this young Kaleb was.

Kaleb was only a few years older than the Prince and had been training under the tutelage of Guy for years. He was too young to have been a Forces soldier prior to this training, so Farren wondered why he was able to bypass the usual steps of becoming a Gallant.

It was customary that a man be enlisted into the Forces for at least four years before they were eligible to go through the training and testing to join the Special Forces ranks. Kaleb, though, was being trained as a Gallant without prior military service. *There had to be a reason,* wondered Farren.

Farren slumped further against the tree and put his hands behind his head, closing his eyes to listen to the sounds of nature. Farren suddenly heard a sharp, whooshing sound in the air and opened his eyes. An arrow sailed towards him from above and before he was able to get out of the way it embedded itself in to the ground between his legs.

He was so shocked by the sudden appearance of this deadly projectile he was unable to let out an audible shriek. His eyes just widened in astonishment. Seeing another one flying towards him he shook himself from his stupor in time to role to the side and avoid it. This time it had landed directly at the base of the tree where he had been laying.

He drew his two jukos and crouched ready for retaliation. Two more arrows flew towards him and he nimbly dodged them with little effort. After waiting to see if more arrows would come, he shouted to his hidden assailant.

"Who is out there? Who dares fire at the Prince of Briva?"

A laugh could be heard from a distance and Kaleb stepped out from behind the cover of a few trees downstream towards the waterfall.

"You sound so formal and assertive when you shout like that. Nothing like the infamous Scourge of Valoria Bazaar," shouted Kaleb.

"Oh, it's you."

Kaleb smirked at Farren's embarrassed expression. He held his bow at his side, not hiding the fact he was the hidden attacker. He quickly erased the smirk from his face, trying to conceal his amused satisfaction. His sharp facial features; thin mouth, narrow chin and pointed nose, emphasized his stern military focus. That being said, it was obvious Kaleb was not above having a little fun every once in a while.

"You could have killed me, you know," said Farren.

"If I wanted you dead, you would have been dead. That was just a test." Kaleb shouldered his bow. "Come with me."

He started walking downstream towards the waterfall. Farren quickly followed.

"What do you mean a test? That second arrow landed right where I was sitting. If I hadn't jumped out of the way..."

Kaleb continued walking, while Farren tried to keep up as he beseeched his trainer for answers.

"Exactly. You were able to dodge the second arrow. A soldier must always be aware of his surroundings. He should never let his guard down. If I had meant the first arrow to hit you, you would be dead," instructed Kaleb.

Farren contemplated the comment and, while he felt the idea could have been explained in a more subtle manner, he could not argue the importance of it. He continued to follow Kaleb until they approached the waterfall.

Below was a recess in the open plain, with a small pond at the base of the waterfall. The area of grass was about the size of the training corral at the royal stables, or just large enough for a Gallant bowman to practice his expert marksmanship.

The grass was clearly worn from frequent usage, but some parts were beginning to grow back since its abandonment. A few scattered trees dotted the area, used for shade and targets for bow practice.

"This is where we will train. Up until the end of the war, this is where all soldiers were trained to become Gallant members." With a nod of his head, Kaleb indicated to Farren a large stone staircase that lead down into the bowl.

Down on the training grounds, Kaleb began unpacking a bag of supplies he had brought down for training. Farren stood eager with anticipation, but with a sense of foreboding at how difficult the training would be. Kaleb spoke without looking up as he unpacked.

"In fighting, there are three chief virtues; speed, strength and control. We will assess your abilities in these three virtues today. So first, I want you to scale those stairs." Kaleb blindly held up his arm, pointing towards the ragged stone steps that they took to enter the grounds.

Farren's face turned to a look of excitement to hear his first task and he turned to run off towards the base.

"Fifty times. Up and down," continued Kaleb.

Farren froze in shock.

"While you do that, I will set up the next two tasks," he finished. "And take off that padded vest. You will not be needing that today."

Farren's jaw dropped and he turned to Kaleb in disbelief. Not hearing Farren's retreating footsteps, Kaleb turned to look at the stunned boy.

"What is the matter? I gave you your first task."

"Fifty times?" blurted Farren. "That is insane." Farren pointed towards the stairs, hoping for a hint of compassion from his trainer. Kaleb, though, was not amused.

"When I talk of speed, I do not just mean speed of hand, or speed of thrust, or speed of foot. There is also endurance. You do not want to be caught in a large battle and have yourself killed because you could not outlast your opponent. Losing to a lesser enemy while you are trying to catch your breath is a dishonorable way to die," said Kaleb bluntly.

Kaleb again returned to his work unpacking. Farren, abashed by the lecture, slowly turned and trotted off towards the stairs. Kaleb watched the young Prince begin his assent and smiled.

Nearly four hours later, Kaleb lay under the shade of a tree near the waterfall pond, doing his best to imitate Farren's carefree demeanor when he first arrived. He had been mentally counting Farren's progress on the stairs as he relaxed under the shade.

After many water breaks and near disastrous tumbles, Farren was stumbling his way down the stairway for the fiftieth time. Kaleb could hear his frantic heaving and moans of exhaustion.

At the final stair, Farren nearly miss-stepped and gave way to fatigue too quickly, but he pushed forth enough energy to keep himself afoot and collapsed to his knees instead. He slumped into a ball on the ground, his back heaving as he gasped for air.

Kaleb heard the collapse and peered at Farren through one eye. He shook his head in dismay, but with a smile on his face. He rocked himself up into a sitting position and then got up and walked over to Farren.

Kaleb reached out a small leather canteen of water. "Here, drink up."

Farren turned his slumped head to spot the canteen, then swung a limp arm up to snag it. He quaffed the entire canteen and then handed it back, still showing a little fight in him.

"Don't stay slumped like that forever. Your muscles will tighten up and the next exercise will be far worse," said Kaleb. Farren flung his head back, staring up into the beating sun. He groaned loudly. "Get up. No time to sit around," ordered Kaleb, as he turned and started walking towards the pond. "We're going into the pond next."

Farren willed himself to stand, moving one limb at a time like a puppet coming to life. He had no energy left to argue with the stern young trainer. "I didn't think it possible, but you're worse than Master Guy," Farren groaned as he began his mechanical shuffle towards the waterfall pond.

Farren finally walked up next to Kaleb, who was standing at the edge of the pool. "The next virtue is power," said Kaleb. He calmly reached out a hand and nudged Farren into the water. Farren no longer had the strength to recover his balance and he flopped ungracefully into the stillness.

He floundered his way back to the surface, gasping for breath. "What was that for?!" he complained; the cold water seemingly revitalizing his energy.

"I just thought it would be easier than listening to you whining about having to jump in."

Farren rolled his eyes, but did not argue because he realized Kaleb was right again. This kid was wiser than he first appeared to be. *He is definitely a student of Master Guy,* Farren thought to himself.

"Power is an essential virtue in battle," Kaleb started again. "If your attacks have more strength behind them, you will wear on your enemy quicker. A more powerful attack is a more decisive attack. The most powerful assault is one that does not require a second strike. You can only achieve this through increased strength."

"Then, why am I in the water?" questioned the sodden prince.

"You will practice your sword moves and footwork in the water." Kaleb tossed a wooden sword to Farren. "The resistance of the water will make each movement more difficult, therefore will build strength."

Farren nodded his acknowledgement and then turned to begin his work.

"Tie these around your ankles as well. They will keep you anchored to the bottom," said Kaleb as he tossed a set of small weights attached to ropes into the water.

Farren dove down and retrieved the weights and tied them to himself. Without complaint he went to work. *Attack, advance, parry, sidestep, cut, defend, retreat, lunge, thrust,* Farren repeated in his mind as he wrenched his body through the thick, cool water.

After a few hours of water training, Kaleb started clapping his hands together to get Farren's attention.

"Alright, Alright. Your time is up, Young Master." Kaleb circled the edge of the pond to face the front of the exhausted young prince.

Amazingly, he had kept a nice steady pace the entire time, seemingly drawing energy from the cold water. He stopped his movements, letting his head fall back and float on the water. He breathed heavily, but with no excessive gasps or moans. He was exhausted, but did not feel the need to make a show of it.

"Excellent! You kept pace, which is outstanding. Your movements were a bit dull and sloppy, especially as you tired, but that is to be expected. You are coming along nicely," said Kaleb. "We will take a short break. I brought you a change of clothes." Kaleb pointed towards the tree where he rested earlier; a change of clothes, water and a small snack were laid out underneath.

Farren struggled to get out of the wet single suit that clung tightly to his body. He lay naked on the grass to let the slight breeze dry him and the beating sun warm his body. The snack was a bland military ration of potatoes, bread and cold slice of overcooked beef. Farren only noticed the energy it gave him as he quickly consumed it. He drank the entire canteen of water and then put on the fresh, dry single suit brought by Kaleb.

He took a few deep breaths to calm himself and closed his eyes to feel the warmth of the sun on his face.

"Alright," he said aloud to himself.

He pushed himself up off the ground and wandered over to where Kaleb was calmly eating his rations. Kaleb turned and showed an expression of slight surprise. He finished chewing, and set the rest to the side. "Alright then. Let's begin."

At the far end of the waterfall pond, a series of flat rocks jutted out of the water creating small platforms scattered throughout the area. Kaleb hopped out towards the middle of them and Farren followed, much less gracefully. They faced each other and Kaleb tossed Farren another wooden sword. He held one as well.

"The final virtue of battle is control. You can be the fastest and strongest fighter in all of Paks but, if you are unable to control those abilities, you will be unable to use them effectively and will easily be defeated. Control is the most important of the three virtues. You must be able to control your body as well as your mind. Instinctive awareness is the first step towards acquiring that control."

Kaleb suddenly swung out his sword. Farren managed to raise his sword in defense, but he was put off balance and he slipped from the rock and into the water.

When Farren rose back out of the water, Kaleb yelled at him in a commanding voice. "Not good enough! Get back up."

Farren scrambled back onto one of the rocks and this time got himself into a ready position.

"Instinctive awareness is the ability to have complete knowledge of your surroundings without deliberation. Without thinking, you should have known that there was another rock two feet back and to the left of you that you could have stepped back onto. You should also know that after the splash of your last fall it is now wet, so the traction will be poor and you should take caution." Farren turned to see the rock and quickly examined the rest of the area as well.

"In a battle, there will be many different things occurring all around you. You won't be able to keep complete focus on all of them, so instinctive awareness is key," Kaleb continued.

Farren focused on his every word. Without speaking, Farren nodded.

"Let us begin again," warned Kaleb. He swung out his sword again.

Soaked and exhausted, Farren lay naked on the grass in direct view of the sun. He had nothing left. After hours of training on the rocks, Farren had finally succeeded in fending off all of Kaleb's attacks, nimbly stepping from stone to stone, only to slip on the final stone and fall into the water.

"You improved quickly," lauded Kaleb, who sat next to him in the grass.

The sun was a few hours from setting and the temperature was starting to drop. Farren sat up and grabbed a pair of loose cotton pants. After he tightened the waist he sat back down next to his trainer.

"But, not enough," Farren brooded.

Kaleb laughed. "Don't beat yourself up. There have been many fully trained soldiers who have done much worse than you did today. I myself did not do as well as you my first time." Kaleb gave Farren a hard pat on the back, and then took a long swig of water from his canteen. "You should be proud of yourself."

Farren smiled and then fell back onto the grass. "It felt good," Farren commented. "I only wish I had started it sooner."

"It's never too late. You have plenty of time to improve."

They both sat staring up at the retreating sun. "So, how is it you became Master Guy's apprentice?" asked Farren, breaking the peaceful silence. "Your training does not seem to follow the normal procedure?"

A flock of birds streaked across the sky, and the bottom edge of the sun hit the horizon, making the sky dim ever so slightly. A slight chill came over them both as the sun dipped. A bell tolled in the distance towards the city. Kaleb lowered his head, his smile slowly faded at the chime. "That my friend is a story for another day."

12

The bells of the council chambers rang loudly. The sound reverberated throughout the city. They needed to be loud, so all Councilmen, wherever in the city they may be, could hear them.

The day was ending. The shops of the bazaar were packing up and the rest of the citizens were heading home after a long day of work. Soon the lights of the Seduke District would brighten and those that still had energy left from their day would drink to their hearts' content.

Tonight, though, all councilmen would still be working. When the bells of the council chamber tolled, that meant an emergency meeting was being summoned. Not since the beginning of the war had those bells rang.

It took time for the hundreds of aged men to shuffle their way into the chamber from throughout the city. Many were annoyed by the late and sudden summons, but they were generally more curious and concerned about the reason why they were being called. "Not since the war," they all muttered.

As the councilmen filed in, the chambers continued to grow louder with chatter and confusion. All wondered why they were summoned, but no one seemed to know. To add to their confusion, Supreme Regis Bishop sat at the table in the center of the chamber; the spot normally reserved for Head Council Grey. Anton stood next to the Regis, waiting for the chamber to fill; not uttering a word to anyone.

While Anton did not show it, he was just as confused about why they were there as everyone else. The Regis had come to his chamber and demanded he call an emergency council. He did not give an explanation and immediately left before Anton could ask for one.

Since the council generally never convened at night, the room was poorly lit with the fading light outside. Glow lights were dispersed throughout the room, but they were little help. Shadows stretched across the walls as the councilmen continued to enter, adding to the ominous feel of the proceedings.

Coal entered the chamber, for once alert and intrigued at the start of a council meeting. He had not had a chance to see the Supreme Regis since he had woken and unexpectedly charged out of the infirmary. Bishop had shut himself in his quarters since then, refusing to speak to anyone.

Coal had spent many hours trying to sooth his sister's anxiety; reassuring her that Bishop was not himself and it may take him time to recover from the traumatic events that he experienced.

Kara had never seen Bishop act so irrationally. He had never once raised his voice at her in anger. The startling outburst from her husband had sent her into a daze. She could not comprehend what had happened, nor could she find a reason for it. So, until then, she continued to walk around as a confused soul, longing for answers.

Bishop, on the other hand, seemed impassive as he sat at the center of the chamber. Even with the hundreds of eyes bearing down on him from the seats, his expression was unchanged. He was a man who had a purpose and everyone in that chamber wondered of its details. The last few councilmen filed in. Every spot was full. Not a single councilman would miss an emergency meeting.

Anton watched as those men took their seats. He cleared his throat and the chamber quickly quieted. "Good evening, Councilmen. I apologize for the inconvenience of this meeting," he started. In truth, he minded little of the convenience of these decrepit men, most of whom used their position for unlawful and personal gain. Formality in this instance was a must, though, so he forced his way through it.

"Listening to the chatter before the assembly I can tell that many of you would rather I get to the heart of the matter, so I will not waste time. Today's gathering was by request of the Supreme Regis, who has joined us today. We are all thankful that he has fully recovered from his ordeal in the Shroud. We were all praying for his swift recovery. But now, he wishes to speak to us on a matter he assures me is of the utmost importance. Our great ruler wishes to speak before us, so I humbly, and with great pride, hand the floor over to him."

Anton turned to the side and stepped back, to allow Bishop to take his place. He placed his closed fist to his forehead, thumb first, and bowed his head down as Bishop passed. The rest of the chamber rose to their feet and did the same. It was the formal salute that all councilmen were required to perform in the presence of the Regis.

"We open our minds to accept your wisdom," they all chanted.

Bishop stood at the center of the stage and scanned the crowd around him. The councilmen sat back down silently. It seemed like eternity, but for almost a minute, the chamber was dead quiet. The councilmen held their breath in anticipation.

When Bishop finally finished examining his surroundings, almost like a predator observing his prey, he spoke with a loud, demanding tone. "Councilmen, I know you all are curious as to the reason we are here but, unlike the Head Council, I will take my time in stating my ultimate reason."

Bishop continued without pause. He either did not notice the surprised reaction in the crowd, or he received the desired reaction, so proceeded quickly to maintain his advantage. "When I left the city on my mission to Coroge, I planned to pass on a message of peace. I returned, though, empty-handed and barely alive. This is what you already know. Upon my return, you all wept and prayed for my safe recovery, as you should for your leader."

Coal listened quietly to his friend's strong speech. He, more than anyone, had been waiting to hear the details of what happened on the mission. Due to the council's incompetence, Coal had been unable to solve the riddle of this attack on his own. He had been waiting for Bishop to awake so he could have his answers, but the Regis had disappeared too quickly for him to question him. As he listened, he was disturbed by the cold and emotionless way that Bishop spoke about such sensitive circumstances. This was not like him.

"I am now cured and I stand before you to tell you why you are here."

The council all shifted to the front of their seats. "I stand before you all today for one purpose. I am here to state my declaration of war against the sect of Vertura."

This time Bishop stopped. He was letting it sink in. The shock of it quieted the entire chamber. Even Anton was in disbelief and it took intense control to not show it. He stood up from his desk.

"War?" he questioned. "On what grounds, Your Highness?"

The moment Anton finished speaking, the rest of the chamber went into an uproar as if he broke a levy of silence. Now words could flow again. Councilmen began shouting, some in raving support, but most in anger and confusion.

Bishop silently turned to face Anton, ignoring the shouts from the crowd. He almost looked happy to discover someone would question his word.

"What is your reason for this declaration? Was it the Creed that attacked you in the Shroud?" continued Anton.

Bishop responded impassively. "Those cowards used the cover of the mist to ambush us. Every one of my guard was killed and I was barely able to escape with my life into the trees. They are without honor and their actions require an immediate and severe response. This cannot go unpunished." He spoke only to Anton, as if Anton were the only one worthy of hearing his explanation.

Coal had not moved, or spoken, but still listened intently, wanting to hear Bishop speak. Coal had realized something was different about the Regis and feared for the worst, but this was beyond anything he was thinking. *War?*

Coal needed to know more. He rose to his feet. "Supreme Regis?" he shouted.

This time Bishop's head shot around, his eyes glaring in the direction of Coal's voice. Instead of amusement, now he showed irritation towards the person who interrupted his conversation. He eyes finally focused on Coal standing in the crowd.

Coal did not show concession and did not hesitate to speak. "My men tell me there was no sign of an enemy at the ambush site. Nor was there any sign of foreign weaponry or traces of a retreat. In fact, by examination of the scene, your wounds and the wounds of your men, they deduced that it was animals from the Shroud that attacked, not a military force. Are you sure you saw what you thought you saw, Your Highness?"

Bishop now turned completely around, facing Coal. "Do you doubt the word of your Regis? Do you call me a liar?" retorted the Regis, now with force and emotion.

While this was clearly not the same Bishop he knew, Coal did not back down from his stance. Normally, it would be unwise to question the Regis so openly, but Coal felt it was necessary. "I do not question your word, nor do I call you a liar. I just know that in the face of terror and death, one's mind can fabricate something that is not there. Think strongly, Bishop! Was it truly the Creed?" pleaded Coal.

Coal knew that by using the Regis' first name in the council chambers he would attract scornful eyes, but he hoped it would cause Bishop to see reason and remember who he was. He was not acting like himself. As predicted, a few faint gasps were heard in the crowd at Coal's bold remark, and it appeared only to enrage the Regis further.

Head Council Grey stepped in to try to subdue the tension. "Commander Lucer. Your remarks have merit and are duly noted, but remember, in this chamber you are to refer to His Highness as either Supreme Regis or Your Highness, no matter your personal connection to him," warned Anton.

Coal respectably bowed his head and took his seat.

"As I was saying, Commander Lucer has an excellent point, Your Highness. Are you sure of this? This is a bold action even for Minor Leo. You were on a mission to sign a treaty of peace. I do not believe he would be so brash."

"I am not a man whose mind is so weak that he cannot distinguish between a beast and a man," quickly rebuked Bishop. "And the Creed are easily distinguishable from other men, as you know."

Bishop continued to look towards Coal as if examining him. Even though he had been quieted by the Head Council, Coal was content that his voice was heard and that his point of view was being discussed. As long as he could listen and gather the necessary information, it did not matter who it was that was asking the questions.

"If you are sure of what you saw, then this is a disturbing circumstance," pondered Anton aloud.

"Even so, it may not mean we have to go to war," voiced Councilman Rieven from his seat. "It is possible that it was just a band of renegade Creed that held a personal grudge against us. The Minor may not be involved."

Bishop's agitation was clearly growing as the discussion continued. He did not believe there would be so much dissension among these weak-minded old fools. Clearly there were a few that were stronger than the others.

"And if not? What happens if the attack was sanctioned by the Minor himself? If an attack on my life is not enough to force us to action, they will know how truly weak we are. The Creed feast off weakness."

"It is a simple situation that involves looking at the costs and benefits, Your Highness," said Denuke. "If we attack the Creed and we are wrong, then we have started another bloody war. If we do not attack and we are wrong, than we have only shown weakness and hesitation. Those are two things that can be regained, unlike the lives of thousands of people."

"And do you think that the Creed will just sit there and deliberate about our weaknesses?" shouted the young Councilman Balyct from his seat high atop the chamber.

Anton grimaced silently when he heard the young Hayes speak. He was hoping no one would speak out in favor of the Regis. This impetuous youth was going to be more of a nuisance than he had thought.

"The Creed will not sit and squabble as we are doing. They will attack us if we show our weakness, just like they did before. They need little reason," Hayes finished.

Bishop smiled at the sight of a strong voice in his favor. He feared that there was not a soul strong enough in this crowd to show opposition to the others. Anton knew that there were many in the crowd who still held a vendetta against the Creed and many more who were looking for a way to get in the good graces of the new Regis. This could be their opportunity.

Anton realized that he would be unable to sway the Regis' decision, but he could offer an immediate alternative while still presenting the same final goal. He needed to be delicate in his wording and persuasion.

"You know as well as I, Your Highness, that the citizens are still weakened by the last war, and to start another would damage your reputation," explained Anton. "As a young ruler, you need to tread softly. You cannot start a war without solid proof. So, when you are able to show that proof, I will give you my support."

The sun was now fully set outside, so the glow lights showed a more dominating and consistent light, as they were the only source of illumination, but the chamber was still ominous. The silence between breaths added to the uneasy feeling that still lingered in the room.

"I find it amusing that you believe I require your support," scoffed Bishop.

The heads of the councilmen shifted to Anton, waiting for a response.

"An act of war, Your Highness, can only be sanctioned by a majority vote of the council." Anton emphasized the royal title, adding a hint of forcefulness that hit the Regis right where Anton intended. "And, as Head Council, I am the only one who is permitted to initiate a vote of any kind. So, you could say that you require my support." He paused to add tension, and bowed his head. "Your Highness."

With his point expressed, Anton just waited to see the Regis' reaction. He feared he might have pushed the agitated ruler too far, but it might have been necessary.

Bishop boiled. He did his best to hide his anger, but to the trained eye it was clear that the Head Council had gotten to him. It was a well-laid trap and Bishop knew he could not afford to get snared, but he could not back down and abandon his position.

"Spoken wisely, Head Council," said Bishop. "How would you have me show my proof? What is it you require from me?"

Anton was impressed by the Regis' restraint. "I would have you send an inquisition to Coroge. Question Minor Leo directly. We could ascertain his guilt that way. Minor Leo has too much pride to lie about such a thing and he would also see this action as both cautious and strong."

Murmurs of agreement echoed through the chamber. Bishop could see that he could not argue with Anton's request, but felt it also gave him time to build upon the little support he had. This was merely a well articulated delay to an inevitable end.

Bishop merely bowed his head slightly in respect to Anton. "I agree to the terms."

Sitting in the crowd, Coal studied Bishop. *He concedes, but only for now. What is his true motive? I need to stay close to this and decide for myself what is behind it all.*

"If it pleases Your Highness, I will send one of my own men. This is a situation that requires the utmost speed and care," announced Coal.

"We will gladly accept the offer. Your men are the best, Commander. We all wish them safety on the journey," Anton responded.

Bishop silently looked back at Coal. He showed no sign of friendship or recognition. Bishop looked at Coal like he was an agitation that needed to be removed and it worried the Commander.

Anton was relieved to have ended the discussion without much dissent in the council and without a declaration of war, but he knew this was not the end of it.

Anton gestured to the council that the meeting was finished and the men began to quickly file out, wanting to get home to their families or immerse themselves in the pleasures of Seduke.

At the entrance into the chamber, a young man stood wearing a long, ashen cloak with the hood up. In the low light, his hair was a dull gray, with a slight tint of blue like it had faded in the sun. He had been staring down at Bishop intently, but quickly turned and left when the other men began to disperse.

For the men that were leaving, it was going to be a cold, windy night.

13

It was a clear and cool night and a stiff breeze chilled the body even more. It was odd, but the breeze seemed to penetrate even through the cover of buildings and alleys. Coal, with his full-length woolen coat hugged around him, hurried his way back from the council chambers. The wind only added to the chill that he still felt from the night's emergency proceedings.

He could not erase from his mind the blank look that Bishop gave him at the conclusion of the meeting. Bishop looked at him like he had never once met him; like he was a stranger. Coal only wished he could get closer to Bishop to talk with him and discover what it was that was bothering him. Unfortunately, the Regis had not permitted anyone to enter his chambers for some time. Neither Farren nor Kara had spoken to him either.

Two young boys scampered by Coal holding wooden swords and with sling shots at their waists. They noticed Coal and immediately hesitated, fearful that they had been caught out after curfew. But Coal was so deep in thought he did not notice them. They realized the Commander's stupor and ran off before he came around, thankful for their luck. The sounds of the night were out in full force. Insects were buzzing, Speckled Owls hooting, and the faint shouts and music from the lively Seduke district echoed off of the wooden facades and cobblestone streets. The strongest sound, though, was the howling and whistling of the wind.

Where is this wind coming from? Coal wondered.

The wind only briefly tore Coal's thoughts away from the new worry that he now faced.

Is Bishop really a threat?

He knew he had to send a man to Coroge but, rather than question Minor Leo on his guilt, Coal needed to tell him of the situation. Warn him even. While Coal trusted Bishop unequivocally, the evidence was undeniable. The Creed were not responsible. *Why is it then, that Bishop is targeting the Creed? What happened between Bishop's departure and now that has changed him so?* These are the questions he needed to answer.

Coal felt it ironic that he now was trying to protect the Creed from his friend, when just a few days ago he disobeyed Bishop's order and had his men follow him, to protect him from the Creed.

He turned the corner of the street and another gust of wind hit him, making him shiver. He turned his head to protect his eyes, and when he looked back up he saw a cloaked figure. He felt a sudden hint of danger and readied himself for an attack, but the figure did not move.

The hood of the figure's cloak was up, so Bishop could not see who he was. His cloak seemed to just gently sway in the wind while Bishop struggled to stand erect against the force.

The figure reached up and lowered his hood to reveal the face of a young man similar in age to Coal. His hair was short and sharp, dull grayish-blue. He was tall and strong with lean muscles. His face was pale, smooth, and somehow inviting. The face made Coal relax slightly, but he kept his hand near his sword.

The man walked forward until he was a building's length away and stopped. He spoke with a gentle, soothing voice. "Are you the man they call Commander Coal Lucer?"

The question neither calmed Coal, nor made him uneasy. It would seem normal for someone to feel fear at the sight of a strange man on a dark night, but the way he spoke seemed to block any fear from entering Coal's mind. Coal did not know this man, but he somehow knew he had nothing to fear from him.

"That is what they call me. And what is it that they call you, stranger?"

The man's cloak blew open slightly and Coal caught a glimpse of the hilt of a sword.

"My name is Kyte Valen. I come bearing a message for you." Kyte spoke gently, but with little emotion or inflection behind the words.

"A message has a source. Where is it you come from, Kyte, and why is it you come to me at night on an empty, dark street?" probed the Commander.

Kyte paused, contemplating whether he should answer. His eyes shifted suddenly when he heard footsteps behind him. A city patrol guard appeared at the end of the street and yelled down to them.

"Is everything alright, Commander?" he asked.

Coal noticed the uneasiness in his new acquaintance and wondered why it was he was fearful of this man. Or, maybe it was that he did not want anyone else to hear him.

"Everything is fine, Patrolman. You may go about your duty." The man bowed his head. "While you are at it, there were a few youngsters running around a few blocks down. Make sure they find their way home safely," Coal added, smiling to himself.

The patrolman continued on his way and Kyte's tension loosened. Coal waited for the mysterious young man to speak. "This is something I will say only to you," Kyte said. "You may be in more trouble than you know."

Bishop was furious. He had called the emergency meeting of the council to start his war but it had ended in a peaceful alternative. *Damn that Anton Grey!*

Bishop had not expected such resistance from the council, but he would sway them soon enough. It did not matter what the messenger to Coroge discovered, he would have his war. He just needed to find the right key to turn a majority of the council. Anton Grey may have a strong weight over the council, but every man could be bought.

The key may be that young councilman that spoke out. I need to meet with him soon.

The carriage that drove him back to the palace jostled on the stone pavement of the city. The roughness annoyed him and the wind buffeted the side of the compartment. Bishop pitied the majority of the council. They were ancient old fools that had long lost their hauteur. It was the select few that held the group together. They were the mortar that he must loosen to bring down the wall.

The carriage came to a stop and a palace guard opened the door for the Regis to exit. After closing the door behind him, the guard turned to speak but Bishop waved him off silently, knowing the guard would ask if he wished for a palanquin to take him up the stairs to the palace gate. He would walk.

At the top of the stairs, the guards at the base of the gate came to attention, forcing energy into their tired bodies. It was indeed late.

"Open the gate!" shouted one of the guards.

After walking through, Bishop motioned to a guard to get him a horse. He did not desire to walk through the palace grounds tonight.

After entering the palace he quickly made his way to the small dungeon gate in a far, secluded hall. A guard stood near the gate.

"I wish to speak to a prisoner," declared Bishop.

The guard bowed his head and held his fist to his opposite arm in the Forces salute. "His Highness wishes to speak to a prisoner this evening," he shouted into the gate.

There was a long pause and then a faint voice responded from inside the door. "Speak the phrase and you shall be admitted," it said bluntly. The guard whispered an answer through and the gate started to rise.

As the gate rose, it revealed another guardsman, bowing his head in the presence of the Regis. "Welcome to the palace dungeon, Your Highness," the man said.

Without acknowledging the man, Bishop walked past him into the darkness. The first guard returned to his post.

The dungeon guard quickly followed the Regis. "Which prisoner is it you wish to speak to, Your Highness?" he questioned nervously.

"I know where he is kept. You need not worry about guiding me."

It was damp and cold, but it kept out the wind of the night and therefore felt warmer than the outside. Their footsteps echoed loudly as they continued to move endlessly downward. The restless moans of the prisoners funneled their way to the center stairway, but they did not seem to faze the Regis.

"Be quiet!" shouted the guard.

They reached the bottom and Bishop took the right tunnel at the dead end. None of the other cells in this wing were filled but he stopped at the end and turned to stare into the final cell.

The murderer of the late Regis and Lady, Datro Cervon, lay on the stone floor, staring at the ceiling as he always did. When the Regis' and guard's footsteps stopped, the gaunt man turned his head to see Bishop standing at the entrance of his cell, arms crossed behind his back, staring at him.

Datro began to laugh loudly. His time in the depths of the prison had withered his appearance, but he did not seem to have lost any of his energy and madness. "So, it is you!" he shouted. "I was thinking it would be that irritating commander again; always asking the same questions and expecting a different answer. And they think I am mad!"

Bishop turned to the guard and nodded for him to leave. He quickly returned to his post. Bishop then turned to the crazed man, waiting for him to silence.

"He would always look at me with that righteous glare of his, like I would cower and fear him. I actually found it kind of amusing, but I managed to hold in my laughter," Datro continued to banter. "But, here you are. You have finally come. I was beginning to worry," said Datro. He rolled up into a cross-legged sitting position.

"I see you are doing well," commented Bishop.

"The first thing I hear from you and it is a joke. At least you are trying to fit in, I see. Everything going according to plan I hope?" Bishop glared silently at Datro, who grinned uncomfortably. "That bad, huh?"

"Just get to work! You know what you have to do," ordered Bishop as he turned and walked back down the hall.

"It would be my pleasure, Your Highness," Datro shouted after him with a tone of devilish sarcasm. He patted his folded knees and sighed heavily, smiling from ear to ear.

As Bishop exited, he turned to the guard at the top of the stair. "Release the prisoner. Make sure he is fed and safely returned to his lab. Tell no one."

The guard hesitated, but bowed his head and saluted. "Uh... yes, of course, Your Highness. I will release him immediately"

Inside the Gallant training room, the tension was looming. The moonlight poured in through the giant stained-glass windows and created a faint kaleidoscope of color throughout the room. There were glow lights, but Coal had not lit them.

After the insistence of the mysterious young man, Kyte, Coal had brought them there. This late at night the building would be empty, so they could talk in private.

The mystery of this man kept Coal in a constant uneasy state, but he had showed no sign of threatening action.

The walk to the palace grounds was silent and awkward. Coal attempted to goad more information from this Kyte, but he stayed silent, only speaking to tell Coal he was here to deliver his message, nothing more. Even stranger was that Kyte seemed to react to any sound around them. His paranoia caused concern for Coal. It was as if he was being followed.

Inside the training room, Coal closed the large wooden doors and turned to Kyte. "Is this sufficient, stranger? There is no one else here to listen."

"No one you can see. That is something now that you must concern yourself with. Danger can be anywhere."

The comment was strange and Coal could not determine if it was a warning or a threat. *Is this man playing with me?*

"Where do you come from, Kyte Valen, and what is your message? What is this danger you speak of?" Coal was beginning to become frustrated by this man's delaying and secrecy.

"I do not come from any sect or city that you know of. I do not belong to any government or enemy of your own."

"Quit wasting my time and tell me why you are here!"

"You insist that I tell you about myself and then you get angry when I try to do so. You let your emotions get the best of you. You are impatient. These are not good qualities in a warrior."

"First you waste my time and now you insult me? You really are not from around here are you?" barked Coal. "I do not have the time for this. There are issues that require my attention. These are troubling times in the capital." Coal turned to walk away.

"Your troubles are far worse than you know, Coal," said Kyte. "War with the Creed is the least of your worries."

Coal stopped and turned back to the young man. He chuckled and said, "Have you ever met a Creed soldier, Kyte?"

"I cannot say that I have."

"Then you would not be saying that," said Coal.

"Yes, but have you ever met a *Tellurian* warrior?" responded Kyte.

Coal froze as he continued to walk out of the room. When he turned he had a skeptical yet intrigued look on his face. "Of course I have not met a Tellurian, you fool. They do not exist. Now either you tell me who sent you, or you leave here immediately. My patience has ended." Coal said as he drew his sword.

Kyte sighed and shook his head. "If you insist. I was hoping to explain myself more before I passed on my message, but you will not allow it. Now it is certain, judging by your reaction to my last comment and your refusal to listen to what I have to say, that you will believe the message as much as you believe in the existence of Magi. Nor will you believe who the message comes from."

Coal took another step closer, moving the point of his sword nearly inches from Kyte's impassive face. "Get on with it," he said.

"If you insist. I come bearing a message from your Supreme Regis and friend; the man who fought valiantly against a powerful enemy and the man I found gripping to life in the Shroud. The man that is now dead."

Coal's sword point pressed hard up against Kyte's skin and blood started to drip down his face, but Kyte did not move. Even with the point of Coal's sword at his face he did not act to defend himself. Coal's eyes were burning with hatred and malice.

"What did you just say?" growled Coal.

"Hold in your anger, Coal Lucer. I did not kill him. I am not your enemy."

"Oh, really? You are insane. You say Bishop is dead, but I have seen him myself. If you were there in the Shroud, then you know what happened to him. You know that he was attacked and returned here bloodied."

"Strange, I know. That, I cannot explain."

Coal could not determine if he was furious or confused. This man spoke as if truthful, but what he spoke was nonsense. The Commander could not determine what his motive was. He did not act dangerously, but he was surely mad. He had not even drawn his weapon.

"Tell me where you come from. Who are you really?"

Kyte let out an exasperated sigh, lowering his head. "I cannot tell you that."

"Quit playing me for a fool!" Coal shouted. His anger had finally overcome him and he pushed forward with his sword. Before his sword met its mark, though, Coal was blown backwards several feet. Coal stumbled, but kept his footing; his sword clattered to the ground.

"I am not your enemy, Coal Lucer. Your enemy now is something far worse."

Coal was shaking. Not from fear, but from the intense cold feeling that filled his body. He gripped his chest and breathed heavily. "What was that? What just happened?"

Coal stared back at Kyte, who just stood silently. With the strange sensation coursing through his body, Coal finally started to notice Kyte's features. They were strangely familiar.

"This cannot be. Was that magic? You are an Aerious?" Coal said with a questionable tone.

Kyte smiled slightly. "You find it hard to believe, I see. You are probably thinking that we should be extinct; dead after the Great War. That is far from the truth," Kyte explained.

"Then, why are you here now, after so many years?" muttered Coal. He picked up his sword and gathered himself.

"I live in the Shroud. That is where my clan is in hiding. I found your friend Bishop washed up on the bank of a river that runs through the Shroud, at the base of a large cliff. He was alive, but just. I was hesitant to help him but, you see, I am the last of my clan, so I felt that our secrecy was not nearly as important, anymore, as his life," Kyte retold. "He was weak but could still talk slightly. He told me who he was and that I should come and warn you."

"Warn me of what?"

"When I rolled him over I found a wooden needle sticking from his chest." Kyte held up the small splinter of wood to Coal. "Do you know what this is?" he asked. Coal shook his head. "This is a Tellurian poison needle. One prick from this and you are surely dead. I know of no cure."

It was strange to Coal that he was not more shocked when listening to this story. Under ordinary circumstances, he would never find it normal to be speaking to an Aerious and have him telling him a story about Tellurians, but he seemed to accept it without fear. *Nothing seemed ordinary anymore.*

"Are you saying that he was killed by Tellurians?" calmly questioned Coal.

Kyte nodded. "That is why I am here. He told me that the Tellurians were coming and that I should warn you. That is all he said, before he died."

Coal was so engrossed in the story that he had lost track of the one thing that still bothered him about this whole thing. "If you truly talked to Bishop, than who is the man that returned? Who is the man I saw in council today? How do you know that the Bishop you met was really him?"

Kyte rustled around in his cloak and pulled out a small object and tossed it to Coal. "I took that from his finger. My mother once told me that the leaders of your people wear rings to represent their power. I assume that is what that is."

Coal stared down at the large gold ring, moving it around in his finger tips. The sense of calmness finally drifted away and he felt intense sadness and anger. He examined the ring, seeing the Kaiser crest with the Hym'Shailan Dragon. He held in the avalanche of emotions, but could not bring himself to raise his head and look at the man who just told him his friend was dead.

"I am sorry, Coal Lucer. I am sure he was a good man."

A tear streaked down Coal's cheek but, at the same time, he could think of nothing else but revenge. The conflicting emotions multiplied inside of him and even his military control could not hold them in completely. Kyte felt his grief, but could do nothing for him. Having delivered his message, Kyte turned to walk away.

"Stop," said Coal. Kyte turned his head around and saw Coal's sword again pointing at him. "You are just going to leave? You know what we face, yet you will do nothing?"

"I cannot let myself be exposed. I was foolish to even come here, but I gave your friend my word," Kyte responded.

Coal had wiped away his tears and now expressed an air of complete determination. His friend was dead, but there was a danger to the city and this man was someone he could not let go.

"Soon, everyone will know that the Magi still exist, so hiding yourself will not change that. What will you do? You said yourself that you are the last of your kind. You would rather hide yourself in the Shroud and live out your days in solitude than help us stop an enemy that you yourselves could not defeat?"

Kyte had a sense that he would not be able to leave this place peacefully. The moonlight reflected from Coal's determined, unblinking eyes, adding to his appearance of unwavering resolve. "Do you intend to fight me, Coal Lucer? You know you cannot defeat me and yet you insist?"

"My purpose is to protect this city and all of Briva. If that means that I die in the process then that is what will happen. Besides, I have always wondered how well I would fair against a true Magi."

Coal's comment had a lighthearted tone, but he did not smile. He held his sword strong and steady. He was not carrying his kidon, so he was at a defensive disadvantage, but he assumed that even the short sword would do little against this Aerious' attacks. He did not even know what kind of powers Kyte would have.

Still, with his back turned, Kyte concentrated on his enemy, waiting to see if this man would truly strike. A slight moment before Kyte was about to speak, as if Coal knew, Coal again lunged forward with his sword. In a flash, Kyte dropped down, drew his sword and spun around in a whirl. His sword clashed against the Commander's sheath, which he had removed to defend himself, and the sound reverberated through the hall.

"Metal inlayed into the sheath. I see you are accustomed to fighting with two swords. Impressive," said Kyte.

Coal swung down with his sword and Kyte pushed off of his bent knees and jumped back out of reach. The moment the balls of his feet hit the ground, he launched forward again. He attacked the right side, forcing Coal to use his sword to block the blow instead of the sheath. Coal forced Kyte's blade upward and he lost his balance, allowing Coal to swing his sheath and forcing Kyte to block the blow with his forearm.

Kyte cringed when the sheath contacted bone. Coal quickly lunged with his blade but Kyte parried to the side, giving him the time to completely regain his balance. They began to circle each other, eyes keen to any movement towards the other.

Coal focused on the Aerious' fluid motions. His movements seemed to require no effort and he did not exert himself more under pressure. Coal feinted with a forward swing of the sword, causing Kyte to defend, but Coal then swung his sheath upward. Kyte nearly dodged the blow, the tip of the sheath grazing his chin.

Surprisingly, with incredible speed, Kyte snatched the sheath in mid swing. Then, without a pause, he brought his sword around to attack Coal's open side. Coal quickly countered by bringing his sword over to defend and then trapped Kyte's blade in between his side and arm. Knowing he did not have the time to attack directly, Coal quickly thrust the butt of his sword upward and contacted Kyte under the nose. Because of the blow, Kyte released his sword and stumbled backwards. He wiped his nose, seeing the blood on his hand. Coal tossed Kyte's sword to the side.

"Why did you not use your magic?"

Kyte continued to wipe the blood from his face and then smiled. A drop of blood fell from his hand and splashed onto the floor, adding yet another stain on the once pristine granite floor. "My magic is only to be used against my enemies, Coal Lucer. Those who fight against Tellurians are not my enemy."

Coal relaxed, letting his tired muscles rest. Sweat began dripping down his face. The duel was quick, but it took every ounce of his strength and concentration.

"So, you will help us?" Coal asked.

"I refuse to let myself just fade away in solitude." Kyte bowed gracefully, arms out like the wings of a bird. "You have my sword."

An Aerious bowed before him. Today was a day Coal would remember for the rest of his life, yet he knew there would be little time for him to reminisce in the days and weeks to come.

Bishop is dead and the Tellurian's are coming.

14

The palace servants rushed about frantically as the day began. The maids worked to keep everything clean in the hallways and meeting rooms. The floors were washed, the windows cleaned to a perfect sheen and even the grooves in the intricately designed frames of the artwork gracing the walls were meticulously dusted and shined. It did not matter that hardly anyone ever entered the palace. It must always be immaculate. Once the royal family awoke, they would then go about cleaning the private quarters.

The chefs had been working tirelessly to prepare the Regis' morning breakfast; a thick strip of smoked wild ham, three lightly cooked eggs, freshly baked bread, toasted, and an assortment of fresh fruit. Lately, Bishop had been more irritable, so the chefs took extra special care to make sure his meal was perfect. Fortunately for them, Farren never desired his morning meals cooked for him. He tended to just grab something from the kitchen himself on the way out the door and the Lady Kara had requested little in the past few days, keeping to herself in her quarters. They had more time to focus on His Highness' meal. The servers stood at attention to await Bishop's arrival. He usually arrived precisely at dawn, but he was already late. The chefs were beginning to worry his food would begin to become cold or dried out.

The dining room of the palace was long and narrow, in order to follow the flow of the table that sat in its center. The table sat up to fifty people and had only one end. The other end came to a point, therefore there could only be one person at the head of the table. Two grandiose chandeliers hung low from the ceiling, seeming to bring the high vaulted ceiling down towards the seated occupants below. Two sets of doors came into the room, one to the kitchen and the other to the hallway. The doors to the dining room creaked open and the servers and chefs came to attention. The servants relaxed with an exasperated sigh as Farren sauntered in.

Head server, Kapett, stepped forward to great him. "Good morning, Young Master. Have you come this morning to gather energy before you head off for the day?" Kapett, like most of the palace staff, enjoyed Farren's company and lighthearted presence. It was a reprieve from their tense daily duties.

"Good morning to you too, Kapett." Farren called most of the staff by their first names and tried to insist they do the same for him, but they all politely declined.

"You are more than welcome to help yourself to the kitchen, as always. We are just awaiting the arrival of the Supreme Regis."

"I do not think my brother will be coming to breakfast this morning, Kapett. I saw him working in his study. It does not seem like he has any interest in moving anytime soon."

Kapett and the other servers let out a sigh and let their shoulders slump. "Do you think it would be prudent to take his meal to him, Young Master?"

"I wouldn't," Farren warned with a wry smile.

Kapett gestured to the other servers to begin taking the food back to the kitchen. *The chefs will not be happy about this,* he thought.

"Thank you for the warning, Young Master. We would have been standing here for quite a while if you hadn't told us." Kapett bowed his head to show his appreciation.

Farren gave him a friendly nudge with his arm. "Always happy to help, Kapett. I don't like to see you guys pushing yourself too hard for our sake."

"If you do not mind me asking, Young Master, is the Supreme Regis feeling alright? He has been a bit... secluded... as of late."

The servants continued to clean up the food, and a few angry shouts could be heard from the chefs in the kitchen.

"I don't think it is anything to worry about. Just a little stress is all. He will be back to his old self in no time, I'm sure," smiled Farren. His smile held a little doubt in it.

"I am sure you are right. We all hope that is sooner, rather than later. His comforting smile is sorely missed around here," said Kapett. "Now, if you would like, you are welcome to help yourself to your brother's breakfast. I am sure the chefs would be delighted that their hard work would not be completely wasted."

Farren laughed, happy to see the head server add a little sarcasm to his normally stiff, formal demeanor. "Thank you, Kapett. I would be delighted to dine on the Supreme Regis' own specially made fare," Farren retorted. After a shared laugh, Farren told the head server why he was really there. "I actually came here for another reason, Kapett."

"What is it the Young Master desires?"

"Kara has been taking my brother's change a little hard, so I wanted to try to cheer her up this morning."

"A noble gesture. What is it I can do to help?"

"I wanted to bring her a nice breakfast. She has been requesting very little lately, but I think maybe her favorite breakfast would help. The chefs would know better than I what that may be."

"I will do what I can, Young Master. The chefs will be delighted to help cheer up the Lady Kara. I will send up the food as soon as it is ready."

"If you would not mind, I would like to take it to her myself."

"Of course, Young Master," said Kapett, bowing slightly.

Since Bishop had returned from his journey, Lady Kara had found it difficult to be around him, so she had been spending her nights in her old room from when she was just the wife of a Prince, not the Supreme Regis. She had found it comforting, being in surroundings that reminded her of the old days when their lives were filled with much less stress.

She sat out on the balcony, overlooking the castle grounds. It was peaceful hearing only the sounds of the birds that nested in the trees and the rustling branches of the willows as they swayed in the wind. She enjoyed the peace, but what she wanted more was the company of her husband. This new man that was pretending to be her husband was no more than a fraud. She would find a way to get him back. She just was not quite sure how, yet. She was surprised by a knock at the door.

"Who is it?"

"It is me, your faithful and obedient servant, Farren Kaiser, My Lady. Would you permit me to enter, so that I can serve you your morning meal?"

She almost broke out in a girlish laugh, but suppressed it to a chuckle. She walked quickly over to the door, running on her toes so she did not trip on her long, silk, sleeping gown. When she opened the door, Farren was bowing, his head almost to his knees.

"I have brought you your breakfast, My Lady."

She finally allowed herself to laugh loudly as she looked down at the back of Farren's bent head. Farren rose, a broad grin across his face. Kara jumped onto him, hugging him tightly.

"Lady Kara, do you think this appropriate? What if the Regis finds out?" Farren joked.

Kara let him go and playfully pushed him backwards, almost knocking over the cart of food he had brought. "Oh, be quiet, Fare."

He was happy to see her smiling. "So can I come in, My Lady?"

"As long as the food comes too and you drop the act."

Farren turned and began pulling the cart in behind him. "I think I can handle that." Kara closed the door behind him. Farren looked around the room as he entered. "This place brings back memories," he said. A large, four poster bed was pushed against the far wall, drapes hanging from the sides. A few large, scenic paintings hung on the brilliant ivory colored walls. In one corner was a large dresser with mirror and a few couches were sitting nearby.

"I know. It seems like only yesterday that I used to spend my nights here," reminisced Kara.

"From what I have been told, you actually did spend the night here last night," said Farren.

Kara rolled her eyes at Farren, shaking her head at his jest.

Farren was pleased to see that she wasn't so depressed he could not raise her spirits. "I asked the chefs to make your favorite meal. I hope you like it." Farren uncovered all but one of the plates of food on the cart and Kara grinned in delight. She picked a few pieces of fruit from one of the platters and began to munch on them.

"So, what have you been doing these past few days? It has been kind of lonely lately without you around." The comment was mainly to make her feel better, but there was definitely truth behind the words.

The question clearly made her a little uneasy, but she tried to cover it up. "It has been a little crazy lately and I have just been trying to avoid it all. It's peaceful here."

"Did you know that I've started my training? I had my first session with Master Guy's apprentice. You should come and watch one of these days. We are out in the old training grounds. It's nice and peaceful out there, too."

She forced a fake smile. "Maybe I will. I always did like to watch Coal and Bishop train with each other. And I could use some fresh air."

They both stood there for a silent minute. Farren could tell he had said something wrong because she had returned to her saddened state. He never was that good at talking to girls, even her. There was little else for him to say, so he just went to the heart of the matter.

"It's going to be alright, Kara. He'll come back to us soon."

"I know," she muttered. It did not seem that she believed it, though.

Farren sighed. "Well I think I will leave you to your breakfast then. I have other things to do myself," he lied. "You should go for a walk on the grounds. It's a nice day," he said as he turned and exited the room.

Well, that went well, he thought as he closed the door.

Kara dropped herself onto one of the couches against the wall and stared up at the ceiling. No matter what she did, she could not remove her nagging thoughts of Bishop from her mind.

Gathering a bit of energy, she kicked herself up from the couch and walked over to the cart of food. She picked up another piece of fruit and popped it into her mouth. She then took the cover off the final plate of food and laughed, looking down at a passater, a sweet breakfast pastry, topped with strawberries and cream in the shape of a smile.

She picked up one of the passaters and walked back out onto the balcony. The sun was high enough now that the temperature was beginning to warm and she saw servants beginning to enter the grounds to trim and groom the greenery. It was going to be a beautiful day.

"Maybe a walk would be nice."

Councilman Balyct hated mornings the most. He lived alone in a moderately sized house on the fringes of the residential district of the city nearest to the city square. He was usually awakened early by the crowds heading to work or the restaurants for an early breakfast.

He lazily prepared himself a burnt piece of toast and a glass of juice. He sat munching on the pitiful meal as he contemplated his day. He had spent the last few years pushing himself to his limit to get to where he was, but today he had no desire to rush into work.

Hayes was the youngest man on the council, having been elected into the position after his many years of excellent work helping with the rebuilding of the city after the war. He also helped to revitalize the massive foreign trade network that was centered around Valoria and had been damaged severely by the fighting. He was considered a maverick of sorts, and many of the elder councilmen did not like his brash attitude and straightforward views. He spent little time caring about what others thought of him, instead spending his time working towards his goals and making Briva a better place in his eyes.

After forcing down the gritty toast and washing it down with the juice, he went to his room to change. On a day when council was not held, he wore a plain pair of dress pants and vest with white long-sleeved shirt underneath. It would be too hot to wear a coat, so the shirt and vest would do. He combed his hair enough to make it presentable and wandered out into the streets.

He found it difficult to maneuver through the masses of people walking to and from their early morning destinations. The smells of the restaurants on the city square had him frustrated. He now wished he had gotten up a little earlier and stopped for a better breakfast, but now he no longer had the time.

After forcing his way through the square and residential areas, he made his way to the council building. In the early morning, the sun created a massive shadow on the ground surrounding the raised structure. There was little conversing between him and the other councilmen, aside from the occasional "good morning" or nod of the head, as he found his way to his study. A few councilmen did give him disconcerting looks, which made him wonder about the reason.

When he opened the door to his study he was shocked to find Bishop sitting in a chair in the corner, legs crossed, waiting for his arrival.

"Your Highness," he blurted. "I was not expecting you." He bowed, fist pressed to his forehead.

Bishop got up from the chair and walked up to greet Hayes. "I hope you do not mind that I took the liberty of letting myself in. I was told you would have arrived by now."

"My apologies. I woke a little later than desired this morning." It was a half truth that he deemed sufficient to explain his lateness. *Of all the days for him to come and see me.*

"No need to apologize. I am just here to ask you a few questions and seek your assistance on a matter."

Hayes brightened. It seemed that he was finally starting to make a mark and be noticed. The Supreme Regis was requesting his assistance. All that Hayes had worked for was for this. The highest position he could attain was Head Council, and that position was chosen from the councilmen by the Supreme Regis. If he could get in the Regis' favor it would be a monumental step.

"I would be honored. I hope I can be of some assistance."

Bishop smiled and sat back down in the chair in the corner. The room was small, but cozy. Three of the walls were lined with bookshelves, sparsely filled with scrolls and texts, and two high backed chairs sat in the corner. A glow light rested on a small table between the chairs. Hayes used the area to relax and read. His desk was in the middle of the room, covered with papers and scrolls.

Hayes quickly organized the papers on his desk before going to sit next to the Regis.

"I remember you from the council meeting the other night. You spoke out in favor of my petition for war," Bishop said, getting to the point immediately.

"I am sorry I was not of more assistance in getting the petition passed, Your Highness. Head Council Grey has significant leverage over the council. He is a very proud and well respected man."

"So it seems," muttered Bishop. "Let me ask you this, Councilman Balyct. Do you think you have the ability to turn the council against him?"

It took Hayes a moment to finally realize what the Supreme Regis was asking him to do. "You want me to try to sway the minds of the council in order to undermine the Head Council's authority?"

"I only ask you to try to convince the other councilman of our point of view. You do not need to do anything you might consider unlawful. I suspect that there is already much distrust of the Creed in the minds of many of the councilmen?"

"Yes, of course. All of these men lived through the war. Many have not forgiven the Creed for what they did."

"Then, it shouldn't be too difficult to change their minds, should it?"

While Bishop seemed calm during the entire discussion, Hayes was feeling an intense pressure being forced upon him from the Supreme Regis. He was asking Hayes if he wanted to help, but to Hayes there seemed to be only one answer he could give.

"I will do what I can, Your Highness. It is my desire that the Creed are punished as well. They should be held accountable for what they did to you and what they have done to this city."

Hayes was satisfied that he showed some resolve, but worried that he might have overstated his ability to actually complete this task he was being asked to do. This was his chance, though. He would work as hard as was required to please the Regis.

"Tell me, Hayes. Why is it you despise the Creed so much?"

He was shocked by the personal question, but could not refuse an answer.

"They are a vile race, Your Highness. They think only of battle and victory. They are barbarians and have no place in this world."

Bishop smiled at Hayes' hate-filled expression. "That is not a reason, Councilman that is a definition. Why is it you hate the Creed?" Bishop insisted.

Hayes paused and let out a heavy sigh. "My wife, Your Highness. My wife was killed during the war." Thinking back, it made it difficult for Hayes to speak of it. "It was on the first day. She was outside the city, helping her father on his farm. The farm was in the path of their first assault. The fields were burned and my wife and her family murdered for no reason. They are barbarians," he said. Hayes' eyes were filled with tears and his jaw started to tremble.

Bishop again responded calmly. "I am sorry, my friend. It is difficult to have to deal with loss. It was much the same for me when my parents were killed. I still find myself struggling at times with my emotions. It is only human." He spoke of emotion, but his face showed none. Hayes was too emotional himself to notice the Regis' unnaturally stoic face.

"You have my word, Your Highness. The council will vote in your favor soon enough," Hayes asserted, after gathering his emotions.

"Thank you, Councilman. I leave the rest to you." Bishop rose up from the seat and left the study with a satisfied smile stretching across his face.

16

The complete silence was beginning to bore into Syd's mind. He couldn't take it anymore. Silence was the point of the secret meeting room inside the Gallant Building, but that knowledge didn't seem to make the quietness any less irritating to him. All he heard was the breathing of Guy and Kaine sitting nearby and the creaking of the chair he sat on as he leaned back in it, putting it on two legs.

"I hope those legs snap on you," Kaine muttered from the side of his mouth.

Syd shot him an annoyed glare and leaned forward, dropping the chair back to its four legs. Kaine and Guy did not seem to be bothered by the silence, both just sitting peacefully in quiet contemplation. That, in itself, bothered Syd as well.

"How can you two just sit there?"

"It's quite simple when your mind has the capacity for original thought," quipped Kaine.

Syd quickly went to draw his sword, but Guy interjected. "Quit it boys. This is not the time for it. The commander should be arriving shortly. I don't think it would be wise to be fighting with each other when he walks in."

Syd despondently clicked his sword back into its sheath and fell back into his chair. Kaine snickered to himself, not once opening his eyes during the whole argument.

The two regularly quarreled, often ending in a fight. They had known each other since they were little and, while they were not related by blood, they were brothers nonetheless. Their fights were often started due to their brotherly attitudes towards each other and their distinctly different personalities, but there was never any true hatred between them. Guy and Kaine went back to silently waiting for Coal's arrival, while Syd methodically banged his head against the wooden table.

"You know I find it a little unsettling that we have been in here twice now in the past week when we haven't used it once since the war. What could it be about this time?"

"If I knew, I wouldn't be so impatient sitting here," said Syd.

"How about we just sit and wait for the commander to get here to tell us. Huh, boys?" calmly suggested Guy.

"How can you be so calm, old man? With everything that has been happening lately, do you not find this a little unsettling that the Commander ordered us here?"

"I would say I am more intrigued than unsettled. It is odd that he chose this place for the meeting, but if it was an emergency he would have been here long before we were," explained Guy. "And I would appreciate it if you did not address me as old man."

"As long as you keep calling us boys, then I'm going to call you old man. It seems appropriate to me," responded Syd.

Guy smiled with amusement at Syd. Suddenly, a groaning sound echoed down from the hallway leading into the room and a rush of wind blew past them. Once the groaning stopped, they heard footsteps coming towards them. They all rose to their feet and prepared to salute. Coal walked into the room from the dark hallway, followed closely by Kyte.

"Commander," the three Captains shouted.

"Captains," he responded with a nod to tell them to sit back down.

The three men looked curious at the unexpected appearance of Kyte, but none said anything. Coal sat down at the head of the table, but Kyte stayed standing behind him. Coal noticed the men's wandering glances. "Is there something you would like to ask?"

"Who is he?" blurted Syd, pointing at Kyte. "Only the Regis and high level members of the Forces and Gallants are allowed in here. I have never seen this man in my life."

Kaine shook his head in dismay at his impetuous friend.

"And for good reason, Captain," coolly responded Coal. "He is not from here."

Syd was about to continue his flurry of thoughtless questions but Kaine stuck out his hand to stop him. "The oaf is right, Sir. I would assume that this man has something to do with the reason why we are here, so it would be in our best interest to know who he is and where he comes from."

"If you would have waited a brief moment, I was going to introduce him. Of course he is the reason why we are here, that is obvious. I would not bring him here otherwise. His name is Kyte Valen. Anything past that he has requested to be kept secret."

"Secret? Come now Commander, I did not think that we kept secrets in the Gallants; especially from each other. It was you who set that law into effect."

"I know our laws, Captain. I do not need you to remind me," said Coal, agitated. "These are uncommon circumstances. The only reason he is still here is because I agreed to these terms."

"So, we are just supposed to continue this meeting as if he is one of us and nothing is out of the ordinary," asked Syd. "This is ridiculous, Commander, and you know it."

"Hold your tongue, Captain. I understand that I have broken one of our laws, but I am still your Commander and you will follow my orders. Kyte asks only for us to respect his privacy and we will do so. Do I make myself clear?"

"I do not recognize the name Valen," said Guy, ignoring the tension. "I do not believe it is a Brivan name. I am not as familiar with Feran surnames, but it is not familiar. Where do you hail from Kyte? Surely you are not Matroz; you do not have the look."

Coal sat speechless for a moment, unable to find an answer. He wanted to lie, but could not find a good one. He was about to speak, but then Kyte finally broke his silence. "You are quite right. I am no Matroz, that is clear," he said. "Nor am I Brivan or Davati. I live alone in the Shroud, but I belong to no sect or people."

"That is ridiculous. No one lives in the Shroud. It is too dangerous," said Syd.

Kyte turned to Syd and said plainly, "What do you know of the Shroud? Have you traveled into the mist and seen what lies inside?"

Syd was a little shaken by the pointed accusation, but then his confusion quickly turned again to annoyance. "Of course not," interjected Kaine. "The mist clouds everything. It is suicide to enter."

"But, if there was a way to counteract the mist, then the Shroud is no more dangerous than any other forest in Paks. In fact, the mist then becomes your ally."

"How in hell do you counteract the mist?" Kaine asked, directly.

"He is an Aerious," said Guy, confidently. Guy had been silently observing the rest of the conversation and examining Kyte. He had finally come to his conclusion. Kaine and Syd turned to him with awestruck looks.

"He is an Aerious," he stated again. "Look at him," speaking to Kaine and Syd. "The gray-blue hair, the lean slender body. Even if he lives alone, as a human, he would claim a sect as his birthplace."

Kaine and Syd turned back to look at Kyte, examining him as if looking for a sign that would say what he really was. Coal smiled.

"I do not know how you do it, Guy. Apparently I should open up a book or two myself sometimes."

"So, it's true then?" asked Kaine. "This man is an Aerious? He is one of the legendary bird men?" Coal nodded. "Incredible. I did not think they really existed. I do not blame you then, for wanting to keep your identity a secret." Kaine, seemingly satisfied with the answer, relaxed back into his seat.

"So, then the next question is, what is he doing here?" asked Guy.

"That is what we are here to discuss," said Coal. He gestured to Kyte to sit and he pulled up a chair next to the Commander.

"Wait a second," interrupted Syd. "That is it? That is all you two need to be convinced of this farce? This is preposterous. There is no way he is an Aerious. They do not exist. I want proof. I want proof that he is a Magi."

Coal responded quickly. "I have seen the proof myself. That should be enough for you."

"Sorry, Commander, but I want to see his powers with my own eyes," Syd grinned.

"I am a bit curious myself, Commander," added Kaine. "What is the harm in it?" Coal shook his head in dismay

"I do not think this is the place for a demonstration," said Kyte.

"Let us see it, Aerious," urged Syd.

"If you insist." Kyte silently took a few steps back from the table and put his hand out in from him, palm up. The three Captains sat forward in their chairs. Guy was trying to hide his anticipation a bit, but he was just as excited as the other two.

A draft started to stir in the small, stone-walled room. The breeze picked up speed and then started to circulate, with Kyte at the center. Kaine's shoulder-length, wavy, brown hair began to whip violently and the men were forced to shield their faces from the buffeting wind. The circulation intensified and began to condense into a small cylinder. The few empty chairs started to rattled and were about to get sucked up into the wind but the Captain grabbed them. Luckily, there was nothing else in the room that could have been whipped up in the maelstrom.

As the hurricane of wind constricted, it passed over the Captains and the chaos seemed to stop entirely. They all looked up to see a large ball of wind confined to Kyte's hand. It continued to constrict and, as it did, the speed of the wind created a whistling sound. Finally, the constricting stopped and a ball of high-speed wind circulated in his palm. It emitted a faint glow and high pitch whistle.

The men stared at the ball like eager children, Syd unconsciously stuck his hand out to touch it. When Kyte noticed Syd, he quickly clapped his hand shut and the ball disappeared. The men blinked and shook their heads as if a trance had been lifted.

"I hope that was enough proof for you." Coal laughed to himself, a sense of satisfaction washing through him.

"I'll say," shouted Syd. He leaned over and gave Kyte a friendly pat on the back.

"That was incredible. To see it with my own eyes is unbelievable," said Guy. "You have a truly amazing gift."

"Thank you," Kyte politely responded.

"So, if you three are satisfied, is it alright if we start this meeting and discuss what we came here to discuss?" asked Coal.

"Actually, Sir, I have one last question," said Kaine as he turned to Kyte. "If Magi truly exist, then where have they been for the past five hundred years? Have they been in hiding? Are there more out there?"

"That is more than one question, Captain."

"Can you blame me, Commander? I mean, this is an unprecedented moment. This is a Magi in front of us."

"It is quite alright, Coal. Your Captain is absolutely right. I do not blame him for being curious. I would be as well," said Kyte. "To answer your first two questions, my people and I have been in living in the Shroud for centuries. I would not necessarily say that we were hiding, but we kept ourselves separate from the happenings of the rest of the world. I asked a few times when I was younger why we never left the

Shroud, but no one would tell me. I like to think, that after decades of war, we just wanted to live peacefully. To answer your last question, until now, I did not know if any others still existed. I assumed there were others, but I have never met one, nor did any of my people ever speak of others."

"Until now?" asked Kaine.

"As you assumed before, Kyte is related to the reason why we are here," interrupted Coal. "He came to me last night to inform me of some disturbing news."

"I think that the appearance of a Magi after centuries raises a lot of questions, Commander," said Guy. "Whatever the reason for his hiding up until now, any news that would bring him out of that hiding would inevitably be disturbing."

"Have you encountered more Magi?" pressed Kaine.

"Stop asking questions, Kaine, and just listen," said Coal. He paused momentarily, trying to determine how he would word his next phrase. "There really is no good way for me to say this, so I will just say it plainly. Kyte has informed me that the man that you brought back from the Shroud is an imposter. The real Bishop is dead."

It took several moments for the comment to finally sink in and Coal received the exact reaction he was expecting; disbelief.

"Are you serious, Commander?"

"To bring a Magi in front of us is one thing, but this is just ludicrous. It is not possible."

Kaine and Syd did not seem willing to believe it and Guy, as always, sat calmly in his seat contemplating. "Do you not think that the Commander would have reacted the same way hearing this?" Guy turned and looked intently at Coal. "Bishop was his friend. If the Commander believes this, then it must be true."

"The man we brought back looks exactly like him. The resemblance is uncanny. You heard him speak as well. We had been following the caravan and we found him not far from the initial skirmish. It has to be him," said Kaine.

"Kyte tells me he found the real Bishop on a river bank at the base of a cliff."

Kaine looked at Syd before leaning over and muttering something into his ear. They whispered for a few more seconds. "There was a cliff nearby when we found him," Kaine turned and stated. "If what you say is true..."

"The real Bishop was thrown from the cliff and the imposter took his place before you were able to arrive," finished Guy.

"But, what about the wounds? Those were real enough," questioned Syd.

Coal explained. "Deception. If we found him unscathed, after the entire caravan was slaughtered, we would have thought something was amiss."

"It makes sense, but where is the proof?! We are going on the word of a man we just met," argued Syd.

Coal tossed Bishop's ring onto the table and it rolled to stop in the middle. Without picking it up, they all knew what it was. "Kyte gave this to me. You all know what that signifies. I noticed in council that his ring was missing."

"That proves nothing. He could have attacked Bishop himself and taken the ring."

"Then why would he come here, Captain? Why come here and expose himself to us if he was the attacker, when he could have just hid in the Shroud and no one would have suspected?"

Syd realized his folly and sat back into his chair.

"Then who was the attacker? Surely this was not done by one man and it could not have just been beasts from the Shroud," asked Guy.

"This is where your final question comes into play, Captain," said Kyte to Kaine. "Your assumption was correct. After centuries, I have indeed discovered the existence of other Magi. Your Regis told me one thing before he died. He told me that the Tellurians were coming and that I should come and warn Coal," said Kyte.

"Oh Almighty, so they are alive as well," gasped Guy. "So, what about the Ignati? Do they still live?"

Coal quickly interrupted. "This is not the time to indulge your historic curiosities, Guy. This is a serious matter."

"This is insane. Tellurians?! This is getting out of hand."

"We just saw Kyte's powers, Syd. Why is it so much more unbelievable to think that Tellurians are involved as well," said Kaine. "In fact it makes perfect sense. Tellurians have the ability to transform into animals, correct?" he asked Kyte."

"Yes. Each one can transform into one particular animal."

"That would explain the wounds on the men. It would also explain how the men were over-powered so quickly," Kaine finished.

"But, it still does not explain this imposter," said Guy. "As you have said, he is the spitting image of Bishop. We saw him up close and unconscious. If he is a body double, he is the greatest double I have ever laid eyes on."

"I know. The thought has been simmering in my mind since Kyte first told me," said Coal. "I cannot explain it. That is one of the things we need to discover. Who is this man?"

"And we also need to know why? Why are they here? What are they up to?" added Kaine.

All the men nodded their heads in agreement except Syd, who still seemed lost. Rather than continue to flounder around in his confusion and look the fool, he sank bank into his chair and surrendered.

"That is what we need to find out," said Coal.

"Why don't we just kill him and get it over with?" asked Syd.

"To everyone but us we would be killing the Supreme Regis. That is the worst crime you can commit. No one will believe our story. There would be no proof. We would be hanged as traitors and the Tellurians would still be out there and no one would know," explained Coal. "This needs to be done secretly. We tell no one unless it is necessary." He was no longer explaining, but ordering. The men knew when their Commander gave them an order and they all nodded in agreement.

"What should we do then, Sir?" asked Kaine.

"First, we need to warn Coroge. For whatever reason, this imposter is targeting the Creed and they need to be warned. If the petition for war is passed and we attack, they must know the reason. We cannot allow hostilities to erupt between us again. I am sending Kyte to go warn Minor Leo. He knows the way through the Shroud best and he can travel quickly."

"I will personally keep an eye on this imposter. I must ensure he does not make any serious moves and I will also try to slow down the petition for war in the council. I want Kaine and Syd to search for information. Look into historical records; ask around the public, whatever you have to do to try to decipher what they could be after. Make sure to be discrete, as well. Kyte tells me that Tellurian spies can be anywhere, disguised as anything."

"Guy, I would like you to keep an eye on Farren and my sister. Kara is already shaken up by the apparent change in Bishop's personality. I do not want either of them finding out, or getting themselves hurt."

After Guy's acknowledgement of the order, Coal's expression turned more somber. "Now, I know this is hard to fully grasp, but it is true. It took me time to believe it. Bishop is dead," he said.

When Coal said it again, a sudden realization came over the three Captains. While Coal was much closer to the Regis, they all had some sort of relationship with him, so it was difficult to accept.

"All we can do now is fight back against those that are responsible and protect this city like we were trained to do. You have your missions, now go and complete them."

Coal's statement was clearly the finish to the conversation, so none of the men spoke up after the fact. They all stood, saluted Coal and left down the tunnel. Kyte was the last one to leave before Coal stopped him.

"I must warn you Kyte. The Creed are not as welcoming as we are. Do not expect to just waltz into the city and demand to speak to the Minor. You must tread carefully."

"I have heard stories of these men. They fought against the Tellurians during the Great War. They are strong."

"It is not their strength you need to worry about, it is their stubborn pride."

"Thank you, Coal. I will do all I can." He bowed before turning and leaving down the hallway.

17

Alexia Pyke sat in a decrepit laboratory chair with her elbows firmly planted onto her desk and her face cushioned against the soft soles of her hands. The notes she read were boring and, for the most part, completely incorrect. She found it sad that she was so uninterested in her own work.

She leaned back and lifted her arms for a nice stretch, forgetting there was no back to the chair, and almost fell backward onto the floor. She managed to grab the edge of the desk before the chair tipped completely.

The lab was quite large, encompassing most of the basement of the Science Society building. The entire perimeter of the room was lined with tables strewn with all sorts of scientific instruments, including test tubes, grotesque specimen jars, heating plates, planting stations, chemical jars and an array of hand tools.

Since the head researcher, Datro Cervon, was arrested and taken away, Alexia had tried to concentrate on her work, but most of her time ended up being spent cleaning the lab because she could not focus. As Datro's chief assistant, she was involved in all of his research, so she had much she could be doing. However, until his sentence was carried out, she would always be fearful of him coming back and discovering she had made progress on his work without him. He did not tolerate that kind of forward thinking.

Because of that, the lab was spotless and had been for some time. On a normal day, papers would be strewn across tables and broken glass would be everywhere. Fires and explosions were also quite common.

There were a few rooms adjacent to the main lab, one for storage and filing and another for Datro's personal lab. Aside from Datro, Alexia was the only one allowed to enter the lab, but she tried to avoid it at all costs. He used the lab generally for live experiments and testing, so it often had a smell that caused her to want to vomit.

She despised the man for the sorts of things that he could do without thought or pause, but she also respected him for his genius and relentlessness. She was not surprised when he was finally arrested but she still found it unbelievable that he was capable of something like murder.

Datro had held a deep hatred of Bishop's father, Lien, for many years because he had reduced the funding put towards Datro's research during the war. Datro had been close to a breakthrough he claimed would have helped them annihilate the Creed, but Lien said that they did not have the time to sit and wait for him to finish his research. Their need was more immediate so, instead, Lien focused their efforts and funds on weapon construction.

Alexia sighed and let her head fall against the wooden table. When she picked up her head a paper stuck for a moment to her oily face. It had been sometime since she had showered and she was beginning to notice. She had light brown hair, cut to about chin length, and soft brown eyes. Her hair was beginning to show clear indications of dirt and oil, the hairs clumping together and sticking out in some places. These were the times she wished her hair was long enough to neatly pull back and hide her dirtiness.

Even in her disheveled state, she had a cuteness to her. Her face was round, with a slightly squared chin to add distinction. Her slenderness was not from exercise or fitness but, rather, from a lack of time to eat very much because of her work. She was of average height and a girlish figure, which was generally hidden beneath her loose research coat.

She got up from her chair and started organizing the papers on the table to return to the side room. She wouldn't be getting any work done today. It was too nice of a day to be stuck in this basement pretending to work on experiments that weren't hers. If only they would decide on Datro's fate quickly, then her life could continue.

If Datro was sentenced to death, she would become the head researcher and she would be able to control which experiments they would be performing. Until then, though, she had to sit around hoping.

It's time for a shower. Maybe I will go into the square for some lunch, too.

As she was meticulously filing away her papers, she heard a loud crash from the main lab and she jumped. She rushed back into the room to find Datro standing in the doorway looking exhausted and confused.

"Sir?"

Datro did not seem to notice her and just continued examining the room, looking for something.

"Sir, I thought you were arrested. Weren't you being held in the dungeons?"

"I was released by the Regis," he said simply, not bothering to explain further. "What happened in here?"

"I, uh, cleaned up, Sir."

"What did you do with my data; my experiments?"

He began frantically darting around the room, checking all the tables as if his papers would just reappear if he looked long enough.

"I organized all of your papers and filed them away, Sir."

"What have I told you about touching my work?" he screeched.

Alexia was still in shock at the sudden appearance of the head researcher and now she was at a complete loss for words. She was certain that she would never see this devilish man again, but here he was.

"Sir, I thought…"

"You thought I was going to be hanged, didn't you? Foolish girl. You thought this was all going to be yours, huh?" He franticly waved his arms around to emphasize his statement.

He ran into the side room and for a few seconds there was quiet. Alexia took the moment to catch her breath and analyze the situation. *They let him go?*

A few seconds later he came running out again. "Ahhh! That room makes no sense to me," he shouted. He continued to dart around the lab, but with no visible destination.

"Did you need any help, Sir?" Alexia nervously asked.

"The experiment that we were doing before they… those fools… took me," he muttered. "Do you remember?"

"Of course, Sir."

"Get the data and papers out and get it going again," he ordered. He finally stopped scurrying around and spoke sternly.

"What will you do, Sir?"

"I need to gather some more information. I am going to Herous."

"Herous? But why Herous, Sir?" she yelled, as he turned and rushed out the door again.

"Just get to work Alexia!" he shouted back from up the stairway, the voice faint.

As quickly as he had arrived, he was gone. Alexia just stood there shocked. *What just happened? Surely they did not let him go. I did not hear anything about this.* Being cooped up in the lab, it was not uncommon for her to be completely unaware of the happenings of society, but surely the release of the Regis' murderer would have reached her ears nonetheless. This troubled and puzzled her.

She was not sure what was going on, but she knew what it meant. Back to work. She let the confused thoughts drift away and her shoulders slumped as she let out a deep sigh. *Well, there goes my shower.* She turned and started searching the side room for the records she needed. It was going to be a long day after all.

18

Once nightfall came, Seduke became a haven for every type of person in the city searching for any pleasure they could think of. Glow lights danced throughout the streets, illuminating storefronts and lighting up colorful signs pointing people in the direction of fun and enjoyment.

Unlike much of the rest of the city, which was constructed of stone and wood of bland and uninviting colors, Seduke was bright and vivid. The taverns and entertainment houses were painted to seduce the customer into entering, so brightness and flashiness was common. Beautiful, scantily clad women stood outside the storefronts attempting to entice the men with promises of companionship, alcohol and a night of fun.

There were three main types of entertainment in Seduke. There were the taverns, where men went to drink and be merry with his fellow man. Then there were the hosted taverns, where men went to drink with the company of a female hostess who entertained him and kept them company. Finally, the show houses put on fantastic performances involving women, music and dancing and were a big hit with even the women of the town.

The women outside the stores wore tight, colorful dresses that accentuated their curves and lean bodies. The necks were cut low and long slits were cut along the leg. Some of the show houses had women dressed in more extravagant or revealing garments to show the theme of their show to give a sneak peak at the performance.

The sun had not quite set, so Seduke was not awakened into its full, exotic form. The women were beginning to arrive at the stores for a late night of work and the noises of the taverns setting up drifted out into the street. Many of the taverns were already open and a few of the hosted taverns had begun to open also; their women standing out front to invite the early comers inside. Kaine and Syd had been wandering the streets for a few hours, but they were not there for the normal reasons.

"Ahhh, I can't take this anymore! Where is he?!" shouted Syd. They had set out in full Gallant regalia, but now Syd's collar was unbuttoned, his hair was a mess and his normally forceful and strong stride was turning into an exhausted shuffle.

"Quit your whining, will you? It's not helping anybody," calmly responded Kaine. "Guy said he would be here somewhere. We just have to keep looking."

"I don't really care what the old man said. It's torture walking through all the taverns for hours and not having a drink." Syd was beginning to plead.

"Forget it," commanded Kaine. "Have you forgotten why we are here? We need to find information. Guy says this man can help us. This is a mission. It does not matter whether we are in Seduke, or not. We do not drink while on a mission."

Kaine was just as frustrated, which is why Syd's constant complaining was beginning to get to him. This was not an ordinary mission for them, but failure was never an option for him.

"Then let me put it this way. It is clear he is not out right now. We came too early. Let us just sit and have a drink for a little while, gather some information and wait for the crowds to come. It is not long until sundown and it would be a waste of time to continue walking around anyway when there is barely anyone out."

Kaine stopped, leaned back his head and sighed. "Fine, Syd. We will stop for a while," he conceded. "But, once the crowds begin to arrive, we are back to work."

Syd silently cheered at his success, then started to frantically search for a place to go. It had been some time since he was able to indulge himself in Seduke. His Gallant duties did not permit him the time to do so, he did not know quite where to start.

After the meeting with Coal and the others, they had been on an intense search for information to help in the battle against the Tellurians. They were unsure of exactly what they were looking for but, at this point, anything would do. Guy had told them of a man that could help them.

"He is an old friend of mine. His name is Seno Pierson and he was the former head of the Valorian Historical Society. If you are looking for information about the Magi, he is the one to ask," Guy had told them.

That had brought them to Seduke. Guy had said he was bound to be somewhere in the district at night; indulging frequently in the entertainment since his removal from the Society.

Now, Syd wandered the streets in an uplifted mood, trying to decide where it was he wanted to sit and have a drink. After turning a corner, a tall, blonde woman approached them. She was wearing a loose flowing silk dress, tighter around her chest to emphasize her curves, but it was short to show her long, sleek legs.

She took Syd by the arm and nestled close into him. "Good evening, gentlemen. Are you looking for some company?" she asked sweetly. She looked into Syd's eyes shyly and smiled; a subtle seductive technique she had mastered well.

Kaine could tell that Syd was being quickly taken in by the woman, so he attempted to break her spell and intervene. "We are on a mission, so we are just looking for a quiet place to take a break, nothing more."

She turned and widened her eyes in obviously exaggerated shock. "Oh, you are soldiers then? I do love a man who puts his life on the line to protect others."

She turned back to Syd and placed her hand on his chest. "Oh, I can tell. You're so strong."

Syd was beginning to become flustered, but was enjoying every moment of it. "Well, actually, we are Gallants," he boasted.

Again, the woman feigned surprise and giddiness. Kaine was not amused. The woman looked over and saw Kaine's annoyance. "Why so serious? You are in Seduke. You should be enjoying yourself."

Syd gave him a cheerful nod and smile of agreement.

"We do not have the time. I am sorry," Kaine insisted. "Maybe another time."

"But, this is the best time. We are not yet busy, so there are plenty of girls available to keep you company. I won't even charge you extra." She turned to the door of the tavern and shouted in. "Neesa!"

Kaine tried to voice his disagreement, but she was not paying any attention to him. A second later another girl walked out of the tavern towards them. She was smaller and had short-cropped, wavy, dark brown hair. She had a similar, loose flowing dress on, but with a much more slender, girlish frame. The dress was held up by two thin straps and it seemed to just float above her body as she glided towards them.

"This is Neesa," the blonde woman introduced. "She is one of our newest girls."

Neesa walked up to Kaine and bowed her head slightly. "It is nice to meet you." Her voice was sweet and innocent, matching her look perfectly. Kaine groaned loudly, upset that he was clearly beguiled, and knew it.

"And my name is Ana," added the tall blonde. "We would love it if you would come inside and have a drink with us. We have a wonderful selection to choose from and our girls enjoy keeping the patrons company while you relax; especially strapping young soldiers such as yourselves."

"That sounds good to me. Lead the way!" shouted Syd gleefully. "My name is Syd, by the way, and that is Kaine."

"It is nice to meet you both," Ana added. "Shall we?" She turned and walked Syd into the tavern. He was almost skipping as they went.

Neesa finally picked up her head and looked at Kaine with her light blue eyes and smiled. Kaine rolled his eyes. "Are you going to come inside?" she asked sweetly.

Kaine shrugged, finally realizing there was nothing he could do. He started walking towards the door and Neesa gently grabbed onto his arm and walked with him. He glanced up at the sign above the door that read *Ana's*.

I should have known, he chucked to himself.

The inside of *Ana's* was just as bright as the outside. If there was one word to describe it, it would be *plush*. A long bar stretched across one wall and the others were draped with colorful sheets of silk. Dozens of large, crescent-shaped booths dotted the floor where a customer could sit and enjoy his drink with plenty of company to surround him.

There were dozens of glow lights lining the walls and booths, with colorful shades to create a nice pleasurable mood. There were aromatic herbs being burned which gave off a scent of citrus and cinnamon. The overall feel conveyed relaxation and bliss.

Ana led Syd to a booth in the back and sat him down.

"Girls," she voiced.

Three of the tavern's girls came quickly tip-toeing over and stood next to the tavern owner. All three were equally as beautiful as Ana, but a bit younger. All wore loose flowing, short silk dress of various colors. It was a clear theme for the tavern. They all also displayed a broad smile and a distinct willingness to please.

"Yes, Ma'am," they all said in unison.

"Make sure these two men are well taken care of," she instructed, also gesturing to Kaine who was just walking through the door with Neesa.

"Of course, Ma'am." They all turned together and smiled at Syd. "It would be our pleasure."

The girls nimbly scooted into the booth next to Syd, pressing themselves up next to him tightly. Neesa ushered Kaine into the booth as well and sat next to him on the end.

"So, what would you like to drink? Are you Herousian Ale men, or would you like something a little more potent, like some drystol or pintare?" asked Ana, after they were settled into the booth.

Syd was about to make a comment, but Kaine quickly made the choice. "Two ales would be fine. Thank you, Ana."

Ana smiled at Kaine and bowed her head in response. "Of course. They will be right out." A moment later, two more girls glided over to bring them their order.

The first three girls were all nestled around Syd, avoiding Kaine, who was giving off a clear sign that he did not want to be there. Neesa, still sat next to him, unsure of what to do. There was an awkward moment, just after the drinks were served, when no one did anything. Kaine quickly snatched up his ale and started drinking.

Syd watched and started laughing. "There we go. That's the spirit."

The three girls giggled softly and Neesa silently smiled. She cautiously inched her way closer to him.

The three girls entertaining Syd were much more energetic and talkative than the shy Neesa. "My name is Lyn," announced the short redhead. "And this is Elise and Liona," she pointed to the two blondes on his left.

Syd smiled back at the three perky girls. "I'm Syd and that is my friend Kaine."

"Are you two in the Forces?" asked the short blonde, Elise, as she playfully glided her hand along Syd's uniform.

"Well actually, we are Gallant Captains," Syd announced.

"Syd!" Kaine growled angrily.

"What's the harm in telling them?"

"If the Commander finds out..."

"He won't find out. Just relax and have some fun," said Syd.

"Don't worry, handsome. We don't go around telling people about who comes here. It would be bad for business," explained Lyn. "There are many men that come in that would rather not have their presence here be known. Discretion is part of the business. Your secret is safe with us."

"Just relax," said Neesa soothingly. She squeezed against his arm a bit tighter and smiled at him. Her smile just seemed to melt his worries away. Kaine wondered if that was part of the game –a practiced trait to keep the customers coming back- or just how sincere she truly was.

"You hear that Kaine? The Commander won't find out, so don't worry." Syd tipped his beer back and quaffed it, letting out a big refreshing sigh when he finished.

A few other customers started to enter, so the place was beginning to come alive. Girls in their flowing silk dresses scampered around the room, giggling and laughing. The deep hardy laughs of the men they entertained seemed to be quieted by the cloth sheets lining the walls. It was an effective and decorative way to keep the noise at a minimum and the conversations as private as possible.

"So, you are Gallants?" admired Elise. "I always wanted to meet one. You are the strongest fighters in the kingdom, right?"

"That's what they say," he boasted, laughing raucously.

"What do you have to do to become one?" asked Liona.

"You have to be a Force's soldier for at least four years, then you can go through the written and physical tests involved. If you pass, you become a Gallant."

"Wow. Those tests must be pretty hard," Liona lauded.

Kaine softly chuckled to himself at the little ridiculous display of adulation.

"So, how do you two know each other?" Neesa asked him.

"Me and Kaine?" shouted Syd, overhearing the question. "We go way back."

Kaine shook his head at his boisterous friend, who seemed to be getting louder as the time went on. "Syd and I were friends since we were little," Kaine explained. "Our fathers were in the Forces together."

"We were attached at the hip, him and me," added Syd.

"Are your fathers Gallants too?" asked Lyn.

They both paused and exchanged a knowing look. "Our fathers were killed late in the war. So was Syd's mother."

"Awww, poor babies," the girls said, apologetically. They all hugged closer to Syd and Neesa looked up at Kaine thoughtfully.

"We joined when we were of age and never looked back," finished Syd.

"It must have been tough," said Neesa.

Kaine finally looked down at her and smiled. "Yeah, but we had each other. We made it through." He looked back at Syd and they both softly laughed, reminiscing about old times.

"Another round of drinks!" called Lyn, breaking the silence. Elise and Liona both cheered.

"No, no. We should probably get back to work. It's starting to get dark, so we need to go find him," said Kaine.

The girls all booed in unison. A second later Ana came walking up to the table. "Leaving already, you two?"

"We have to get back to our mission," explained Kaine. "We only stopped to let the time go by and wait till the streets busied some more. We're looking for someone."

"If he is a regular around these parts I'm sure he's been here before. I keep track of everyone that comes through here. What's his name?"

"Seno Pierson. Former head of the Valorian Historical Society."

"Seno, of course, he is a regular here. He is quite the lady's man, or so he likes to think. Tonight is one of his usual nights, actually. He should be in at some point," said Ana. She turned to point to a tall brunette wandering around the room with a tray of drinks. "Soline there is his regular girl. I'm sure if you just wait around for a while he will show up. No need to get up and exhaust yourself in searching for him."

"You hear that, Kaine?" Syd shouted. "I knew it was a great idea to sit down and wait for a while. Let's just sit back and relax for a bit."

The three girls cheered. "Relax!"

Kaine shook his head. "Fine, but we are not drinking too much. And you will let me know immediately when Seno arrives," he stated to Ana.

"Of course, Sir," she agreed. "Get these men another round!"

The girls cheered again and Neesa leaned her head up against Kaine's shoulder; happy that he was staying for just a while longer.

The sun was now fully set and Kaine and Syd could hear the streets outside fill with excitement. Almost every booth at Ana's was full and not even the sound-proofing of the room could control the laughing and shouting that filled the tavern. Now that the sun was down, the room was a warm glow of oranges, reds and yellows from the glow lights.

Kaine had been doing his best to keep Syd under control, but to no avail. Syd had clearly had too much to drink, but Kaine found no reason now to berate him for his stupidity. He found it funny to watch his good friend intoxicated and surrounded by beautiful women.

He was content and enjoying himself with Neesa, who he discovered was actually a genuinely sweet girl. They had talked for the past few hours and he was beginning to wonder why such an innocent girl was working in a place like this. He did not want to ask though.

Ana came up to the table amid the laughing from Syd's side of the booth.

"Your man has arrived, Sir," she said to Kaine. She turned and pointed to a middle-aged man standing just inside the door.

"That's him?" he asked.

She nodded. "If you intend to make a scene, please try to take it outside, would you please?"

"Do not worry," he assured. He looked over at Syd and realized he wouldn't be much help. "Could you try to keep him here?" he asked Neesa, gesturing to Syd.

"I can try," she giggled.

He got up and started walking over towards the door. Seno, who was dressed in an old vest, slacks and a wrinkled dress shirt, started walking towards a booth with Soline. The clothing was probably from his old days in the Society and he had clearly let himself go, his stomach was starting to protrude. He was cleanly shaven, but his thick, brown hair had not been trimmed for some time.

Kaine followed them and went up to the booth after they sat. Seno looked up at him in surprise. "They must be short on girls tonight. Oh well, get me a drystol with a bit of callip juice would you, Lad? In a tall glass, too, I'm getting a late start." He turned back to Soline, not realizing that Kaine had not moved. A few moments later he turned again. "What's wrong? Did you not understand my order?"

"I'm not your server, Seno Pierson," said Kaine.

"Then, what are you doing standing in front of my table? I got here first, Lad, get your own girl." He draped his arm around Soline's shoulder.

Kaine grabbed his sheath and sword and pulled it forward to show Seno. It took Seno a moment, but he saw the sword and then realized what Kaine was wearing and his attitude changed.

"A soldier, huh? Gallant too, I see. Good for you, Lad. What is it you want with me?"

"I need some information. I hear you are the man to talk to."

A girl quickly scampered over and placed a drink on the table. Seno picked it up and took a sip, clearly trying to act as calm and relaxed as possible.

"Alright, ask away. I'm always happy to spread a little knowledge."

"Not here," stated Kaine. "You're going to need to come with me."

Seno nearly spit up his drink in surprise. "Whoa there, Lad, I just got here," he said. "Let me have a few drinks first and then I would be happy to go anywhere you want later. How is that?"

"I've been waiting too long already. You're coming with me right now."

"And what if I refuse, Lad? You going to slice me up with that sword of yours?" he said arrogantly.

Kaine reached down and grabbed the hilt of his sword and began to draw it when Seno jumped up. "Alright, alright. I get the picture," he blurted. He quickly downed his drink and started to shimmy his way out of the booth. Kaine stopped Soline as she tried to walk away.

"Could you go back and get my friend, please?" he asked her.

She gave him flirtatious wink. "I would love to, Handsome."

Seno slowly inched his way out of the booth and walked up to Kaine. "Always with the swords, you lot. Can't solve a problem peacefully, can you?" he muttered.

Syd stumbled towards them with his three girls in tow and all still laughing together. "You found him! Hooray!" he shouted. The girls responded with a chant as well.

"Let's go," Kaine ordered.

Syd and the girls stumbled past him and out the door. Ana stopped Kaine on his way out. "I assume you will pay your bill on your next visit then?" she asked slyly.

Kaine laughed. "Of course. On my honor as a Gallant."

"Good," she responded. "I know that Neesa would like to see you back as well. She seems quite smitten with you."

He turned and spotted Neesa, giving her a nod and a smile. She blushed and bowed again as she did when Kaine first arrived.

Kaine gave Seno a push out the door into the crowded street. "Time to go. I have waited around long enough for you."

Seno might as well have lived in Seduke itself. His house was just outside the physical border that separated Seduke and the Residential District, but the lights and sounds still stretched easily to his front door. It was almost like he had a signal that alerted him that he needed to head out for the night.

Because of Seno's incessant squabbling and insisting, Kaine had decided to take him to his house for their questioning. He did not see any reason why not, and Seno was giving him plenty of reasons why. It was difficult to get them there through the crowds with Seno being obscenely uncooperative and Syd in a very flirtatious and drunken state. Every time they passed a show house or hosted tavern, Kaine had to wrestle Syd away while keeping an eye on Seno as well. Luckily, all it took to convince Seno to stay put was the glint of his sword. Eventually, he stopped trying to sneak off at every opportunity.

Now that the night was in full swing, the streets were a cacophony of noise and entertainment. Street performers were now out, staging shows involving everything from fire-breathing to dangerous displays of sword-skills and knife throwing. Some of the show houses had a few of their performing girls out in the streets giving potential customers a taste of what to expect.

Kaine was relieved to finally make it to the edge of the district.

"Alright, where do I go next?" Kaine barked at Seno.

Kaine put his arm on Seno's shoulder to give him another push, but Seno shrugged him off. "Let's stop with that now, Lad. I told you I would take you and that is what I am doing. No need to get physical. You have nothing to fear from me. Just keep an eye on your friend there," he gestured towards Syd, who was beginning to look a little sick.

Kaine shook his head in dismay. The fool would make it up to him later, that was certain. He grabbed Syd by the arm and started pulling him along as Seno guided the way to his house.

Seno's home was large, especially since there was only one occupant. It was built of the usual stone of most other houses in the area and had a large balcony hanging out over the front door from the second floor. Inside, the area was almost entirely open, with only his room and bathroom separated from the rest of the house. The kitchen was large, but clearly unused and the lounge area opened up to the second floor with an iron spiral staircase leading to the upper level. There was even a small bar in the corner with a handful of crystal glassware and a few nice bottles of expensive wine and alcohol. From what Kaine could tell, it was the most used thing in the house.

Upon entering the house, Seno immediately went and poured himself a drink.

"I hope you don't mind, Lad, but I was rudely interrupted before I got my first drink," he stabbed. "I would offer you one but I know you would gruffly decline and your friend there clearly doesn't need anything more."

Syd had slumped himself into one of the couches and proceeded to slowly fall into a stupor. Kaine was content with just letting him be. After Seno finished making his drink, he gestured to Kaine for him to follow.

"Let us go talk upstairs. I find it a little more comfortable." Before Kaine could argue, he started to walk up the spiral stairs. Kaine followed reluctantly.

The second floor was a large open library with a small fireplace in the corner and a few large, cushioned leather chairs, tables and glow lights. Kaine could tell that Seno spent most of his time here when he wasn't out on the town. A glass of melted ice and the remnants of an old drink sat on a side table, and a few coals were still warm and glowing in the fireplace.

Seno plopped himself into a chair in the corner, setting his new drink next to the old one. Kaine sat in a chair across from him and eyed him suspiciously.

"So, what is it you want to know, Lad? Must be pretty important for a Gallant captain to come and ask it. I do not talk to soldiers very often. They are rarely interested in anything but their swords. It must have been Guy that sent you. He is the only one of you with a knowledgeable head upon his wide shoulders. He also doesn't know how to leave a poor man alone." Seno was relaxed and not intimidated by Kaine. He propped his feet up on the table in front of him.

Kaine sat, straight-backed and regal, trying to express that he was not here to joke around, but it didn't seem to affect the old historian. "The Magi. What do you know about them?"

"The Magi? You surprise me, Lad. That is not what I was expecting. Now I'm curious about why. Why is it that a soldier is asking about the Magi? It's an interesting topic, to be sure. Not many people asking about the Magi these days; at least not in a serious context."

"Why, is none of your concern. I am here for information, not to indulge in your curiosities. Just tell me what you know."

"That's not the way to act towards someone you're asking a favor from. You should work on being more courteous."

Kaine bolted up from his seat and drew his sword, pointing it at Seno. Seno did not flinch. "I am not asking for a favor!" Kaine shouted. "I do not ask favors from cowardly drunks. I am ordering you to tell me."

"What are you going to do, Lad? Are you going to kill me? Then what would your options be? Who would you go to?" Seno took his feet off the table, sat up and picked up his drink. "Ask yourself one thing. Why would I leave the tavern and come here with you? You wouldn't have done anything to me in that tavern and we both know it. Here though, you wouldn't hesitate to throw a few punches, am I right, Lad? Then why would I come here?" He finished the rest of the drink and clanked it back onto the side table. He nodded to Kaine to sit down. Kaine reluctantly sheathed his sword and sat back down. "I was always going to cooperate with you, Lad, but is it too much to ask to get a little feedback? I am a curious man by nature and by trade. I like to gather information."

"No matter how much you try to convince me, I cannot tell you anything. This is a Gallant matter of the utmost secrecy."

"You can trust me with anything, Lad. I have nobody to tell. I am a man of knowledge and history. All I desire is information for my own curiosity. Besides, I am the laughing stock of the Council and I spend my days drinking with harlots. Who am I going to tell, huh?"

Kaine sighed, calming himself. Seno was right. They had nowhere else to turn. He was their only lead and they could not go back to Coal empty handed. "You tell me what you know and if the information is good, then I will tell you what you want. But only after."

"You drive a hard bargain, but if that is your final offer then I guess I don't have a choice." He got up from his seat and started searching through the books on the shelves. "You know the stories don't you? The legends about the Magi, their powers, what they looked like, what the world was like when they ruled?"

"Of course, everyone does."

"Everybody knows the legends, of course. They were the greatest of bedtime stories. What people do not realize, is that the legends are true, to an extent. Some, like all legends, are exaggerated, but based on fact. The Magi existed and ruled during what was known as the Emerald Ages. Lad, those were beautiful times."

"How would you know how beautiful they were? That was hundreds of years ago"

Seno chuckled to himself. "Books, Lad. Books are a wonderful thing. They bring the past back to life." He found a book, pulled it out and kept looking.

"Then, where can I find some books about the Magi?"

For a moment Seno did not respond. He pulled a few more books off the shelves and then turned around and sat back down. "You can't," he finally responded bluntly.

Kaine looked down at the three very ragged, dusty texts that he had dropped onto the table. "Then, what are those?"

"Don't get ahead of yourself there, Lad. Let me finish my story." He smiled, obviously enjoying himself. "You know the Magi Wars, right?" Kaine nodded. "Decades of fighting between the three races of Magi that, about five hundred years ago, came to a sudden end. The Magi disappeared and we were free to start our Kingdom. That's the legend. As far as everyone knows, the Magi are gone and only we remain."

"But, that's not true?" Kaine asked, sensing that there was a "but" coming.

"Exactly. You've got a brain in there, don't yah?" he grinned as he pointed at Kaine's head. "The reason why the war ended is still unknown, but we do know that the Magi are still out there."

"Then, why doesn't anyone know? Why does everyone believe that they are all dead?"

"Yes!" Seno shouted. "You are brighter than I expected, Lad. That is the question." He leaned forward in his seat. "To my knowledge, there are no records of the Magi, or the Emerald Ages, anywhere in the archives here, or any city or sect in the kingdom. I spent the better half of my life looking. The Creed claim to retain many texts, but they keep them closely guarded. So how does every scrap of information on such an important part of Paks' history disappear?" Kaine just shrugged. "You are so close, Lad. Come on now. Who has the authority to destroy that much information?"

"The Supreme Regis?" said Kaine, apprehensively.

"Exactly!" Seno shouted gleefully.

"But, why would the Supreme Regis want to destroy the history of the Magi?"

"Supreme Regis Henri I was the ruler just after the war. Along with many other undesirable personality traits, he was a coward. He feared the Magi and wanted them to be wiped from Paks completely, but, of course, humans did not have the power to do something like that in those days. What he decided to do then, was to wipe the memory of them from people's minds. Hundreds of people in those times went out searching for the Magi, trying to discover where they had gone to and what had happened. The people were fascinated by them, so Henri had every text that mentioned the Magi burned and every person that went out in search of them conveniently never returned. It was a genocide of sorts. After a few generations people began to forget, the stories turned to legends and the Magi had disappeared."

"That is insanity. Why did the people let something like that happen?"

"Some people fought back, but it did not matter. Some books escaped the carnage, but over time they were tracked down and destroyed." Seno glanced down at the books in front of him and smiled.

"Except those?" questioned Kaine.

"My great, great, great... well, really old, grandfather, Alexander Pierson, started the Valorian Historical Society. I am from a long line of historians and scholars. He wrote many books about the Magi in those days; published many as well. Most were burned, but these are his personal diaries. They were not published so they were not known and were missed during the burning. He hid them for decades, risking his life to save them. All I know comes from these."

Seno nudged them towards Kaine, who leaned over and picked one up. "These will tell me all I need to know about the Magi?"

"They sure will, Lad." Seno watched as Kaine flipped through the pages, eyes widened in intense curiosity. "So," he finally interrupted, breaking Kaine from his focus. "Now it is your turn, Lad. We had an agreement."

It took Kaine a second to realize what Seno was talking about. "You are a smart man, you figure out why I am here." Kaine grabbed the books and got up to leave.

"I think I already have, if you will indulge me," blurted Seno. "It is obvious you are not here because of your own curiosity. You said this was a secret Gallant matter, which makes it military. If what you are looking for is information on the Magi, and it is a military situation, I can only assume that the Magi have returned and that you are looking for a way to fight them. Am I correct, Lad?"

Seno said it so assuredly that Kaine was taken back. He could not even find the words to lie to the man and tell him he was wrong. In fact, he was exactly right. Kaine's silence gave Seno the answer he needed.

"I knew it. And if these Magi are a danger, it has to be the Tellurians. They were always the provocateurs." Kaine still gave no response. "Almighty, I never thought I would see the day," said Seno.

Kaine stood silent and in disbelief. *How could he put it all together so quickly?* He decided it was no use to try to convince the man otherwise now. Seno was too sure of himself for that. "You must tell no one, Seno," begged Kaine.

Seno ignored the order and kept talking. "What have they done? What are they after?"

"We do not know. That is why I am here," pleaded Kaine.

Seno's excitement was palpable; like a child on their birthday. "Tell me everything. Don't leave anything out." He jumped up from his chair. "Wait! I need another drink first."

19

"Councilmen, please calm down. This is a place of debate, not incessant squabbling!" shouted Head Council Grey. Shouts were erupting from all around the chamber and Hayes was standing amid all of it, in front of his specified seat. He stood silently for the shouting to calm. For a moment it did not seem like the other Councilmen had any intention of calming down, but Anton finally asserted himself and used all his strength to shout the men to silence.

"Now, Councilman Balyct, I ask you to please try to avoid stirring up too much of a commotion. This is a civilized place; we are civilized, educated men, not animals."

"I did not tell these men to start yelling, responded Hayes."

"But, you knew full well that your argument would stir up controversy."

"Controversy is what this council is built upon, Head Council. If we did not debate and argue, we would not have a purpose."

"Yes, but debate can be done respectfully and without anger," Anton pressed, looking around the room at the now silent chamber.

Hayes, as of late, had been more and more vocal during council proceedings and even outside of them. The talk amongst the Councilmen was that he was protesting the decision made by the Head Council to delay the attack on Coroge. He was talking to the other Councilmen and advocating an immediate declaration of war. He was preying on the men's hatred for the Creed and exploiting it. Anton was already seeing a change in the Council's opinion towards the issue. It was becoming more and more difficult to control the men during meetings.

Hayes continued, "These men are shouting and speaking out because they have something to say and you are denying them the chance to say it. You casually dismiss their opinions and declare yours as the only one that truly matters."

"This chamber is here so that all men can voice their opinion, but they must do it in a respectful manner. If you wish to argue that we take a more direct approach towards the Creed and discuss the chance that they are involved in the Supreme Regis' attack, then I will wholeheartedly advocate that, but I do not tolerate shouting and childish bickering in my chamber. Do I make myself clear?" responded Anton.

Hayes smiled. "Of course, Head Council."

Anton was not sure of this young upstart's motives, but he could no longer take a passive approach towards him. The council was normally quiet and reluctant to take any big steps, but his brashness was rallying them. These elder councilmen had more grudges than most against the Creed and they had much to gain if the Creed were to fall.

"I do not deny that we need to take strong action towards the Creed, but I also believe that we must not act too brashly. You are telling me that we need to strike now, when they least expect it, but I ask you, what if we are wrong? What happens if the Creed are innocent? We were going to sign a treaty of peace, said Anton."

"You ask us to take a defensive approach against the most brutal men in the kingdom? This is why they have preyed on us for centuries and why they attacked us without pause twenty-five ago. What if we attack them and they are innocent, you ask? Then we have the upper hand and defeat an enemy that has needed to be defeated for decades," Hayes responded.

It seemed as though Hayes was drawing confidence from the rest of the council. He had an answer to every question that Anton had and spoke more confidently than Anton was expecting. In a way, Anton respected Hayes' confidence and ability, but he could not allow his opinion to sway the rest of the council.

The councilmen were beginning to stir again, but Anton hushed them with a wave of his hand. Councilman Rieven stood to voice his opinion. "Councilman Balyct, I recognize your frustration and do not disagree with it, but would it not be wise to defer to someone who has been through a similar situation?"

"And how did that solution work out, Councilman? I assume you are referring to the Head Council. What happened before, when you decided to take a defensive approach?" Hayes paused to give Denuke time to respond, but the elder councilman could not find the words. Then Hayes turned to Anton. "How can we expect anything to change in this world if we continue to make the same mistakes as those before us?"

"He's right," shouted Councilman Sengure from the middle of the chamber. "I am sorry, Head Council, but we need to be more direct. We cannot allow them to take advantage of our indecision and weakness. For once, we need to be the ones to attack, no matter if there is a reason."

"For decades I have regretted my decision to reduce patrols along the border. I made a mistake that cost thousands of lives and I have, and will continue to, take responsibility for it," Anton said, with his head lowered. "What I am not willing to do is risk more lives because I am regretful and want to make up for past mistakes. We are not sitting idly by and doing nothing. As we speak, a messenger is going to Coroge to demand answers. We will discover the truth before we make such a drastic decision as war," he shouted.

"They have attacked the Supreme Regis..." bellowed Hayes, who jumped back up from his seat. "...and we are responding by asking them if they did it? The murder of the Supreme Regis is the worst crime in the kingdom. Action must be taken." Hayes was almost quivering as he finished his demanding statement.

For a moment the chamber was silent, shocked at his outburst. Not even Anton could respond. Then, calamity erupted and cheers echoed around the room. Most the men in the council were now cheering for the maverick councilman and his emotional speech. Anton looked over to Denuke, and the elder councilman shrugged. Anton did not know how to salvage the rapidly deteriorating situation. He had realized at some point that this may have been the inevitable result, but he never thought it would come this quickly.

"I demand an immediate vote for a declaration of war," yelled Hayes, taking advantage of the emotional uproar. The cheers continued to spread.

Anton had lost complete control. He had not experienced such helplessness for twenty-five years. For once in his life, he was not sure what to do. He was out of options. All he could think to do was to stall for more time.

"By law, when a council vote is requested, a one week recess must occur before the actual vote," said Anton. "If you so desire this decision, Councilman Balyct, than the vote will occur at the next council meeting."

Anton was relieved to be saved by a technicality, but only for the moment. He now needed to use this one week to campaign amongst the men to try to reverse Hayes' influence. The cheers of the men turned to groans as they heard the Head Council state his law and drain the enthusiasm in the room.

Would one week be enough time? Do I still have enough control to manage this situation? It seemed like yesterday that he was sending Bishop to Coroge to sign a treaty and now they could be one week away from another war.

How could it have come to this?

20

The port city of Herous had been around longer than any other city in the kingdom, but much of it was brand new. Along the water, the oldest buildings still stood; built of stone, resisting the pressures of time. Since Herous was the largest port city in Briva, it had been expanding quickly because of the trade network and the longest stretch without war in centuries.

The city sat at a natural inlet of the Great Waters, making it a perfect port. The inlet protected the harbor from the rough waters, which made the port serene and safe. The harbor also stretched the entire length of the city in a large arc, with hundred of docks and platforms for loading and unloading cargo. Hundreds of merchant ships arrived and departed from Herous every day. Most of the ships were headed for, and arriving from, the sect of Layalta, which was comprised solely of islands in the north.

Because Herous was expanding so quickly, much of the new construction was done with wood, because it was faster and easier to build with than the usual stone. Buildings were colorful and had much more variety than the capital city, giving Herous a very youthful and fun feel.

A large outdoor market spread along the length of the harbor where merchants sold their goods, and where fisherman tried to dispense of their fresh catch before it turned foul. Fresh seafood was a Herousian favorite. Mussels, clams, crab, shrimp and dozens of varieties of fish were pulled out of the Southern Waters daily. If you did not like seafood in Herous, you would have starved.

Herous was home to a large merchant class, therefore there was a variety of people from many walks of life that lived in the city. The bluffs at the far end of the harbor outside the city, were where the wealthiest of the merchants lived. Their homes were so extravagant that many sailors used them as a visual marker when coming into port.

The clopping sounds of a horse's hooves were heard reverberating sharply in the street, as Datro Cervon galloped into the city. He halted quickly and dismounted. Horses were not allowed to be ridden in the city, but since there were many merchants that came and went by horseback, one could walk them anywhere in the city grounds.

Datro did not seem to fit in amongst the lively, colorful bunch running throughout the city. Unlike Valorians, Herousians delighted in dressing brightly and acting foolish and youthful. A typical young man in Herous would wear ankle length knickers, a bright vest with arm guards covering the forearms. Most men wore hats as well, ranging from berets and gatsbies, to derbies and fedoras.

The women of Herous were young and independent. Most of loved to experience their youthful years on their own and in an exciting place, before settling down with a man in the capital, or out in the countryside. They wore a variety of fashions, from the colorful versions of the popular sun dresses worn in the capital, to more recently popular knee length skirts, with a tight, sleeveless top. Herousian women enjoyed being bold and individualistic.

Datro found the color and excitement of the city annoying. *Don't these people have a purpose?* he thought callously. Even the crisp, ocean air bothered him. He just wanted to get what he came for and return to his lab.

Near the harbor stood the old stone buildings that first comprised the city. They were mostly government buildings and a few houses where the original wealthy lords and merchants who started the port lived.

The harbor was fairly empty in the late morning, with most of the merchant ships and fishing boats gone for the day. The market too was not yet in full swing. No foreign goods had yet arrived and fisherman were not back with their daily catch. Datro found the quietness delightful.

Datro was starving and the loud growl from his stomach broadcast it, but he did not want to stop anywhere here too long. He approached one of the old brick buildings and tied up his horse out front. The sign read, *Herousian Maritime Library and Museum.* There was a large front doorway with pillars, archways and colorful banners hanging along the façade. He groaned at the added ostentation to the historic building.

He wandered in and quickly passed by the displays in the foyer of Herous' history as a port city. At the end of the hall he took a stairway that lead downward. At the level below was the library. All records of merchant ships, fishing expeditions and naval fleets were kept in this library since the end of the Emerald Ages.

There were few guests walking around in the mustiness. Only a few workers who were keeping the library organized and clean could be seen. Datro continued past the main section of the library and down another hallway. Towards the end of the hallway, Datro stopped at a closed door. He looked around to make sure no one was around and then knocked. No one answered, so he slowly turned the handle and entered, locking the door behind him.

The room was clearly used as an office, with a small desk along the back wall and another side table strewn with papers and books. A raggedy old couch sat against the other wall. Datro examined the room for a moment and then rushed over to the couch. He shoved it out away from the wall and then got down on his knees and started probing the base of the wall with his hand. He found a spot on the wall and gave it a hard shove inward. It seemed to move, so he pushed again. After a few more vigorous efforts the stone pushed in about six inches revealing a small handle in the floor below.

Datro got to his feet and grabbed the handle. He struggled mightily, and a small trap door rose from the floor. The door was disguised using the same stone on the floor, so the door was extremely heavy. Datro had to move the couch back even more and shoved over the desk as he struggled to get the door open. He slowly let it down onto the floor and then stopped to catch his breath.

He looked down into the dark hole. There was an old wooden ladder built into the side of the wall. He grabbed a small glow light from the desk and then started his descent. About thirty feet down, he could feel the room open up and he held the light out to see a large room.

After jumping down to the floor, he looked around and found a few more glow lights, which he used to get the room better lit. It was one large open room with a high ceiling. There were tables lining the perimeter and a few in the middle. Some large shelves full of scrolls and texts were set into the far wall. It was a lab, similar in arrangement to his own in Valoria.

With glow light in hand, he wandered over to the set of shelves and started sifting through the papers. They were delicate and almost fell apart in his hand. There did not seem to be any organization to the papers and he sneezed violently at the dust that was kicking up as he searched. After almost half an hour, he finally stopped at a large text. It was hand bound with string and the title, "Experiment 5.7A; Notes and Findings," was scribbled across the cover. Datro dusted it off and started gingerly turning through the pages. After a few minutes of searching, his face lit up with a toothy grin. He slapped the cover shut and rushed out of the stuffy darkness.

2J

The Hanine Pass Inn was a lavish structure standing at the base of the immense Bardon mountains. It stood out breathtakingly and not by accident. Kyte spotted the building from miles out into the Central Plain, its bright façade contrasting with the earth tone colors of the mountain's silhouette.

Even though the inn was erected at the base of a mountain and nowhere near any large city, it seemed to be plucked straight from Valoria's lavish upper class district. It was built from a combination of mountain stone and wood from the Pine on the far side of the pass, giving it a unique look. The main structure was stone, with the roof, front deck and accents made of wood. The wood was painted white and shades of red to give it a rustic and classy feel.

Kyte's journey, so far, had been uneventful, but he did not expect that to last. Taking advantage of the mist, Kyte had flown over the Shroud atop his giant eagle, Drek, before landing and walking through the Central Plain on foot. While it was dangerous to travel the plain by oneself, Kyte had done it many times and knew the way well. At the base of the mountain, the Hanine Pass Inn was the gateway between the three largest sects; Briva, Vertura, and Fera. The extensive market caravans that traveled between the sects took the pass. The only other way to reach the other side was to travel hundreds of miles north to the coast and circumvent the mountains altogether.

After a long and sleepless night in the Inn, Kyte checked out and started his trek through the pass. While wandering past the stables, he received some friendly hellos from a few early-rising merchants and some miserable grunts and moans from other travelers who were most likely involved in the commotion in the tavern that kept him up all night and were just now regretting it.

The entrance to the pass was smooth and flat, giving the illusion of an easy trek, but not far down the path the terrain started becoming far from painless. Over the years, workers had done their best to flatten and smooth the path, but the mountain did not agree with their goal. Thousands of men had been killed during the work, so the idea had been abandoned as a silly dream and the path left unfinished, despite the complaints of the merchants.

For a healthy, fit man walking on his own two feet, the terrain would be considered a vigorous exercise, but for anyone on horseback, any large, lumbering animals, or wheeled vehicles, the terrain was so daunting it was almost not worth the effort or danger.

Since the pass was the only feasible way to traverse the mountain range, merchants made the trip despite the difficulties. Over the years, though, the merchants had created tricks to help them with the terrain, like the breeding of nimbler horses for riding or stronger ones for pulling vehicles. They also experimented with the wheel placement on their vehicles and placement of goods inside them to help with balance and maneuverability. Kyte watched some of the caravans and marveled at the ingenuity of the humans.

They definitely do not lack heart.

Kyte bounded up the rocky slope, passing quickly by all other travelers. The inclines were rigorous to climb, but heading back down the other side, he discovered, was far more treacherous. Loose rocks slipped from under his feet many times, forcing him to inconspicuously use his magic to keep his balance. A subtle, small burst of air under a foot or against his chest was all he needed to keep himself from tumbling down the mountainside.

Occasionally, he assisted a fellow traveler, but he tried to avoid as much contact as possible, keeping his hood up and speaking little.

On the second day, he came to the split in the pass where the roads separated to direct traffic to either Fera or Vertura. The pass was built at the point where the Bardon Mountains intersected the small Grace Mountains that formed the border between Fera and Vertura. This way, only one pass, forked at the center, needed to be built rather than three separate paths to connect the major sects.

Many caravans were pausing at the intersection before proceeding towards their final destination. Kyte took the moment to rest and have a small meal before quickly continuing on. The sun was beginning to get high in the sky and he wanted to get to the Pine quickly so he was not caught out in the open pass in the heat of the day.

On occasion, Kyte would spot a Striped Mountain Fox peering down on them from a high ledge, or a Plains Hawk circling over head. It was not uncommon for travelers to be attacked and killed by the dangerous wildlife, especially if they were traveling alone.

It had taken him longer than he wanted, but he finally reached the Pine. The sun was beating down on him and he was sweating profusely under his cloak, which he refused to remove in case someone would recognize his Aerii features. The shade of the thick evergreen trees of the Pine was a welcome reprieve from the open, rocky pass.

The Pine's canopy was thick, creating a very dark and open forest floor because no sunlight escaped through to help grow the underbrush. Many species of trees grew in the Pine that grew nowhere else in Paks. There were the common evergreen-like firs, pines and spruce, but there were also the Pine Cedar and the Everfir Oak, whose structure looked like a massive oak tree, but its limbs held needles instead of leaves.

Because of the lack of other plant life in the forest, there were few small scavenging animals and consequently very few predators. Therefore, the Pine was a dark, yet peaceful, place.

Kyte sighed in relief at the cool shade and he took a long drink from his canteen. Since it was getting late in the day he was no longer running into other caravans coming from the other direction and he had moved quickly, so he had passed most travelers following his same path. He was alone now as he peered into the dark forest and he was happy to be able to make the next part of the journey without prying eyes.

There was a large path cut into the forest to allow for large caravans, but the darkness still made it hard to keep your direction. He walked slowly along the path, admiring the unique trees. The darkness of the Pine was similar to the mist of the Shroud, so he felt at home, but he did not feel in constant danger here, as he did in the Shroud. He found it ironic that a peaceful forest like this was what surrounded the capital city of Coroge, where such brutal men lived.

The view was unchanging as he walked for hours. Even though it was always dark in the forest he could begin to tell that it was getting darker outside the trees. The temperature was dropping and the few shadows that were there were fading. He felt a chill and suddenly the serenity of the wood gave Kyte an ominous feeling. He stopped and examined his surroundings.

A twig snapped behind him and Kyte spun around quickly to spot the speeding shadow of an arrow racing towards him. He threw his forearms up in front of his face, pulsing a shield of wind. The arrow struck the wall of wind and shattered. When he opened his eyes, a man was racing towards him, sword drawn. His skin was as dark as the forest around him. Kyte quickly drew his sword and readied himself, but then another arrow shot out from the trees to his left. He threw up another shield of wind, stopping the arrow, but it distracted him enough to allow the first man to get close to him. The man swung his sword down at Kyte, who blocked it, but fell backwards and dropped his sword. The man did not pause. Taking advantage of Kyte's situation, he attacked. From his back, Kyte shot a sword of fast moving air out of his palm, impaling the man in the chest as he tried to attack.

Kyte pulled the sword of air from the man and he slumped to the ground, dead. Kyte quickly had to roll to the side as three more arrows buried themselves in the ground where he had been laying. He got to his feet, darting his eyes around to see where the next man would come from.

Two more men burst from the darkness, one rapidly shooting arrows from a compact crossbow. The other man had two swords drawn. Kyte's shield of air protected him from the arrows, but it was a dangerous distraction, so he shot a burst of air at the man and he flew backwards, hitting a tree and shattering his crossbow. Kyte then turned and defended the attack from the second man with his wind sword. The sharp, magical sword cut through the man's metal blade, but the man knelt, spun around and swung his second sword. Kyte blocked it again, and then kicked up his knee, contacting the man in the jaw. He staggered backwards and Kyte cut him across the chest.

Kyte heard the angry roar of the crossbowman behind him and turned, slicing his wind sword through the air, sending a sharp current of wind at him, cleanly slicing the man through the middle.

Kyte was breathing heavily, but did not let his guard down. A moment later one man stepped slowly into view. Like the others, his skin was black, but he stood almost seven feet tall and he was built as strongly as the trees that towered around them. The man stood there, staring at Kyte, then looked around at the dead bodies of the three other men. He slowly drew his sword from a sheath on his back. The sword was enormous, almost as tall as he was and nearly a foot in width at the hilt. The man's muscles rippled as he held it.

Kyte stared at his sword of wind and then back at the man's sword. He surged more air into his sword, increasing it in size. The speed of wind circulating through the sword made it hard to control, but Kyte grabbed on with two hands and drew forth the strength.

The two men charged at each other and the clash sent a shockwave of air out in all directions. They attacked furiously back and forth, not a word being said between the two of them. Kyte then swung his sword and the man ducked under it. The current of air sliced through the trunks of the trees behind him and they both dodged out of the way as they fell to the ground. Using the commotion as a distraction, Kyte lunged forward and attacked, finally cutting through the man's sword, the tip crashing into the ground. The man surprisingly kicked out his foot and sent Kyte sprawling back several feet.

With the man now weaponless, Kyte darted forward. Without warning, the man leaned over and began picked up one of the trees that had fallen to the ground just moments earlier. He howled with the exertion, but the tree slowly rose. Kyte, who was now in full sprint, could not stop his assault as the man took the tree and swung it savagely towards Kyte. Kyte tried to block the blow with a shield of wind but the blow was so strong he flew sideways, hitting hard into the trunk of a giant Pine Cedar. He slumped into a pile, unconscious.

The man let out a large sigh and dropped the tree, letting it crash into the ground. He slowly walked over to the body of Kyte and stood above him. He leaned down and pulled back Kyte' hood, revealing his blue, gray hair and Aerii features. The man smiled.

"Exactly as I thought," he said with a deep, bass voice. "To think I would run into one of you on such an ordinary day." He got up and looked around at the carnage they had created and the bodies of the other men strewn around.

"Well fought, Aerious," he whispered.

22

Syd woke with a groan, his head pounding and his stomach in knots. He had not felt this much pain since his last duel with Coal. As his vision focused he looked around, trying to figure out where he was. The room looked vaguely familiar but he could not figure out why. Nothing came to mind when he tried to place it, but his mind wasn't really working well. The room was dimly lit and it opened up widely above him. As he looked around, he lost his balance and fell off of the couch he was awkwardly laying on, the cushions tumbling down on top of him.

With a groan, he stumbled to his feet, getting dizzy as he rose. Before he fell again, he caught himself on the arm of the couch and took a moment to let the spinning stop. When he rose he became aware of a sharp ache in his neck and back. He was still in complete uniform, but it was awkwardly twisted about him. His sword and sheath were on the floor on the other side of the room. As he made his way that direction, he heard some faint talking that seemed to come from the floor above him. He spotted a staircase that led upward and struggled his way towards it. Every step felt like a drum pounding on his skull.

At the top, was a small library and sitting area and when he reached the final step, he caught his foot and stumbled. The talking stopped. Kaine peaked his head around the corner and looked at his pathetic friend. A second later Seno's head appeared as well.

"So, the lad's awake, finally," Seno chuckled. "Still hurting though it seems."

Kaine shook his head in disappointment and walked over to help Syd up and into a chair. He handed him a glass of water and Syd downed the entire thing greedily.

"How long have I been asleep?" Syd asked.

"Most of the night. It's almost morning, Syd," groaned Kaine.

"I don't remember anything."

"For good reason, you fool. You drank half the alcohol in the tavern."

Syd turned his head in confusion, trying to figure out what Kaine was even talking about. Kaine noticed his obvious disorientation and groaned in annoyance.

"Do you even remember what we were doing out last night?"

"Of course. We were looking for the historian, Seno." He paused for a second. "Wait, did we find him?"

114

Kaine dropped his head and let out the loudest groan so far. Syd looked at him, wondering what he'd said to cause such a reaction, then looked up at Seno, who smiled at him and waved.

"Is that him?" Syd asked.

"Of course it is, you clod!" Kaine shouted.

"So we found him…"

Seno started laughing, almost falling backwards off his chair and Kaine finally gave up, jumping up from his seat to get himself something to drink. Syd still looked around at them confused. Seno came up and patted him on the shoulder.

"It's alright, Lad. I've been there a few times myself. More than I would like to admit. Drink the water and it will fade soon. You are still young, so you should bounce back quickly."

A faint light could be seen starting to peek through the closed shades on the windows in the room. Kaine and Seno had been up for hours, discussing the situation with the Tellurians and what to do about them. Seno soaked up all the information like an eager child. He was more excited about the appearance of a Magi than the trouble that could arise from them coming back, though, so Kaine often had to force the man to concentrate on the real situation at hand.

"We needed to take a break anyway, Lad. I haven't focused so much on one thing in a long while." Seno wandered over to his small bar where Kaine was and started to make a drink for himself. "You want anything, Lad?" he shouted back to Syd.

"You're joking, right?"

Seno chuckled. "I just thought I would ask."

They both made themselves a small kiho riser, a common morning drink used to refresh the mind or cure a rough night, then sat back down in their chairs.

"So, what have you two been talking about then?" Syd asked, breaking the silence.

Seno took a big sip, smacked his lips and set the drink down on the side table. Kaine drank in thoughtful silence. "Your friend and I have been having a long discussion about your new predicament."

Syd shot a look over to Kaine. "Oh great, you told him? The Commander is going to kill us for this."

"I did not tell him. He guessed," defended Kaine. "I couldn't really deny it. Besides, I didn't have a choice."

"Don't get too mad at him, Lad. It was obvious from the point when he asked about the Magi. You don't get many questions about them these days. It didn't take much after that to put it all together."

"He knows what he is talking about, Syd. Once I told him everything, he has been working with me to find a way to fight them." Kaine turned and picked up the big diary they had been looking through. "This book has everything we need."

"So, it tells what they're after? Why they are here?"

Kaine started to flip through the book furiously. He came to a page and turned it to show Syd.

"It talks here about the Magi Wars. Do you remember hearing the legend of why the war started?" asked Kaine.

Syd leaned forward to look at the pages as Kaine spoke. "Something about a Tellurian that rose up and tried to overthrow the other Magi, right?"

"The Grand Master," added Seno. "The child prophecy of the Tellurians that made them believe they could rule the entire kingdom."

"Exactly." Kaine jumped up from his chair and began to pace the room as he talked. "He was the one who started the whole war. Everything that happened was because of him. And get this. He could transform into a human."

Syd looked up from the book, "Wait, I thought that Magi could only transform into animals."

"That's why he was considered so special, Lad," said Seno. "He was the first and only Tellurian to be able to do it. The Tellurians were very religious creatures, so when something like that happens, they see it as a sign."

"So, they started the war because one of them could transform into a human? I thought we were nothing compared to Magi. Why would they care?"

"I do not think it had anything to do with the fact it was a human, Lad, but rather that it was something that had never happened before. Fanatics do not really need a reason for anything."

"Okay, that makes sense. So, they started a war and everyone died. How does that help us? We need to know how to fight them. We need to know what their purpose here could be."

"Yes, of course. That is what I am trying to get at. This one Tellurian was able to transform into a human. That means that he could make himself look like any human he wanted," said Kaine. He sat silently for a moment, waiting to see if Syd would catch on to his point.

Finally, Syd's eyes widened. "You don't think?"

Seno smiled and said, "Exactly, Lad; we have a Tellurian ruling our kingdom."

Syd, who was still a little dazed from the night, found it difficult to wrap his head around the comment. He looked over to Kaine for answers, but Kaine gave him a shrug.

"You say that Bishop is dead and that this new person is an imposter. We know that the Tellurians are involved as well. This imposter looks exactly like Bishop and, from what you say, he sounds just like him as well. It must be a descendent of the Grand Master."

"I know it sounds crazy, but after what we have been through lately, it really isn't that unbelievable. It actually makes perfect sense, Syd," added Kaine.

"I know, but..."

"It's a lot to wrap your head around, Lad," added Seno.

Syd flopped back into his chair and sighed as he stared up at the ceiling. "This is not at all what I was expecting, but you are right, it does seem to make sense." He pondered it for a moment before saying, "For the sake of the argument, let's say it is true. We are being ruled by a Tellurian. So, what do we do now?" he asked. "Do we know what they are after? I mean, this sounds like a very complicated plan. Why not just attack us?"

"I would assume their aim is the same as before. They want to take over." commented Seno. "But, they may not have the strength to do it. With the powers of the Supreme Regis, they control the Valor Forces. If you combine that with their own powers, they would have a very strong army."

Syd sat back up and started flipping through the pages of the book.

"Coal tells us that this imposter is trying to start a war with the Creed. He is pushing pretty hard in the council to get the motion passed," added Kaine.

"Why the Creed?" asked Syd, without looking up from the book.

"Think about it," said Seno.

"Please don't make me think right now," quipped Syd.

Kaine laughed. "The Creed are equal in strength to the Forces. Back during the Magi War, they were the only ones that fought against the Tellurians with the other Magi. They are a threat, so the Tellurians want to try to eliminate them first."

"That's good, Lad," said Seno. "The Creed do know quite a bit about the Tellurians. Or, at least they claim to."

"Hey, look at this," commented Syd as if he wasn't even listening to Seno's response. He started reading a section from the book. "I remember the day when the Tellurians attacked the city. Never before had they even paid attention to us humans in Valoria. Why they attacked, I do not know. I did hear rumor, though, that they were after a weapon that the scientists were producing. What kind of weapon could the Magi want from us?"

"The Hand of the Almighty," blurted Seno. Both Syd and Kaine looked up at him. "He talks about it more, later in the book."

"What is it?" asked Kaine.

"It was a secret experiment set up during the war to try to battle the Tellurians. The Tellurians were beginning to get aggressive and humans were dying as a result, so we tried to fight back."

"But, what was the weapon?" urged Syd.

"No one knows. It is hardly ever spoken of in any texts I have read and, when it is, it is only vaguely. I do not believe that anyone outside of the group running the experiment and the Regis at the time knew any of the details. To the best of my knowledge, it was never completed."

"Did the Tellurians get the weapon?"

"I do not believe so. The Hand of the Almighty was said to have been such a powerful weapon that it would have instantly turned the war in the favor of whoever possessed it. If the Tellurians captured and completed it, we would have known."

"If it was something that strong and they failed to get it the first time, then…" thought Kaine, out loud.

"…they wish to find it this time, so their success would be ensured," finished Seno, unsure of himself.

"But, it was never completed, right?" asked Syd. "What good would it be to them?"

"Even if, over these hundreds of years, someone has not found a way to complete it, the Tellurians would find a way. They would not have waited this long if they did not know they could have it," said Seno.

They all nodded in agreement.

"Then, we must find it before they do," asserted Syd. His enthusiasm was great, but Seno did not seem so assured.

"I have never once read of where it might be located. It was created in the utmost secrecy. There are no actual records of the experiment."

"Is there anyone who would know? Could the information have been passed down through generations, like these books were to you?" asked Kaine.

Seno slumped back into his chair and thought. He took the final swig of his drink and placed it back onto the table. "I do not believe that Bishop, or even Lien, would have known. Something that secretive probably would have been undertaken specifically by the Regis at the time, not even passed down to his successor. That leaves only the scientists performing the experiment, who would have been compelled to complete the experiment, no matter the politics." He paused for a moment, leaving Kaine and Syd in suspense. "They may have left some indication of the experiment, but kept it secret amongst themselves; possibly even continuing the research without the Regis' consent."

Again he paused. "Spit it out, Old Man!" shouted Syd.

Seno turned and chuckled at Syd, but then his smile turned to a grimace. "I can think of only one man who might possibly know, but you are not going to like it."

Rage reverberated throughout the outer hallways of the palace as Coal and his two captains walked briskly onward. The anger, combined with the echoing of their hard footsteps against the granite floor, gave anyone ahead of them warning that the Commander was coming and that he was not in any sort of pleasurable mood.

"Are you sure?" hissed Coal. "He is one of them as well?"

Kaine and Syd did their best to keep up while still holding their composure, but it was difficult. The Commander walked with a purpose.

"It fits, Sir." Kaine looked around to make sure no one else was listening and then quieted to a whisper. "It explains everything. We are in a more difficult situation than we originally anticipated."

A few palace servants walked into the hallway from a side room but quickly darted back in when they spotted the three bearing down on them. Coal did not seem to be bothered by the people's fearful glances.

"And this weapon?"

"Nothing substantial, Sir. All we know is that they tried to steal it before and were unsuccessful. It is said to have tremendous power."

"With the influence of the Supreme Regis, they could easily find and complete it," Coal thought out loud.

Both Kaine and Syd nodded in agreement.

"But, why draw so much attention to yourself when you could just sneak in and steal it? Deception is their greatest strength," questioned Coal.

"With the power of the Supreme Regis, they have control over the Forces as well," blurted Syd.

"We must assume that their numbers are not as great as they were back during the Magi Wars, so they need as much strength as they can muster," added Kaine. "It is quite an ingenious plan, Sir."

Coal finally turned back to them and grinned. "But, they did not factor in that we would find out. They have lost their greatest advantage."

They were quickly led through the dungeon gate and Coal ordered the guards to stay put. Even in the dimness of the stairway, Coal's silhouette was easily distinguishable and he began to hear angry shouts from the prisoners as he walked downward past the side tunnels where they were locked away. Many of the prisoners were arrested by Coal himself, so derogatory words were shouted; many with personal emphasis. Coal calmly deflected them.

"And, you think that he is the only one that would know where to find the weapon?"

"That is what Seno believes, yes. He is likely the only one that would know."

They continued down the stairway, silently. The shouts from the prisoners were beginning to fade away as they went further. There were far fewer men held this deep in the dungeon.

Finally, they reached the end and headed down the side hallway. It was deathly quiet as they reached the final cell and peered in. All they saw was emptiness.

"Are you sure this is the correct cell, Sir?" asked Syd cautiously.

"Yes, of course. I have been here so many times, I could find it in the dark. I can even smell his stench lingering."

They stood silently for a few more seconds before Coal erupted. "Guard!"

The sound nearly shook the stone around them and they could hear it echo its way up towards the entrance. After a moment, there were hurried footsteps and the guard appeared before them with a concerned look. He quickly saluted and bowed his head.

"Yes, Sir?"

"Where is this prisoner?" Coal asked calmly.

"Uh..." the guard stammered as he looked back and forth between the cell and Coal. "He was released, Sir," he responded apprehensively.

Kaine and Syd took a wary step backwards from the Commander. Anger could almost be seen emanating from him, but he held his cool. "By whom?"

"It was the Supreme Regis himself, Sir. He came down nearly a week ago and ordered that he be released immediately."

"Why was I not informed?" Coal's voice was beginning to fill with anger.

"He told me not to tell anyone, Sir. I was only following orders. I would have informed you immediately in any other instance. You have to believe me, Sir."

Coal drew in a large breath and shook with rage. He looked down towards the floor to try to control himself while he thought. Kaine gestured to the man to leave with a quick turn of the head. The guard slowly and warily disappeared back up the stairs.

Kaine and Syd stood quietly, waiting to see if their Commander would say anything. Finally, Kaine decided to break the silence.

"His disappearance does seem to prove our hypothesis. He is involved somehow." He paused to see if Coal would respond. "But, they have gotten to him first. We were too late."

Coal's roar sounded like that of a lion as he released his rage. Kaine and Syd merely hung their heads and let the piercing sound echo around them. When the sound finally dissipated, he turned and glared at them.

"Find him!" he seethed.

Alexia was close to falling from her chair in exhaustion. Her elbow was resting on the table, and her hand was awkwardly squished into the side of her face, when Datro burst into the lab. Just before she slipped into a deep sleep, she was jolted awake by his sudden appearance.

She had spent the last week recovering Datro's notes and information on his previous experiment and bringing it back up to speed. Jars of liquids and herbs were brought down from the shelves and side room and a series of instruments were lined up along the table. A heating pad was lit and warming a glass beaker of liquid.

Alexia quickly wiped the line of drool from the side of her mouth in order to hide her languor. Unfortunately, the disheveled appearance of her hair and her half open eyes did little to assist in the charade.

"Have you got it going, Alexia?"

"From what I can remember and decipher from your notes, yes," she responded energetically. She quickly got up to show him what she had done. "I have arranged the needed ingredients and have mixed an initial formula," she said, pointing to the heat pad. "It has been at moderate heat for a few hours."

Datro walked over and observed the liquid, wafting the scent up to his face. He drew in a deep breath. "Not quite, but I wouldn't have expected perfection from you," he said coldly. "Your measurements are a bit off and the heat is a bit too high. It cannot be allowed to even approach a boil, or else the compound will begin to break down."

Alexia grimaced, but did not let it get to her. She was used to his disapproval. He was not a man to laud anyone for their good work or assistance and it was fortunate that Alexia no longer found it disheartening when he ignored her success.

Datro tossed a large book onto the table, nearly toppling the beaker and its contents. "Don't worry, though. Your failure does not matter. I now have what we need. This will tell us what we have been missing, so we can finally complete it."

"Is that what you went to get in Herous?"

He nodded as he flipped through the book excitedly.

"If that will tell us how to complete the experiment, why have you not retrieved it until now?"

He did not bother to look up at her as he responded. "Because Lien was having me watched. He did not trust that I would follow his orders and stop my experiments. I needed to make it seem like I was working on what he wanted me to."

"So, then Bishop is allowing you to continue, despite what his father believed?"

Datro chuckled. "In a way, yes. Bishop is very much in favor of my research. In fact, he is encouraging it. A lot has changed about the Supreme Regis." He turned the book toward her and pointed to the page. "This is the final piece of the puzzle. This is what we have been working towards for all these years. With this, the experiment will be complete."

"What is it, Sir?"

"It is a precious gem hiding in the Shroud; a diamond in the mist. Once I retrieve this final piece, then our success is assured." He slammed the book shut. "Keep the preparations going as before. I will return again soon," said Datro as he raced up the stairs and disappeared as quickly as he arrived.

Alexia stood starring at the doorway, still stunned by what happened. "What have I gotten myself into?" she mumbled under her breath.

23

The room was dark and austere. That was all Kyte could ascertain as his eyes slowly opened and adjusted to the dimness. All he could see was mist on the cool air as he breathed. He tried to rise, but a sharp pain shot up his back and he crumpled back onto the bed. His entire body was sore and he could barely move.

The bed he lay in was comfortable, but plain, and there was little in the room besides a table to the side of the bed with a glow light, a large wooden door in the far wall and one small window which was letting in a faint ray of light.

Where am I? How did I get here? he thought, as he again struggled to rise up to a sitting position. He propped himself up on his forearms and then pushed up to slump forward. The pain caused him to groan and when the blanket fell off of his body, he noticed the extensive bandages covering his chest and arms. A few of the bandages showed stains of blood starting to soak through.

After examining the room for a few more minutes, he took a deep breath and swung his legs off the side of the bed. After another pause, he slowly lowered himself onto his feet. He winced in pain as he put weight onto his right leg, so he shifted over to his left.

He was not wearing any shirt and he could see that the bandages covered almost his entire torso. He was, though, wearing some loose cotton pants drawn at the waist with a tie. He could feel bandages impeding his movement along his right leg as well.

When he reached the door, he found it securely locked. There was no other way out. The window was too small to force his way through, so he started to use his magic to try to open the door. He manipulated small air currents within the lock of the door and lightly undid the locking mechanism with a click. He slowly opened the door to find a short hallway that seemed to open up into a larger room at the end.

He cautiously and painfully slid his way down the hallway to the open room. When he did reach the end, a hand reached out from the side of the entrance to halt his advance.

"That's far enough," grunted a man.

Kyte looked over to see a tall, dark skinned man standing guard at the entrance into the larger room. He wore a sharp, black, military uniform that was only contrasted by gray buttons and accents around the collar, shoulder and cuffs. It was similar in style to the Valor Forces, but with a far darker color.

The man also held a spear that had a remarkably long, curved blade on the end that Kyte assumed was specially forged. It took Kyte another moment to realize that another man stood on the opposite side carrying an equally deadly looking weapon that resembled a dual-sided axe blade, though longer and sleeker.

Kyte looked back to the first man. "Where am I?"

The man ignored his question and grunted a command. "Return to your room and we will alert the General that you are awake." His face stayed impassive and neither man even looked over at Kyte.

Kyte was confused by their emotionless demands, but he did not want to attempt an escape in his condition, especially since he still did not know where he was or even how to escape the room he was in.

The first man turned his head to the other and nodded a command. The second man hurried out of the room through the door at the far side of the room. Kyte watched him leave, trying to catch a glimpse of what lay beyond the door, but he saw little. The first man turned and silently gestured to Kyte to return to his room with a tilt of his head. The man obviously was strong and he did not seem worried about an attack from Kyte.

Is he ignorantly confident, or is he that strong?

Kyte decided to retreat for now and turned to limp back to the room.

It had been almost an hour as Kyte sat on the edge of the bed in the bare room. It was clearly a holding cell, but not for criminals. They seemed to be treating him as a suspicious guest. After returning to the room, he noticed a glass of water on the small table and drank it with caution.

How long have I been here?

His thoughts wandered, as he tried to remember what happened before he woke up in this place. He looked out of the small window, but saw nothing but a vast forest and a range of mountains past it. He was high up in a large structure, so he could see far into the wilderness around him. Even with this advantage, he could see nothing that helped him remember.

Kyte's mind returned from its wandering when he heard the clicking sounds of the door unlocking and slowly opening. An enormous man strode through the door. He wore the same black uniform, but a few red insignias and markings on the breast and shoulder signified he was of a high rank. The man showed no sign of aggression but Kyte still felt in intense sense of danger from the man.

Then it occurred to Kyte. This was the man that he fought in the forest. Without pause, Kyte formed his sword of wind and crouched to attack. Before he lunged forward, though, he winced at the pain in his leg and then his back gave way as he doubled over. The man never once showed any sign of distress.

"That was foolish," the man commented.

"Who are you?" Kyte forced, breathing heavily. "Where am I?"

"I am surprised you are awake already, but you are an Aerious, after all," the man grinned. "I am told you have advanced healing abilities." Kyte showed a hint of surprise, then realized after the fight they had it would have been obvious what he was. "Your injuries, though, are not healed yet, so you should rest."

"I cannot stay here. I need to deliver a message," declared Kyte. He struggled to stand back up.

The man started to pace the room, circling Kyte like a predator. "And to whom must you deliver this message? This is dangerous country to be wandering around alone in, even for you."

Kyte stood firmly, his chest out. This man was clearly trying to intimidate him and, even with his injuries, Kyte refused to bend to his will. "I need to speak to Minor Leo Lockhardt. I must get to Coroge as quickly as possible."

The man stopped and stared at Kyte. "No one speaks to the Minor without…"

"If you do not help me willingly, I will not hesitate to force you to. You already know what I am, so you know what I am capable of," interrupted Kyte.

The man was slightly shocked, but then started to laugh boisterously. The laughing irritated Kyte even more than before. "I respect your courage, Aerious, but, even for you, that is an impossible task. You are held captive right now in a military outpost in the Pine, hundreds of miles from the capital. Even if you managed to escape here, in your condition you would be struck down long before you were able to reach the walls." Kyte did not laugh and the man seemed to find it funny that Kyte was so serious. "I do wonder, though, what an Aerious wants with the Minor. We have not seen or heard from a Magi in centuries and yet, here you are."

"I bring a message from Commander Coal Lucer. Coroge may be in danger," Kyte said plainly.

The man's expression changed immediately upon hearing Coal's name. He now showed no hint of humor. "The Commander sends us a warning? Ha!" he yelled. "You should know that the Minor was deeply upset that the Supreme Regis did not show himself for the treaty. I do not think he has any interest in listening to your message."

"I need to pass on the message," urged Kyte.

"Fine, Aerious, tell me the message and I will determine if it is vital enough to pass on to the Minor."

"I will speak only to the Minor," Kyte responded quickly.

The man seemed annoyed by the words. "Anything that you must tell the Minor, you can tell to me," the man insisted.

Kyte examined the man again, trying to determine what it was that made him so imposing. Sure, he was a man of great strength, but Kyte had never felt so fearful in the presence of a human before.

"Who are you?" asked Kyte.

"My name is General Weston Lockhardt," he asserted. "The Minor is my grandfather."

24

Year 2: Month 3: Day 49: of Experiment 5.7A

The experiment trudges onward, despite our failures. We are close though, I can feel it. Yokin nearly destroyed the lab this morning when he decided to bring the substance to a boil, despite our warnings. An explosion left the lab in ruins and Yokin is in the infirmary. I cannot blame him, though, for wanting to try everything we can. Nothing seems to work.

Jone seems to believe it is a problem in the mixture ratios, but I am not certain. I think there may be an ingredient we are missing; a control agent that helps stabilize the reaction and protect the subject. What that ingredient is, I am not sure.

I dread my days since the Regis has forced us into trials. We are far from a working substance worthy of initiating trials, but we must bend to his will. The war is strengthening and the battles are beginning to stretch to our borders. He is being pressured to make an extremely unethical choice. Each day a subject is brought in for testing and each day a corpse leaves. The only comfort I have now is not knowing where these men come from, or who they are. I had never thought of ignorance as a virtue.

I have now been making the other researchers conduct the trials. The pain and suffering that the subjects go through is beyond displeasure. Even the thought of it brings me to tears. I have closed myself in a side room where I can only hear the muted echoes of their screams. I now spend my days fighting to find the answer that will lead us to the final solution and these men's salvation.

Year 2: Month 4: Day 11: of Experiment 5.7A

I was correct. There is an herb that grows in the Shroud that may be the answer. The Magi consume it to strengthen their control over the natural energy and increase their power. This is exactly what we need. I have ordered a team to retrieve it. I do hope that they are successful. The Shroud has become a stronghold for the Tellurians, so they will need to tread softly.

I have ordered an immediate delay on testing as well, until we can obtain the herb and combine it with our substance. There is no need to continue until we have it. The Regis has congratulated us on the finding, but I am wary to begin celebrating before the new substance is completed and tested. Until then, I will continue to dread each day.

Year 2: Month 4: Day 30: of Experiment 5.7A

The attack was swift and brutal. It was the first time that the Tellurians had targeted us and no one can seem to contemplate why. For what reason would they attack our city? We have never once attacked them, or contributed to the war, unlike the Creed. Even stranger is the fact that they attacked Herous, rather than the capital. If they were aiming to weaken us, then surely Valoria would have been their target.

It does not matter now, because the Tellurians were killed despite their overwhelming power. The damage was immense and many innocent people perished, but we were able to defeat them. That says a lot about our resolve as humans.

Despite the successful defense, I am still troubled. The team sent to the Shroud has not returned and I worry that they have been killed. Even though the herb will be difficult to find in the mist, it has been too long. The Almighty is not gracing us with his benevolence, it seems. This experiment looks to be doomed to failure no matter what we sacrifice.

Year 3: Month 6: Day 11: of Experiment 5.7A

It is over. The experiment is a failure. No matter what we try, it does not work. We still have been able to secure samples of the herb from the Shroud. The first team never returned and the other three that we sent disappeared as well. After that point we could no longer get any volunteers to go in search of it. I know that it is the Shroud and it is fraught with danger, but I am beginning to believe there is someone out there actively trying to stop us. If that is true, they have succeeded.

We can no longer continue. Regis Joran has long since cut our funding and left us stranded. Yokin, Jone and I refused to accept defeat, so we powered on, but now it is futile. Without the herb, the solution is unstable. No matter what else we try to use to replace it, it does not work. I cannot continue to subject innocent men and women to these tortures. I cannot sleep at night as it is. Their screams haunt my dreams. I am unsure if I will ever be able to live with myself, especially now in failure.

If we continue we will only bring more death. The Regis is still unaware of our work, but if he ever discovers that we have continued, we will be sentenced to death for sure. The last thing I ever wanted to do was accept failure, but it is the only course. We must leave this experiment, and the death that has followed it, with what little humanity we have left. I only hope that someday a more intelligent and stronger man will take up the challenge and complete it. Until then, I hope that we can survive. Paks needs this weapon. Humanity needs it. It will finally bring us out from the darkness and into the light.

> -Excerpts from the laboratory notes of Rubon Ull; 2nd Head Researcher of the Valorian Science Society.

25

A splash kicked up as Farren fell awkwardly into the waterfall pond. He resurfaced with a gasp, spitting the salty taste from his mouth as sweat flowed down from his forehead. He clung to one of the stones as he caught his breath.

"Better," commented Kaleb, who has standing on a stone a few feet away. His clothes were wet as well from a few plunges and he had cast off his shirt to the grass as it was beginning to weigh him down. He was barefoot and now only wore a pair of light sparring pants that clung to his body due to the wetness.

"I thought for sure I had you," complained Farren, as he dragged himself back onto the stone.

Kaleb spun his sparring sword around in his hand mockingly as Farren recovered and stood back up. He fished his wooden sword from the water and readied himself again.

"Your footwork was good, but I caught you looking down at your feet. It was only a split second, but that was all I needed." Kaleb demonstrated by poking him in the chest with his sword. "Keep your eyes on your opponent at all times," he added, tapping Farren under the chin. Farren nodded in compliance. "Your swordsmanship is improving quickly too, despite the fact I haven't been able to train with you lately."

"I have been observing some sparring sessions in the training room. There is a lot more to fighting than I thought."

"Yes, of course there is, but you should not think about it during your fights. You train hard enough that it becomes instinctive. That is why you train. The moment you start to think, you are dead," said Kaleb. "But, it is clear that observing the sessions has helped you. Your movements are sharper and there are fewer extraneous movements. Your progress is quite impressive."

"Thank you." Even though Kaleb's guard was down and he did not show any signs of attacking, Farren kept up his defense. It was not above Kaleb to attack unexpectedly to teach a lesson. Besides, Farren's skin was beginning to wrinkle because of the water and it was getting hard to hold onto his sword. Falling in again was not an option.

Kaleb grinned at his student's attentiveness. "Nice focus. You are learning. Good."

A small fish jumped out of the water near the waterfall and Farren glanced over. Kaleb thrust forward. Farren noticed the movement out of the corner of his eye and dodged to the right but slipped on the wet stone and fell in.

"But, not enough it seems," mumbled Kaleb.

Farren flopped his arms back up onto the stone and groaned. "Stupid fish."

"Don't blame the fish, Farren. The fish did not look away from his attacker. The fish did not lose focus."

Farren clung to the rock for a moment as he sulked in his failure. The cool water felt nice against his weary body and he slowly treaded water to take the strain off his shoulders.

"Come on. Get back up here so we can keep going," pushed Kaleb.

"Give me a second, will you? It's a bit tiring having to drag myself out of this water all the time."

"Then, all the more reason to practice, so you won't fall in as often. Besides, that was not a request. It was an order."

Farren met Kaleb's forceful stare. He was about to drag himself up when they heard the sound of hoof beats and looked up to see Guy appear at the top of the grounds stairway. He was riding a spotted brown and white horse, and pulling another horse with him.

"Kaleb!" he shouted. "You have a mission. You need to leave immediately."

Kaleb tossed his wooden sword onto the bank and started hopping his way out of the pool. "Looks like you have lucked out. We will break for the day."

Farren sighed and smiled as he let go of the stone and floated onto his back. "Thank the Almighty."

Kaleb grabbed a dry shirt from a pack on the bank and put it on. "You need to continue practicing while I am gone. You're lacking concentration. Your movements are good, but you are losing focus." He packed his remaining things into the bag, took a swig from his canteen and then threw the pack over his shoulder. "And get yourself out of that water, you're beginning to wrinkle like an old woman," he shouted back as he ran off towards the stair.

Farren laughed and started swimming his way to the bank.

At the top of the stairs, Kaleb attached his bag to a clasp on the side of the saddle and then hoisted himself up onto the spare horse. "What is the mission?"

"You are to head to the Shroud to capture the criminal Datro Cervon. He was seen heading there this morning."

"Why is he heading for the Shroud?"

"We do not know. There is talk that he just returned from Herous yesterday and is now on the move again. He is involved in the plot somehow and he needs to be captured. You are alone on this mission, Kaleb," added Guy with a concerned look. "And you know what is out there if you are discovered?"

Kaleb nodded seriously. "I will move swiftly and cautiously, Master. I know the importance of the mission and I will not chance failure. Magi are not ones to meddle with lightly. Nothing is certain. Caution before valor you always say."

"Good. Coal was not certain you were ready for something like this, but I assured him you were and we have little other choice."

"Thank you, Master. I will not let you down."

Guy handed Kaleb his sheath belt with his hand blades and they both saluted each other with a fist to the opposite arm.

"Be safe. Show them how strong we Gallants are."

Kaleb grinned, gave Guy a nod, and galloped off down the path.

Guy watched his apprentice ride off. A hint of concern passed through his mind. He had trained Kaleb well. He was one of the strongest fighters in all of Paks. *But these are Magi,* he thought. Kaleb was right. These are uncertain times.

He looked down into the grounds to see Farren changing into a dry pair of clothes. "Train hard, Young Master. I hope you are ready when the time comes. You will need to be strong, or else your world will come crumbling down around you and you won't be able to stop it."

26

Kyte trotted along slowly in the darkness of the Pine. A company of Creed soldiers rode alongside him, as their horses slowly took them towards Coroge. Kyte had on his cloak, but the hood was down. There no longer was any reason to keep his identity a secret. The massive form of Weston Lockhardt towered over him atop his horse, managing to cast a shadow on him even in the darkness.

They had been riding for nearly a full day in the Pine and there was no sign of the darkness ever ending. Only a few times had Kyte even seen movement in the forest, usually from a bird that had landed in a high tree branch in order to rest its tired wings before taking off again a few moments later. The quiescence that Kyte once found peaceful was now beginning to wear on his mind. Nowhere, had he ever seen such a lonely place.

Weston had thought to bind Kyte's hands for the journey, but then realized it was foolish to think that would make a difference, so he allowed Kyte to ride free amongst them. Weston's men were all ferocious looking fighters and their array of weaponry was just as frightening. Kyte now understood Coal's warning about the viciousness of these people.

Kyte was not used to riding horses, especially for an extended period of time, so he was beginning to get sore and was wondering if they were ever going to reach the city. Not a single word had been spoken by any of the men since the onset, so Kyte did not dare speak up to ask.

An orange, hazy glow started to appear in front of them and grew in intensity as they rode closer. When they were near it, Kyte could feel the warmth of the sun as the glow hit him. The edge of the forest was abrupt, with only the light to warn them of its end. A wide open field stood on the other side and standing in front them was the base of the Fortrer Mountains. When Kyte's eyes adjusted to the light, he witnessed something not even his Magi eyes could have imagined. An enormous city that looked to be carved into the side of the mountain itself stretched out in front of him.

He struggled to not gape at the marvel of it. The city of Coroge was a fortress and an engineering marvel; an enormous cavern blown out of the mountain. The city walls, which thrust from the side of the mountain on either side of the city, were carved from mountain rock and stood nearly twice the height of Valoria's walls. The only thing that could be seen behind the walls was the palace, which was entirely built into the mountain, with only its entrance and high balconies visible to the outside.

A team of Creed soldiers rode up on horseback, weapons drawn.

"Put up your hood, Aerious," ordered Weston. "We do not want to start a wondrous rumor of your appearance."

Kyte took a moment to shake away his amazement and then dutifully draped the hood over his head.

"General," one of the soldiers shouted as they approached.

"Pion," greeted Weston. They saluted each other by putting a strong fist up in front of their chest, forearm held horizontally. They pounded their fists and forearms together in welcome.

"What brings you back to the city so suddenly? You just left a few days ago. I know you like your time in the Pine more than our bustling city. You would not come back needlessly," Pion asked. He turned and noticed Kyte and eyed him suspiciously.

"I need to speak to the Minor. There is news from Valoria."

"He should be in the palace. He will be glad to hear of news. His frustration still boils since the absence of our Supreme," he responded without taking his eyes from Kyte."

"He is our guest," reassured Weston.

Pion hesitated. "Very well." He turned and they all started riding off towards the gate.

As they rode towards the city, Kyte saw hundreds of soldiers patrolling the open plain and across the edge of the Pine. Kyte wondered about how impossible it would be to try to attack the city. The edge of the forest was far from projectile range, so no one could hide in the trees and fire upon the city, but on top of the city walls it seemed possible that a large projectile weapon, such as a trebuchet, could reach the forest edge.

The Doranian River stretched across in front of the walls preventing anyone from trying to scale the walls using ladders or towers. Kyte could tell that the river had been redirected in order to acquire maximum defense.

These people's lives are built around war.

At the bank of the river, the walls towered in front of them. He could barely see the top of the mountain itself over the ramparts. They curved outward, swiping an enormous arc in front of the city. The draw bridge that stretched across the river was down and they galloped across its thick iron surface.

They skidded to a stop at the gate, which, compared to the immensity of the wall, was like a grain of sand in the Southern Desert. What the gate lacked in size, it made up for in impenetrability. It was nearly as thick as it was tall and solid iron, mined from deep in the mountains. A massive counterweight was lowered on the inside of the wall to slowly raise the door and allow safe passage to and from the fortress city. Not even the destructive powers of the Ignati could think to break through it.

The gate began to slowly inch its way up. Kyte could hear the moaning sounds of the mechanism that opened it, straining to hold under the intense weight. A loud thud shook the ground as the counterweight lowered completely. Rows of Creed soldiers stood on either side of the gate as the men rode through. They all saluted as their General galloped past. Kyte's appearance drew many suspicious glances. Even with his hood up, his appearance was clearly foreign.

"You are famous already," chuckled Weston. "Not often do we allow outsiders within the walls, even in peacetime. An occasional dignitary or politician may make a visit, but you are clearly neither. Even merchants are forced to sell their wares in the market just outside the gates." He waved the rest of his men off and they all turned and left for their regular posts. "This way."

The city itself was just as imposing and severe as the walls that surrounded it. Just inside the gate, there was a long passage open up to the sky, with a stair that led up to the city streets. In the unlikely event that the gate was breached, forces would be stationed at the top of the passage and they could fire down on the attackers with any manner of object: arrow, rock, or boiling oil.

At the top of the passage, the city opened up and the towering mountain hung over them like a monstrous wave crashing into the beach. Stables stood near the entrance, where patrolmen could keep their horses. An array of weapons shops and smithies also stood among the stables where the soldiers could repair their weapons or bring them in for a quick sharpen.

The guards standing along the top of the wall all stood erect, not slouching even the smallest degree. Each one kept a keen eye on the horizon and watched the tree line for movement. There had not been an attack on the city for decades, but they stood vigilant.

The streets were solid grey rock, the same color as the mountain, and the buildings were built with wood from the Pine. There were no decorations or brightly colored facades. The buildings were built to be practical, nothing more.

"Your architecture is... interesting," commented Kyte. "There is strength and power to it, that is obvious, but there is no beauty."

"We Creed have a much different view on how we run our lives than the Valorians. We do not allow ourselves to be distracted by luxury."

"You speak as though luxury is weakness. Taking something beyond its basic form is not wasteful. That is how we make it better."

Weston eyed the bold speaking Aerious. "Are you saying we are weak because we do not paint our homes or grow pretty gardens in our fields?"

"I am saying removing luxury and beauty from your lives is preventing you from becoming even stronger. In the prime of the Emerald Ages, the Aerii and the Ignati lived in excessive luxury. It was far beyond anything that you could even imagine. Our strength came from our wisdom, not from our swords or our magic. We created beautiful things, we did not destroy them. Strength is more than just steel, rock and fire, General."

Weston scoffed at the comment and fell silent as they continued to ride up the winding road that slowly led up towards the palace. The city was built on the side of a sloping hill that led to the palace and the tops of the buildings created a stairway effect as one looked up towards the mountain.

Kyte took in the sights of the city as they rode. There were no children running around freely, playing games in the streets or laughing at silly jokes. There was little noise aside from the clanging sounds of iron on iron and the hoof beats of horses against the street. It seemed that every person in the city had a purpose and worked tirelessly towards it. The women mainly worked in restaurants, taverns and shops, but some toiled in the fields, which was a job usually held by older men who were past their fighting prime.

Kyte was amazed at the strength of these people, but could not help wonder what they gave up for such strength. Every person saluted the general as they passed, as if the entire population was soldiers, but they did not stand in awe and went immediately back to work.

"I do wonder, General, why it is you were not so amazed to find out that I was a Magi? I was under the impression that the humans thought we were extinct."

"It is true that most humans believe that, but we Creed fought in the war ourselves. We knew the result and therefore knew that there were some Magi remaining, albeit very few."

"Am I the first Magi you have met?"

"Personally, yes. And, actually, you are the first we, as a people, have encountered for centuries. It seems that either you are dwindling in number, or are getting much better at keeping yourselves hidden," Weston said, with a questioning tone.

"As far as I know, you may be correct on both assumptions. I am the last of my clan and I have not met another Aerious for years. I had heard rumors of others as a child, though, but I have not met one."

"I am sorry for your loss," Weston added solemnly. "To lose one's family is devastating. I myself have felt that pain and I do not wish it upon any other man."

The city ended abruptly and Kyte saw only an open stretch of rock and a barrier stretching out a distance away. As they approached the barrier, he began to see the rim of a deep chasm plummeting downward. Kyte could see the bottom, but the shadow of the mountain late in the day made it difficult. It stretched the full length of the city and was immensely wide. A lone bridge stretched across it and the barrier stretched the length on either side to prevent people from falling in. Kyte stopped his horse suddenly in disbelief.

"What is this?" he asked in shock.

Weston responded quickly, knowing that Kyte would ask. All visitors did. "The mountain gives us protection from attack, but it also brings with it dangers. Rocks tumble down the slope and crash down towards the city and during the winter months there have been avalanches as well. The palace is safe, of course, but the city is vulnerable. This chasm is here to protect the city from those dangers. It swallows up anything that tries to swallow us."

Kyte looked up at the side of the mountain and imagined the destruction that a large avalanche could rain upon the city and how it took something like this to stop it. He pictured the wall of snow racing towards them and then crashing down into the chasm, throwing clouds of icy particles into the air. There really was no force that these people could not defend themselves against.

As they rode across the bridge, Kyte felt uneasy as he looked into the chasm's depths. It was not the height that bothered him, but rather the thought of how intensely passionate these men were to their goals and how dangerous that made them.

At the base of the palace, Kyte looked up at the mountain that towered over them. It was almost like an overhanging roof to keep out the rain, protruding out and casting a vast shadow across the ground in front. The gate was open, as it always was when there was no immediate danger. Not since the Magi Wars, had there been any reason to fear the palace being breeched. If an enemy was strong enough to make it this far, then the Creed would have already lost. Guards at the gate dutifully took their horses and they walked in.

While the Creed did not believe in excess and luxury, their architecture was inspiring in its grandeur. Magnificent columns were etched out of the mountainside to line the front of the palace, with depictions of long fought battles and conquests carved into the arches and above the gate. A tall, triangular entranceway was also carved out above the gate and three balconies peaked out of the façade across the top. The middle balcony was the largest, and was used on occasion when the Minor addressed the citizens.

The entrance hall was colossal. The ceiling reached up to what seemed like the peak of the mountain. It had a conical shape with the upper levels circling the hall with balconies. Very little natural light was let in, so hundreds of glow lights circled the walls on every floor, giving the entire room a haunting glow. It was nothing like the brightness of the palace in Valoria.

At the far end of the hall, there was a giant stone stairway that led to the first level of balconies, but then each level after that could only be accessed through stairwells in the side passages, giving the hall a layered appearance. Kyte could only imagine how far into the mountain the palace passages went.

The first level above the entrance was where the three balconies in the front of the palace could be accessed and where the only light, aside from the gate itself, came in. With the sun low in the sky, a bright orange light shown in and intensified the orange hue from the glow lights. Kyte noticed a large carving in the floor of the hall. Three swords were laid across each other, each tip pointing towards a depiction of one of the Three Guardian Moons. The center sword was much broader than the other two. It was the symbol and crest of the first ruler of the Creed, Rune Warrik, whose vision designed and started the construction of the city.

Before the conclusion of the Magi Wars, the rulers of the three sects were not known as the Supreme Regis and the three Regis Minor. There was no human kingdom; no united Paks. The ruler of the Creed was known as the Fathos, and Fathos Rune ruled for nearly seventy years.

Weston noticed Kyte staring up in awe. "Impressive isn't it?"

"I cannot fathom even how it could have been built?" said Kyte.

"Do you mean it is unbelievable because we are human?"

Kyte eyed Weston suspiciously, but then smiled. "Because it is spectacular and beyond imagination, whether built with magic or by hand. I have seen nothing like it and I have seen many great wonders created by humans. Times have changed over the centuries. Humans are far stronger than they once were. You do not have to prove yourself to me, Weston Lockhardt," added Kyte.

"You are right, I do not," said Weston, sternly. With that, Weston started walking off towards the stairway. "This way," he shouted back.

At the top of the stairs, a large hallway stretched forward into the stone. Like the entrance hall, the passage was lined with glow lights down its entire length on either side. The passage was plain, with no decorative artwork or archways. As they walked, they passed many side passages and rooms hidden behind large wooden doors, but they kept going straight ahead. The passage must have gone into the mountain nearly a mile and, even then, it seemed to keep going. At some point no more doors or side passages popped up and it was just forward. For most of the walk, neither spoke. Finally, when the silence seemed to bore into his mind, Kyte broke it.

"Since I have come from my hiding and met you humans, I have noticed an intense hatred between you and the Valorians. I do not know your history as much as I would like, but I assume that it has been this way for some time."

Weston seemed to ignore the comment for a moment, continuing to walk silently. Finally, he responded calmly. "It goes back almost to the Emerald Ages. Our societies are fundamentally different, as you no doubt have noticed. What we deem as important in our beliefs is far different than what they do, and so we have quarreled since our two societies began. After the Magi Wars, we both grew and became stronger and so the quarrels escalated into battles and then into wars."

Finally the hallway stopped and a large stairway stretched upward, seemingly endlessly. Staring upward, an image of the palace stair in Valoria flashed into his mind.

Not so different as they might believe.

Without pause, Weston started walking up the stairway as he continued to talk. "The Valorians think we are barbarians. They believe that we know nothing other than war. Their arrogance is what drives our fury. We believe in strength and honor above all else, but that does not mean we are barbaric."

"Has there ever been a peace?"

"If you consider peace as a time without war and bloodshed, then yes. But there has never been a time when we have lived together and cooperated as friends."

Kyte could sense a small hint of regret in Weston's voice. "Do you wish there was? A peace, I mean."

"The Valorians are weak," he responded quickly. "We would gain nothing from being friends with them."

The stairway was so long that Kyte was beginning to tire in his weakened state, but finally a large doorway started to appear at the end. At first it seemed to be a normal sized door, but as they approached it continued to grow until it reached almost thirty feet high. Nothing in this palace was small.

"If you believe the Valorians are so weak, then why is it you have never defeated them? Why is it they rule this Kingdom and not you?" asked Kyte as they reached the base of the door.

Weston turned and glared at the Aerious, but said nothing. The question was clearly digging at his pride, but there was truth behind it and Weston realized it. In reality, Weston had always realized that truth, but had ignored it. He turned and started to push the giant door open. "The Minor awaits you, Aerious. Tell him what you have told me and maybe he will show you some compassion." As the doorway opened up, a bright, orange light shone through and Kyte had to cover his eyes.

"But, do not expect it," added Weston.

27

ayes had not been this excited since the first time he met his wife, nearly twenty five years ago. She was a fantastic beauty, short blonde hair with stunning blue eyes, and her body was slim and lithe from years of dancing. Alice was her name, and she was a performer in Seduke. The moment he laid eyes on her he could not look away, but, of course, that was the same for every man that saw her. She had no lack of suitors, normally drunken patrons who assumed they could force her affection.

It had taken time and months of delicate maneuvering, but Hayes managed to win her trust and take her on a date. Alice did not often open herself up to affection, but when she did, she had much to give. They married less than a month later. Hayes had loved her with all his heart until the day she died; until the day that the Creed appeared outside the city walls. Now, all that mattered was making something of his life, so that her sacrifice was worth it. He walked with a purpose and an energetic quality about him. This would be the day that got him his revenge.

To most of the citizens of the capital, today was just a normal day. The story of the impending war was being kept a secret until the vote was cast. The people went about their day without a worry or care, not realizing that soon their lives could be drastically changing. Hayes walked past the massive fountain in the city square, with the sunlight glimmering off the metallic, chiseled bodies of the four Valor Forces soldiers as jets of water cascaded all around them. The soldiers stood in a circle with their swords held up high, meeting at a point in the middle. Hayes stopped to admire the fountain. The sight of the soldiers giving him a sense of reassurance in his plight.

As he wandered closer to the council building, the tension in the streets was beginning to build. He was met with accusing glares but, more often than not, he was given a supportive nod and smile. The vote would be close, but he was confident of his victory. He had put in too much work to fail now.

For weeks, Hayes had been petitioning the council members and trying to persuade them of his view. Hayes was not above doing anything to achieve his goal. For many of the councilmen, it did not take much to convince them, but others were much more obdurate. Since the day when the Supreme Regis had visited him, he knew that there was nothing more important for him now than winning this vote. When a councilman did not agree, he convinced them. When they were not convinced, he took matters into his own hands. Most of the men in the council were men of conviction and character, but courage was not a trait greatly shared. It was obvious that the Supreme Regis wanted the war and Hayes was his puppet, so it did not take much to sway most men. The wrath of the Supreme Regis was enough to strike fear. When that did not work, most of the men could be bought or even threatened.

Hayes was astounded at how easy it was for him to threaten these powerful men. Even when the men pleaded for him to be rational, he did not waver. Living the last twenty years of his life alone had left his ethical compass twisted. Hayes' ambition was all he had left.

He did not react to the glances and comments as he made his way to the chamber. His face showed only a stoic resolve. The walk up the steps to the building seemed to stretch endlessly and time slowed. Inside the chamber, it was eerily quiet. Normally, the councilmen were in chaotic conversation as they tried to discuss the week's events and what was to be debated that day. Today, every head turned to watch Hayes enter the chamber. The bang of the door echoed as it closed behind him and he froze at the sight of all the staring faces. Chief Council Anton stood in the center of the stage calmly looking up at him.

During the past week, Hayes had begun to notice a change in the attitudes of the councilmen. Before, his campaign was moving along flawlessly as he turned councilman after councilman, but then the men began to resist. They were becoming more stubborn and resistant to his influence. After some time, he started to hear rumors that the Chief Council was making a stand and campaigning himself. It was inevitable that Hayes would run into opposition, but he did not think that the Chief Council still had enough influence to make a significant push. It was a mistake to underestimate the man.

Hayes met Anton's stare respectfully and nodded his acknowledgement before taking his seat. He tried to avoid eye contact with everyone else. When the rest of the council realized there would be no grand entrance or commotion, they returned to their own quiet contemplations. After a few more minutes, Anton announced the start of the meeting.

"I am thankful to see you are all excited to be here this morning," announced Anton theatrically, lightening the mood in the room. Many of the men chuckled at the remark. "Normally, we would start the session by opening the floor and allowing you all to voice any problems or grievances you may have, but to ignore the obvious situation weighing on everyone's mind would be foolish. Therefore, I propose that we initiate the vote immediately." Anton stared directly at Hayes as he spoke, displaying a confident semblance.

Does he know something that I do not? wondered Hayes.

Just as Anton was about to speak again, the main door at the top of the chamber opened and the Supreme Regis walked in. Of course, it was not truly Bishop, but only one man in the room realized this. Clad ostentatiously in full royal regalia he strode into the room. His flowing green and gray cape flapped violently as the door created a draft when it closed behind him. Bishop's piercing brown eyes looked around at the staring faces.

"Am I too late for the vote?" he asked aloud. When no one responded, he said "It seems not. Excellent! Do not mind me, gentlemen. I am but an observer," he reassured as he found a seat towards the top of the chamber and sat quietly down.

Even if he was just there to observe, the appearance of the Supreme Regis would create a massive discomfort for most of the men. The Supreme Regis would now witness, first hand, the face of any man that dared to defy his wishes. Any councilman that was toying with the idea of acting courageously and voting against the war was now second guessing his intentions.

Hayes grinned at Anton's obvious distress.

"It is an honor, Supreme Regis," announced Anton with a councilman's salute.

The rest of the council was about to salute but the Grand Master put out his hand. "No need, councilmen. As I said, I am only here to observe."

They all sat back down, apprehensively.

"As I was saying," muttered Anton. "I think it would be foolish to delay the vote, so let us begin. Even the Supreme Regis has graced us with his presence on this historic day."

The tension in the room raised quickly, each councilman inching to the edge of their seat. The Supreme Regis sat casually in his chair, legs folded.

"If I may, Chief Council" shouted Coal from his seat high in the chamber. The tension shattered like glass. Everyone turned to look at the Commander as he stood. "I wish to speak before the vote is cast. I believe I have the right."

Anton silently nodded and the entire council shifted in their seats to hear what Coal had to say. The Commander rarely spoke out in Council. As a military man and friend of the Regis, Hayes hoped he would speak in favor of the war, but there was talk of him meeting with Anton a few days ago. No one knew what they spoke of.

"For those of you who do not know, my name is Commander Coal Lucer. I would be lying if I told you all that I enjoy this process we call diplomacy. My seat on this council is strictly a formality because of my position as Commander of the Gallants. I dread each day that I come into this chamber and listen to the squabbling of you men as you decide the fate of the people based on your own ambitions." Coal began to wander slowly out to the stairs and down towards the center stage. Men glared at him as he derided them, but he appeared not to notice. "We are about to take a vote on a war that none of the people of Briva even know about. For the past weeks, we have campaigned against one another and threatened each other and not once has anyone thought about what will happen to the people."

"Get this fool off of the stage!" shouted a councilman.

Anton glared furiously at the man. "The Commander wishes to speak and has the right. You will not interrupt or you will be thrown from the chamber." Anton was nearly shaking with rage and the man fearfully returned to his seat. Coal reached the stage and Anton gestured for him to take the center. The chamber quickly quieted.

"As most of you know, the Supreme Regis and I have been friends for most of our lives." He stared passionately up at the Supreme Regis, forcing a friendly smile at the imposter. The Supreme Regis gave him a friendly nod in return. "But, in this instance, I must put our friendship aside. We, as councilmen, are here to make decisions that best suit the people, not ourselves or our friends. This is a war that will take the lives of thousands of men; men that have families, wives and children. Our lives will be thrown into turmoil and pain. Do any of you here even remember why it is that we are starting this war? You have lost yourselves in your own cowardice and greed. You have forgotten why it is you are sitting here in this chamber." Coal spun around, throwing his hands up as he shouted. "I am a man of war; a soldier, but that does not mean that I wish to slaughter innocent lives just for the sake of one man's ambition," he ended, glaring up at the imposter.

Even Anton seemed surprised at Coal's poignant rebuke of his friend. It was dangerous to speak ill of the Supreme Regis, even for Coal. Everyone shifted their attention to the Supreme Regis, to see how he would react. The Supreme Regis shifted in his seat but kept his composure.

He rose to his feet. "A passionate speech, my friend, I would expect nothing less," he said as he started to make his way towards the stage. "But, unfortunately, I *do* remember why it is we are starting this war. I do remember the day that I was attacked and nearly killed by the barbarians we know as the Creed. That is the reason," he finally shouted. "You asked for proof, but since it seems that your messenger has not returned from Coroge, I am to assume that he has been killed as well. Is that not proof enough?" The councilmen were beginning to murmur and come alive. "You say that a war will throw the people's lives into turmoil, but how can the people truly live, knowing that those monsters are still out there. If they dare attack me, then they surely will not hesitate to attack our city. I am not starting this war because of my ambition, friend, I am starting it to bring peace to Briva once and for all and rid us of the shadow that has been cast over us for centuries."

When he finished, he was standing face to face with Coal, neither one flinching. For a moment the chamber was silent again, but then it erupted. The councilmen all cheered in unison and Hayes grinned broadly. Anton dropped his head in disbelief. The Supreme Regis allowed the councilmen to continue their cheering for a few minutes before turning and silencing them, gesturing for them to sit.

"The shadow was about to be lifted. We were going to have our peace, without the war," said Coal.

"Until the Creed decided that they did not want that peace and attacked me."

"We still do not know for sure. Allow me a few more days to confirm the attack before we make this leap into chaos. Why pay the high cost for peace when there is a chance you could still get it for free?"

"Peace never comes without a price, friend. We must take it ourselves. No more sitting around and deliberating. All of those in favor of declaring war against the sect of Vertura please rise," shouted the Supreme Regis. Nearly the entire chamber got to their feet. Anton and Coal looked around in disbelief. Only a few remained seated; Councilman Rieven among them. The Supreme Regis smiled as he turned to face Coal. "I am sorry, old friend. It seems that I am the better man."

Coal's face did not react. It stayed impassive even with the chaotic scene around him and the creature that killed his friend standing right in front of him. It would have been so easy to just kill him now, with the whole chamber watching, but Coal knew what the consequences would be. No one would believe him.

"*Were* the better man," snapped Coal.

The imposter's smile turned to a glare.

The Supreme Regis slammed the door behind him as he stormed into his office. After leaving the raucous council chamber, he walked quickly back to the palace and straight to his private study. The joy and exhilaration of his plan taking a giant leap forward quickly disappeared after the end of the meeting. There was something weighing heavily on his mind.

He stripped off his cape and threw it viciously at the bookshelf on the back wall, causing a series of books to crash to the floor with it. He stood in the middle of the room for a moment, hands on his hips, appearing ready to erupt with anger.

A fluttering of wings could be heard in the shadows. "Did the vote not go our way?" whispered an unknown voice. A second later, a decrepit looking creature stepped out into the open.

The Supreme Regis was silent for a moment, his head still down in deep thought. "The vote went as planned, Corvus. We are now officially at war." He did not look up and his face stayed stern and emotionless.

Corvus eyed him blankly. "Then, what is the problem?"

"I believe the Commander may know."

Corvus took a step back. "Do you mean about the plan? About us?" he stuttered.

The Supreme Regis finally turned and glared at Corvus with his brown human eyes. He did not respond, but did not need to.

"How is that possible? We have taken every precaution," added Corvus, almost apologetically.

"I do not know."

"Are you sure about this?"

"Yes. I could see the truth when he looked at me. He had murder in his eyes. He knows I am not his friend. To what extent he has knowledge of our plan, I do not know, but he surely knows I am not who I am claiming to be."

"Then, what do we do? We did not plan for this."

"We continue. We do not hesitate. The commander is but a thorn. He can do nothing. If he tries again to get in our way, you kill him. Am I clear?"

Corvus smiled. "Why not kill him now?"

"No. Not yet. There is no telling what he knows and who else knows it. Killing him will only create suspicion and attract unwanted attention. For now we will keep an eye on him. Send a few of our spies to follow him."

Corvus showed a tinge of disappointment, but held his emotions and bowed. "Of course, Grand Master. It will be done."

"Good. That is settled. We cannot take any chances. Not now. We must move forward," urged the Grand Master. There was a long silence. "Is that all?"

"Yes, Grand Master, that is all."

"Then leave me. I have much to think about."

Without hesitation, Corvus bowed and launched his avian form from the window and flew off. When the Grand Master wanted to be alone, he was to be left alone. He continued to stand silently in the room, staring at the floor. He did not like it when plans did not go as intended, especially this one. He had waited too long for one simple human to stop him.

What will you do, Coal Lucer? Will you try to kill me, as your eyes so desired? Do you even have the strength to do it?

28

To the west of Briva stood the sect of Fera. In contrast to Briva's temperate climate and flat landscape, Fera was a luscious land speckled with hills, mountains and jungles. It was impossible to travel very far in the countryside on foot as the jungles were extremely dangerous and the mountains caused severe exhaustion and disorientation when traveling. Anyone who dared to venture into the forest was quickly devoured by its inhabitants, either by the carnivorous animals, the infectious insects, or the poisonous plant life. Despite human ingenuity and cruelty, the jungle knew of more ways to kill than humans would ever know.

For decades, the land stayed uninhabited, cast aside as a wild land that could not be tamed. Despite the harshness of the terrain, the people known as the Davati flourished in it. Over centuries, they learned to adapt to the land and utilize its dangerous treasures. Some would say that they escaped the dangers, rather than adapted to them. Either way, they managed to live in a land that many considered inhospitable.

Their capital city, Caradice, sat atop a high plateau in a small mountain range in the southwestern tip of the sect. The plateau was impossible to traverse by conventional means and few humans had managed to climb up the sheer rock face that led to it. In order to live in the safety of the plateau, the Davati had created the most technologically advanced creation in the kingdom; the airship.

How the airship actually flew was the most highly guarded secret in the kingdom. No foreign scientist had ever been allowed to study the ship's design and anyone that had ever tried to steal the secret was quickly dispatched of. The technology of flight gave the much less powerful sect an advantage over the mighty Creed and Brivans, who were left to struggle as the Davati soared overhead.

The technology, though, was not entirely perfected, even after centuries. Therefore, its capability as a military advantage peaked at nothing more than a severe annoyance. Only one warship was ever successfully built and utilized and, for fear of losing it, the Davati had never used it in an actual war. Despite its failings as a weapon, the technology had greatly increased the standard of the Davati's everyday life. Small airships dart around the capital in designed routes, taking people from place to place, and home to work. Adventurers and merchants use them to travel around the sect and to the borders. Small airships could land in flat outcroppings and plains, amongst the hills and trees. It was strictly forbidden to fly an airship outside the borders for fear that the ship could be shot down or captured. The severest restrictions were put on airship use in order to ensure absolute control of the technology.

The only battleship that had ever been successfully built was nicknamed *Fionetta,* after the wife of Minor Leneker Grommen. It was his vision that saw the ship's completion. The ship was visually stunning and looked nothing like its miniature counterparts. Its bow was pointed, with a flat flight deck stretching the entire length of the ship. The top deck was flat, so that smaller airships and personnel could land and take off, and various ordnances could be launched down onto the enemy. The size of the ship was breathtaking. It would have trouble landing, even in the expansive reaches of the Valorian Palace grounds.

Not since its completion had the spectacular ship ever left Fera, so there was no blaming the citizens of Valoria for their reaction when the behemoth airship and its fleet of smaller companions soared over the city, nearly eclipsing the light of the sun. The ship was flying so high that most people did not even notice it until the massive shadow covered the streets. They looked up in shock and complete disbelief, as if the sky itself was falling. For minutes, the entire city was still and silent, only soft gasps left the mouths of the Valorians.

As they stared up at the black silhouette across the sun, the image began to grow as the ship lowered down towards them. As it approached, the air began to stir, kicking up dust and dirt, forcing people to cover their faces. When it became obvious that the ship was going to land in the grounds outside the city, many people broke from their daze and began to sprint towards the gate to try to see it as it landed. The commotion began to grow as more and more citizens followed suit and the streets crowded. At the gate, the guards were refusing to let the citizens through and a crazed mob was growing.

Coal, along with Kaine and Syd, was hurrying through the palace grounds when they spotted the airship. They all stopped and stared up in shock. "Is that what I think it is?" gasped Kaine.

"So, it seems. This does not bode well for us." responded Coal thoughtfully.

Syd turned his attention to the other two, seemingly lost in their private conversation. "What is it?" he blurted.

"It is the battleship built by the Davati, you idiot. What else could it possibly be?"

Syd turned an annoyed eye towards Kaine, who was still looking up into the sky. "I don't know, maybe some magical Aerii creation or even the Almighty itself coming down to spite the Tellurians. Stranger things have been happening lately."

"Do you know what this means?" asked Coal, still in serious contemplation.

"It means we are in far worse trouble than originally feared. That thing is massive. How in the Almighty's name does it even fly?"

145

"If we knew that, don't you think we would have one of our own?"

"Shut up you two," shouted Coal. "This is serious. The Davati have never let an airship leave their borders, let alone the *Fionetta*. Their intention is obvious."

"What do you think the Tellurian did to convince them? Do you think they know?" asked Kaine.

"I doubt that Minor Fanix knows the whole truth. The creature would not risk exposing his plan to the Minor on the chance he would not agree. That being said, I do not think it would have taken much convincing to get Fanix to join in on a combined attack against Coroge. He despises the Creed as much as we do."

"Yes, but to go to this extent? Their battleship has never left their borders. For all we know, it has never left the ground at all."

"It will take a lot to destroy Coroge, you both know this," Coal reminded them. "The Corogean walls have never been breached by any army. This is a convenient way to get around them. That is why the ship was built. It has just been the Davati's fear that has kept it grounded all this time."

"The Tellurian must have been planning this from the very beginning," added Syd.

"Even before the vote was cast, I assume. It would have taken weeks to even deploy their fleet."

Coal gave his two Captains a worried look. "Things do not seem to be going our way. This is worse than I expected."

"So then, what do we do, Sir?"

"The Davati only worsen the situation, they do not change it. We must hope that Kyte has made it to Coroge and warned the Creed. What they intend to do with the information is up to them, but for now I think we must focus our efforts on this weapon we assume they are creating. There is not much else we can do on our own right now," sighed Coal. He turned and started hustling back towards the city. Kaine and Syd quickly followed. "Guy has sent Kaleb after Datro, but I want you two to go to his lab. There might be something there. I will try to speak to Minor Fanix. I have met him before. I may be able to convince him that this road is not one he should go down."

"Will you tell him about the Tellurians?"

Coal stopped. "Only if I must," he pondered.

"Let us hope it will not come to that. But, if something happens," said Kaine. "If there is trouble and we need to find a place to meet, where will we reconvene? It cannot be anywhere where they will expect us to go."

The three of them thought for a moment, until Syd smiled and said, "I know of a place."

Even in the palace, servants and aides rushed around in panic and confusion when they heard the news of the Davati fleet landing outside the city. Most of the citizens of Briva had never seen a Davati airship and only a handful had seen the battleship, so it was an astounding sight. It was like the Almighty was coming down to judge them.

Upon hearing the commotion, the Grand Master came out of his study. An aide stopped suddenly in front of him. Her curly, light brown hair was a mess and sticking out in various places. She had run clear across the grounds and to the top floor of the palace. She bent over for a moment to catch her breath. The Grand Master stood annoyed as he waited for her to speak.

"The Davati are here, Your Highness. They landed their fleet outside the city walls." It seemed that she expected him to rear in shock, but all he did was smile. "Do you know why they are here?" she begged. He brushed past her silently, leaving her confused. "What should we do, Your Highness?" she shouted after him. He gave no response.

It had taken longer than he had expected, but the Grand Master's plans were finally falling into place. He was successfully in control of the throne, the war was set into motion in the council, he had secured an ally, and soon Datro would complete the weapon that would insure their victory. The Creed would soon be destroyed and then there would be no one to stop him. He walked happily through the palace halls with a wicked grin stretched across his face.

As he turned a corner, he saw Kara sprinting in his direction. When she spotted him, she let out a sigh of relief and ran harder. She leaped in to his arms, hugging him tightly. He stood motionless, arms at his side.

"I just heard, the Davati are here with their battleship. What is going on?" she gasped, with her head buried into his chest. When the Grand Master did not respond she looked up at him. "What's wrong, Dear?"

"I am in a hurry," he said sternly.

"Where are you going?"

"I need to speak to the Minor."

"Do you know why they are here? Are they going to attack us?"

The Grand Master's impatience was beginning to run out and he tried to push her away, but she clung tighter.

"Does this have something to do with the war you have started?" she asked, tears starting to form in her eyes.

"That does not concern you. Now, let me go." His anger was starting to show in his voice.

"Of course it concerns me, Bishop, I am your wife. You used to tell me everything. You used to confide in me, trust me. What has happened to you?" Her tears were now flowing, and she struggled to keep her composure. Her voice was trembling as she finally let out the feelings that had been building for weeks. "I know that a lot has happened and that you went through something very traumatic, but let me help you. I can help you figure everything out."

The Grand Master could no longer contain his frustration and he pushed her away with a shove. She stumbled, but then leapt forward again to embrace him. He slapped her hard with the back of his hand. The blow forced her to falter and she fell to her knees.

"I told you to let me go, girl," he growled as she knelt on the ground, stunned. He turned to walk off but Kara grabbed his ankle. When he looked down at her she was still staring at the floor in shock, but her hand held firmly onto him. He tried to shake free but she held fast, so he rose up his arm to strike her again. Before he could swing, she released his ankle. A tear hit the floor below her downturned face and she began to shake. The Grand Master stood motionless for a second and almost felt a twinge of pity for her, but shook it away. "Your old Bishop is dead. Remember that," he said as he turned and raced off down the hall.

More tears splashed off the stone hallway, but Kara never lifted her head to watch him walk away.

Guy had not heard from the Commander all day and the appearance of the Davati was a clear sign that something big was coming. The Tellurian was acting quicker than they had originally imagined. The news from Kaine and Syd about the creature was disturbing, but logical. Since he could not locate Coal for alternate commands, he was racing through the palace to attempt to locate Farren and Lady Kara. If he did not have any further orders, he was going to follow through with his original ones. Those two must be kept safe.

A male palace servant bumped into him as he turned the corner on the second floor of the palace. Everyone was trying to get into the city and catch a glimpse of the once-in-a-lifetime event. The halls were nearly empty now, which made it easier to move. The quietness was evident as he raced through the entrance hall and the faces of the past Supreme Regii looked down at him. They had never seemed so ominous.

It had only been a day since he had sent Kaleb to the Shroud after Datro Cervon and he had not stopped worrying. His apprentice was strong, but his training had never prepared him for what could be waiting for him. The Shroud on its own tested a man, but surely the Tellurians would be protecting Datro and they would not let Kaleb near him. Fighting a man was one thing, but fighting a Magi was something far different. Guy tried to shake the thoughts from his mind.

I trained him well. He will be fine, he reassured himself.

As he approached the royal chambers, he spotted Kara shuffling down the hallway. Her head was down and she seemed completely distraught.

"Lady Kara!" Guy shouted, but she did not respond. "Lady Kara!" She continued to shuffle along as if she didn't even hear him. He ran over to her and grabbed her by the shoulder. "Lady Kara." He turned to look at her but she still held her face down. Her hair was ruffled and her stance showed a sense of guilt. "Are you alright, Lady Kara?"

"I'm fine, Master Guy," she muttered, still keeping her head down. "I was going to go down to see the Davati airship."

Guy tried to bend down to look at her face but she lowered her head more. Finally, he tipped her head up by the chin. She offered no resistance, but tried to turn away. Her eyes were puffy and red and there was a clear bruise appearing on the side of her face. She sniffed lightly, finally turned and looked up at Guy.

"What happened?" asked Guy seriously.

"It is nothing, Master Guy."

"I am not your brother, Kara. I am not going to scold you or get angry at you… or at whoever did this," he reassured.

She stayed silent.

"Who did this Kara?" Guy insisted.

"It is all my fault," she cried. "I shouldn't have stopped him. I shouldn't have gotten in his way. He said he was in a hurry."

"It is not your fault. Never tell yourself that," he said forcefully. "Was it Bishop?"

She hesitated. She wanted to say yes, but could not get herself to do it. She opened her mouth, but the words would not come.

This changes everything, thought Guy.

Guy imagined what would happen if Coal found out. The plan would be ruined. He could never control himself. He would attack this Tellurian in a blind rage. Someone would end up dead and nothing good could come of it. Guy would have to solve this himself. It was his duty to keep them safe. "It's going to be alright, Kara. I will talk to him."

"No!" she sobbed. "He is not the same. He won't listen."

"I know, Dear. Just let me talk to him. I will try to sort things out."

She stared up at him like a lost child. Her look was a mix of gratitude and fear. Her eyes quickly shifted and then widened in shock as she looked past him. Guy spun around to see Farren standing at the end of the hall. He was drenched in sweat from training and his two juko were sheathed at his side. His eyes were unblinking as he stared at them both.

Guy realized he had heard everything. "Young Master, you must not be hasty…" Guy managed to say, before Farren turned and ran off down the hall. "Farren no!" he shouted.

Kara grabbed tightly onto Guy's coat. "You have to stop Farren, Master Guy. Bishop will hurt him!"

"I know. I need you to get out of the city. Go to the old training grounds where Farren trains. I will meet you there. Do you know where that is?"

"Yes, of course," she stammered. "But I don't understand. What do you mean? You are leaving me?"

"I need you to trust me, Kara. I want you safe."

"But, why do I need to leave?"

"Just trust me," Guy insisted. "You are in grave danger. We all are. You must leave here while you still have a chance."

She nodded as the tears continued to flow. Guy jumped to his feet and ran after Farren.

29

Since reading the hidden research notes, Datro had set out for the Shroud in search of the final ingredient for his experiment. After years of working on the weapon, he felt like he was only inches away, yet it turned out there was much more to do than he had expected. The final piece was a precious herb that grew in the murky shadows of the Shroud. In the notes it was called the Haze Creeper and was said to have a whitish, green appearance and a slight minty taste. It could be found growing low across the ground and, in the mist, it was almost impossible to find.

While initially Datro's spirits were up, he was now getting weary of the never ending search through the mist-covered forest. Sweat dripped from his forehead and his shirt was drenched in the salty liquid. He had taken off his coat and discarded it somewhere in the bushes. His legs were beginning to stiffen and he was tired of constantly bending over to examine every plant, just to discover it was not what he was looking for. At first, he was cautious of every stirring sound he heard amongst the trees. Now, however, he just assumed that it was the Tellurians keeping a close eye on him. They would not let him out of their sight. Their presence was obvious since he had left the city. Not once had he been attacked, or even seen a wild creature.

It had been hours since he had entered the Shroud but, because of the mist, he was unsure exactly how long it had been or how close to night it was becoming. He was unsure how he would escape this place if he ever did find the plant, but he assumed that the Tellurians would guide him. He was too important to them to be left to wander to his death. He caught his right foot on a root, stumbled and fell to his hands and knees. He grunted when his knees hit.

"Dammit!" he shouted aloud, pounding the dirt with his fists. He slumped onto the ground and turned onto his back as if to stare up at the sky, but he could see nothing but mist. Taking a deep sigh, Datro took this opportunity to rest his legs and close his eyes. He splayed his arms out to the sides in an exaggerated motion of relaxation and his arms landed softly on a bed of vines.

He awoke suddenly and bolted to a sitting position. A few seconds with his eyes closed was all it took to drift off in his exhausted state. *How long have I been asleep?* It was difficult to tell, since there was no night and day in the Shroud. Nothing had

151

changed. He smacked himself in the forehead in frustration and fell back again to the ground.

"Where is this damn plant!?" he bellowed.

A wispy scent of mint sailed across his nose as he lay staring up into the grayness. After a few relaxing seconds, something clicked in Datro's brain and he turned his head to the side. His right arm was lying in a bed of whitish-green vines that had started in the ground and were growing up the side of the gnarly Gregormore above him. Then a smile emerged and he started to laugh hysterically, still stretched out flat on the ground. After hours of exhaustive searching, it took only one stumble. His laughing finally ended in a fit of fatigue-induced coughing and he ripped a handful of the vines from the ground and inhaled the minty aroma heavily.

He turned over to his knees and started ripping out more and shoveling it into jars that he produced from a bag slung around his shoulder. He wasn't sure what state the plant needed to be in to be added to the formula, so he needed to keep it fresh as long as possible. He even tried to shovel dirt in with some of the samples to ensure they kept fresh. After nearly tearing down the tree in the process of collecting as much of the Haze Creeper as he could, he got to his feet and brushed himself off. He looked around to decide which way to go, but could not determine where he had come from.

Surely the wretched Tellurians would return soon and guide me back to the path.

A rustle came from the trees behind him and he turned, expecting to see a Tellurian wander out of the mist. Instead there was a young human man standing in front him, sword pointed at his face.

"So, that is what you were after then," Kaleb murmured. "Is that for the experiment; the weapon?"

It took a moment for Datro to get over his shock, but he gradually gathered himself. This boy standing in from of him looked quite strong. There were lean, tight muscles evident under his gray uniform. He held his sword powerfully and with clear conviction. The uniform was puzzling as well. It looked like that of a Valor Forces soldier, but it was entirely grey, with no insignias. At his waist, were two more small blades, sheathed on either side. It was obvious that this boy had been following him, *But for whom?* Datro wondered.

"Who are you? Why are you following me?"

"Don't play the fool. You know exactly why I am following you. And who I am does not matter. All that matters is that you come with me. I am taking you into custody?"

"For what crime?"

"Stop! You know full well what you have done and are planning on doing, Datro Cervon. Do not try to deceive me with such questioning."

Datro was actually enjoying heckling this young boy, who seemed quite set on his point of view. He was courageous and had an honorable look, but he was too anxious. "If you claim to know what my purpose is, young man, then you know full well who I am working for. You are a foolish boy for coming here, despite your honorable intentions."

Datro was beginning to emit a haughty air and Kaleb's confidence was dissipating. Kaleb held his sword steady, but Datro could sense his nervousness.

"I know everything. I know about the Tellurians and about the weapon you are making for them. I know that they killed the Supreme Regis, as well. They will not succeed. We will stop them."

"Who is *we*, boy? Who sent you?" Datro began to take a few steps forward, but Kaleb held steady. "That uniform is different, I do not recognize it. Are you from Valoria?" Kaleb tensed. It was clear he was from Valoria, but it was not any uniform he had ever seen. "Wait, I know what it is. You are a Gallant trainee. So, it is the good old Commander then. I should have known. It was only a matter of time until he discovered I had been released. Then, all he had to do was find me. I am confused, though, why he sent a trainee to get me. Surely he knows that one trainee will not be enough."

Suddenly, a pack of wolves lumbered out of the mist, surrounding Kaleb. He calmly turned full circle, examining his situation. They stalked slowly around him as Datro continued to banter devilishly.

"The Commander was always quite ruthless, wasn't he? He sent you on a suicide mission, boy. How can you pledge yourself to a man who has so little regard for your life?"

"My Master would never send me on a mission if he did not believe that I could succeed," Kaleb responded with conviction.

"Your bravado blinds you to reason. You stand in front of five Magi and you think you can escape? You are such a foolish boy."

Kaleb smirked. "That's what they always tell me."

Datro scoffed, finally annoyed with the conversation. A Tellurian in its true form walked up behind him. "They will take care of the boy. We must return to the city," the Tellurian ordered.

Datro stared, irritated, at the grinning Kaleb before spinning around and running off with the Tellurian leading. Kaleb took a step forward to follow but the wolves all growled and closed in a few paces.

"Alright then," said Kaleb, as he took his sword and stuck it into the ground. "I will have to take care of you lot first and then it will be his turn." He quickly snagged his two hand blades from his side and expertly spun them around in his hands before grabbing on tightly and bending down into a ready position.

The blades were unique, with a closed grip that fit his entire hand, and the blades extended out, one down the backside of his forearm and the other across his hand, parallel to his knuckles. The blades were short, about the length of his forearm, but he was an expert at close combat. He combined his blade skills with powerful martial arts that created a unique and deadly fighting style.

"You always said you would give me a fun first mission, Master. You sure do know how to pick them. This will be a good story to tell when I return."

Kaleb's smirk broadened as the first wolf attacked.

30

The Grand Master stood irritated as the palace gate slowly creaked its way open. *Just another thing that is trying to stand in my way.*

Some of the palace guards tried to strike up a conversation with him, but they quickly gave up when they realized he had no intention of contributing. The rumors of Bishop's new personality were spreading quickly now.

The moment that the gates were open wide enough, he quickly walked through and waved to a guard to retrieve him a horse. He was in no mood for a peaceful walk through the grounds. He needed to get out to the Minor as quickly as possible. For once, there was even a slight hint of excitement in the Grand Master. He wished to see this behemoth battleship that the humans had created first hand. It was difficult for him to believe that anyone, especially humans, could master the skies as well as the Aerii.

Just as the guard was leading a horse over, a blood-curdling bellow reverberated its way to the Grand Master from just inside the palace. "Brother!"

The Grand Master turned to see Farren come sliding to a halt on the far side of the gate just as it began to close. The guard closing the gate hesitated, confused by the situation.

"Brother!" Farren shouted again as he started to march towards him. He slid through the small crack of the gate and stopped a short distance away, a look of pure rage spreading across his face. His deep, audible breaths showed that he was trying to contain his anger, but was having little success.

"What is the problem, Farren?" responded the Grand Master with a sigh. He turned to the guard with the horse and waved him to leave them. Another nod told the guards at the gate to give them some privacy. "Why the angry face?" he added, turning back to Farren. "Has something happened?"

The calmly stated question was like a punch to the stomach and it only managed to enrage Farren further. "Why, Brother?!" he seethed, with sweat dripping down his face.

"You will have to be more specific, Farren."

"You know what I am talking about. Do not talk to me as if I am a child."

Farren started to convulse, but still managed to hold himself together. The reaction amused the Grand Master. "Are you talking about my lovely wife, Kara? I ran into her in the hallway. I told her get out of my way, but she wouldn't listen."

"She is your wife!"

"So, she should obey me," growled the Grand Master. "When I tell her to move, she should move. When I tell her to smile and be my pretty wife, she should obey. That is what a wife does."

Listening to his brother talk that way started to make the Young Prince weep with frustration and anger. Tears streamed down his reddened face. "What has happened to you? You have changed more then I realized. It is like you are a different person altogether. Kara does not deserve this, brother. She is better than both of us."

"Better than you, perhaps. She did not weep as much as you are, that is for sure. She is quite appealing to look at also, I will give you that, but she is just such a foolish little girl. Her incessant squawking was beginning to wear on me," explained the Grand Master.

"Quiet! If you say one more bad thing about her..." Farren seethed.

"Shut your mouth, boy!" the Grand Master exclaimed. "She got what she had coming to her. I asked of her one thing and she could not do it. All she had to do was leave me alone and no harm would have come to her. Instead she opened her mouth and meddled where she did not belong. She deserved what happened to her," he yelled, almost laughing as he said it.

Farren's eyes glowed with anger and he screamed with rage as he drew his two Juko and raced towards the Grand Master. The Grand Master stopped laughing and returned the stare with a content smile. He did not draw a weapon, or cast any magic. He just stood and smiled as Farren ran towards him. With wild swings and thrusts Farren attacked, but could not manage to connect a blow. The Grand Master just calmly dodged and retreated, never once even raising his arms from his side. With an emotional surge, Farren shot forward and swung quickly out with one of his swords. The Grand Master leapt backwards to evade, but this time the tip of Farren's sword managed to cut through his coat and draw blood. Farren did not stop and brought his other sword across for another attack when the Grand Master suddenly stuck his hand out and grabbed the sword blade in mid swing.

The sudden stop in motion surprised Farren and his shoulder nearly snapped under the pressure. The Grand Master quickly twisted the blade back in the other direction. The Grand Master's excited expression from before now was filled with anger as he stood, holding the sword in his bare hand.

Farren looked down at his brother's hand which had seemed to turn to wood from the wrist down and was not even bleeding from the impact. The Grand Master tossed the sword to the side.

"That was foolish, Farren. You should have stayed away as well. But now it's too late."

Before Farren could react, the Grand Master kicked out with his leg, sending Farren sprawling backwards, falling onto his back. Like a predatory beast, the Grand Master raced forward and pounced onto Farren, straddling him with his knees and pinning his remaining sword arm with incredible strength. Farren struggled to break free but could not even budge the Grand Master's vicious grip. He grunted as he continued to resist but the pressure caused such a pain that he thought his wrist would break, so he submitted.

The Grand Master raised his wooden fist to strike him. "If only you would have stayed out of my way."

"Stop where you are!" came a loud shout from behind them.

The Grand Master turned to see Guy standing in the gateway with an arrow pointed directly at him. "Let the boy go." he ordered.

"You could just as easily hit the boy. Don't be foolish."

"Would you like to see just how accurate I can be?"

The Grand Master let out a low growl as he got up off of the young prince and backed away a few steps. Farren scrambled up, keeping his eyes on the Grand Master.

"Farren," Guy said with insistence. "I need you to leave the city and go to your favorite spot."

"But..."

"Farren! I need you do this for me. Find a place to hide in the city tonight and Lady Kara will be waiting there for you at sunrise. Take the horse."

"He is not the same, Master Guy! He will kill you."

"I know, Farren. That is why you need to leave. I am not sure how long I can hold him off."

The thought of his brother killing Guy made Farren freeze in place. He was unsure what he should do.

"Go, Farren. Kara will need you," bellowed Guy. Hearing Kara's name shocked him out of his stupor, but he still hesitated, looking back towards Guy. "Someone will be there to protect you."

"That someone had better be you," said Farren.

Guy smiled and then Farren turned and ran over to the horse. He mounted quickly and galloped off towards the front gate. At no point did the Grand Master attempt to stop him. It was as if he was amusingly waiting for their little side performance to finish so the main act could resume.

"So touching, but ultimately a useless gesture. I will find them both." Guy held steady, never once removing his gaze from the Grand Master. "How long can you continue this stalemate? Are you even sure that arrow will make it to me?"

"You underestimate us, Tellurian."

The Grand Master let out a raucous laugh. "Ah, so you are one of the Commander's men. I had a feeling that he knew. How, I still have not determined, but you will not be able to stop us. Not now."

"I am not here to stop you, or your plan. I am here purely to protect the boy. That is all."

"How admirable of you. But, as I said before, he won't make it far, no matter what you do."

It was nothing for Guy to stare into the eyes of a monster and not falter in his belief. He had lived a long and virtuous life and would gladly give up what remained of it for the safety of another. His duty was to protect and that is what he intended to do.

"He is stronger than you think. As are all humans. You may think you have already won, but you are far from a victory. The Commander will never stop, the Creed will not be defeated and that weapon you intend to create will never be built."

"If you know of the weapon, then you know your fight is futile. Even without it, you could not hope to win. I am a Magi. I control the energy that flows through this world. You think that I underestimate you? Ha! Humans are nothing but pawns. That is what they have always been and will always be. You are the one who underestimates us, Human."

The ground around Guy started to shake and, unexpectedly, a thick vine shot up and latched onto his arm. Without pause, he fired his arrow. The Grand Master swiftly stuck out his hand, transforming it back into wood, to stop the arrow, but the arrow penetrated too deeply and still contacted flesh beneath. He let out an inhuman wail as he pulled the arrow from his hand and grabbed his wrist in pain. More vines had shot up and grabbed onto Guy, pinning him to the ground. Guy stood, with one knee to the ground, as the Grand Master seethed in agony.

"So, you do bleed. Or is that a result of your current form?" taunted Guy.

The Grand Master glared back at him, his eyes showing the yellow, predatory eyes of his Tellurian self. He stopped his screams and walked over to Guy, who knelt calmly, as if in no danger at all. The Grand Master drew his sword with his bloodied hand and knelt down in front of Guy so he could look at him straight in the face.

"I will exterminate every last one of you humans as if you were insects. You are nothing compared to me." He took his sword point and put it on Guy's chest. "You should be honored. After the Supreme Regis, you have been the second human to be killed by my own hand."

With an effortless push, he jabbed the sword straight through Guy's heart. Guy let out a small gasp, but then smiled just before slumping over. The vines disintegrated into dirt, letting him fall to the ground.

"I will never understand you humans," muttered the Grand Master, seeing Guy's smiling corpse.

He took a rag from his pocket and wiped the blood off his sword. A large crow fluttered to a halt behind the Grand Master. The Grand Master stared down at his bloodied hand.

"Find the Commander and his men and kill them all," he muttered, not turning. "And have Pardos track down Farren and the girl. Where one goes, the other will, as well. I am sure he has been getting restless, having to stay hidden."

The crow only cawed, before turning and flying off in to the fading sun.

31

In the state district of the city, the last few citizens were leaving work and heading home for the evening. Since this district housed the offices and workplaces of every business related to the Regency, it quieted down quickly at the end of the day. Not many who worked in this district desired to stay there any longer than required.

It would only be another hour or so before the sun set completely and the sky was now flooded with yellow and pink light. Combined with the shadows of the buildings, the color created an eerie feeling for anyone walking the streets. Fortunately, neither Kaine nor Syd seemed to notice.

They walked swiftly through the shadowy, stone streets. The buildings in this district were not as uniform as other districts, because many of the different government buildings continuously tried to out-do each other in decadence and grandeur. High arches, pillars, and curved facades were common. No building in this district was the same as another.

The main building of the Valorian Science Society was one of those buildings that went beyond practicality and focused on ostentation. The entranceway stretched up three floors, with two pillars holding up the pyramidal overhang. The entry was also entirely made of geometric, glass sections, so it was sometimes difficult to even find the door. Inside, the décor emphasized sharpness. It seemed as though everything had an edge and it formed distinct shadows in the low light. The ceiling of the open antechamber was also a glass dome made of various geometric shapes, which, in the day time, redirected the light from the sun to illuminate the entire room, no matter where the sun was in the sky.

Kaine and Syd walked up to the front of the building and looked up at it. The glass was shining a curtain of red light across the front and inside the entrance hall.

"Well that is quite disquieting," commented Kaine.

"Quite what?" asked Syd.

Kaine rolled his eyes. "Spooky. It means spooky, you idiot."

"Oh…" responded Syd. He turned back and looked at the building. "Yes, it is isn't it. I think it is the glass that does it."

Kaine rolled his eyes again. He heard a slight rustle in an alley behind them and quickly spun around, strung an arrow, and fired in the blink of an eye. His arrow struck a small cat that had peeked its head out into the street. It let out a high pitched screech and slumped dead. Kaine sprinted over and knelt down next to it. As he grabbed for his arrow, the cat disintegrated into dirt.

"You do not see that every day," commented Syd, who had just walked up behind him. "Is that what happens to a Tellurian when it dies?"

"It seems so. It has been following us for some time now. They are onto us. Keep your eyes open."

"Finally, a little action," Syd smirked. "I haven't been in a real flight in far too long."

Kaine gave him a friendly punch to the stomach and then picked up his arrow before running off towards the building. A group of shadows silently followed after them.

If there was one word to describe Minor Fanix Ayr it would be *hawkish*. He had a long, sharp nose and a thin face that ended in a pointed chin. His light blonde hair was cut close to his scalp on the sides and styled to a point in front on the top. He was tall and thin, with whipcord like muscles. Many were deceived by his appearance and assumed him frail. That was usually their first, and final, mistake.

A series of support struts had been lowered out of the bottom of the *Fionetta* so it could neatly rest on the grassy plain outside of Valoria. Large areas of grass had been blown away and flattened near the ship's bulbous engines, exposing the dirt beneath. The dozens of smaller airships that had been flying along with it had landed on the deck of the battleship and were being tied down to protect them from any unexpected gusts of wind.

The Minor walked from the hatch that lowered out of the underside of the battleship with two personal guards walking beside him. He wore a handmade Davati Airmen dress uniform, specially sized to form to the Minor's slender build. The jacket, sky blue with accents of light grey, the Airmen colors, clung tightly to his chest and arms. The pants, too, were form fitted and his thin legs made him look even more bird-like. Over the top of the uniform he wore a large, blue cloak. The collar was high, reaching up to his ears, and it was tied near the chest. The inner lining was made of soft Drambole fur, a small, white, fox-like creature that lived in the very highest points of the Grace Mountains.

"How did the Captain say she was running?" Fanix asked his guard.

"As well as could be expected, Your Highness. The engines are working flawlessly and there were no unexpected complications, as of yet. He was more worried about the landing than anything and that too went without difficulty. I hope that the Supreme Regis will not be too upset about us destroying a bit of their precious grassland."

"That is the least of his concern, I can assure you. He has much more important things to be worrying about. Did we lose any of the attack ships?"

"No, Your Highness. They are all safely landed and stowed on the top deck. All are running smoothly, as well."

"Excellent. It seems that she has held together nicely despite her lack of action over the years. My forbearers may have been a little overcautious with her. We have held her in the shadows too long. It is about time she had the opportunity to stretch her legs and flex her muscles." He turned to the other guard. "Airman, I want you to alert the Captain to have the men stay put for now. Once I speak to the Supreme, I will return to give them their specific orders. They have the night off."

"Thank you, Your Highness."

"But, they are to stay on the ship," he shouted back, as he walked away. "No one is to enter the city."

The man quickly nodded, before running back into the ship.

"Do you think it wise, Your Highness, to let the men have the night off?" asked the remaining guard. "Valoria offers them many chances to get themselves into trouble during the night."

"That is why they are confined to the ship, Babon, but they do need a chance to let out a bit of that energy they have been building up in anticipation for battle. We need them with level heads when the fighting starts."

Babon, the Minor's second in command, nodded and decided to let the issue go. If there was one thing he had learned from being the Minor's personal guard, it was that you never second guess his orders or explanations.

Unlike the Minor, Babon was a tall and well-built man. He had shoulder length blond hair that he usually kept tied back and round facial features. His eyes were gray and inviting at most times, but could command aggressively when required. Intensely loyal, but intelligent and outspoken, Fanix trusted him with everything.

After reaching the bottom of the hatch, Fanix looked around expecting to find a big welcome, but no one was waiting. The sky still held a tint of yellow-pink sunlight and the hundreds of glow lights that lined the outer surface of the ship lit the area well, but he could see no one waiting.

"This is not quite the welcome I was hoping for."

"I'm sure someone will be along shortly, Your Highness. It could be that they were not expecting us so soon."

"Get me my horse. We will meet them half way, then. After that journey, I have no intention of sitting around and waiting any longer."

"Of course, Your Highness." Babon bowed and ran back into the ship to retrieve the horses.

Minor Fanix looked off towards the city. In the quiescence of the open plain, he could easily hear the music and voices of Seduke beginning to erupt.

"So it begins."

Outside the city walls, the lights abruptly ended. The sun still offered a bit of illumination but, none-the-less, Coal rode his horse wildly down the dirt paths, relying on his memory rather than his sight. He had been riding these paths since he was little. He knew them better than most. The chilly night air buffeted across his face, making him squint his eyes, but he did not slow. He needed to make sure to reach the Minor before anyone else.

As Coal came over the top of a small hill, he could see the light from the battleship in the distance. The eeriness of the rows of reddish light was unsettling. Two shadows appeared in the center of the light and they seemed to be growing larger. Coal slowed and as the sound of his horse's hoof beats quieted, he could hear the hooves of two more horses approaching.

"Who goes there?!" Coal shouted. The surprised whinnies of two horses reached Coal as the shadows stopped suddenly.

"His Highness, Minor Fanix Ayr. And, who might you be, stranger? You seem to be in quite a hurry."

Coal trotted closer to the two figures until he could make out their faces. Babon rode forward to meet him, intent on protecting his master from any unfriendly aggression. Coal saw Babon's hand ready to draw his sword.

"Commander Coal Lucer. I am here to greet the Minor."

Babon relaxed and the Minor trotted up next to him.

"Commander, it is excellent to see you," he said with a straight face. Coal knew that the Minor rarely smiled and the welcome was indeed cheerful despite the lack of emotion.

"A pleasure to see you as well, Your Highness." Coal looked around to see if he was being accompanied by anyone else. "Has no one come to greet you?"

"You are the first, Commander. Were you not coming to escort us? Is the Supreme Regis too busy to grace us with his presence?"

"I am unaware if the Supreme Regis is planning to come to greet you. He may be on his way as we speak, but I do not know for sure. I am actually here to speak to you for other reasons."

Fanix raised his brow in interest. A long silence caused Babon to tense up again, looking to his master for any sign of distress, but Fanix turned a slight smile.

"So, the Supreme Regis does not know you are here? You are walking a dangerous path, Coal. I do not think that the Regis would be too happy to know you circumvented his authority to come to see me."

"A chance I was willing to take," Coal responded firmly.

Coal's seriousness caused Fanix to break out into laughter. Even his laugh had a piercing, bird like pitch to it. Babon was confused by the unusual outburst from his master, but did not react. "I always did like you, Coal. You do not let anyone push you around, do you? You say what you mean. I respect that. I suspect that you wish to speak alone?"

Coal nodded.

Fanix turned to Babon. "Go back to the ship, Babon. I will be safe here with the Commander."

With a slight hesitation he bowed his head and rode off back towards the haunting lights.

"Do you wish to go somewhere a little more private?" Fanix asked.

"There isn't time. Besides, we are quite enough alone, don't you think?" he said looking around him at the darkness.

"As you wish," his hawkish glare returning as he dismounted from his horse. "I find myself extremely curious about your reasons for being here and, if I do say so myself, I am very rarely curious about other people's actions."

Coal dismounted as well, and brushed himself off. "Well, what I have to discuss with you, I think, may be worthy of your rare curiosity. I can almost guarantee it will also be quite unexpected. I am actually here to try to stop you from joining forces with the Supreme Regis."

Fanix's eyebrows rose in surprise. "Indeed it does wet my curiosity. I would have assumed you, of all people, would be eager to wage war against the Creed. An allied force of our two sects would almost ensure victory. You must know this."

"Trust me, Your Highness, I wish the Creed destroyed as much as you, but that is not my reason for asking this of you."

"Then what is, Commander? I cannot image many reasons that would stop you from having a chance to kill the murderer of your father."

"Are you trying to rile me, Your Highness? You do not have to remind me who killed my father. I was there."

"Not at all. I am just trying to make sense of your reasoning. You have wished vengeance on Minor Leo for decades. You now have your chance and you seem to be refusing to take it."

"I will have my revenge, I do not doubt that. Don't begin to think that I am passing up my chance, because I will have none. The Supreme Regis cannot be trusted. He is planning something more than what he is telling you."

Speaking of distrust and betrayal would normally concern someone, but the Minor did not seem alarmed. He casually walked over to a large rock and eased himself down onto it.

"And you know this for a fact?"

"Of course. I would never have come to you if I didn't."

"How did you come by this information?"

Coal hesitated, forcing himself to stop before saying something that might endanger their secret. He was not sure yet if the Minor could be trusted.

"The Supreme Regis and I are good friends. He confides in me many things that he would normally not tell others."

"And yet, you seem to be betraying his trust. You speak of his betrayal, but it seems that is what you are doing as well."

"For the greater good," he insisted. "The kingdom comes before any friendship."

"Always the good little soldier, aren't we? Sometimes I think you would sacrifice your own sister if your duty called for it." Coal stiffened with anger. "But alas, that's what makes you such a good leader, I suspect. You are good at making the tough decisions."

Coal had expected the Minor to be difficult, but Fanix seemed to be trying to deliberately anger him. It took a considerable amount of will to restrain himself. He could not even find the words to respond without angering the Minor. He still needed to try to convince him of the danger.

"So then, tell me Coal. What is the Supreme Regis planning? What is he not telling us?"

"He has no intention of sharing the spoils of war with you. You are just a pawn to him. Once you defeat the Creed, then he will toss you aside."

"Those are harsh accusations, Coal. It is hard to believe that our beloved Supreme Regis would do such a thing. Coincidentally, the Supreme Regis has told me that he has no want or need for Vertura or the land that it inhabits. His only desire is that the Creed are destroyed. He has promised us complete control and rights over the land and its resources."

"He will not let you live, Fanix. Once he is done with the Creed he will come for Fera, you can be sure of that."

"I beg to differ."

"You cannot trust him! He's...."

"He is what, Coal?" Fanix shouted back at him. "...a Tellurian?!"

Stunned may not have been a strong enough word to describe what Coal felt at that moment. For all his attempts to hide that fact, Coal had never thought that the Minor himself would know. Surely the Tellurian would never have told him. It seemed as though he underestimated the Tellurians.

"You know? You know and yet you agreed to follow them?"

"They are Tellurians, Coal. They will get what they want, no matter what we do. So, either we fight back and die, or align ourselves with the winning side and come out of this as victors."

"I should have known from the beginning. I suppose I did not want to believe it. You were never one to do what was right. You are a coward, Fanix."

"Better than a fool," responded the Minor.

Coal heard a faint sound behind him and he turned just in time to duck away from a faint black shadow that flew inches by his head. Turning back to the Minor, he saw Corvus fall neatly from the dark sky onto the grass next to Fanix.

Fanix turned to the Tellurian. "We have an unexpected visitor."

"I can see that," growled Corvus.

"It looks as though you and your Master have gotten sloppy. How is it that the Commander knows?"

"We are unsure, but he and his men will not be a problem for much longer. You can be assured of that." Corvus starred at Coal with blood-thirsty eyes.

Fanix noticed the Tellurian's urge to fight. "I assume that you can handle him."

Corvus hissed devilishly at Fanix. Realizing Corvus' intent, Fanix walked back over to his horse and got back on. "I am truly sorry, Coal. I never wished for this. You are a good man. If only you had more sense than pride, you would have chosen the other side. There is only death awaiting you now."

"For me, there is only one side."

Fanix smiled grimly. "What I wouldn't give to be young and virtuous again. But alas, I will be the one who lives out the day and you will be lying dead in a field with no one watching."

"Only a coward needs someone watching," shouted back Coal, as Fanix galloped off towards the city. Coal turned his attention to the creature.

"Stupid human, you should never have messed with our plan. It no longer matters how you found out, because you and your men will not live through the night. Your sister and the boy will be found and made to watch as we drive a spear through your skull and mount your head atop the palace walls."

"You killed my friend and now threaten my family. You are the fool, Tellurian," said Coal as he drew his swords. "Shall I bring *your* head back to your master, or just leave it in the plain to rot in the sun? Your choice."

The sun was now completely set and the darkness in the grassland was almost absolute. The first of the Three Guardians, Vala, was peeking its head above the horizon, but its light did little to illuminate the landscape. The field of tall grasses looked like a swaying ocean in the faint moonlight as a swift breeze cut across the ground. The rustling of the grass was all Coal could hear and, for once in his life, he felt a tinge of fear.

After the initial clash, Corvus had faded back into the darkness and Coal was doing all he could to sense where the sly Tellurian was. In the dark, he stood completely still and tried to listen for the footsteps.

Can the Tellurian see better in the dark? What kind of advantages does it have?

Behind him, Vala inched upward and lit up the ground enough for Coal to sense a shadow behind him. Corvus dove down towards him, transforming as he swooped from the sky. Coal quickly rose up his kidon to defend against the attack, pushing Corvus away with a mighty heave.

Corvus had two small daggers and quick, powerful legs that he used to strike concussive blows. His motions were smooth, fluid and, in the darkness, nearly impossible to follow. Coal's kidon was effective at defending, but he did not have time to strike with his halmon, so he was being pushed back.

Corvus sprinted forward and leapt into the air, flipped, and came down hard with his heal. He had transformed his leg into hardened wood, so it glanced unscathed off of Coal's blade. He then spun around with a kick, contacting Coal in the shoulder. Coal grunted under the impact, but he held firm. Coal swung out wildly with his halmon, forcing Corvus to retreat backwards. Corvus quickly threw his daggers at Coal, who jumped to the side and rolled back to his feet. When he looked back at Corvus he had his palms planted on the ground and was chanting silently to himself. Coal felt the ground below him rumbling, so he jumped sideways and a spike of earth shot up from the ground where he was standing. He fell roughly onto his side, dropping his halmon. Corvus, though, did not let up and another spike shot up, narrowly missing Coal as he rolled sideways. Soon the entire ground around Coal was rumbling and erupted with sharp spears of dirt. One sliced through the side of his leg, but he managed to get to his feet.

"Is this all that you have?" shouted Corvus. "I thought you were one of the strongest humans? Over the centuries you humans have not even become stronger. You are just as weak as you once were."

Coal's chest was heaving as he caught his breath. Blood was running down his leg and dirt was caking around the wound. He could feel the wetness, but it did not bother him. His adrenaline was coursing so fast that he could not even feel the pain.

"I was looking forward to this fight because I thought you could test me. I have seen more fight from a child. You cannot even lay a finger on me. Even your friend Bishop fought more valiantly than this," Corvus scoffed with a devilish grin.

Coal searched around for his halmon but he could not see it in the darkness. He would have to find a way to fight with just his kidon. Corvus started to run at him and then flipped forward with a somersault, his hands briefly contacting the ground. A second later a vine whipped out of the ground and wrapped around Coal's leg. It surprised him for a second, but he concentrated on Corvus as the Tellurian swung his leg around towards Coal's head. Coal caught the leg in mid air and then kicked out forward with his own leg, contacting Corvus in the back and blowing him forwards. Before Corvus could recover, Coal ripped his leg free and lunged forward. Corvus ducked under his first swing, but Coal continued to jab and swing, not letting the Tellurian retaliate. Using only the kidon, Coal's movements were much faster, but he was still finding it difficult to land a significant blow. After evading a quick jab from Corvus, Coal caught him with a hook to the mouth stunning the Tellurian for a moment.

Corvus licked the side of lips, tasting the blood. "Better," he hissed with a grin.

As the fight continued, the Guardians continued to rise and the grassland began to brighten, but they did not notice. Sure, it was becoming easier for Coal to see Corvus' movements, but his thoughts were so concentrated on the fight it had not occurred to him.

Coal had been trying to stay on the offensive, not allowing Corvus to cast any powerful magic, but he was beginning to tire and could not continue at that pace for too much longer. Sweat was pouring down his face, stinging his eyes. The blood that had once been dripping down his leg was now dried and hardened. He wiped the sweat from his brow with his sleeve, but it did little to help because his sleeve was already soaked. Aside from a few cuts around his lips and face, Corvus seemed unharmed and only slightly winded.

Corvus whipped out his leg and Coal put up his sword to defend, but Corvus had softened the wood in his leg and the sword stuck into it. The momentum of the kick tossed the sword off into the grass. With a swift kick to the chest, Corvus sent Coal reeling onto his back. Instantly, Corvus slammed his hands onto the ground and vines shot up from the ground and grabbed Coal, pinning him to the ground. He struggled to rip himself free, but the vines continued to regrow themselves as Corvus kept his hands planted onto the grass. Corvus then got up and pounced towards Coal, but Coal managed to rip free and roll to the side; Corvus' fist buried itself into the ground where Coal once laid.

Corvus' devilish enthusiasm was waning and it was being replaced by extreme annoyance.

"You are beginning to bother me, Human. Why won't you just give up and die?"

Coal struggled to his feet, his back hunched and his lungs gasping for air. "Because, there is no way I am letting an ugly little creature like you kill me. I would never be able to face my father if I let that happen," he chuckled.

Like a wild animal, Corvus growled viciously and raged towards him. Coal dodged the first few attacks but then he got caught with a punch and a sweeping kick to the side of the head. Corvus continued to attack, snarling wildly as he went. Finally, Coal fell to the ground and could not force himself back up.

"Did you really think that you could stop the Grand Master? You could not even put a scratch on me, human. You are weak."

Coal began to crawl away slowly, his arms barely able to hold his weight. Corvus laughed. "Where do you think you are going?" Coal started to crawl faster. "You can't escape me. You have lost, Human; accept it and face me." Coal ignored him and continued to crawl faster. Finally, Corvus chased after him. "I said stop!"

As Corvus ran up to him, Coal stopped and swung around fast, kicking dirt up from the ground where his sword had been lying. As the blade sliced through Corvus' chest, he let out a high-pitched scream, grasped his chest and fell to the ground. He writhed around in the grass, clawing at the grass and continuing to screech. The shock was nearly as painful as the cut, which was deep. Finally the Tellurian's hysteria subsided and he laid on the ground in disbelief as Coal stepped up to him and stomped his foot down onto the wound. The scream traveled far in the flat grassland.

"I do not run from a fight. Remember that, Tellurian." Corvus glared up at Coal, his anger showing through the pain. "I may not be as strong, or have the powers of a Magi, but I am not alone. We will stop you. I will destroy your master."

"Die, Human! You are not worthy enough to fight him," Corvus howled as he slammed his hand on to the ground. The ground began to shake, but before anything happened, Coal quickly stabbed him through the chest. This time the scream was quick, as all the air in his body escaped him. The rumbling stopped and Corvus' body went limp.

Coal let out a sigh and dropped to his knees. He looked down and watched as Corvus' body transformed into a crow and then disintegrated into dirt. The Commander had never before been pushed so close to death and his emotions were running rampant. He looked off at the distant lights of the *Fionetta*. "Damn you, Fanix. I never thought you would fall so far," he said aloud. "You have doomed us all."

32

F arren could not stand still, because his nerves were jumping wildly. He did not sleep a wink, yet he was not tired. He knew the moment the front gate would open and was there to leave when it did. Unlike Kara, he had not bothered to disguise himself because it was not unusual at all for him to be running around the city. The guards at the front gate thought it a bit odd he was up quite so early, but they still smiled and greeted him cheerfully. He had quickly nodded back as he ran out through the gate.

The Prince had stayed in his band's hideout overnight. It was a small, abandoned building inside the bazaar that was originally a storage building, so it had a wide open space on each floor. A few couches and chairs, along with a few tables and chests where they kept their contraband were strewn around. He had laid awake all night on one of the couches, staring at the ceiling.

Now he paced back and forth beneath the tree near the waterfall pond at the training grounds. He knew it was still early, but he could not drive the fearful thoughts from his head.

What if something has happened to her?

There was nothing he could do but wait. He tried to stay underneath the tree to avoid the rain, but many of the leaves had already fallen off, so it provided little shelter.

It was difficult for him not to think about the night before and what had happened. Bishop had been acting strangely for some time, but Farren was content with blaming whatever happened on the mission to Coroge and all the stress he was under. There was a part of him that knew that something more had changed, but he did not want to accept it. What happened the night before was far worse than he could have imagined, though. It was as if Bishop was a completely different person. Bishop would never hurt anyone, especially Kara. There was something going on far greater than he could imagine and it seemed as though Master Guy knew. If Guy knew, then Coal would as well. Once he and Kara were safe, he would find Coal and discover what was going on.

A faint voice jolted him from his thoughts. He looked off towards the top of the stairs, waiting to see if someone would come into view. The voice grew louder and soon he could make out the words.

"Farren! Farren!"

A second later he saw Kara appear on the hill top. She skidded to halt, panting.

"Farren!" she shouted again.

"Kara!"

His heart jumped and an exhausted smile spread across his face. After catching her breath, she looked down at him and smiled. She then started to run down the stairs towards him. Seeing that she was drenched and covered in mud, he started to run towards her, hoping to meet her half way. She stumbled, nearly falling onto her face, but she did not slow down. The excitement on her face made Farren even gladder to see her.

When she was about halfway down the stairs Farren stopped in mid-stride, his eyes widening. Kara saw his expression and turned around. At the top of the stairs stood a monstrous black panther, its eyes fixed on her. She froze in shock. Her smile faded as she heard Farren scream. "Kara, run!!"

She turned and started to sprint down the stairs faster than she had ever run before. It did not matter that she was close to collapse, her body was forcing her forward.

The panther started to bound down the stairs towards her, quickly catching up with its long, powerful strides. Farren was running at her, trying to get there first. There was no way he could fight that thing off, but it did not matter. As she came to the bottom of the stairs, the panther leapt at her. Farren froze in shock. The panther pulled back its giant paw to attack, but suddenly a burst of wind rushed past Farren and collided with the panther, sending it flying back into the stairs. The gust of wind had nearly knocked Farren off his feet, but he managed to turn and see a young, cloaked man with grayish-blue hair descending down towards him on a giant eagle.

"We need to get out of here, Prince Farren! It is not safe. Grab Lady Kara!" the man shouted as he approached. He jumped off of the eagle and ran over to him.

Farren's mind was racing. Kara was just attacked by a giant panther and now a mysterious man riding an eagle came down from the sky. His confusion was so great he could barely force out a response. "Who are you?" he blurted.

"My name is Kyte. I am a friend of Commander Coal. You can trust me. We need to get out of here. You are in grave danger."

Farren did not know what to think. Nothing made sense anymore. His brother attacked Kara, likely killed Master Guy, and now this. He did not know what to do anymore.

"Prince Farren" yelled Kyte.

Farren jolted back to reality. He looked over at Kyte, whose face was filled with concern and urgency. Then he looked at Kara, who stared back at him with red, tearful eyes and a look of sheer panic. His mind started to focus again. There was still one thing that still made sense. There was one thing that did matter, and that was to save Kara. She was nearly stiff with fear when he grabbed her arm and started to pull her away. He saw that the panther was regaining its composure and getting up, so he pulled harder.

"We need to go, Kara. Come on!" he urged.

They started running and Kyte ran with them, keeping an eye on the panther. The beast finally looked up and saw them attempting to escape, so it transformed itself into its Tellurian form and placed its hands onto the ground. Vines shot out of the grass near them. One snagged Kara around the ankle and she immediately hit the ground, striking her head hard and falling unconscious. Farren and Kyte skidded to a stop and turned to see her. Before they could run back to get her, a giant wall of earth rose up in front of them, blocking their path. Farren ran up to it and started to pound his fists on it.

"No!"

Kyte grabbed him and tried to restrain him.

"Prince Farren, we need to get out of here now."

"Not without Kara!"

"That thing is too strong for me. I cannot hold it off long enough. We need to leave, or we will all die."

"No! I will not leave her!" Farren shouted.

Kyte tried to pull him away but Farren was struggling so hard that he could not drag him along. Finally, Kyte struck him in the back of the neck, knocking him out. He threw him over his shoulder and jumped onto the eagle. As it flew off and out of the training grounds, the wall of earth crumbled into a heap and the Tellurian was standing behind it, watching them escape. Kara's limp body was tucked under its arm.

33

It was early, but there was still much to do. Neesa rushed about the restaurant, cleaning tables in preparation for the night's customers. After cleaning the tables, she needed to set them, polish glasses, sweep the floor, fix the curtains and organize the bar. It was her first time setting up, so she had arrived early to make sure that she had enough time and she did everything perfectly. She did not want to mess up the first day.

Neesa worked fast, but carefully, making sure not to miss a single spot. She wore a simple grey dress; one that she did not mind getting dirty while working. As she cleaned, she brushed her forehead, wiping away the sweat.

A hard knock came at the door, startling her, and she let out a quiet shriek. She stood motionless for a moment, confused about what to do. Nobody had told her if she should answer the door when the restaurant was closed. The person knocked again, this time even harder. Ana was in the back room working, but Neesa did not want to bother her.

"Is there someone there?" the person shouted. "We need help."

It was a man's voice. "Please, someone open up. My friend is injured"

The commotion brought Ana out from the back. "What is all the noise about? Neesa?"

"There is someone at the door. I do not know what to do. They say that they need help and one of them is hurt."

Ana cautiously walked up to the door. "Who is it? State your name and your business here."

"My name is Kaine Ducale. I am a member of the Gallants. My friend and I were in your restaurant not too long ago. My friend Syd is injured. He needs medical attention."

Kaine! Neesa thought in surprise.

Ana quickly opened up the door and Kaine was standing just outside, Syd draped around his shoulders. It was still raining and they were both soaked, but that was not what worried her. Ana looked at them both and the state they were in. Syd's left arm was limp and covered in blood and a deep cut ran down the side of his face. Aside from the fact his clothes were in tatters and he was on the verge of collapse, Kaine seemed unharmed. She quickly urged them in.

"Oh my goodness, what happened? Are you alright?"

"Nothing too severe. I think his arm is broken, but that is all."

"Oh, do not try to act all tough around me. I know men quite well, Captain, they are not as tough as they like to seem. Put him down over there on that table," she pointed. "Neesa, go fetch some water and rags and there should also be some medical supplies in my office."

Neesa stood staring at them both in shock and did not move.

"Neesa!" Ana shouted.

She jumped in alarm and looked up at Ana.

"Go!" she insisted. "And see if you can find some dry clothes, as well."

Neesa ran in to the backroom.

"How did this happen?" asked Ana, turning her attention back to Kaine as he laid the half-conscious Syd onto the table. Syd groaned in pain as he was lowered down onto his back.

Kaine looked up at her and grimaced in dismay. He turned away without answering, examining Syd's arm.

"So, that is how it is going to be, huh?" she murmured.

"That is how it must be, Ana. I am sorry, but I cannot tell you. It is for your own safety."

"Do not give me that line, Captain. If you were really that worried about our safety you would never have come here," she rebuked. Kaine lowered his head apologetically and Ana sighed to relieve a bit of her irritation. "But, of course, I would never turn you away. I am sure you realized that."

"You are right. I am sorry, Ana. There was little other choice. We were on a mission and ran into some trouble. We came here because there are few we know who we can trust right now."

Ana's expression changed from annoyance to concern as she looked at the somber Kaine. He seemed quite distraught and sincere in his statement. Something was truly bothering him, but nothing he wished to speak of.

"In that case, I am honored. To believe you would think so highly of us after meeting only once."

Kaine smirked. "Well it wasn't entirely my idea," he commented, looking over at Syd.

Ana started laughing. A moment later, Neesa burst out of the backroom door carrying a bucket of water, medical supplies, bandages and clothes.

"Here you are, Ma'am."

Ana rustled through the medical supplies and picked up a container of powder that she poured into the water. After mixing it in, she soaked a cloth and handed it Neesa.

"Help Kaine, Neesa, while I tend to this fool over here."

"I am fine, really," insisted Kaine.

"Don't listen to him, Neesa. Tend to his wounds and get him cleaned up."

Neesa took the cloth and looked over at Kaine apprehensively. "Do you have any cuts or wounds that you want me to look at first," she asked shyly.

Kaine could not manage to mutter a response as he looked down at her coy expression. With a knowing smile, Ana watched as the two attempted to interact. She then turned her attention to Syd, who still lay on the table. She dipped another cloth into the water and started to wash the blood of his arm. He grimaced, retracting his arm quickly.

"Ouch," he groaned

"What are you, a Gallant or a child? Quit your complaining."

Syd finally cracked his eyes open and grinned happily. "Hello, my love," he whispered.

"Hello, you big oaf," she smiled. "At least your personality is not injured as well. That would be a travesty. You seem to have gotten yourself into some trouble."

He laughed slightly but groaned because of the pain. "Nothing we couldn't handle. But, that is not important right now. How have you been? Did you miss me?"

"Every night since you have been gone, of course," she said with a sarcastic chuckle. "You know me. I am a sucker for a man in uniform. Now sit still."

She started to wash his arm again, ignoring his complaints. She washed gently, noticing the bruising along his forearm, and the bulge where the break clearly was. The cut along his face was deep and would undoubtedly leave a scar.

It's a miracle he is even conscious. He must be even more stubborn than I thought. Who could have done this to them? And why?

Turning back to the other two, she was happy to see Neesa was cleaning the cuts on Kaine's back. Neither one was speaking to each other, but it was better than nothing.

"So, Captain," she interrupted. Kaine turned to look at her. "What happened to you two? No matter how much you try to convince me, this was no typical scuffle. You say that you do not know who you can trust. That makes me think that there must be some trouble in the Regency, or maybe the Forces. Should I be worried?"

"You realize, Ana, that I cannot tell you anything without the Commander's consent. I am truly sorry. I hope you can understand."

"Does this have to do with the war?" she asked, ignoring his refusal to give any information.

"The war?" Kaine said, trying to act the fool. "Well, uhh…"

"You can keep your secrets, Captain, but don't you dare try to lie to me. I know men too well. You cannot run a place like this without hearing things. Men speak of many things under the influence of alcohol and in the presence of a beautiful woman. I know many things that I am not supposed to know. Besides, that enormous airship outside is evidence enough. The Davati do not fly that around for pleasure."

He rolled his eyes, admitting to the accuracy of her assumption. "I cannot seem to keep a secret from anyone these days," he muttered. "Yes, it is related, but that is all I can tell you without permission from the Commander. There is much more going on than anyone else knows."

Neesa finished cleaning his injuries and put the cloth back into the water.

"Thank you, Neesa," Kaine smiled as he started to put on a dry shirt that she had brought out.

Her eyes widened and she turned her face away, trying to cover up her blushing. She then remembered what she was wearing and how dirty she was, got even more nervous, and turned away completely. Kaine sat, mouth agape, wondering what it was he had said.

Ana shook her head in dismay. "Where is the Commander?" she asked.

"We were supposed to meet him here, if anything went wrong," said Kaine.

"I hope he is alright. Should he be here by now?" asked Ana.

"Under normal circumstances, yes, he should be here. But, these are far from normal circumstances,"

Ana looked towards the door in concern.

Syd forced himself to sit up. "Don't worry. It will take a lot to stop the Commander. He'll be here."

"Wait, I think I see him!" one of the patrolmen shouted. "Over there! He just ducked into the alleyway!"

Once he around the corner and out of sight, Coal made a run for it. Luckily, the crowds had no interest in making way for the patrols, so Coal could smoothly duck in and out of cover before the guards could catch up. Using that tactic, he had managed to make his way this far. He needed to make his way to Seduke, but the patrols were closing in.

After confronting the Minor and getting attacked by the Tellurian, Coal was on the run. Surely, now that the Tellurians knew that he was on to their plan, they would not hesitate to kill him. He found a place outside the walls to sleep the night and to wait for the gate doors to open in the morning. It was unsafe for him now to make his presence known. With the power of the Supreme Regis, they could easily have him arrested, if not killed behind the scenes. He was concerned for the rest of his men and needed to make it to *Ana's* as quickly as possible. He had underestimated the Tellurians' abilities and, for once, was unsure that his men would be alive.

He quickly ducked into an alley on the far side of the street and continued walking casually. His cloak was too recognizable now, so he took it off, left it in the alley, and joined the crowd in the street.

After entering the city that morning he had quickly found a place to clean up and cover his wounds as best he could. The gash down his leg would have drawn unneeded attention. He also purchased the cloak at the first stand he found in the bazaar in hopes it could disguise him, but he was wrong. Coal was too recognizable around the city to go unnoticed. Besides, it was not much further to the Seduke District and now that he had been spotted in the cloak, it was as much a hindrance as it was helpful. The patrols would be looking for a man in a cloak and might not notice him if he did not have it on. The final hurdle would be once he made it to Seduke, where, during this time of day, the district would be close to empty and there would be no crowds for cover. He needed to be able to get to *Ana's* unseen.

Coal continued to walk calmly through the crowds, even though he could hear the shouts of patrols behind him. He didn't dare turn to look, lest they see his face. Up ahead, the street opened up into the large central square where it split and lead to the different districts. Luckily, it was near the middle of the day and there were many people visiting the square's restaurants. It was not quite as crowded as the bazaar, but there was still cover. Coal turned quickly towards the road to Seduke and caught a glimpse of a patrol entering the square from the bazaar. He turned his head away and picked up the pace. He made the turn to take the street to Seduke, when he heard a man cheerfully yell his name.

"Commander, is that you?"

Coal cringed at hearing his name and peaked over at the patrol. One of the men looked over and their glances met.

"There he is!" he shouted, and all the men quickly made chase.

Coal darted past the small crowds and entered Seduke. There was no point in acting casual now. He needed to lose them, and quickly. If they were anywhere close by when he entered *Ana's* they would search the area and find him eventually. Without the crowds, there were very few places to hide, but he could run much faster. He hadn't noticed how much his leg was bothering him until now, but he kept running through the pain. He turned down a side street and tried to lose them by using the alleys and buildings, but it did not seem to be working. Without the crowds, not only could they see every move he made, they could hear him as well. As he ran through one of the alleyways, he made another turn and skidded to a stop as he looked up at a dead end. There were no doors to enter or places to climb. He was trapped. The sounds of the patrolmen reached him and he knew they were coming through the alley. There was nowhere for him to go. A second later the men appeared.

"He's here!" the first one shouted to the rest.

Soon, the rest of the patrol came and circled Coal with their swords drawn.

"There is no place to go, Commander. You cannot escape. Just come with us. There is no need for violence," the man added as he saw Coal reach for his swords.

"And why must I go with you, Soldier? Have I done something wrong?"

"I have been ordered to take you into custody. That is all I need to know."

"You are ordered to take your superior officer into custody and you do not ask why? Was it that easy for you to believe that I was guilty of such an act that it warranted hunting me down?"

The man's confidence clearly wavered as he second guessed his motivation. "There is nothing for me to question, Sir. I have my orders. I hope you can understand that," he affirmed.

There were eleven men in the patrol and while Coal knew that most patrolmen were not well trained in combat, it would be difficult to fight through eleven men without injury, but there seemed to be no other way. He started to draw his swords, but was stopped.

"What is wrong with you fools?!" a voice shouted. All the men looked around in confusion, trying to find out where the voice came from. "Is this how you patrolmen treat your superiors? I always knew you were a shabby bunch." The men's confusion increased and even Coal was baffled at the sudden turn of events.

"Who are you?" one of the soldier's shouted.

"Me, you ask?" Reme's face appeared from atop the building behind Coal. The sun was shining right behind him, so it was difficult to distinguish him. All the men covered their eyes and squinted to look at him. "My name is not important. I am but a keeper of the peace and a symbol for justice," Reme howled theatrically.

"Aren't you that boy that's always running around making trouble in the bazaar?" asked another patrolman.

"Ah, so you know of me?" he smiled. "My fame is well known throughout the city."

"Get out of here, boy. This has nothing to do with you."

"But, that is where you are wrong. I'm not sure if you know, but this is our territory and I don't like it when people are threatened in my territory."

"Alright, that's enough. If you don't get out of here I am going to come up there and get you myself."

"Oh, really? I would love to see you do that, actually."

The patrolman growled in annoyance and realized that Reme had called his bluff.

"And what are you going to do exactly, if we arrest the Commander? Are you going to throw sticks at us until we submit?" The man grinned in satisfaction, thinking that he had made a clever retort, but suddenly a small stone rocketed out of nowhere and hit him in the back of the head. He screamed in pain and grabbed his head.

"What on Paks was that?"

"I don't know about sticks, but I always found stones to be quite affective," goaded Reme. Coal chuckled at the theatrics.

"Alright, that's it, boy." The man raised his sword, but another stone flew in and hit his hand, making him drop it and yelp in surprise.

"Hey, there's another one up there. I just saw him over on that building." shouted one of the patrolmen.

They all turned to look where he was pointing. The first patrolman shouted up at the roof. "Show yourself."

Dash slowly stood up to reveal his presence.

"Dammit, Dash," groaned Reme. "You were supposed to stay hidden so they got all confused and scared. It would have been so much more intimidating that way. Now, what are we supposed to do?"

The men all started laughing.

"Sorry, Rem. You know I didn't even want to come, anyway. Man, that chair was real comfortable back at the hideout, too," he reminisced. "But, no, you insisted that we go stick our noses where they didn't belong."

"I don't even know why I bother with you anymore, Dash," he sighed.

"That is enough of this charade," interrupted the first patrolman. "You two get down here right now, or we will arrest you, as well."

Reme looked at him like he had forgotten he was there. "What are you talking about, Mister? The situation hasn't changed, so why on Paks would I let you arrest me. In fact, now there is one more of us, so you and your men leave now, or we will continue to pummel you until you beg for us to stop. The choice is yours," said Reme.

"You have got some nerve, boy." He turned to a couple of the men behind him and motioned for them to find a way to the top of the building. When they turned around to run out of the alley, dozens of other boys appeared along the rooftops, all with their slingshots aimed down at them.

"I wouldn't do that if I were you," said Reme. "You see, there is not a kid in the *Kaisers* that doesn't have a severe loathing for you patrolmen and they have excellent aim, too. I've seen Typ over there hit a five rin coin from across the center square. So, if you value your eyes, or maybe some of your more manly parts, then I suggest you leave."

The first patrolman looked up at the boys in disbelief. He could not decide if he was annoyed or concerned. He looked around at the other men, but they all seemed as confused and apprehensive as he was.

"What should we do?" asked another patrolman.

The man groaned in aggravation, then pointed up at Reme. "This isn't over, kid. Next time we catch you, it won't just be a warning." He looked back at the Commander and then spun around to leave the alley, waving for the rest of the guards to follow him.

After they left, the kids lowered their slingshots and relaxed. Coal watched as they walked away, trying not to laugh before he looked up at Reme.

"Thanks a lot, boys," he shouted.

"After all that, you are still going to call us boys? How about a little respect, Commander?" chided Reme.

"You are right, I am sorry," smiled Coal. "Thank you, men. You saved me."

"Anything for a friend of the Boss," shouted Reme. "Besides, I expect a reward at some point in the future. We don't do this sort of thing for free."

Coal had met Reme many times, but the boy seemed much different now. There was a much more confident air about him.

"If you insist. I suppose an award is well deserved."

"Excellent. Now, it looked like you were headed somewhere, Commander. Might we be of assistance?"

"I am looking for a hosted tavern called *Ana's*. Do you know of it?"

Reme grinned. "I know the place, but I didn't think you were into that sort of thing."

"I'm meeting some of my men there. It is important."

"Sounds serious, Commander. I am not used to seeing you running from patrols. I know it is none of my business to ask, so I won't. The Boss trusted you, so that is all that I need to know. If you are in trouble, we will help. Follow me, I know a shortcut," and he disappeared atop the roof.

34

arren's head was throbbing and, for a moment, he thought that he was beginning to go blind. His vision was clouded. He saw nothing but dark forms on a white backdrop. There was a definite musty and damp smell to the area as well. It took a few moments for his vision to clear up until Farren realized it was a thick mist that surrounded him.

He was lying in a hammock made of strong strands of rope that looked to be comprised of the bright white hair of some animal he had never seen. It stretched between two gnarled Gregormores and curved comfortably around his body like it was made especially for him. When he tried to rise up, his head pounded, but he still managed to push himself into a sitting position. The hammock seemed to open up for him as he moved and it swayed only slightly as he swung his legs out and onto the ground.

He looked around at his surroundings. There were numerous small wooden buildings erected around the area and hammocks were strung up around each one. There were dozens of such buildings, but they all seemed deserted. Farren was clearly somewhere in the Shroud. The mist was all around him, but strangely it seemed to be held back by some invisible force. He could see the area around him clearly, but beyond that, the mist covered everything.

It was cool, especially in the shade, so he rubbed his shoulders to warm himself up. There were some clothes neatly folded at the base of the tree and he threw on a gray cloak. It was warm, but still light and smooth to the touch, like silk.

He slowly got up to his feet and started to walk around. The silence was calming, yet a bit unnerving. There were always sounds in the Shroud, no matter how insignificant. Wandering into one of the huts, Farren found little. There were more hammocks that hung from the ceiling, a small table with a few chairs, and an area that most likely was used for cooking. Despite the emptiness, it was remarkably clean, like one had just recently moved out.

The uneasiness of the place was fading now, as his head began to feel better. As he looked out into the mist it seemed almost peaceful, even though he knew that behind it was darkness and evil.

Farren kept walking around the area, but was beginning to think he was alone. As he approached one of the last huts, he heard some noise. He approached slowly and stuck his head into the open door. Kyte was standing on the far side of the room, with his back turned.

"So, you are finally awake Prince Farren. I am glad," he said without turning.

Upon hearing his name, he walked into the room. Kyte turned around and put a bowl of hot soup down on the table next to him. In front of Kyte was a large pot, steaming over an open flame. The flame was burning through a few logs that sat atop a wooden cooking area. Remarkably, the fire did not seem to burn through the table, but just the logs.

"I imagine you are hungry. I have made some soup. It is mostly vegetables and spices from the forest, but there is some wolf meat as well, so it should get you your strength back."

Farren approached slowly and sat down. The man was familiar and seemed friendly, but Farren was still a bit apprehensive. In the end, his hunger won over and he ate voraciously.

"Who are you?" he finally asked after taking a few spoonfuls.

Farren was afraid that the man would be upset that he did not remember him, but all Kyte did was smile. "We have only met briefly and under extreme circumstances. My name is Kyte Valen and I am a friend of Commander Lucer."

"Where is this? Are we in the Shroud?"

"This is my home. It is a small village deep in the Shroud. We are safe here."

"You live in the Shroud? How is that possible? It is difficult enough just to pass through it."

As Kyte took the pot from the flame he said, "My family and I have lived here for centuries. We adapted to the forest and learned to protect ourselves from the dangers."

"Did Master Guy send you? He told me that someone would be there to protect us?"

Kyte looked confused. "I am afraid not. I just happened to come upon you on my return to Valoria. Why would Captain Guy have sent me? Has something happened?"

"To be honest, I am unsure what has happened at all. Nothing makes sense." He stopped eating and lowered his head. "My brother has changed. He is starting a war, and has attacked Kara and me. Guy confronted him long enough to let us both escape," he murmured. "And now he has Kara, and Master Guy is surely dead," he recalled emotionally. "My brother's arm… it seemed to turn to wood when he attacked me. I still can picture the vicious eyes he looked down at me with."

"Your brother?" asked Kyte. Concern stretched across his face.

"Yes," said Farren. "He was like an animal."

Farren's emotions started to emerge, but there was more anger than sadness in his eyes. He pounded his fists down on the table and soup splashed up out of the bowl.

"What was that thing that attacked Kara and me?" he wondered aloud.

"I understand your frustration, Prince Farren. There is much that is occurring right now. You have been in the middle of it, but blind to its happenings. While we thought that you would be safer not knowing, things seem to be progressing faster than anticipated. I have been away from the city, but I can see that the situation has changed. Keeping you in the dark now would be unwise."

"What do you mean, we? Do you mean Coal and his men?"

"Yes," affirmed Kyte. "These are grave times Prince Farren; much more than you know."

"But, what was that thing that attacked us? It... used magic."

"I'm going to tell you what is happening, Prince Farren, because I believe you have the right to know. It may take some time to sink in, or even believe, but I think that it may settle the storm of thoughts and emotions that are swirling inside you."

The seriousness of Kyte's tone scared Farren. His anger towards Bishop seemed to drain away for fear of what Kyte was about to tell him.

"You were right to say that the creature that attacked us was using magic, and strong magic at that. Prince Farren, that creature was a Tellurian, one of the three Magi."

Farren could not find the words to respond.

"You have heard of the Magi, I assume, Prince Farren?"

Farren stammered, "Yes, of course. They are myth."

"Far from it. That is what you have been led to believe, as have most humans in the past centuries. But, believe me, Prince Farren, the Magi are quite real and quite alive. As you might have already guessed, I am one as well."

"You are an Aerious." It was said almost as a question, but Farren realized that he had already known it was true.

"Yes," smiled Kyte.

"What are you doing here? Why was the Tellurian after us? What does it have to do with my brother?"

Kyte just smiled at the Prince's confusion. "That is where it gets difficult, Prince Farren. You see, the man that is sitting on the throne and hurt Lady Kara and you -the one that you so vividly despise at this moment- is not your brother." Kyte paused as he waited to see Farren's response, but he showed only confusion. "That man is not your brother, Prince Farren. Your brother is dead."

Kyte was right. The storm in Farren's mind was stiller than the deepest waters. The words were there, but they just floated around without a destination.

Farren managed a whisper. "He is dead?"

Kyte only nodded, solemnly.

"But..."

"As I said Prince Farren, that man is not your brother. He is a Tellurian as well. They have the ability to change themselves into another creature, and this one can apparently change into a human. Before I left for Coroge, we were uncertain who this imposter was. But, when you said it seemed like your brother's arm turned to wood, it made me think. That is one of the Tellurian's abilities. Despite the improbability of it, it is logical. He must be a Tellurian."

Farren refused to believe it. "How do you know this? If they can change themselves, how could you ever tell?"

"When your brother was on his way to Coroge, he was attacked not by the Creed, but rather by the Tellurians themselves. The man that returned was not your brother, it was the Tellurian. I found your brother in the Shroud. He was alive, but barely, and he told me everything." Kyte reassured, "I know this is hard to believe, Prince Farren, but..."

"Of course it is!" Farren cried. "You tell me that my brother was killed by Magi. You tell me that one has taken his place, and you expect me to just believe it all to be true?"

"Death is hard to understand, Prince Farren, especially when it is unexpected. You have suffered much and that is regrettable, but now you need to be strong."

"What do you know of it? You don't know how I feel. I have nothing now. My parents and my brother are dead. I am all alone, so how can I be strong?"

"Look around you, Prince Farren. This was once the village of my entire clan," he said. "Now, I am all that is left. While our situations are not exactly the same, I do indeed know how you must feel. I have seen much death and felt much loss. I was truly alone, but you are far from it. You have many people that still love you and need you. You need to be strong for them."

Farren was beginning to calm. "If he was still alive, why did you not help my brother? You are a Magi, surely you could have used your magic to heal him," he asked despairingly.

"There was nothing I could have done for him, Prince Farren. There are some things that are even beyond the Magi's control."

Their soup was no longer hot but, then again, neither one of them was hungry anymore. Farren folded his arms onto the table and rested his head.

"You are strong, Prince Farren, I can see that as plain as I can see your face. While I did not know your brother well, I could tell that he had that same strength. It is admirable to be faced with such danger and loss and to think more about the safety of your friends. Am I right, Prince Farren?"

Farren raised his head. "What will they do to her?"

"I cannot know for sure what will happen to Lady Kara, but it is safe to assume they will keep her alive. They now know that their plan is revealed and they will use her as a hostage."

"Then, we need to save her."

"I have sent a message to Commander Lucer, informing him of what has happened. If he wishes to try to save her, that is his decision, but she will be safe for now. We have a far more crucial mission, though, Prince Farren."

"What do you mean?"

"I just returned from Coroge, where I spoke with Minor Leo. While he thanked me for the warning about the war to come, he proclaimed that it was ours to fight."

"He is not going to help?"

"No. We are alone in this war, Prince Farren."

"But, they control the Valor Forces, the Tellurians and now the Davati. How could we possibly fight them?"

Kyte rose up out of his seat. "That is why we must look for aid from another source. One that they will never expect."

35

The Grand Master pounded his fists down onto the desk and bellowed, "What do you mean Corvus is dead?!"

Minor Fanix stood on the other side of the desk next to his chair, not at all fearful or perturbed by the Grand Master's furious mood. His hawkish features were emphasized by his stern expression. "I found what I assumed to be his remains in the grassland not too far from my ship. Tellurians turn to dirt when you die, correct? There were signs of a fight. Commander Coal must have killed him."

"What was the Commander doing that far from the city? Did you speak with him?"

"Coal came to me to try to warn me about you and your plans. He seems to know a lot about what is happening. Apparently you have not been as careful as you claim with your actions. Coal is not a good enemy to have. He will cause us many problems."

"Cause *me* problems, human? There is no *us*. Learn your place," growled the Grand Master. "And I am fully aware that the Commander knows of what is happening."

The Grand Master slowly walked around the desk and into the open room. "How he knows is still a mystery to me, but soon it will not matter. The plan still moves forward as scheduled," he continued. "I am surprised, though, that Corvus was defeated. His arrogance must have gotten the best of him. The scouts that I sent to guard the lab have disappeared and, while Datro returned safely from the Shroud, it seems there were complications there also."

"As I said, Coal and his men are no ordinary fighters. They are the best in the kingdom. You should not underestimate them."

Fanix righted the small glow light that had fallen over on his desk. They were in his private study aboard the *Fionetta*, The Grand Master finally came out to meet the Minor after a demanding request sent by Fanix to the Palace by Babon. The room was at the bow of the battleship, sticking out past the top landing deck. Behind Fanix's desk was the bow of the ship, which was covered entirely by glass so the Minor could look out at the land when flying. It was a large, open room with very little to fill it, aside from the desk, which sat in the very middle, and a few bookshelves. Its starkness made it seem even larger than it actually was.

"It is obvious now that you are correct, human. They will just be more of a hindrance than originally expected. That is all they are, though; just a hindrance. It was a mistake for them to make such a bold move so early. Their element of surprise was lost."

"I don't believe that he ever thought that I would have known. He was shocked when I revealed my knowledge of your identity. His plan was to warn me and hope that you were trying to trick me into doing something that I did not want to do. He was wrong on many accounts."

The Grand Master walked over to the windowed wall and gazed out. "I was forced to tell you of our plan, but that does not make you an essential part of it. Remember that, human."

Fanix felt a welling of contempt, but controlled it. "Yes, Your Highness," he nodded graciously. "It is our honor, as humans, to be allowed to fight alongside you. While that honor is more than enough reward itself, I also remind you of our agreement."

"Do with it what you want," he waved indifferently as he turned back around to gaze out the window. "Vertura means nothing to me. When the battle is finished, the land is yours."

"I thank you, Your Highness. You are most generous."

From the entrance to the chamber, a voice echoed.

"Grand Master."

Minor Fanix flinched in surprise. He turned around to see a Tellurian standing behind him, head bowed in reverence. He had not heard even a footstep to warn of the creature's approach. The Tellurian was short and thin, but with whipcord strong muscles.

"I bring word from Pardos, Master. He has the human girl and waits for your orders."

"What girl?" questioned Fanix.

The Grand Master ignored his inquiry and continued to question the Tellurian. "What of the Prince?"

"It seems that he has escaped, Master."

"Are you talking about the Lady Kara?" The Grand Master's annoyed glare answered for him. "Why have you been forced to capture her? What has she done? And the Prince? Have they discovered our plan, also?"

"*My* plan!" the Grand Master snapped. "She has been captured because she was becoming an annoyance. I do not think that either one of them knew anything, but now they certainly do."

"This could either be a blessing or a curse," said Fanix. "The Commander loves his sister. Her capture will send him into a rage and it will be difficult to control him. Then again, we can use her as a hostage, if it comes to that."

"I assure you, it will not," said the Grand Master. "I do not need a hostage to defeat a human." Assuming his conversation with Fanix was over, he turned back to the Tellurian. "How did the Prince escape, Astero? Surely he wasn't able to fight off Pardos. Pardos never lets his pray escape once he is on the scent."

"It seems," Astero said reluctantly, "that he was aided by an Aerious, Master." The Grand Master snapped to sudden attention.

"You cannot be serious. An Aerious? Are you sure?" blurted Fanix.

Astero glared at the Minor and refused to respond.

"Pardos is sure it was an Aerious?" repeated the Grand Master.

"He says that the Aerious descended from the sky on his eagle and attacked without warning. He managed to capture the girl, but only just. The Aerious took the Prince and escaped."

"So, they *do* survive," the Grand Master seethed. "Centuries, we searched for them."

"I know, Master," Astero said. "Pardos is not taking this lightly either. You know him."

"He will be incensed, that is certain. We were certain that they were gone. The infection that we spread through their clans should have killed them all. Yet one decides to show its face at the precipice of our plan. They always were an annoying race."

Fanix asked, "What will you do?"

He put his palms down on the desk and lowered his head to think. After a few tense moments, he spoke without raising his head. "Was there only one? Did Pardos say there was only one Aerious?"

"Yes, Master. From what we saw, there was only one."

"That doesn't mean that there aren't more," added Fanix.

"I know that, you fool. If there are more out there, then they will pose a formidable threat. However, if it is only this one, then we should not have much trouble. Either way, this Aerious must be tracked down and killed."

"I agree completely, Master. There are too many uncertainties and dangers that he poses to just ignore him."

"Where is Pardos now?"

"There is a small ravine not too far from here where he found the girl. It provides the most cover for him to stay with the girl without being seen by any humans. It is an old area used for training by the human soldiers."

"We will go to fetch the girl and keep her here on the ship. I cannot chance having her in the palace where she could talk with any of the servants." He turned to Fanix. "We will take one of your small ships."

Fanix bowed. "Of course, Your Highness. It will be arranged immediately," and he walked quickly to the door.

"Astero, I need you to gather a group of our fastest Tellurians to help track down this Aerious. Do it quickly, we need this inconvenience dealt with promptly."

"Of course, Master. I will do it with all haste," he hesitated before leaving. "Master, Pardos will want to have the chance to track down the Aerious and fix his mistake."

"He will have that chance, but not alone. You go with him. I will not accept failure in this instance."

Astero bowed, then turned around and transformed. A beautiful, bright orange butterfly fluttered away out a small window on the far wall.

The small airship sped through the air like a silent hawk. The only sound it made was the air rushing past it. Farmers and merchants gazed up at it as it soared by, remarkably close to the ground. They could feel the current of air that trailed behind it as it passed overhead.

While the Grand Master was in a furious mood due to the appearance of another Magi, he was still quite amused by the intricacies of the ship.

"I have to admit, human, that these ships of yours are quite amazing. I would not have thought that you humans could build such things."

Fanix had been quite reserved since the earlier discussion and he responded with only a slight nod of acknowledgement. "Thank you, Your Highness. It took many years to design them. The reward did not come without its difficulties."

The particular ship that they rode in was a transport ship used specially by the Minor, so the interior was more lavish than the spartan ships used for battle. Two seats were positioned up front for the pilot, which in this case was Babon, and in the rear were two long seats stretching down each side of the interior. The seats were upholstered with blue and gray silk, with the Davati insignia etched into the back.

"How is it that they fly? I am intrigued." the Grand Master probed.

Fanix kept his face indifferent as he responded, "I am not familiar with the scientific principles that the ships follow. I am no alchemist."

"Even so, I would assume that, as the leader of your people, you would have at least a general understanding of how such an important innovation works."

Fanix only responded with a contrite, "Again, Your Highness, I am no alchemist."

The Grand Master was slightly perturbed by the Minor's passive obstinacy, but decided to ignore it. He looked out the window at the landscape as it rushed by. In the distance he could see the ravine where the training grounds were and sat up straight to prepare for arrival. They exited the ship through a door in the back and stepped down onto the dying grass. Leaves blew by on the ground, swirling around the Grand Master's legs.

Pardos was waiting as they exited, having left his hiding spot near the ravine face by the waterfall. He had Kara in tow, arms tied in front of her and mouth gagged. She was covered in dirt and her hair was a mess, due to her constant struggling. At the moment, though, she seemed devoid of energy and her head was bent over in defeat.

The Grand Master and Fanix walked around the airship and approached Pardos. Kara heard footsteps and weakly raised her head. When she saw Bishop's face, her eyes widened and she started struggling to get away. Her muffled screams eked out of the gag in her mouth and tears started to well up in her eyes.

"She seems downright terrified of you. You have made quite the impression on her," commented Fanix.

Pardos glared hatefully at Fanix. "What is the human doing here, Grand Master?"

"We have gone over this already, Pardos. You know that we are using him as a part of the plan. I was with him when Astero brought me the news and we used his ship to come here. I need you to start to accept this so we do not have any problems."

"We do not need them," said Pardos, in his deep bass voice.

The Grand Master was growing impatient. Turning to Fanix he said, "Take the girl into the ship. I need to have a word with my warrior."

Fanix walked up cautiously to Pardos who frustratingly shoved Kara towards him. She collided with the Minor before pushing away and trying to escape. Fanix grabbed her dress around the shoulder and started to push her towards the ship.

After Fanix disappeared, the Grand Master turned back to Pardos. "I have had enough of this, Pardos," he growled.

"I have not," responded Pardos. "We don't need to abandon our pride as Magi in order to complete the mission. Our pride is far more important."

"The mission is everything!" the Grand Master bellowed. "I do not care what we must sacrifice to ensure that we succeed, because there is nothing else, Pardos."

"We can have both, Grand Master. You just need to have faith that we will win. The power that we hold is more than enough. You have forgotten what it is to be a Tellurian."

"I am the chosen one, Pardos. I am the *ideal* Tellurian," he preached. "Besides, I would rather have ensured victory, than have to pray for a chance at it. Remember your place in it all. You do not question my authority."

Pardos held back his rage, keeping it at a muted snarl. He could not bear to hear his Master speak such heretical words. His belief in the glory of all Tellurians was absolute, but the prophet of that belief was telling him to abandon it. Pardos did not know what to believe anymore. With difficulty, he bowed his head.

"Good," said the Grand Master. He grabbed Pardos on the shoulder reassuringly. "I cannot have you losing conviction at this point in the plan. I will need your strength when the time comes."

"I will fight for my brothers no matter the circumstances, Master. You know that."

The Grand Master grinned. "I know you will, Pardos. But, right now, I need you do something far more important." He turned around and looked up at the waterfall. "This Aerious of yours must be found and killed. I cannot have it intervening in our plan."

"Of course, Master. I take full responsibility for my failure and I thank you for giving me the chance to correct it. I will complete the mission you gave me those many years ago. The Aerii will not be allowed to stop us again."

"Good. I am sending others with you."

"That is not necessary, Grand Master. I was caught off guard before, but it will not happen again."

"This must be done quickly, Pardos. I am sure that you are strong enough to take on one, but if there are more of them out there, you will need help." The Grand Master walked right up to Pardos and spoke at a firm whisper. "I will not accept failure again."

Pardos nodded. "And I will not permit it."

The Grand Master started to walk back to airship. "This world has room for only one race. We need to cleanse it of its impurities," he shouted back.

Inside the airship, the Grand Master smiled devilishly at the restrained Kara. She was still struggling despite there being no place to run. He reached out and caressed her cheek. She trembled as he ran his finger down her face.

"Do not worry, my dear. I have no intention of hurting you." Suddenly grabbing hard onto her hair, he whispered devilishly, "You are far more valuable to me alive."

36

Over the years, there were many instances when Alexia doubted, even feared, how Datro went about his experiments. She admired him for his ingenuity and genius, but sometimes he took things farther than she thought ethical. To say that he was driven was far too much of an understatement. Success was his only compass and nothing else mattered to him. She thought back to all of those moments in the past and realized that they were nothing compared to what he was about to do.

A man thrashed about in an attempt to free himself from the restraints that held him to the large testing table in the middle of the lab. His frantic shouts did not seem to bother Datro as he stood, completely focused on his task, at a table against the far wall. Alexia, on the other hand, could not seem to concentrate on anything with the man's anger filled screams behind her.

"Let me out of here! Who do you think you are?" The table shook as he attempted to pry loose his arms and legs.

"Shut him up will you, Alexia," said Datro nonchalantly.

Alexia stood, mouth agape, staring at Datro in astonishment. When she looked over at the crazed man, he was staring furiously and fearfully at her with dark brown eyes. He had a rough beard, dark black hair and, judging by his clothes, she assumed he was a farmer or field hand. His grubby appearance added to her presumption. She looked back at Datro, who was still working, and then back at the man.

"Um, Sir? I don't know what I should do."

"Gag him or something, Alexia. I do not care how you do it, as long as you shut his mouth. I am trying to work."

She looked around the room and found a thick rope left over from tying him to the table. As she walked towards him, he again started to struggle to get free.

"What are you doing to me? What gives you the right to take me from my home and..." His voice cut off to a mumble as Alexia wrestled the rope into his mouth and tied it around his head. She looked down at him with an apologetic, guilty stare before turning away.

"Explain again, Sir, what it is that the Haze Creeper will do?"

"Dammit, Alexia. Would you pay attention? It is a stabilizing agent. It helps balance the solution and prevents it from overwhelming the subject and ripping them apart from the inside. Too much of it and the solution is ineffective, but too little and the solution is too volatile."

Datro poured a small amount of liquid from a large beaker into a test tube and then placed it in an ice bath. "Since they never were able to procure any in the original tests, we have no information to go from. We will just have to test blindly to see what will be the proper proportion.

The liquid was whitish-green and it had a minty aroma. After a few seconds, he pulled the test tube out of the ice and walked over to the man. Alexia backed away to make room for him.

"To answer your previous question, my good man," he said to the test subject still struggling on the table, "the Supreme Regis gives me the right to do this to you. I do not know why you are complaining. You have been chosen for a historic event. You should be kissing me, not spitting in my face."

The man could only respond with moans.

"Are you not excited, Alexia? After all of our work, we finally have a chance to finish it. Certainly, there is still work to do, but at least it is within our grasp."

She forced a smile. "Of course, Sir. You have been working towards this for a long time. I am glad to see it completed. That being said, I am not sure it is wise to begin human testing so soon. I mean this is the first complete solution we have created. You read the notes, so you know what happened to the subjects from the original tests."

Datro turned slowly and looked at her with a blank stare. "Do you not approve of my methods, Alexia?"

"I was only thinking that we should wait..."

"Wait?" he asked, confused. "The Supreme Regis demands results. I demand results. So, there is no time for pointless tests and recalculations. I have waited far too long. The fastest way to a complete solution is with real life experimentation. This man is willingly sacrificing himself for that cause," he insisted.

The test subject's expression turned from anger to fear, and his eyes screamed with panic as he began to realize his situation.

Datro bent down and whispered into his ear. "You are a true patriot. You do not realize it yet, but if you make it through the experiment, you will be rewarded with everything you have ever dreamed of. You will have true power."

He smiled at the man and then said to Alexia, "Hold him down and remove his gag."

"Look at him, Sir. He does not want this. There has to be another way." Her cheeks reddened and tears began flow.

"Alexia!" he shouted.

She jumped in alarm but still shook her head no.

"Do it!"

With her head lowered, she slowly walked over and quickly started to untie the rope. Looking down at the man made her sob even more, and tears dripped down onto his face. She had to turn her head away from him because she could not handle his frantic moans for help. The moment the gag was out, he began pleading for his life.

"Please, you do not have to do this. I have done nothing. I am but a simple man; I do not want riches or power." He looked up at Alexia, but she still refused to look his way.

Datro stepped up to him and held out the test tube. "Now, my good man, I have here a truly remarkable substance. I am not going to tell you what it does, because that would ruin the surprise. All you need to know is that it has the ability to do truly remarkable things."

"You mean, like kill me?" he shrieked.

"Well yes, there is that," Datro responded casually. "But then, there is always risk when you are seeking a reward such as this."

"What is it going to do to me?"

"Now, now, do not get ahead of yourself. You needn't worry about such trivial things. It will be much more exciting if it is a surprise."

The man was sweating profusely and, while he was no longer struggling to escape, he still trembled. "And, if I refuse?"

Datro chuckled. "Mister...." He paused, trying to remember the man's name. "Oh, what does it matter? You are strapped to a table and the only thing between you and escape is this vial. Do you really think you have a choice?"

The man didn't respond.

"Let me answer for you then. No." He started to circle the table. "Either you take the solution and you *may* die, or you don't and I kill you myself." He lifted his hands and smiled. "Come now, there seems to be only one logical choice. If you are a betting man, then surely you must go for the better odds."

Having to choose which way to die was more than the man could bear. He breathed heavily in silence, and his mind was blank with fear and doubt. Alexia continued to stand a few feet away, looking in the other direction. He could hear her sniff as she tried to erase her tears. There would be no help from her. He was on his own. Finally the man looked up at Datro and nodded.

"Excellent!" he cheered. "Now, all you must do is drink this."

"Then what?"

"Then we wait."

Datro leaned forward and picked up the man's head to help him drink. The man hesitated for a moment before letting the substance pour into his mouth. He coughed slightly as it went down too quickly, but then he finished.

"Alexia, hold his head."

The assistant took a deep breath and turned around. She gently lowered his head back to the table, then grabbed on to hold it still.

"It is all up to you now," Datro murmured to the man. "You must do all you can to try to control it."

"Control what?"

"You will see."

For minutes there was nothing. Datro calmly stood next to the table and waited. Finally, "My heart," the man said. He started to breath heavily. "It is racing."

Alexia could feel his body begin to heat up and her hands were becoming covered in sweat. She squinted her eyes shut and grimaced as she could sense that something was beginning. A few moments later, the man started to pull on the restraints. Alexia gripped harder onto his head, but it was difficult. Datro continued to silently observe.

The thrashing became extremely violent and his muscles seemed ready to burst. His screams were deafening, but Alexia could not put the gag back in as she tried to hold his head still and Datro did not seem interested in helping. After minutes of excruciating pain, the man fell limp and the lab became quiet. Alexia continued to keep her eyes closed, not wanting to see him and the proof that he truly was dead.

Datro put his ear to man's chest to check his heartbeat. "Nothing," groaned. "Not even a hint. I did not expect success, but that was downright dreadful."

He walked back over to his papers and started shuffling through them. Meanwhile, Alexia still held frantically onto the man's head as if she could will him back to life. Her arms were trembling and her breathing labored. Datro did not show any sign of noticing her distress as he flipped through his papers.

He said, "Get rid of the body, Alexia, and secure another. We have much more work to do."

She lowered the man's head and a tear dripped from her sorrowful eyes. She let her head drop down against the man's unmoving chest. After not hearing movement, Datro turned and said, "I said get rid of the body Alexia. There is no time for your dawdling. We are at the precipice of my work and we will not rest until it is completed. I will not be tolerant of your paltry efforts this time."

Struggling against her emotions, and with the little strength she had left, Alexia pushed herself back up and started to un-strap the man's corpse. There was no use resisting. It was going to be a long next few weeks. Resisting would only make it worse.

37

The knock was loud and it startled Syd awake from his fatigue-induced sleep. He was lying on his back on one of the couches. When he jolted awake, he cringed at the pain in his arm, which he had instinctively swung to attention, forgetting its broken condition.

It had been hours since they had arrived, and both Kaine and Syd had been treated and cleaned up. Syd's arm was wrapped and splinted and both donned new clothes that Ana had provided.

At first, both of them were vigilant and awake, waiting for Coal to arrive. However, as the hours went by, Syd could no longer keep his eyes open. The injury and physical exhaustion were too much for him to withstand any longer. As Syd slowly drifted to sleep, Kaine continued to stay up, waiting for Coal's arrival. The night's events were turning through his mind over and over. They were lucky to be alive, but that did not give him relief.

Neesa had done her best to keep him company. She brought him food and drinks and talked with him from time to time, but he seemed consumed with his thoughts and responded very little. She understood his feelings, but could not help but grow a little disheartened when she was ignored.

Ana was in the back, still trying to prepare the tavern for the night's usual crowd, despite the difficult circumstances. With Neesa helping the two captains, Ana needed to finish the setup and was now preparing the bar. Having work to do was keeping her mind off of what was occurring and what could possibly occur once the Commander arrived. Even though Kaine refused to tell her the specifics of what had happened to them, she was making her own assumptions; none of which were making her feel at ease.

When the knock came to the door, it stunned everyone in the room out of their common daze. Ana quickly ran up towards the door, telling Kaine to stay back with a wave of her arm.

"Who is it?" she questioned.

"Hey, Miss Ana, it's Reme and Dash."

"Ah, boys it is good to hear from you. It has been a while since we have last met and I always do enjoy your company, but I did not send for you. I do not mean to be rude, but what is it that you need?"

"Well, you see, Miss Ana, I have this friend of mine out here that would love to come in and have a few drinks with his two chaps. Assuming you'll have him, that is."

Kaine walked up to the door and asked, "Commander?"

"I am here, Captain."

"It is good to hear your voice, Commander."

"Yours as well. I would like even more to hear it without a door between us, though."

Kaine hurried to unlock the door to let them in. Reme and Dash sauntered in first, with Coal behind them.

"Man, I love that whole military, secret code talk you soldiers do," Reme said. He turned to Ana and bowed his head slightly. "Good to see you, Miss Ana."

"Always a pleasure, Reme."

Syd slowly got up from the couch in the back as Coal walked in. He was trying to hide his limp, but Kaine caught the slight shifting of weight.

"Are you alright, Sir?"

"I will be fine, Kaine. There is nothing to worry about."

Ana turned and shouted to Neesa, who was standing near the back, not wanting to intrude. "Help the Commander, won't you Neesa?"

She quietly nodded and ran off to fetch the medical supplies.

"There is no need, Miss, it is nothing. We are already overstaying our welcome as it is."

Ana smiled. "You men are all alike. Sit down, Commander," she insisted. "And Neesa will get you cleaned up." For a moment Coal stood motionless. "That was not a request, Commander." As she walked over to the bar to get him some water she turned. "And call me Ana. No need for formalities here."

Reme walked up next to Coal and gave him a friendly nudge in the side. "I think she likes you, Commander." Coal gave him an exasperated glare. "Just making an observation, that's all," said Reme before walking away.

"Commander," saluted Syd as he finally made his way from the back.

"It looks like you took a bit of a beating, Syd."

"They caught me off guard, that is all, Commander. It won't happen again, you can be sure of that."

"It looks like you ran into a bit of trouble yourself, Commander," said Kaine, looking down at Coal's leg.

"Nothing that wasn't taken care of," he assured coolly.

Coal looked over at Ana, who was behind the bar prepared some drinks. "We can trust her, Commander," said Kaine.

"Are you sure?"

Kaine shrugged slightly, "As sure as I can be right now, Sir. She took us in and tended to our injuries. She is a good person and we don't have many options."

Syd gestured towards Reme and Dash, who were both at the bar talking with Ana, "It looks like you found a few new friends, as well."

"They helped get me out of a difficult situation. I probably would not have made it here otherwise. They are a bit more dependable than you might think."

Neesa finally came out and knelt down next to Coal with a bucket of water and rags.

"Commander?" she asked.

He nodded with a grateful smile. "Thank you."

She rolled up his pant leg and started to wash the deep gash where Corvus had cut him. The dirt was thick around the wound and had started to seep in deeply as well, but he did not even flinch as she scrubbed away.

Ana walked up with some water for the three of them. "I suspect you are hungry, Commander? Can I get you something?"

"That would be great. Thank you, Ana."

"It is my pleasure, Commander. You have two fine men here, if I might say so. It is not common these days to find men such as yours. Believe me, I know my men well."

Coal smiled and thanked her with a nod.

"Would you like something as well, boys?" she asked Reme and Dash as she walked back towards the kitchen.

"Always, Miss," they cheered in unison.

After she left into the back, Coal turned to Kaine and Syd.

"So, did you find anything? Was there anything in the lab?"

"We did not even make it down into his lab, Sir. We were being followed, and once we got into the building they attacked in force. There must have been a half a dozen of them."

Syd added, "They came out of nowhere. It was like fighting shadows, Sir."

"So, you couldn't get into the lab?"

"Not even close. We barely made it back as it is."

"They must have known, then. They discovered we know somehow. Either that, or he was having us followed as a precaution. It might have been because of my speech in council."

"Either way, Sir, we are in a difficult situation. We have shown our hand and have given up our slight advantage," Kaine murmured. "Has there been any word from Guy or Kaleb?"

Coal grimaced at the realization. "Nothing. They did not know where to rendezvous either. If they are alive, they could be anywhere and have no way of finding us."

Syd piped up after taking a big swig of water. "The old man wouldn't go down that easy. He will find us eventually. He has that frustrating ability to somehow know everything."

Coal and Kaine nodded in agreement.

"What about Kaleb then? The mission was a tough one to begin with..." Kaine paused. "...And now. I know the boy is strong, but we may have to fear the worst."

The silence was uneasy, but none of them wanted to admit to the difficulty of their situation. The thought that one of their own was dead and there was nothing they could do was not a feeling they were used to.

Ana walked out of the back with two trays of food and, after dropping one in front of Reme and Dash, who attacked it with ferocity, she brought the other over and set it down in front of them. The men stopped their discussion.

"Ah, sudden silence," she joked. "It seems that I am not privy to the conferences of important military men, quite yet."

"It is not that we do not trust you, Ana," explained Coal.

She held up a quieting hand. "No need, Commander. I understand completely. These are matters that do not concern a lonely woman such as me. These are problems for men and soldiers." She began spreading out a few plates on the table "Besides, I will just probe Neesa here for the information later," she winked.

Neesa blushed. "Ma'am, please."

Coal then realized that Neesa had been there the entire time and grimaced at his ignorance. They all heard a slight tapping sound and looked around to see where it was coming from. At the front of the tavern, a small sparrow was pecking at a high window.

"Stupid bird. It probably wants in from the rain," said Syd.

"Don't be such a brute," chided Ana. "That bird has never done anything to you. You would probably want in from the rain was well."

The bird continued to peck and Syd could not stand it. "That is it," he bellowed. He tried to jump up from his seat, but a sharp pain shot through his arm and he fell back down.

"Calm down you fool. You are going to hurt yourself," said Kaine. "Don't let a little bird get the best of you."

"Wait, look," pointed Neesa. "It has something wrapped around its leg."

Kaine got up and opened up the front door. The rain had started up again, but the overhang at the front of the building protected him as he stepped out. The bird fluttered down and landed on his hand. He untied a small piece of paper from its frail little leg and let it fly away. As he walked in and closed the door, he unraveled the paper and read it silently.

"Is it a message from the old man? He does not know we are meeting here, but I do not doubt he would find a way to reach us," said Syd.

As he read, a grave expression spread across Kaine's face.

"What is it, Kaine?" asked Coal.

Kaine didn't respond.

Coal pressed, "Captain?"

"It is from Kyte, Sir."

Surprised, Coal asked, "Has he returned from Coroge? Was he able to talk to the Minor?"

"Well yes, but that is not the reason for the message." He turned and looked reluctant to continue. Coal got up to go over to him, but Kaine finally decided to go on. "It seems that they have captured Lady Kara while she tried to escape with Farren."

Coal stopped in his tracks. Both Syd and Kaine looked at him and waited for a response. For what seemed like hours, the room fell silent. His expression slowly turned to one of rage rather than shock, but he still did not respond.

"What did you just say about the Boss?" finally shouted Reme, from across the room.

"Farren is safe. Kyte was able to protect him, but Kara was taken." He insisted to Coal, "Kyte believes she will be safe. They will most likely use her as a hostage against us, so they will not harm her."

"Whoa," jumped up Reme. "Who took her? Who in their right mind would attack the Prince and abduct the Lady?"

Syd spun around angrily. "Quiet, Reme! Not now."

Reme froze. Coal continued to stay silent.

"Kyte also believes that Guy has been killed as well. He sacrificed himself so that they could escape," added Kaine.

"Dammit, Old Man. Why did you have to go and be a hero?" said Syd.

Sensing that the tone of the situation was getting too thick, Neesa quietly packed up the medical supplies and disappeared into the back room.

"Sir?" asked Kaine. "What are you thinking?"

Both Kaine and Syd waited warily for a response. Knowing their Commander's penchant for emotional outbursts, especially when dealing with his sister, they expected the worst. Unable to hold in his emotions any longer, Coal sent dishes flying across the room with one swift motion. They smashed against the wall and scattered everywhere. When the calamity subsided, he finally looked up at Kaine, but did not speak. His expression said everything.

"What should we do?" asked Kaine.

"I do not know, Captain. I just do not know. Of course there is part of me that wants to storm into the palace and kill that son of a bitch right now, but even I know that would be foolish."

"I think we all feel that way, Sir."

"If that is what you want, I am with you for sure, Sir. We have to get Kara back."

"No, Syd that would accomplish nothing. We cannot give up quite yet. Besides, Kyte is right. Kara is safe for now."

"Then what *do* we do?"

Coal sighed, "I do not know."

Reluctant to interrupt the conversation, Ana said, "I am sorry, Commander, I don't mean to interrupt, but we will be opening shortly. My girls will be arriving anytime, so it will not be safe any longer. There are many soldiers and councilmen that come here."

"Just when I was getting comfortable," groaned Syd.

"I guess we need to find a new place to stay. Where do we go, Sir? There aren't many places I know of that would be safe. The patrols will be after us," said Kaine.

After a short silence, Reme came sauntering over from the bar. "You need a place to stay out of sight for a while, Commander?"

"Do you know of one?"

"We have a hideout. Safest place you'll find in the city. Patrols haven't found it yet, so we shouldn't have a problem with them."

Coal looked to his Captains, who shrugged their acceptance. Coal tried to stand and he groaned as pain shot up his leg. Ana stepped up to help him to his feet.

"Thank you."

"My pleasure, Commander."

"We will need time to sort things out and make a strategy. It may take some time," added Coal.

"It's okay with us. Stay as long as you want. Just do not expect royal accommodations."

"Alright then, let's get going. The longer we stick around here, the more danger everyone will be in."

They all started to get up and gather their things. Dash tried to shovel as much food into his mouth as he could, and even put a few piece of bread into his pockets for later.

"We will regroup at Reme's hideout and decide our next move," Coal announced as they walked towards the door.

Kaine smiled and nodded to Neesa, who was standing in the back of the room. She beamed back at him.

"Commander," shouted Ana. "Reme and Dash are good boys. They will keep you safe, just like they have me and my girls. I know you are strong, but I want you to promise me one thing."

"What is that?"

"You better bring those men of yours back safe and get a drink sometime. They still have not paid their tab."

Syd and Kaine smiled when Coal glared back at them. "Our pleasure, Ana," shouted Syd. "You don't have to ask me twice."

38

Gone are the days when I could travel the countryside and enjoy the pleasures that it offered. I grow old in body, but my mind is still that of an excited child. I have traveled far and seen much more than most people have seen, but I still continue to long for the excitement that comes when I witness a sight that I have never witnessed.

No matter how much I do see, it still seems like it is not enough. As my days come to an end and I were to choose just one thing that I regret the most, it would be that I was never able to find the *City in the Sky*. Strange that I have seen the grand cities of the Tellurians and the Ignati, both of who are far more unwelcoming, but the grand city of the Aerii has eluded me for decades.

The Aerii are a peaceful and welcoming people, but they put secrecy above all else. I have heard that only those of noble Aerious birth, those of the highest clan, are allowed to enter the city. Even more, they are the only ones that know of its whereabouts. The secrecy of it makes it far more enticing.

For years I searched for it, piecing together bits of information. I went to the clans of the Shroud, the clans of the Lusai Jungle and even the clans in the barren snows of the north. I found it fascinating that the Aerious viewed the grand city, and the highest clan, like we humans view the Magi; like gods. The information that I gathered led me to nowhere. Or rather, it led me everywhere. Each account was as wild as the next, and none matched that of its predecessor.

There were stories of floating islands in the sky, grand buildings at the tallest mountain peaks above the clouds, and even legends that it existed on a different world entirely; apart from this one but somehow out of view. As much as I wanted these stories to be true, there was a part of me that knew there could never be such things.

As the stories became grander, so did my anticipation. I wondered, wherever this city may be, what was contained within it? Would it be buildings of gold and jewels? Were there fountains that erupted with the finest wines? Or maybe it was surrounded by waterfalls, and its roads were rivers in which lived the ancient river creatures of legend. I laugh now as I write, because I realize that my thoughts are even more extravagant then the stories I am told.

There is one account that I remember vividly, and not because it was the most grandiose, but rather the exact opposite. It was when I turned south and trekked up into the Rift Mountains. The mountains themselves were not the tallest, or the most treacherous, but it was not the mountains that I was in search of. The renegade clan that lived there was said to speak to no one and despised all others. I climbed for weeks in the barren rocky peaks and found nothing.

Many a time I sat on the cliffs that looked out over the Southern Waters and wondered if my search was worth the trouble. The provisions that I had packed were nearly exhausted and I had barely enough food to make it back to the base as it was. There was little that grew and lived on the mountains, so there was no hope of finding food as I went. I either continued on and hoped to find my destination in time, or I turned back. Neither option quite appealed to me.

Sometime that night, as if the Almighty had heard my thoughts, I woke to an exhilarating sight. As I write this I realize how odd it sounds, but when I opened my eyes there was a spear pointed at my face. Sure, most people would be scared at such a moment, but after weeks of exhausting climbing in relentless heat, the sight of anything was wondrous.

The man that held the spear was an Aerious, but it was not as obvious as it was for most Aerii. His brilliant, sky-blue hair was pulled back, tied loosely, and the tail hung nearly all the way down his back. His skin was far darker than usual, tanned from the sun, and he wore a tattered cloak, which was likely at one point black, but had lost a bit of its luster. The thing I noticed most, though, was his difference in his expression. It was far from the peaceful and elegant aura that most Aerii emanated. It was unpleasantly clear that the Aerious wanted to kill me, and for no purpose other than that he could.

When he spoke, his voice was raspy but almost as if it was forced to be so. He appeared to be fairly young but, of course, that could mean he was five times my age. Aerii tended to live for hundreds of years. Clearly, since I am writing this story, he did not kill me, much to my delight. Instead he forced me to follow him along through the mountains. It took only a few minutes to find our way to a small crevice in the rocks, which led to a narrow pass. It was nearly invisible, unless one knew where to look, and very uninviting if you happened to stumble upon it. It led to a small break in the rocks and I followed him in.

Inside was a large cavern. I couldn't determine if it was natural or manmade. I smiled in relief to discover that he had brought me back to his village. Well, it was not a village in the normal sense, as it was inside a mountain, but it was a home.

The Aerious, who had not spoken a word the entire time, pushed me along and took me to a small room down one of the tunnels and locked me in. It was clear that I was a prisoner, but, again, I still could do nothing but smile. No matter what they did to me later, I was alive and at my destination.

It did not take long for the leading man of my story to arrive. He looked and dressed much like the first Aerious, whose name I later discovered was Strom, but he was far older. His hair was long and tied back, but it was more gray than blue. His tanned skin was wrinkled and he spoke slowly and deliberately. Remarkably, though, he still moved with unnatural grace. I find myself now, in my aged form, even more jealous of him because of that fact. He spoke with a sophistication that could only be gained through centuries of learned life, and I wondered if I lived as long a life, would I be as wise?

Our first meeting was pleasant and enjoyable, but not of any importance. I realize that I have been rambling, so I will skip ahead to the reason why I tell this story.

Foehn was his name, and it turned out that he was the leader of the entire clan. I told him why I was there and he found my courage and persistence admirable. When I asked him if he had heard of the *City in the Sky*, I remember vividly his response and the conversation that followed.

"The grand city cannot be reached by those that seek it for their own personal reasons, even if they are not of malicious intent. It can only be found by those in true *need* of it. Because of this, Alexander, you will never find it, no matter how hard you try."

"But if I still desired to search for it?"

"You are a strange man, Alexander. Even in the face of obvious defeat you do not falter. Normally I would praise you for your courage, but I think that this is not as much courage as it is obsession. I tell you again that you will not find it, but I sense that you will not be happy unless I reveal to you the secret. Listen well, because I say this only once.

Quest north from where hidden terrors lay, do not lose yourself in the living sea that sways. High into the sky you must climb, in order to find the giants who stand guard, frozen in time. Inside their strong embrace lives salvation, but find it you will not if you are filled with temptation. If you are truly in need and find what you yearn, remember that if you ever leave, you may never return."

I wrote furiously, making sure to copy every specific detail of this riddle that would lead me to my long desired destination, but one thing still lingered in my mind.

"How is it that *you* know this and no one else I have ever spoken to does as well?"

"Because, Alexander, I was born in that place."

-Excerpt from *"Memories of Soon Forgotten Days,"* by Alexander Pierson, 1st Chief Historian of the Valorian Historical Society.

39

If there was one positive quality that could be taken from walking through the Shroud, it was that no matter the weather outside it, the weather inside was always the same. On a beautiful, sunny day it was still dismal and disquieting, but on a rainy, miserable day, its normal dimness seemed almost pleasant in comparison. It did help, though, that Farren walked along in the presence of an Aerious, so somehow everything around him just seemed more pleasing.

They had set out early that morning, or what Farren assumed to be morning, since it was impossible to tell. His normal clothes were in tatters so he discarded them for some garments that Kyte had provided for him. The cloak that he wore was shortened so it was not dragging on the ground, but luckily his frame was similar to Kyte's slenderness, so it fit well otherwise. Underneath, he wore a simple woven shirt and pants and a pair of remarkably light but tough shoes. As he walked, he felt like he was nearly floating across the ground. Over his shoulder, he carried a bag filled with extra clothes and some simple provisions. Kyte supplied him with a bow and arrows, and promised to teach him to use it effectively as they traveled.

"It will be a long and dangerous road," he had told him. "You will need to learn as many skills as possible in order to survive it."

It was difficult for Farren to leave on a journey when there was so much he wanted to do here. He thought of Kara and how much she must be suffering. Wrapping his mind around what Kyte had told him about his brother and the Tellurians was proving far more difficult than he imagined. His brother was dead and he had never even noticed.

Farren could not tell if it was guilt, or regret, or just sorrow, that he felt. He had never had the chance to say goodbye, or even feel the loss. His brother was dead, but he had spent the last weeks thinking he was alive and hating him. He tried to remember his brother as he was, but he could not. This creature had not only taken his brother's life, but the memories of him as well. With much effort, he pushed those thoughts aside and focused on their journey.

Kyte had told him that they would be heading north. It would take only a day to exit the Shroud and then they would be into the Central Plain. Once north of the plains, they would enter the Setting Plateau, which would take them on an exhausting climb up to the legendary Forest of Rising Twilight. There, in the forest, was their destination.

Anything beyond that, Kyte did not say. He said that they could find help there; help that could easily defeat the threat that they now faced. Getting there was going to be the issue. Once far enough north through the Central Plain and away from civilization, they could use Drek to fly a good portion of the way, but when they reached the plateau they would have to go on foot. There were forces there that did not allow anything else.

Silently, they walked along, Farren constantly wary of his surroundings as he had been told to be in the Shroud. It seemed no different than the normal hostile forest that he had visited a few times in his youth, but oddly he felt secure.

"Have you traveled to the Forest of Rising Twilight before?" he asked Kyte to try to create some conversation.

Kyte nimbly jumped over a large root that stretched in the path. "I have traveled much in my days. I have been through the Central Plain, the Southern Desert, the jungles in the west, and even the Setting Plateau, but the Forest of Rising Twilight is a forbidden place. I have looked upon it from afar, but I have never entered."

"Why is it forbidden? It sounds like a wonderful place to go. Why would you not be allowed in?"

"It is a dangerous place, but not dangerous in the way you would think. The forest is a truly breathtaking and beautiful place. There are wonders in the forest that you have never seen and would scarcely believe you are seeing, even as you look upon them. The beauty, though, is the danger. There are ancient powers at work in the forest that can easily trap you inside. As powerful as these forces are, there are ways to escape. Unfortunately, most men are so consumed by the beauty that they do want to leave, and they die slowly, unknowingly, and with a smile upon their face."

Farren stared at Kyte in bewilderment.

"But, do not worry, Prince Farren, we will be safe."

Farren was not ultimately reassured by the comment, but that was not because he did not believe Kyte. It was because he did not need reassuring. It was not fear that he felt but, instead, excitement and anticipation. There was something inside him that ignited at the thought of that place.

"What sort of things are there in the forest?"

Chuckling, "I have told you, Prince Farren, I have never been there. You must wait and see for yourself."

It was fortunate for Farren that the Shroud was held at bay as they walked, because if something were to attack he would never have even reacted. He could do nothing other than imagine what those wonders could be. It captivated him.

The mugginess of the Shroud was beginning to take its toll as Farren tried to cool himself down by removing his cloak and flapping the front of his shirt. While it was not hot, or even that warm, the air was dreadfully stagnant, so it was difficult to breathe.

They continued to walk and, as before, nothing seemed to change. If they could see the sky, the sun would probably have been halfway set in the sky when the disturbance came. Kyte heard a slight rustle in the trees and he quickly strung his bow. Noticing Kyte's reaction, Farren drew his sword and looked around for movement.

"Where did it come from?" Farren asked.

Kyte silently pointed ahead of them and into the trees. He started to inch forward, with Farren following close behind. His bow was up and pointed directly into the trees, not a hint of trembling in his form. The rustling started again but this time a bit louder. Farren tensed up in anticipation.

Suddenly, out of the trees stumbled Kaleb, bloodied and beaten. He fell onto the path in a heap with a groan. Kyte kept his bow pointed at him but did not fire. Farren leapt forward and threw his hand up in front of him.

"Wait, wait! He is a friend."

Farren ran over to him and knelt down at his side.

"Are you alright, Kaleb? What happen?"

Turning slowly to look at him, Kaleb muttered, "Farren?" He coughed achingly. "What are you doing here?"

Every inch of him was covered in blood and he was painted with bruises. The worst was down the lower part of his left leg. His hand blades were tucked haphazardly in their sheaths, but he was missing his short sword. His nose was clearly broken, and he was missing his shoes, so his feet were dyed brown with mud, which covered more cuts and bruises. The largest of the wounds, though, was a large gash in his side that he gripped strongly with both hands.

"That doesn't matter now. You need help. What happened?"

"It was on my mission. I was attacked."

"By who? Who attacked you?"

Kaleb hesitated.

"It's alright, Kaleb. I know everything now."

"You..." he groaned as he tried to sit up. "...know everything?"

Farren helped him sit up and then gave him some water to drink. "Yes. Was it the Tellurians that attacked you?"

He nodded, "I tracked down the scientist, Datro, but the Tellurians were protecting him. He escaped, but I was able to fight my way out."

Kyte finally stepped up. "Were there more? Did they follow you?"

"Yes. They were following me, but I have not seen them for some time. I am not sure if I have lost them."

"Tellurians will always hunt down their prey. In this forest you cannot escape them." He examined the forest around them to see if he could sense anything and then turned to Farren. "We must find a place to make camp in the cover of the trees. I may be able to put up a barrier while we rest that will hopefully divert them. I will need some time to heal him before we can continue on."

They both helped Kaleb up and then disappeared into the trees on the far side of the path. As they left, the forest went quiet. Silence in the Shroud was uncommon, and usually preceded death.

Kaleb grimaced as Kyte finished dressing his wounds. Bandages were wrapped tightly around his waist and a few dressings covered the rest of his cuts. He had washed away the blood, but the bruising was still evident. They had set his nose, but with nothing to hold it in place it would most likely heal crooked. With all of the blood and mud washed away he looked better, but far from good. He was lucky to be alive.

"Now, I will try to speed up the healing process. I need you to stay still," said Kyte. "It will not hurt, but it will feel strange. There will be a chill."

Kaleb took a deep breath and lay back down onto the ground. Kyte placed his hands just above the wound on Kaleb's side and the spot started to glow slightly.

Farren was standing just behind Kyte and watching intently. "What are you doing?" he asked.

"I am circulating natural energy through his body in order to help it heal faster. The energy will invigorate the body's healing abilities and speed up the process."

"So, you are not actually healing him?"

"Not directly, no. It is his own body that heals his wounds. I am just giving his body more energy to do it. It should speed up the process."

"Thank you," Kaleb managed to mutter.

Kyte just nodded with a smile.

They were in a small clearing in the Shroud. Just large enough for them to lay Kaleb down comfortably and allow him to rest. Kyte had cast a small barrier to hopefully prevent the Tellurians from finding them, but it was by no means a perfect deterrent. While a Magi could detect the barrier and find a way through, it was shielding them well from the creatures of the forest. Many times already, Farren had seen an animal walk past them, oblivious to their presence.

Farren watched as Kyte treated Kaleb and he was in awe of the Aerious' powers. Kaleb seemed to instantly relax, his breathing calmed, and his muscles loosened. It almost seemed like the bruises littering his body were disappearing before his eyes.

After a little while, Kyte finally stood up. Farren roused himself from a half sleep, sat down and leaned up against a Gregormore a few feet away.

"I have done everything I can for now. The rest of the recovery will be done by him. It will take some time, but the wounds were not too severe."

Farren went over to Kaleb who was barely still awake.

"How are you feeling?"

"Oh, like a girl on her wedding day," he chuckled, weakly.

Kaleb let out a sigh after the laughter settled. "So, what happened to the others?" he asked solemnly. "If you are here, then something big must have happened. Coal did not want you to be involved, so I assume the worst."

Farren paused momentarily, deciding how to choose his words. "We do not know for sure. I only know what I saw. We assume Coal escaped. There is no way he would let himself get killed that easily. Kara has been captured, but she should be safe for now."

There was an awkward silence.

"What about Master Guy?"

Farren squeezed his eyes closed. He was hoping Kaleb would not ask. He did not know what to say. Guy was like a father to Kaleb, who had been orphaned as a young boy. When Farren did not answer, Kaleb turned his head and looked at him.

"I see." Turning back, he stared up at the trees, smiling.

"He fought so that Kara and I could escape. I did not see him die, but he never met with us in the training grounds. I just assume," he said. Farren's eyes started to dampen with tears.

"Do not weep for him, Farren." Farren opened up his eyes and looked at Kaleb. "He chose his path and I believe that no matter how many times he could go back, he would choose the same thing. He has been looking for a truly honorable death for some time now. I am just glad that he found it."

Farren opened his mouth to speak, but nothing came out.

"Do not blame yourself, Farren. In fact I would bet that Master Guy is grateful to you. You have given him what he has always wanted; a glorious conclusion to a long and wonderful life."

A tear dripped down Farren's face. A mixture of sadness and joy flooded through him. Kyte put his hand on Farren's shoulder. "We need to let Kaleb rest. Even with my help, his injuries will take some time to heal," he said.

Farren nodded and pushed himself up from the ground.

Kyte waited a moment for Farren to gather himself and then said, "Night is upon us, so we will camp here. I did not want to be in the forest when night came, but we have no choice."

Looking around, Farren finally noticed that it was becoming darker and harder to see his surroundings.

"We should start a fire. It becomes cold quickly here in the Shroud and we will freeze without it."

"Won't that give away our position?"

Kyte pulled a small hatchet from his pack and handed it to Farren.

"The barrier will cover up the light. Anything inside the barrier is invisible to anything outside it. Some creatures may be attracted to the heat, but it is a chance we must take. Even with the barrier, we will need to have someone keep watch. I will take first and I will wake you when it is your turn. Now, go collect some wood, but stay close and work quickly."

Farren's eyes opened and it was dark; so dark that he could barely see a foot in front of him. He tried to get up, but he couldn't move. Suddenly, he began to stir and sat up.

The surface he was lying on was hard and cold. His eyes adjusted and he could see that he was in some sort of room. It was small, perfectly square, with no windows. After a few seconds, he became aware of a faint light off to his right and he turned to look at it. There were bars. He was in a cell of some sort. A hallway ran across, outside the bars, and the light was coming from down the hall a distance.

He swung his legs out onto the floor and, with a groan, pushed himself up to his feet. There was something that did not feel right. It was something subtle. It took him a moment to realize what.

I'm taller.

He examined itself, looking at his hands and arms. He felt fine, but for some reason his mind was confused. Walking up to the bars he peered out, trying to look down the hall towards the light.

What is happening?

"Hello?" he shouted. After a short silence he banged on the bars and shouted again. Soon, Farren could hear footsteps.

"Is there someone there?"

There was no response, but the footsteps continued to approach. Soon, a man appeared in front of the cell. He was of average height, but solid build and he wore a black, sleeveless tunic and loose black pants. His hair, also, was jet black and cut short and sharp. Farren could not make out much more in the darkness.

"Where am I?" Farren asked.

"You will soon find out. I must go alert my master that you are awake," responded the man. He turned to walk away.

"What is going on? Tell me what is happening."

"As I said, you will soon find out. I am not at liberty to tell you anything. That is for my master alone. He is the reason you are here."

Growing weary, Farren barked, "Where is *here*? Who is your master? How did I get here? I do not remember."

His heart was beginning to beat faster and he could not control it.

"You were brought here by my master."

"But why? I don't remember anything. Tell me," he urged.

The man did not respond. His face was as impassive as it was when he appeared. Silently, he started to walk away.

The fear and confusion that was building up within him was beginning to overwhelm Farren.

"Tell me!"

Banging on the cell bars, Farren's body started to become overwhelmed with rage. Farren tried to control it, but could not. All he could do was endure the rush of emotion.

His final scream echoed down the hallway. "Who am I? Why am I here?!"

With a shout, Farren awoke. His body was drenched in sweat and he was gasping for breath. Looking around, he realized he was back in the campsite again. Kyte was kneeling next to him, his hand grasping his shoulder.

"Are you alright, Prince Farren? You were shouting in your sleep and thrashing about."

His mind confused, Farren lifted up his hands and examined them. His heart was still racing and the emotions were still there, but they were beginning to fade.

Looking up at Kyte, "I think so," he muttered. "I feel fine now. I am not sure what just happened. I think it was a dream, but it felt so real."

"You seemed quite distressed, Prince Farren. You were screaming and yelling aloud as if you were in danger. The natural energy around you was clearly disturbed. It was strange."

"What do you mean strange? Was there something attacking me? Is this some sort of Tellurian trick?"

"I do not think so. I have never seen anything like it. The disturbance seemed to be coming from you, not directed towards you. For a Magi, that would be common, but for a human it is strange." He reached out a canteen for Farren to drink. "It must have been a terrible nightmare."

"It was not pleasant," he thought out loud. It was not like anything he had ever experienced. *Or was it?* It was similar to the dream he had of his brother being attacked, but it was different. In what way it was different, he could not tell. "So, you think that *I* was disturbing the natural energy? Is that even possible?"

"Improbable, but not impossible," Kyte responded. Just before continuing, Kyte froze. Holding up a whispering finger, he alerted Farren to quiet.

"What is it?"

"The Tellurians are close, I can sense them." He reached for the sword at his side. "But, I do not know yet if they have discovered the barrier."

Farren's heart started to beat fast again. "What will happen if they do?"

"The barrier is not meant to keep things out. If they know that the barrier is here, they will easily be able to get past it."

"What do we do then?"

Without hesitation, Kyte said, "We fight."

He got to his feet and crept over to Kaleb, who was still sleeping. With a gentle shake Kaleb stirred awake. Kyte told him to be silent before Kaleb could even make a sound. "We have visitors," Kyte whispered.

Kaleb nodded his acknowledgement and struggled himself up to a sitting position.

Farren had collected his swords and bow and tiptoed over to them. Crouching in a huddle they discussed their plan.

"How do you feel, Kaleb? Can you fight?" Kyte questioned.

Farren turned in surprise. "What do you mean can he fight? He is lucky to be alive."

"I am fine, Farren," he reassured, as he painfully got to his feet. "I do not intend to be a burden."

"We do not even know yet if we will need to fight but, if we do, it is safer for all of us if he is not lying asleep on the ground."

Kaleb reached out a hand. "Farren, give me your bow. I may not be able to move around very quickly, but I can still shoot."

As they exchanged weapons, Kyte again held up a hand to hush them. Then he pulled the bow from his back and strung an arrow. Without as much as a rustle, a wolf walked its way out of the trees and into view. It sniffed around, apparently unaware of their existence. Kaleb slowly strung an arrow and kept it aimed at the approaching canine. The wolf continued to walk around the area, searching for an elusive scent that it could not seem to find.

Farren suddenly realized that the fire was still going and that the heat would easily give them away, but before he could jump forward and put it out, Kyte stopped him.

"It's too late," he whispered.

Stalking meticulously, the wolf made its way closer and closer to them. Luckily, there was little in their makeshift campsite for it to stumble upon, but the fire was still an issue. Oddly, even though it was only a few feet from the flames, it did not seem to notice it. Farren tensed when it walked within inches of his pack, but it turned and kept searching.

After a few more minutes of searching, the wolf turned and started to walk away. Farren let out a sigh. Just as it was about to disappear back into the Shroud it stopped and lifted up its head. Complete silence fell on the three as they waited to see what it was going to do.

"Behind," Kyte bellowed as he quickly spun around with his bow. He fired into the mist and they all heard a yelp as another wolf came skidding out of the mist towards them, an arrow pierced through its chest. As they all stared cautiously at the limp creature, it disintegrated and left only a pile of dirt.

Kyte turned back around, but the first wolf was now gone.

"Quickly, in a circle," ordered Kyte.

The three of them gathered in a defensive position and Kyte, sheathing his bow, drew his sword. Then they waited. For what seemed like ages, they stood crouched and ready for anything.

Kyte and Kaleb were alert, but calm, both having had experience in true battle situations. Farren's timorous presence was clear, though. He tried to hide his trembling, but the visions of the giant, black panther flashed into his mind. The viciousness of the creature terrified him and he was not sure if he could face something like that again.

After a nervous moment, they were alerted to a loud noise that shook the ground.

Kyte nimbly jumped upon the roots of a nearby tree. "Watch beneath you."

Nothing erupted from the ground, though. Instead, out of the mist, rumbled a group of unusual creatures. They were nearly double the height of a normal man and three times as wide, but their skin was gritty and brown. Like a giant ape, they swung their arms around violently and with brutal force. Kaleb quickly shot an arrow, which buried itself into the face of one of them. Dirt sprayed out from the wound and the arrow started to slowly sink farther into creature's body.

Kaleb's face distorted in a mix of shock and confusion.

"They are puppets," Kyte explained. "Non-living creatures made of earth and controlled by the Tellurians."

To prove his point, Kyte swung out his sword, sending a scythe of wind screaming through the air. It cut cleanly through the creature, causing the top half of its body to disintegrate to dirt and fall to the ground. A moment later, the dirt slowly started to creep its way up the legs of the creature and reformed itself. Once whole again, the creature continued its deliberate advance like nothing had happened.

"Then how do we kill them?"

"You cannot. You must kill the Tellurian controlling them." He toppled another with a burst of air. "I will hold them off, while you two search for the Tellurian."

Taken back by the casual assumption that he could do such a thing, Farren muttered, "B…. but, where?"

"I sensed a burst of natural energy in that direction just before the puppets appeared," he pointed. "It will need to be close in order to control them."

Kaleb was still calm and nodded his recognition, "Alright." As he turned to Farren, he sensed his trepidation. "Do not worry, Farren. We will be fine."

"Prince Farren, as long as the Tellurian is controlling these puppets, he will be unable to cast any more magic. It is just its teeth you must worry about."

Kaleb grabbed Farren by the arms and pulled him along. "Let's go." With a cringe of pain, Kaleb disappeared into the trees with Farren nervously following.

As they darted their way through the misty trees, it was hard for Farren to keep an eye on his surroundings. The roots and low growing plants were tripping him up as he kept his eyes fixated upwards. He looked to Kaleb, who was neatly moving his way through the rutted terrain, to try to feed from his confidence. No one had warned him of quite how different real combat would be.

Falling back to Farren's position, Kaleb whispered, "I hate to suggest this, Farren, but in my condition I am limited in my movement. I need you to take the lead. Try to flush the Tellurian out. I will cover you."

Mustering a bit of courage with a deep breath, Farren nodded.

Kaleb strung up an arrow. "Alright then."

They moved their way through the trees with Farren in the lead. His senses were attuned to every movement, sound and smell. He tried to block out the normal sounds of the Shroud, like the constant drone of insects, so all he heard was what was normally not there

He wasn't sure if it was the knowledge that Kaleb walked behind him, ready for anything, or just a sudden surge of adrenaline, but his anxiety and fear had almost disappeared. All he felt now was anticipation.

After a while, the sound of Kyte's battle with the earthen puppets was fading, easily swallowed up by the Shroud, and the sensation of isolation was setting in. There was no turning back now. Farren heard a rustle and caught a fleeting glimpse of a creature running past them off in the trees. His heart started to race.

Kaleb reassured, "Do not worry Farren, I am still here. Remember your training."

Farren's eyes darted back and forth, trying to catch any hint of movement again. Without warning, the ground just behind him began to shake and he quickly jumped to the side. The earth started to rise up.

"Quickly, Farren, we must run. It is a puppet."

Not pausing to argue, they both sped off in the direction where the animal had been heading.

Out of breath, Farren said "I thought that it couldn't cast anymore magic?"

"It is the same spell. The Tellurian must be diverting some of its magic to try to hold us off." Kaleb stumbled, but kept his balance. "We must find the creature quickly."

Almost like an epiphany, something flickered in Farren's mind. He skidded to a stop.

"What is it? Did you see it?" Kaleb asked.

What he sensed, Farren did not know, but something told him that he must trust whatever this feeling was. "This way," he said.

This time they did not slow, and they ran quickly through the rugged trees. Finally, they came to a small clearing in the trees and stopped.

"It is close."

"How do you know, Farren?"

Farren did not know how to explain it. It was a sensation in his mind, like when he finally recalled a fact or bit of information. With no way of explaining, he shrugged, "I just know."

As if to confirm his inexplicable sense, a vine shot up from the ground and snagged him around the leg.

By reflex, he tried to pull away, but the grip was tighter than he thought and he lost his balance and fell to the ground. Kaleb quickly fired an arrow, severing the vine, and Farren scrambled away.

Before Farren could even think about what had happened, vines started to shoot up all around him. Kaleb pulled back another arrow, but there was a chance he could hit Farren. Farren's movements were so erratic that he dared not fire. "Calm yourself Farren. Use your swords," he pressed.

It was like being caught in a net. The more Farren struggled the more the vines seemed to latch on. Panic was beginning to set in.

Kaleb raced towards him to try to free him, but fell when another vine grabbed him. He quickly pulled out a hand blade and cut himself free. Before he realized, the wolf bounded out of the mist and attacked him.

He put up his arms to defend himself, but the wolf pounced and took him to the ground. Kaleb tried to push the wolf away but he could not find the strength. The impact with the ground crushed the wound on his side and intense pain was coursing through his body. All he could do was hold the creature back enough to prevent its jaws from ripping through his flesh.

Farren managed to tilt his head to see Kaleb fighting to stay alive. He forced back a bit of his panic and battled to rip himself free. With a surge, he freed one of his arms and then started to cut away the vines. He got to his feet and started to run towards the pair struggling on the ground. Seeing Farren coming, the Tellurian shot a spike of earth out of the ground to try to stop him. It barely missed him, but sent Farren sprawling. The distraction gave Kaleb an opening. He pushed the Tellurian off of him and rolled to the side.

Slowly getting to their feet, Kaleb and Farren regrouped. Both out of breath and Kaleb hunched over in obvious pain, they watched the Tellurian closely. Blood started to seep through the bandages on Kaleb's side.

Noticing the stain, Farren asked, "Are you alright?"

"Not really," Kaleb forced out with an exhausted grin, chuckling painfully.

"It seems that Kyte was wrong. He is casting magic at will."

Kaleb took in a few deep breaths. "No, Kyte knows better than us. It must have stopped its other spell and focused on us. We were the more immediate threat."

"Of course it did," Farren groaned.

Ahead of them, the Tellurian got back to its feet and growled; fur stiff in anger. Suddenly, it started to transform. Its legs started to grow longer and thicker, its torso stretched, and its tail shrank. As it changed its form, its fur hardened, turned dark brown and its snout retreated back; changing to an indistinguishable lump amongst the rough skin. Still on all fours, it glowered up at them, eyes raging.

Without as much as a moment of hesitation, the Tellurian slammed its palm down on the ground. The ground below Farren and Kaleb rumbled aggressively and spikes erupted upwards. Sensing the shaking, they both dove out of the way. As Farren rolled to his feet, the Tellurian stormed towards him. Fearfully, Farren swung out with his sword, but it missed its target completely and the Tellurian kicked his foot around in a powerful arc, contacting Farren in the side. The blow nearly shattered his ribs, but instead he crumbled to the ground in a heap as he gasped for air.

Vines burst out of the ground and snared Farren's body, restricting his movement. Farren knelt motionless, anchored to the ground. His eyes were blank, devoid of life, and he barely seemed to breathe. The Tellurian stepped up in front of him.

"Farren!" Kaleb bellowed as he struggled to rise to his feet. The pain in his side was now entirely unbearable and he could hardly move. Even just standing was excruciating. His mind wanted him to surge forward and kill the retched creature, but his body would not allow it.

The Tellurian, about to cast magic on Kaleb, realized that he was no longer a threat and returned his attention to Farren. It bent down and grabbed one of Farren's dropped swords. He pressed the point up to Farren's chest.

The situation was more than Kaleb could bear. They were too far away. He would never make it. He could do nothing, and the pain of that thought was almost worse than the agonizing pain that was sweeping through his body.

The Tellurian grinned at Farren's expressionless face. It was not a pleasing kill for the Tellurian, Farren being defenseless and looking almost peaceful, but a kill was a kill. With a surge of strength it started to push the sword forward.

The Tellurian shrieked and gasped with shock. Looking down it saw the metal head of an arrow sticking out of its chest.

40

he crowd was big and growing bigger. The people pushed together, all trying
to gather close to the bottom of the stairs leading to the palace grounds. A
woman was yelling for her child as she weaved her way through. Unknown to her,
the boy had wormed his way to the front of the crowd and had a front row seat
for the Supreme Regis' speech. The young boy was obliviously pleased with his
situation, while the mother frantically searched around.

There was much speculation about what it was that the Regis was planning to
announce. No matter what the speculation was, though, everyone assumed that it
involved the Davati. There was no other reason for them to be here. *Was it for peace,
or for war?* They would soon find out.

Towards the back of the crowd, near the first set of buildings that lined the
main boulevard, stood Reme and Dash. Dash, as usual, was sitting with his back to
the façade of the small boutique, and Reme stood leaning against it, arms and legs
crossed, with an unimpressed look on his face.

"Oh, how the masses flock," Reme commented.

"Trying to sound all philosophical again?" snorted Dash.

Reme sighed and banged his head back slightly onto the building. "Just making
an observation, that's all. I bet you that half of those people don't even know why
they are standing there. They just saw a crowd, so they joined in."

"So, you are telling me that you wouldn't join in?"

"We're not in there right now are we?"

"That's just because we know what is going on. We are here for a reason. If we
were as oblivious, we would be out there too."

"So you claim, Dash. I, on the other hand, could not picture you at all in that
mob, unless of course there was a nice comfy chair in the middle of it."

Dash stared off in the distance and imagined it. "Touché."

The crowd noise began to amplify and Reme and Dash could hear shouts for
the Supreme Regis, and some fanatical women screaming, "Bishop," as well. Dash
got up and they wandered to the back of the pack.

Sure enough, the Supreme Regis could be seen making his way down the stairs.
A makeshift stage was erected at the bottom, so that he could speak out to the

crowd. It took a few minutes, but he finally reached the bottom. The crowd hushed as he walked up to the stage.

The people stared up at him in anticipation, while Reme and Dash just eyed him with scorn. Of course, the rest of the citizens still knew him as Bishop, and Reme knew this, but it still made him sick to see them all revere him as something he no longer was.

The Supreme Regis, or rather the Grand Master, looked out at the crowd for nearly a minute before finally speaking.

"Fellow Valorians." He paused for effect. "I know there is much that you all wish to know regarding many things, and I know that you all are concerned. I am here to shed light on what *has* occurred and what *is* to occur from this point on. First and foremost, the Davati ship that you all saw land on the outskirts of the city is here for one purpose and one purpose only; to aid us in the war that is to come."

The crowd began to stir, but continued to listen.

"As some of you may know, the Creed have taken action against us. They have attacked me and, thus, have attacked this city. The monster that is the Creed has been haunting us for centuries with their martial ways, therefore it has been decided that it is time to destroy that monster. The council has voted and we have declared war on the Creed. The Davati have agreed to assist us in that struggle, as I am sure you have noticed. With a united front, we will finally be able to defeat them and take revenge for those of you who have lost loved ones at their bloody hands."

A few excited shouts erupted from the crowd, but the Grand Master held up a hand to quiet them. Many more people exchanged worried glances.

"The thought of war may seem troubling to many, but you must imagine the result rather than the action. Imagine a world without fear or worry. We will not have to be scared of an attack or subject to taxes on trade. We will be free of their shadow."

Reme and Dash exchanged glances as more of the crowd began to cheer.

"He is quite the motivational speaker," grimaced Reme.

"It seems that way."

The Grand Master's voice boomed over the crowd as he continued. "I hope that you all will unite together to help us in this battle, because only when we are all fighting as one will we have the strength to win. Therefore, I ask all of you to summon the courage needed for this endeavor. It will be bloody but, if we persevere, it will be quick and the future can begin."

The noise of the crowd was now deafening and Reme and Dash backed away a bit so they could hear each other talk.

"This isn't good, Rem."

"You can say that again. The Commander isn't going to be happy to hear about this. We were in trouble as it was."

After a few minutes of cheering, the Grand Master finally calmed the crowd. The exaltations slowly turned to silence as everyone turned to wait for him to speak again. The Grand Master lowered his head in apparent solemnity, but Reme and Dash were not convinced by the expertly executed charade.

"It is difficult to speak to you about having courage and strength when I myself am finding it difficult in this troubling time." He took a breath to gather himself. "Just yesterday, my brother, Prince Farren, was kidnapped and, if not for the assistance of some Davati soldiers, my wife would have been as well."

A gasp spread across the crowd.

"What makes this even more disturbing is the identity of the kidnapper. It seems that my friend and loyal servant to the Regency, Commander Coal Lucer and his Gallants, have betrayed us all."

The crowd went silent. Reme and Dash quickly scampered back up to the crowd and listened intently.

"It is not evident yet what their motives are, but their actions are undeniable. They may not have allied with the Creed, but what they have done is also beyond simple forgiveness." The Grand Master continued with a firm voice. "Therefore, with much regret, I hereby declare Commander Coal Lucer, and anyone in his service, to be a traitor to Briva and its people. Despite his previous service to this sect, if he is caught he will be charged with that crime and punished to the fullest extent."

Reme was sure that he saw a tear streak down the Grand Master's face and the young teen seethed with anger. Reme had only met the real Bishop a few times, but Farren often talked about his older brother with love and affection. To fake that affection was like a slap in the face to Reme and those that knew and loved Farren and Bishop. Reme reached for his slingshot, but Dash stopped him.

"Not now," said Dash. "That is not why we are here. Coal will take care of him."

Reme reluctantly released his white-knuckled grip on the wooden weapon. They both turned to continue to listen to the imposter make his declaration.

"A reward will be given to anyone who captures him or has information about his whereabouts. This is a grave day in Valoria's history, but let us look towards the future. Let us look at today not as the day that the war began, but the day that the future peace was imagined."

As the Grand Master walked off the stage the crowd slowly started to clap. With apprehension, every citizen started to join in and soon the cheering was echoing down the street. Even as Reme and Dash sprinted back into the vacant city, they could hear it, as if it was chasing after them.

"So, you were right, Sir," sighed Kaine as he stood, leaning up against the wall, eyes peering out the second story window of the *Kaisers'* hideout. "It looks as though we are now outlaws and declared traitors to the people that we are trying to protect."

Coal paced back and forth in the middle of the room. Syd sat in an old beat-up chair in the corner, waiting for Coal to speak.

"It is not as if this is surprising. We were expecting such a move. The Tellurian is smart. Even though we have managed to kill some of his..." he thought for a moment, "...men, we are still much on the defensive. This has been more of a setback then a victory."

"Well then, what on Paks do we have to do to get a victory?" Syd blurted.

Kaine turned away from the window to Coal, but all Coal did was return his worried stare. It was hard for Coal to feel so helpless. He knew that this was a near impossible situation. Nevertheless, it was in his nature to succeed, or at least have an idea how to.

Reme came running up the wooden stairs, the sound of his footsteps preceding him. Dust from the rafters rained down from the vibrations. He instantly froze when he noticed the defeated aura suffocating the room.

"Uh... I found some bread for you," Reme muttered and he tossed a chunk to each one of them. "And here is some water," placing some on a table in the middle of the room. "It's the best we can do on short notice. We don't really keep a supply of food around here?"

"What do you and the others eat then?" Kaine asked.

"We all have families. We do most of the eating at home and if we want a snack while we're here, well... we just find one."

Coal questioned sternly, "Where did you get this bread, Reme?"

"You know, Commander, you are one of us now. You're on the run, so if you want food, or anything else, you may need to partake in some illicit activities. So, don't give me that high and mighty speech of yours, if you plan to eat," he shot back as he plunked down on a couch against the wall.

Syd took a big bite of his bread and started laughing. "He told you, Sir."

Coal looked down at his chunk and then over at Syd and Kaine, who both were eating. With a resigned smile, he took a big bite.

With a mouth full of bread, Syd complained, "I still can't believe that coward Leo refused to help us. You would think he would be dying for a good fight."

"And he will get it," remarked Coal. "They will be attacked no matter if they help us or not. It is just that he does not care what happens to us here. I was expecting really him to." After a swig of water, he added, "But, I was hoping."

Kaine wandered over from the window and sat on the couch next to Reme. "It was a long shot, Sir. At least now the Creed have been warned and they will be able to prepare themselves. They may be able to defeat the Tellurians now that they know what they are up against. Remember, the walls of Coroge have never been breached."

Coal still paced as he visualized the battle in his mind. "Yes, but they have never had to stand against the powers of the Magi. And the walls mean nothing to the Davati as well. This will not be a fight easily won by either side."

"The real question is, what do we do while this battle rages? What *can* we do?" Kaine wondered.

Ever since he had lived through the fight with Corvus, that was the one question that was lingering in Coal's mind. What could three men do against two armies and an unknown number of Magi? It was inconceivable, but an answer needed to be found. No matter what the result, he needed to try something.

"The Tellurian will not take any chance at defeat, so he will throw everything he has at the Creed. The final key for victory is this weapon. Without it, victory is not assured, that is why he needs it."

"Then we destroy the weapon?"

Coal nodded to Syd.

"Sir, the Tellurian has the lab very well guarded. He is not taking any chances. He will not let us just walk in through the front door," explained Kaine.

"Then we will just have to go in through the back." Coal turned to Reme.

Reme smiled and kicked himself up from a lounging position. "You need a way into the Science Society? I can't say we've spent much time in the State district…" Jumping to his feet he began pacing, mimicking Coal. "…but we'll find a safe route. Give me and my boys some time and we'll get you in and out without even a peep."

"How much time?"

Enjoying the idea that he was actively involved in the plan, Reme hummed excitedly as he deliberated in his head. "Two days. Two days and I will get you in that lab and you will finally find out what this weapon is."

41

The Grand Master's speech had created a virus of controversy that spread far and wide. Yes, there were many citizens who were imbued with a simmering energy and excitement for the upcoming war, but there were just as many who were equally disturbed. Most of these citizens were those who had lived through the previous war and knew what it was like.

The Grand Master may have thought that those people would have had a hatred for the Creed because of the war, and that they would be blindly willing to fight again. Their memories of sorrow and death far overwhelmed their feelings of revenge, though. It was those who had not experienced war, the *youth* of the city, who were willing subjects.

High Council Anton Grey was among the battle hardened and the dissenting. Since the vote in the council to initiate the war, Anton had lost all control. There were few councilmen that still looked at him as the Chief Council, but those who did had little courage to make suitable allies. Still, Anton was officially the Chief Council and he still controlled the chamber.

"Do you not see what The Supreme Regis is doing?" Anton yelled out to the other councilmen. He had lost the control of his natural, authoritative voice and was now reduced to simple shouting. "He has frightened and deceived us into initiating this war and now is trying to eliminate those who stand against him."

Now that he no longer held much control, many councilmen had the courage to respond and bellowed their opinions.

"Traitor!"

"Blasphemy!"

"Lies!"

Anton responded with similar anger. "You truly believe that Commander Lucer would betray his sect? Coal Lucer is the most honorable man I know. Far more honorable and courageous than any man in this room," pointing out across the chamber. "I would sooner believe my wife a traitor than he."

"Then, maybe we should bring *her* up here in chains."

Anton shot around and glared in the direction of the comment.

"How dare you," Anton growled.

From the middle of the chamber, Councilman Rieven rose up and turned out to the room. "Gentlemen! We may be on the brink of battle, but we are not savages. We are civilized men and should act as such. Now, I ask that you calm yourselves."

The councilmen hushed.

"That being said, Chief Council, you walk a dangerous line. These are trying times and I know that much has happened, but I would advise that you choose your words more carefully. Control your emotions."

Rieven passed him an insistent look of concern and Anton paused to consider it. Unfortunately, there was little left for Anton but his honor.

"I appreciate your concern, Councilman, but I will say what I must. Coal Lucer is an innocent man and the Supreme Regis has overstepped the laws of our people. He is no longer acting in the best interest of this sect, as he should."

"What are you saying Chief Council?" chimed in Councilman Balyct.

Just seeing Hayes' face seemed to bother Anton, but hearing his voice was far worse. What little self control he had left was keeping him from running up and strangling the man.

"What I am saying, Councilman..."

The doors at the top of the chamber burst open. Every councilman spun around. Half a dozen royal guards marched in, fully armed. Without hesitation, two of the guards strode down the stairs to the center stage, the other four waiting at the door. One stepped up to Anton; abstaining from performing the usual salute.

"Chief Council."

The informality of the encounter and the stern look of the soldier's face was not comforting to the Chief Council.

"What is it, soldier?"

"I have been ordered by the Supreme Regis himself to take you into custody."

Some of the councilmen near the stage started to whisper among themselves, the message being passed up the tiers. Anton turned his head in confusion and responded casually. "For what crime?"

"For suspicion of conspiracy against the Regency and collaboration with the traitor, Coal Lucer."

Anton scowled. *So, that is how he will silence me.*

"You cannot arrest me on suspicion alone, soldier."

As if rehearsed, the soldier responded, "I have been told to give you a choice, Chief Council. Either you come with me and stand trial for your alleged crimes, or you may step down from your position as Chief Council and relinquish your council seat. If you do that, then the Supreme Regis will forgive your momentary errors of judgment."

He knows I am no threat if I am not in the council. By allowing me to step down he removes a potential threat, but If I refuse, I will surely be killed. He has played this well.

"If that is the case, then you leave me no choice," he said regretfully.

Without a word he walked up to Councilman Rieven, removed his Chief Council's ring, and placed it in Denuke's hand. With an acknowledging nod he started to walk towards the stairs. The soldier reached for his arm but Anton held up a hand.

"No need, soldier. I would like to leave this chamber with at least a bit of my honor intact."

Straightening his uniform with a quick tug, he strode out of the chamber with his head held high, all councilmen silently watching in disbelief.

Unlike the cozy confines of the small study in his home, the Valorian Archives were grandiose by anyone's interpretation. It had been years since he had been in the extravagant library and Seno had forgotten how insignificant it made him feel.

The building itself was a tall cylinder. The outside was circled by pillars and gaudy statues, like most state buildings, but the inside was the magnificent part. It was constructed as a series of concentric rings, each stretching from the bottom floor to the very top. The rings were lined on either side with shelves that housed century's worth of texts, scrolls and every kind of historical work imaginable. On each level, a walkway was constructed around the rings so that patrons could access the shelves and each level was connected to the next by stairs. Archways were cut out of the rings at consistent intervals so that one could also access other rings on the same level. Along with the walkways, on various levels there were also tables, couches and chairs to sit and read whatever text you decided to choose. When looking at the complexity of the whole thing, it was a wonder that it worked so smoothly but, like most Valorian architecture, it worked surprisingly well considering its flamboyance.

Having been the Chief Historian of the Valorian Historical Society, Seno had essentially lived in this place for that period of his life. It did not seem as overwhelming at that time, but sometimes it takes an outside view to really understand something entirely.

He sat at one of the tables, the floor suspended out stories above the ground between two of the rings. The height did not bother him. He was far too engrossed in his search. Ever since the meeting with Kaine and Syd, he could not get one single thought out of his mind.

What is The Hand of the Almighty?

There was not a shred of information describing what this ancient weapon was in any piece of work that he had ever read. There were many references to the weapon and its name, but never did it describe what it was or what it did. In the past, he had pondered this mystery, but now that it had so much relevance to them, he could not let it go unsolved. As a man of history, Seno could not justify such an important piece of historical information being forgotten in time.

The giant stack of texts that sat on the far side of the table was proof enough of how long he had been sitting at that desk, frantically searching. He knew that there were no books in the archives that dealt specifically with the Magi Wars, or anything relating to the Magi, but there were plenty of records about other events during that time and there was a chance that something was mentioned about the weapon.

It was a long shot, but he had already combed his own library for any bit of information without success, so this was his last resort. Looking up at the sheer volume of history in the archive, he had to believe that there was *something*, however miniscule it might be.

His hair was even more disheveled than normal, as a result of a shower-less night and the constant grabbing of his head in frustration. A glass of pintare was sitting on the table, creating a small puddle of water; the ice cubes long melted. He fell back into his chair with a sigh and finished off the last gulp of his drink. "Poelis," he shouted.

A few moments later, a small, mousy looking man came hobbling around the corner, His arms were stuffed with books. It was extraordinary that the tiny, old man could carry that many texts but, then again, he had been doing it for many years. After a long life of working in the archives, he was thin and pale. What little hair he had left was gray and his skin wrinkled. Despite all that, he still had a youthful zeal, especially when it came to history.

"Yes, Sir?"

Holding up his empty glass, "I need another drink. Just one cube of ice this time."

Poelis dropped the new books down on the table, having to push over others to make room. "Of course, Sir."

Snatching up one of the new books, Seno started to flip through the pages. "Have you found that text yet, Poelis? The account by Alexander?"

"I am afraid not, Sir. I feel like I am getting close, though. It does not seem to be in its normal place."

"Could it have been taken?"

"Of course not, Sir. Texts are not allowed to be removed from the archives by anyone; not even the Supreme Regis. The exits are closely guarded. It is here. I just need to find it. In the meantime, these are other accounts written by The First and they may have something related to what you are looking for."

Poelis was the oldest of the archive Keepers and had been at the post for nearly sixty years. When Seno was Chief Historian, Poelis worked devotedly under him and did whatever he needed. If there was one person who knew the archives better then Seno, it was Poelis.

"I do not necessarily have the same confidence as you do in these texts, but I will take a look. More than likely I have already gone through them before. How long will it take you to find it?"

"Soon, Sir. I have many of the other Keepers searching as well. I am getting close. There are only a few small areas of the archives that keep texts as old as you are searching for. It is just a manner of time."

Seno pushed out his chair and achingly stood to his feet. His legs and back were far stiffer then he had realized. "Well, in that case, I will get the drink myself. I need to take a break anyway. You must focus on tracking down this text."

"Of course, Sir," Poelis said, with a bow. The old Keeper then turned and shuffled through the archway.

Seno smiled at the eager Poelis as he left, and then looked around at his capacious surroundings. He frowned.

"Oh great, which way do I go again? Poelis!" he shouted, but the miniature librarian was already out of sight. "Well this may take longer than expected. If I were a refreshing drink, where would I be?" he thought aloud.

Seno woke with a jump.

"Sir?" he heard in his drowsy stupor. "Sir, I have found it."

In front of him stood Poelis, holding out a small, leather-bound book in his wrinkled hands.

"Did I fall asleep?"

"It seems so, Sir."

Seno got his feet. "How long have I been asleep?"

"I am unsure, Sir. I do not know when it was you fell asleep." He handed the book to Seno. "But, it has been about five hours since I was last here."

"Oh," said Seno with a startle. "Well, I guess I needed the rest." Looking down at the text, he felt his energy returning. "This is it?"

"I am sure of it, Sir. It is The First's account of the Tellurian attack on Herous. Of course, he did not directly state that fact in the book, but it is the event in question. If what you are looking for is not in here, it will be nowhere."

As Seno opened it up and slowly flipped through the pages, his eyes widened. "Excellent. I believe you are right, you spectacular little man. If my assumptions are correct, this has to be it."

"I am happy for you, Sir. You always seem to have the correct assumptions. I am sure it is there."

Without looking up, Seno said, "Thank you Poelis, excellent work." He sat back down at the table and continued to flip through the pages.

"Sir?" muttered Poelis after a few silent moments.

"Oh, yes," Seno fumbled. "That is all. Go home and rest Poelis, you have done more than enough for today."

"Thank you, Sir." And he shuffled away.

Seno turned his attention back to the book. Eyes wide, as if he was absorbing the information directly through them, he read furiously.

It took several silent, unblinking hours, but finally a smile slowly stretched across the historian's face. As he continued to read, that smile quickly turned to a frown.

42

All of the cleaning and organizing, and all of the work that Alexia had done to make the lab into what she thought was a nice working atmosphere, was for naught. Since Datro had returned, the lab had gradually turned itself back into its chaotic former state. Papers were strewn about, beakers and tubes were smashed and broken, and spilled liquids stained the tables and floor.

Despite all of this, Alexia did not even seem to care. In fact, she did not even seem to notice. What she did notice were the splatters of blood painting the room and the body of a dead soldier lying limp on the table in the middle.

The man's wrists and ankles were bruised where straps had been tied to restrain his struggling. His knuckles and fingers were bleeding from where he banged and clawed them against the table, and his hair was drenched with sweat. Alexia removed the gag from his mouth, which was also stained red, and started to untie the remaining straps that held his head, chest and hips. She did all of this without a peep or a complaint and, after half a dozen other experiments, she did it without shedding a tear. She had become desensitized to the cries and pleas of each subject and the bloody images of their bodies after each failure. It was another day of work, just like any other.

After the body was free, she dragged it off the table and onto a cart sitting next to it. It was difficult work, but she had done it many times now, so she did it quickly. She took a moment to let out a breath and wipe the sweat from her forehead.

"Sir, are you prepared for the next test? Should I acquire another subject?"

Datro, who was working furiously at a table on the far side of the room, did not respond.

Used to his obliviousness, Alexia asked again, "Sir? Another subject?"

"Not yet, Alexia," he mumbled without turning. "Give me a moment." He continued to work for a few minutes, before finally turning to face her.

Unlike Alexia, Datro seemed entirely unscathed. Sure, he was his normal disheveled self, but that was not unusual. His hair was greasy, but undisturbed, and his lab coat was as white as the day he acquired it. Alexia was covered in blood and sweat, her hair was a complete mess, and her eyes bloodshot from lack of sleep.

Still, with what seemed like unrelenting energy, Datro spoke with such speed that Alexia's blurred thoughts could barely comprehend the words. "Did you not see it, Alexia; the moment just before he died? It was spectacular." He paused to wait for an answer, but she was still trying to decipher the words. "There was a flash in his eyes. I do believe he almost had it."

He spun around and fumbled through some papers and pulled one out. "The readings point to it as well. The temperature rose slightly around him and did you see the hair on his arms? It was standing on end. He was creating a charge of some kind."

"But, what does that mean, Sir? That is entirely different than the last subject. There has been no correlation at all between any of the reactions."

"Yes, I know. But it is something. It was hypothesized that the response could be different with each subject depending on the makeup of their internal structure. So, it does not matter if the reactions are different. What matters is the severity of the reaction. That was by far the strongest reaction yet."

"But, the result was the same, Sir. He still did not survive. It does not matter how great the severity of reaction is, or how close the similarities of previous reactions are, if the subject does not survive."

"Yes, but," he shot back as he held up a waiting finger. He grabbed another piece of paper and scurried over to her. "Take a look at this. He lasted twenty-three more seconds than the last subject. That is a much greater jump than the previous one. That man only lasted a few seconds longer than his predecessor. It was clear, as well, that this man was very close to surviving. His body calmed nearly ten seconds before he finally died. Surely you saw it."

He was becoming quite frantic and desperate, and Alexia was not sure why. They had been making steady process in the experiments and this last subject seemed quite promising, up until his demise. It was odd that Datro seemed so troubled.

"Of course, Sir. I too thought that it was going to be a success. It is a shame that he could not hold on a bit longer."

Alexia's heart cringed at the realization that she talked so calmly about a man dying, but that is where she had found herself these past days. She liked to believe that she was the same person she was before, but it was becoming harder and harder to.

"Exactly," he squawked. "If he could have just held on. I do not think that this final experiment's failure was a result of the formula at all. I believe it was a result of the man. I do not think that he had the heart for it, in a manner of speaking. After going over the results, I believe the formula is perfect."

"So, you say the issue was that particular man?"

"Yes. His inner structure was not susceptible to the change. His body rejected it. We need a subject who is more willing to conform to the change."

"In order for that to happen, Sir, we would most likely need to inform the subject of the details of the experiment. But, you said yourself that was not an option. The subject must be oblivious to the final result."

Datro scowled. "Yes, yes. I realize that is what I said."

"Then, do you propose that we inform the next subject?"

"Of course not," he barked. "I said that for a reason. They must not know. We cannot take the chance that they use the result for themselves. We must keep control over them as much as possible, and ignorance is the only way I know of at this point."

"But, Sir, if we do not get a result, then there will be no one to worry about controlling."

Datro pounded his fists down onto the table and shouted, "You don't think I know this?! Of course I realize. But there has to be another way." Again he started to pace the floor, dragging his fingers through his long, greasy hair.

"Well then, Sir, I will dispose of the body and request another subject," She turned and started to strap the body to the cart. "I will try to request that they be more willing, if there is such a distinguishable feature."

Her words clearly did not soothe him. "No. I told you that it would not work."

"But, Sir, we will need another subject no matter what we decide to do. The experiment is not complete."

"We cannot have another subject, Alexia." He said it like it was a giant weight lifted off his shoulders

"What do you mean?"

"The Supreme Regis is growing weary of our lack of results. He said that if we do not report a success and require another subject, then he will send down someone to monitor our work."

"But, how is that a problem? We can still get another subject. Surely this person will not be much of a hindrance."

"I cannot have it," he urged. "I will not allow *that thing* to control what I do."

Alexia was confused by his comment, but brushed it off as stress. "I understand your concern, Sir, but..." she paused. "We still need another subject."

It sounded like Datro almost growled in reaction, but then he calmed. "Yes, I know," he mumbled.

After a few quiet minutes he leaned forward and gripped the edge of the table, dropping his head. He let out a defeated sigh. "Prepare the table," he said. Alexia was confused. "I will need some time to prepare another solution, so you can dispose of the body as well."

"But, for what, Sir?"

When he looked up, Alexia was taken aback by his stare of determination. But she did notice a trace of concern as well.

He said anxiously, "Because I am going to take the solution myself."

43

For the past several days it was difficult for Farren to know if he was asleep or dreaming. Many times when he thought he was awake, he was not, and many times when he *was* awake, he wished that he wasn't. Everything just seemed to blur together. The one thing that was consistent, the one thing that did not seem to distinguish between real or a dream, was pain. Farren had felt more pain in the past few days than he had felt in his entire lifetime. Because of that fact, it made Farren assume that when he "awoke," he was neither awake nor dreaming. He was sure that he was dead.

Not only could he see nothing, he could also hear nothing. It was pitch dark and there was no sound, not even the constant buzz of insects or the whistling of wind. There was just him and nothing more. He also felt no pain. There was no pounding ache in his mind, no dull pressure in his chest, and no longing burn in his heart. For a moment he felt at ease, but then his thoughts reminded him that death was not a welcoming thing. There was much that he needed to do. For once, there were people that were depending on him. He could not afford to die.

And then he heard it; a peaceful, flowing sound. It was almost like the sound of waves out on the vast waters. It seemed to circle around him like a protective cocoon. And then he saw them; small specks of light far above him.

Stars?

When he tried to sit up he felt stiffness. It was not pain, but near his chest it was hard to move. He was delighted to feel something. It was evidence that he may still be alive. Forcing himself up with his arms, he took a deep breath. His eyes began to adjust and he noticed a flowing motion in the area around him. His surroundings seemed to sway with the sounds that he heard before.

"Where am I?" he whispered.

He turned suddenly when he heard a rustle and cringed when the stiffness in his chest spiked to a sharp pain.

"Farren?" a voice called. "Are you awake?"

A shadow pushed through the flowing curtain around him and approached.

When the figure kneeled down next to him, Farren smiled. "Kaleb, oh thank The Almighty."

"Are you alright?"

"Now I am," Farren sighed with relief. "When I woke up, I had no idea what was going on or where I was."

Kaleb settled down next to Farren. "I do not blame you. You were not in very good shape. You are lucky to be alive, in fact."

Farren tried to think back, but could not seem to remember. He knew that they were in the Shroud and why they were there. He remembered when the Tellurians attacked, but then there was nothing. "What happened?"

"Well, when the Tellurians attacked, we split up from Kyte," he started. "He stayed to fend off the Tellurian's puppets while we went after the Tellurian. Once we found the creature, it caught us off guard. My injury was too much for me to handle, so I went down quickly. After that, he targeted you." Kaleb paused. Farren could not see much, but he sensed Kaleb's tone switch. "I could do nothing but watch. If it was not for Kyte…"

"You should never have been in that situation in the first place," finished Kyte, as he emerged from the darkness. "I never should have let you two go off on your own."

"You never could have predicted that the Tellurian would focus on us instead of you," reassured Kaleb. "In the heat of the moment, I would have made the same call."

Kyte's normally serene and smooth voice was much more insistent and stern. "That is where you are wrong, young Kaleb. I should have seen it. It was almost certainly the creature's plan from the beginning."

"Nevertheless, Kyte, we should have been able to fight against it ourselves. Unfortunately, my wound was more serious then I had thought and it seems Farren is not ready for such a fight."

Farren hung his head. He knew Kaleb was right, but that did not mean that he was not troubled by the comment. A real battle was far more intense than he had imagined.

"Do not fret, Prince Farren. I would imagine that you are the only human alive that has fought a Magi in his first true battle. In fact, you are probably one of a handful that have fought a Magi at all and are still alive to tell the tale. It is not shameful to lose such a fight."

"I know," said Farren. But, he did not feel that good about it. He needed to be stronger. If he could not even defeat a single Tellurian, then how could he possibly expect to save Kara? Kaleb was able to fight off many of the creatures at once and Farren only seemed to be a hindrance.

Like every other thought that he had in the past few days, he pushed it aside. He needed to be in the present. He could not afford to think about what was. Looking around again and still seeing nothing, Farren asked "So, where are we?"

"We are in the Central Plain. We left immediately after the Tellurians attacked. There was no telling if there were more lurking in the mist, so we needed to distance ourselves. It does not seem like we have been followed."

"Why is it so dark? Should we not start a fire?"

"In the Central Plain any sort of light can be seen from very far off. It is not safe. If there is anything more following us, then we must take every precaution."

Farren crawled over and passed his fingers lightly through the tall grass, which he now realized was the source of the peaceful sway. "But, I thought that the grass in the Central Plain glowed orange in the dark."

Kaleb groaned disappointingly. "Yeah, that is what I thought, also, but apparently not this late in the season."

"The luminescence dies off in the cold," added Kyte. "The flowers are the ones that produce it, so when they die off, so does the glow. I did say that I was sorry, Young Kaleb."

"I was just a little disappointed, that's all. Don't blame yourself. There will be many other opportunities to come see it."

Kaleb's carefree attitude helped momentarily to cheer Farren up, but there was too much else on his mind for it to last long.

"It is so peaceful out here," said Farren.

"I know," noted Kaleb, "In a disturbing and mysterious kind of way, I suppose. Your mind can get lost in it just as easily as your body can."

Farren noticed the edges of Vala starting to peek up above the horizon and its light began to flow across the plain. He also noticed the eeriness of the miles of swaying grass and the intense silence that Kaleb alluded to, but there was still something serene about it. He definitely favored it to the chaos of the preceding days.

"What do we do now?" he asked.

"We continue on. Our quest does not end because someone is trying to stop it. You do not yet understand the importance of our goal, Prince Farren; what it means to the safety of the kingdom and the destruction of the Tellurians."

"That is because you have yet to tell us. What is it that we are looking for, Kyte? What will we find in the Forest of Rising Twilight?"

Reaching over, Kyte picked up Farren's blanket from the ground and spread it over top of him. "You will know soon enough, Prince Farren. But, for now, you must rest. Once we reach the Setting Plateau tomorrow it will be a difficult climb and you will need as much strength as you can muster."

Farren cocked his head in bewilderment. "But, I thought you said it would take days to travel across the Central Plains."

"On foot, yes, but stealth is no longer important. The Tellurians will continue to follow us. We must make all possible haste. We can no longer worry about being seen by others."

"What do you mean?"

Kaleb let out a little chuckle and, looking over at him, Kyte could not help but smile at the young man's excitement. "Tomorrow, Prince Farren, we will fly."

The short night's sleep was remarkably refreshing and Farren felt revived. It had only been a few hours, but it had been days since he had gotten any sort of sleep without interruption.

Now that Farren could see clearly, he looked around at the vast openness. When Kyte had warned him at the beginning of their journey that the Central Plain was a daunting place, he had not quite understood how that could be.

It was clear to him now. As he looked out, there was nothing. No matter what direction he looked in, he could see only grass. There were slight hills and waves in the expanse, but for the most part it was flat. He thought he could glimpse the faint outlines of mountains off towards the horizon in the west, but he could not be sure.

As he found his pack nearby and started to check the contents, he became aware, again, of the stiffness in his chest. He lifted up his shirt to reveal bandages wrapping his entire torso. He prodded them in various places and winced as he poked at his left side.

"I would not disturb the bandages, Prince Farren. Your wounds will heal much quicker if you leave them alone," said Kyte as he wandered up.

"How bad were my injuries?"

Kyte handed Farren his bow and arrows and smiled. "I think it best that you do not know. You are fine now. We cannot fret on what has happened. We must focus on what is ahead."

Kyte turned around and walked away before Farren could ask him anything else. Farren could still not remember much about what happened that night in the Shroud, but apparently it was much more severe than Kaleb had described. Kyte was right, though. He is alive and that is all that matters.

He tied up his pack and tossed it over his shoulder. He could move easily, but slowly. He tried to avoid any sudden movements. Hopefully, they would not run into any trouble for a few days. He walked up to Kaleb, who was already set to go and clearly anxious to continue.

"Are you ready for this, Farren?" he asked.

"I think so. You have flown before, Kaleb?"

"That is how we got here. Drek brought us here from the Shroud after the attack."

"Drek?"

"Drek is the name of Kyte's eagle." Kaleb responded. "Haven't you flown on him before? That is what Kyte has told me."

Farren remembered back to the day when he met Kyte; when the first Tellurian attacked him. "I have, but I just never knew his name. I was also unconscious, so I saw nothing. All I know is that I flew atop him."

They walked over to Kyte. "Are you two prepared?" Kyte asked.

They both nodded.

Kyte put his fingers to his mouth and whistled. The high pitched sound died off quickly in the openness. Just as it seemed as if nothing would happen, they heard a sharp screech and the light from the sun darkened. Farren and Kaleb turned to look towards the sound but they had to shade their eyes. The shadow continued to grow and finally they could feel beating gusts of wind hitting them. The shadow then lowered itself from the sun's line and the giant eagle's form emerged.

Drek looked, in all but size, like a typical eagle. His feathers were brown with flecks of white and black, his talons sharp and curved and his eyes a piercing yellow. But, of course, he was not a typical eagle. Each feather was the size of Farren's arm, each eye the size of his hand, and his talons were like large scythes. Despite the fact that both boys had seen Drek before, they still watched dumbfounded as he gracefully settled himself to the ground.

Kyte walked up and stroked Drek along his head. He mumbled something quietly to the magnificent bird and then turned to Farren and Kaleb. "He is ready for you."

Kyte hopped up onto Drek's back and settled himself at the base of his neck. Kaleb hurried over and stopped next to the gargantuan avian. He, too, expertly leapt up onto the feathery back with little effort. Then he turned and reached a hand out to help Farren.

Sitting in a row, they stretched the length of Drek's back, but he did not seem to strain at all under the load. Once all three were aboard, he lifted up, ready to go. Farren nearly fell off when Drek moved suddenly, but he felt a gentle push of air hold him up.

Kyte said, "Watch yourself, Prince Farren. I will keep you aboard, but try to hold on as much as you can yourself. Oh, and try not to pull too hard on his feathers. He does not like it."

Drek turned and looked at Farren as if to agree; his piercing gaze more than enough incentive for Farren to grip softly. Farren nervously smiled back.

"Hold on," warned Kyte.

Drek started to beat his wings slowly, but sped them up as he bent his legs and pushed from the ground. Kaleb let out a loud cheer as they lifted from the ground and began to rise. During each wing beat, Farren felt a weightless sensation that turned in his stomach. Once they got far enough from the ground, Drek flapped his massive wings even harder and sped forward.

Once the rising stopped and the flight became smoother, Farren allowed himself to breath. From ground level, the vastness of the plains was spectacular but, from above, it was indescribable. Everything blurred together and even the flow of the grass in the breeze was not visible from that height. The plain seemed small, yet he still could not see the end of it.

Kaleb shouted back to him, "Pretty amazing, huh?"

Farren just smiled. "Yes," he said softly. It was the only response needed. He released his hands completely and leaned back, spreading his arms out into the oncoming air. Kaleb smiled at him, happy to see his friend enjoying himself. Farren had not truly smiled since they left on their journey.

"Do not get too excited, Prince Farren. We have a long journey. You should sit back and rest," suggested Kyte.

Farren nodded in acknowledgement, but then looked down at the small area atop Drek's back. "Um, exactly how am I supposed to do that?"

44

I t was night, so it was a presumed fact that Seduke would be alive and kicking. In fact, it was more than presumed, it was like a law of the land. Despite all of the enticing pleasures that he could have been enjoying, Anton Grey just sat quietly at the bar of one of the older, upper-class taverns, drinking a Herousian Ale. He had come to Seduke that night with the intention of trying to forget his worries, but once he arrived he lost interest. It was not that he found the more risqué activities in Seduke to be uncouth or demeaning -he had partaken plenty in his youth- but after so many years of abstaining from them, it just seemed a bit odd to even think about it.

It had been a few days since his dismissal from the council and he had spent much of it in a state of depression. It was hard for him to accept that he had fallen so far, but the accumulation of events that led up to that point was more than enough for him to rethink his position in the kingdom.

It had been some time since he had really sat down and thought about what had happened over the past several decades during which he held his seat on the council. There had been a war, an uneasy peace, and now the peace had shattered as war was coming again. It was a cycle that seemed incapable of being broken.

He thought about many things. Oddly enough, it seemed that the alcohol was, in fact, enhancing his thoughts. Or, maybe it was that it was making his thoughts more focused; helping drown out the commotion around him. Either way, his thoughts continued to circulate and consume him.

He gestured to the barkeep, who brought Anton another ale. After taking a big swig, he let out a sigh and slumped back into the stool.

"Oh, how the mighty have fallen," said a voice from behind him. Anton spun awkwardly around on his stool and spotted Seno Pierson standing a few feet away. "You look awful, Grey. Retirement does not suit you," added Seno.

"What are you doing here, Pierson? The hostesses are further down the street. You should know that by now," he grumbled.

"Eloquent as always I see, Anton," Pierson quipped back, as he settled into the stool next to Anton. Seno only needed to make eye contact with the barkeep and the man started preparing him his usual drink.

"I thought I might find you down here. I have heard rumors about the council meeting the other day. I was, at first, skeptical, but I now seem to have my proof."

"So then, you have come to gloat in my shame, is it? I seem to remember some choice words that you used towards me when I handed you your resignation, so it is not unexpected." He took another big gulp, then leaned back. "Well then, let me have it."

"Please, Anton, what do you take me for, a child? I am many things, but that is not one of them." The barkeep dropped off his drink and he gently stirred it. "We both know that politics was never my strong-suit. I like to think that it was all for the best, really."

Anton looked at him with a puzzled face, almost as if he could not believe what he was hearing. Seno just chuckled.

"You seem a bit disappointed, Anton. Would you prefer that I start barking obscenities and pounding my fists? Or maybe I should laugh haughtily in your face for several minutes."

Shaking off his surprise, Anton said, "Of course not, Seno. It is just…" He decided to refrain from the comment. "I am sorry, Seno. I presumed too much it seems."

Seno gave him a hard pat on the back. "Do not worry yourself, Anton. It is all in the past. I am sorry, as well, about what has happened. Despite our differences, I always believed there was none better for the position."

He held up his glass for a toast.

Anton, hesitating, tapped his glass. "Well, thank you, Seno. I have begun doubting that myself lately."

"These are difficult times, Anton. Do not judge yourself based solely on what has happened now. You are up against many, with few to assist you. Not many would be able to succeed in such a position."

"I always believed that I was one of those few that could succeed."

"And you are, Anton. As I said, these are difficult times. They are even worse than *you* know."

Anton's sharpness began to return to him. "You were always one to make cryptic statements and confuse with words. I never did like it. If you have something to say, just say it, Seno. What is it that I do not know?"

"There are many things that you do not know, Anton. There are many things that nobody knows these days and they are happening right under our very noses."

Before Anton could respond, Seno stopped him. He nodded towards a table in the back of the tavern and they both walked over to it.

"Now you have me curious. Discretion was never one of your admirable traits. Tell me now, what is it I do not know?" pressed Anton.

"Have you had contact with Commander Lucer lately? I ask only because you spoke so fervently in his favor in council."

"We met..." pausing as he tried to remember. "...A few days before the vote in the council. He came to me to ask for assistance in trying to quell the growing support towards the war." A thought came to him. "In fact, I do remember him being especially vague with his reasons. He would not tell me why, despite the fact that he claimed that he trusted me."

"So, I was right. He came to see you, but did not divulge everything. He was probably just being as cautious as possible. You see, Anton, and I am sure you have surmised this yourself, Coal is at the center of all of this."

"Of course. That is obvious, Seno. What I still do not know is, what is at the center, who is there with him, and why?"

Seno smiled and pointed at him. "That is the important question, Anton. What is most vital is not Coal, but what he faces. When Coal's men came to me, their foe was just an apparition, but now it is more than real."

"I do not mean to sound rude, Seno, but why would they come to you? You no longer hold any office, or have any real power."

Seno almost broke out laughing. "I was as surprised as you are when it happened. But, there is one thing that I still have that no one else does, and that is knowledge," pointing to his forehead. "You see, Anton, we are up against a foe that we have seen before, but have long forgotten."

"Stop with the word games, Seno, and just let it out, would you?" Anton shouted.

The barkeep and the other patrons all turned at the commotion. Seno waived away their looks.

"Sorry. Force of habit I suppose. I do love a little build up before the climax, if you know what I mean."

Anton just shook his head. "Just get on with it, Seno."

"Alright then. I suppose you realize that Bishop and Coal have had a bit of a falling out, as it were?"

Anton nodded. "I would say, a bit, is a little understated. Bishop has changed his views so drastically, it is like he is a different man."

"That is because he is, Anton."

Anton just looked at Seno, confused.

"Do you remember the fated trip to Coroge? What am I saying? Of course you do. You were there when he left. Well, Anton..." He looked around to make sure nobody was listening. "...the Bishop that left Valoria was not the same one that returned to us. Our Supreme Regis is an imposter, and a very inconvenient imposter at that."

Anton leaned in close to the table and lowered his voice. "You are telling me, Seno, that Bishop is not Bishop?" Seno nodded. "That is ridiculous. I have seen him myself; heard him. He is the same man, I am sure of it."

"You are led to believe that, yes. This is no ordinary imposter. That is where I enter the story. You see, when Coal discovered Bishop was not himself, he also discovered something even more disturbing. Coal needed to know who this imposter was and what his motives were."

"Why would he come to you, Seno?

"Coal came to me because I am an expert on all ancient things. I am a man of history. He came to me because this imposter is one of an ancient foe; a foe who many believe to have never existed at all. I am speaking, Anton, quite ambiguously, of the Tellurians."

Anton, who had unknowingly been inching his way to the end of his seat as Seno spoke, slumped back into his chair. "You cannot be serious, Seno. That is absurd. And for a second there I was beginning to take you seriously. The Tellurians do not exist, they are legend."

"Don't be a fool, Anton. Of course they exist. The Magi controlled this land long before we took over and messed it up. They are far from legend."

"Messed it up you say?" Anton said; a bit perturbed.

"You do not know what this world once was. It was far more beautiful when magic flowed freely and the Magi ruled. Paks is a blemished stone compared to the emerald it was."

"I do not need a history lesson, Seno. I know the stories."

"I would not lie to you about something like this, Anton. If you do not trust me, then trust Coal. All I know, I know from him."

Anton sighed and shook his head. Seno just waited as Anton contemplated what he had just been told. It was not in Anton's character to believe in fairy tales and wild stories, but there was something about what Seno was telling him that seemed to make sense. There was a part of him that knew that it was true.

"Let us say, Seno, that I do believe you." He paused. "Why is it you are telling me this? Why now?"

"Because, I need your help, Anton."

"What could I ever do to help, especially now?"

"When I met with Coal's men we discovered that the Tellurians were after something here. They are not just here to control our forces and destroy Coroge, but also to steal a weapon from us."

"What sort of weapon do we have that they could want? I have read many Paksian histories, as well, and I have not heard of such a weapon. Nor do we have any sort of weapon now worth stealing. The Davati airships are a possibility, but they would have attacked Fera then, not us."

"That is because we do not know that we have it. It is something that was developed back during the Magi Wars, but never completed. In fact, the Tellurians tried to steal it once before and failed."

"What is it then? Get on with it."

"For a long time, nobody knew. It was a complete mystery. I had never found anything that ever described what it was, only that the Tellurians wanted it."

"But, you have discovered the secret now. You know what it is?"

Seno smiled. "It took me ages, but I finally found it. I had always looked directly for talk of the weapon, but found nothing. Then I realized that was the wrong strategy. I would need to look for consequences of the weapon; things that happened around it or because of it. Any direct information was destroyed, but if you could piece together little bits from here and there you could come up with the whole picture."

"Get on with it, Seno. I do not have all day," groaned Anton.

"The details are tedious. The real issue now is that Coal still does not know, so I need to inform him. It is vital that he knows, because if not, he will be in for a rude surprise."

Anton then realized what his role was supposed to be. "And you think that I know where he is?"

"Surely you must know something, Anton. You know everything that happens in this city."

"I *did* know everything, Seno. I was only as powerful as my position. Without my seat, I know nothing. Besides, if Coal does not want to be found, you will not find him."

For a moment, Seno was frozen in disbelief, then he sunk into his seat. He was sure that Anton would be able to help him. Now, he was not sure what he could do. There was no one else that he could trust. The secret was finally in his grasp, after decades of searching, but he had no way to use it. If he could not find a way to get this information to Coal, the Commander would be in great peril.

A small group of men at a table on the far side of the room cheered as a young woman strode into the bar. They shouted her name in unison. She laughed, blushing slightly, before sitting down with them. The group attracted some annoyed glares from other patrons. Anton glanced over blankly in reaction to the racket, but he was in deep thought, so he did not really notice them. He turned back to Seno with an enlightened look.

Anton thought out loud, "You said that this information needs to be passed on to Coal, but there is no way to find him. If the information cannot be passed on to him, we need to pass it on to someone else who can use it. It occurs to me, Seno, that in a situation like this, there are few that you can trust because it is impossible to know who is on each side, or even what the sides are."

"You could say that, sure."

"But sometimes, the simplest solution in a situation like this, is the one that you would never think of in a normal circumstance."

Seno perked up. "Quit trying to be cryptic, Anton, and get on with it."

"In this situation, the only one we can now trust, is the one that our foe aims to destroy. This information would be quite useful to them as well."

"You don't mean...?"

"Of course. I believe, Seno, that we need to go to Coroge."

45

It was a spectacular day for the late season in Paks. The sun was out and only a few clouds dotted the clear sky. The temperature was still crisp and cool, but the sun did add a touch of warmth. Despite all of this, Farren was huddled in layers of clothes and blankets as he rested his eyes atop the feathery back of the giant eagle, Drek.

High in the sky and traveling fast, they felt the full force of the chilling wind buffeting against their bodies. With all of the layers, though, Farren was able to keep away the cold enough to catch a few hours of sleep. He slept hunched over and his head resting on his pack in front of him with no room to stretch out. He cared little how the sleep came these days, as long as he slept.

Kaleb was awake, after having slept for a short time as well. Because of the clear day, he could see out for miles below him and smiled at the breathtaking views. Looking behind them, all he could see was yellow and orange grassland but, when he turned forward, he saw shapes on the horizon.

"Kyte," he said. "What is that ahead of us?"

"That is the Setting Plateau, Young Kaleb. It is still some distance off, so you have time to rest and I suggest you do so. We will be going on foot once we reach it."

Kaleb squinted his eyes to try to get a better look, but it was still just a brown smudge on the horizon. "It looks steep. Will it be a tough climb? I have never climbed a mountain before."

"It will challenge you, yes, but the climb itself is not what makes it difficult. If the plateau does not feel as though you are worthy of reaching its summit, it will test you. You will not reach the top unless the plateau wants you to," explained Kyte.

"What do you mean? How could a mountain think or desire something?"

"It is not the mountain itself. There is strong and ancient magic at work there. I do not understand it completely myself. I have only heard stories but, from what I know, I believe that it will allow us passage."

Kaleb did not look reassured. "If you do not understand it, how could you know for sure it would let us through?"

"Because we have an unselfish goal; one that requires great need. We will still be tested, you can be sure of that but, ultimately, it will allow us through."

Kyte looked back at him and gave him an encouraging smile. Kaleb nodded, then looked back out at the horizon.

"Rest, Young Kaleb. Our journey is just beginning."

Farren woke suddenly and found himself wanting to fall backwards. It took him a moment to remember that he was on top of a giant eagle. Then, that falling feeling turned to panic. His arms began to flail as he tried to regain balance, but it did not help. His body suddenly stopped. It still felt like he was going to fall, but he did not.

"Hold on, Prince Farren," Kyte shouted from ahead of him. He had used his magic to corral Farren to safety.

Drek's wings started to beat rapidly, slowing their motion. Farren's stomach felt like it rose into his throat when they decelerated quickly. He then noticed that they were very close to the ground.

Once they slowed, they started to descend and Farren was able to relax. He regained his balance and leaned forward as much as possible, clinging to Drek's back strongly.

He could hear Kaleb laughing ahead of him and assumed it was directed at him, but he did not care. He just wanted to be on the ground again. A few moments later, he felt the sensation of solid ground as Drek's talons touched down. The beating of his wings slowed, then came to a stop. The giant creature tucked them neatly to his side and stood still.

Kyte immediately and effortlessly hopped down to the ground. Kaleb inched his way to the edge and then jumped. Farren took a deep breath and started to shimmy his way to the side as well, but then was reluctant to jump. After a few seconds, Drek gave him a nudge with a little hop and he slid off. When he hit the ground, he immediately fell to a sitting position with a grunt.

Kaleb chuckled. "Very graceful."

"Oh, quiet, will you?" As he got to his feet, he felt the stiffness in his legs from sitting in that odd position for so long, so he stretched them out.

Kyte walked up to Drek, removed their packs and patted the magnificent beast on the side. Drek skipped forward a few steps and launched himself back into the sky. It took him only a few seconds to be almost completely out of sight.

"Where does he go?" asked Kaleb.

"Wherever he desires," responded Kyte. "He is a free beast of Paks, so he does what he wants. Just like he helps me, because it is what he wants."

Kyte handed the two boys their packs. Farren continued to try to loosen up his legs. The bandages around his chest still made his motion stiff, but he was feeling much better. He seemed reenergized from the short and awkward rest.

He looked up at the plateau ahead of them. It was high. He could see the top, but could not see anything that was atop it. The climb did not seem steep, despite the numerous vertical cliffs. There were many paths that showed a nice route. The face stretched for miles in each direction and it was blanketed with vegetation, but nothing very large. It was mostly grasses, bushes and sparse patches of scraggly trees. Like the Central Plain, most everything had turned brilliant yellow and orange in the fall season. It was remarkable that such a large formation could erupt from the flatness of the Central Plain. Kyte walked up to Farren and rested his hand on his shoulder. "How do you feel, Prince Farren? Do you think that you can make the climb?"

"I feel great, Kyte. That is not the cause of my apprehension." He looked back at the plateau with a worried expression. "I have never done this sort of thing before. I barely have left the city at all. I am not sure if I will make it."

"You underestimate yourself. This is a battle, not against a foe, but rather against yourself. You have a strong resolve and a powerful spirit. That can overcome any injury." He put his hand to Farren's wound and started to circulate energy through it. With a bit of surprise he said, "You are recovering remarkably fast, Prince Farren. Your internal circulations have returned to normal, and your bones have even started to mend themselves. Remarkable."

Farren brightened. "I have always healed quickly," he chuckled as he remembered back. "Even when I was younger."

"Well then, you will be fine." Kyte turned back to the rocky plateau. "Once we enter the plateau we will not have to worry about any attacks. The Tellurians will be unable to follow us. The only thing we need to focus on is finding our way."

"How will we get to the top? Is there a special route we must take?" asked Kaleb.

Pointing up at the hillside, he said, "There are many ways to reach the top, each with its own dangers and tests. Take, for instance, that cliff. It stretches vertically from the base to the peak. It is the shortest route, but undoubtedly the toughest. There are much gentler paths, but they are much longer and can disorient you."

Farren scanned the hillside and examined all the different routes that he could see. None of them seemed to be an easy course.

"Then, what do we decide?" he asked. "Do we pick a route that falls somewhere in between those two?"

"Excellent deduction, Prince Farren. In our current conditions, that would be the logical choice. We desire to reach the top quickly, but are unable to take the most strenuous route. But, do not think that the middle path will be the easiest. Each path has its own tests."

"Why is it we cannot just fly to the top?" questioned Kaleb. "Drek could get us up there in no time."

Kyte started to walk forward. After a few steps he slowed, putting his hand out in front of him, trying to feel for something.

He let out a small burst of air from his hand and it hit an invisible barrier. The barrier rippled as the wind hit it. "Because there is magic that prevents it. To get to the top you must make the effort."

The ripple continued outward across the barrier. Both Farren and Kaleb watched, dumbstruck at the immensity of the magical field.

"Does it cover the entire plateau?

"Yes. There are hundreds of barriers and enchantments that exist on the plateau and the forest above. You will not be able to detect any of them yourselves, but you may be able to see their effects." Kaleb stepped forward and put his hand up to the barrier. It passed cleanly through, without as much as a wrinkle. "Only magic of the same type can reveal the barrier but, even then, only the one that cast it can remove it completely."

"Amazing," Kaleb grinned.

"We must get going. We need to get as far as possible today and find a nice spot to camp before night comes. If we do not make it far today, then we will never reach the forest by nightfall tomorrow."

Kyte walked through the barrier and Kaleb quickly followed. Farren tossed his pack over his shoulder and started to trail behind. He had a renewed spirit and energy, but his confidence still wavered. The two fights against the Tellurians were weighing on his mind and he felt unsure that he could rid himself of them completely. He knew, though, that he needed to stay the path. He did not have the luxury of slackening in his resolve. Forward, was his only direction.

As he neared where he had seen the barrier, he slowed down. The power of the magic that had to have been put into the barrier baffled him. Apprehensively, he reached out his hand, extending his finger. Suddenly, he felt a cold rush and a tiny ripple flowed out from his fingertip.

46

Alexia was what one would consider an archetypical alchemist. She enjoyed research and experimentation more than the typical female activities for her age. Because of her attentiveness to her research, she was not concerned with relationships and rarely made any effort to fix herself up, thus men did not even have an opportunity to see the hidden cuteness under her scraggly hair and glasses.

She spent most of her free time reading and thinking about how much she wanted to be back in her lab working, so she had few friends. She had been taught and trained by some of the greatest thinkers in all of Briva.

At one time, she was one of many assistants that worked for Datro, but as the years passed, the number dwindled as the Regency put less and less significance on the projects that Datro was working on. She enjoyed the position, because it allowed her to work on just about anything she wanted, with very few restrictions. Datro encouraged her and the other assistants to think creatively and then follow through with it.

Then, one day everything began to change. Datro started a new experiment; one that he insisted was of the utmost importance. After some time, he forced the other assistants to focus their efforts on his projects and leave their own ideas behind. He started to become aggressive and ill tempered. His fanaticism towards the project led to many of his assistants being fired or leaving for fear of him.

Alexia, for so long, contemplated the change that occurred in Datro and what could have caused it. At one time, she had idolized him for his genius and drive, but now she feared him for it. She had never imagined him as a killer, but now, as she stood next to him, she could see it clearly. His eyes were burning with hatred and, if it were not for the straps that gripped him to the table, she was sure he would have jumped up and strangled her.

"Do it, Alexia," he screeched. His chest heaved under the pressure of his rage.

"Sir, I do not think…"

"I do not care what you think. You are not paid to second guess me, you are paid to obey me. This is how it must be."

Alexia was on the verge of tears, but her emotions were so dulled over the past days, that no tears came. Her mouth moved as she attempted to speak, but only brief, incoherent sounds eked out.

She finally managed to blurt out, "We could go to the Regis again and request more subjects. You do not need to do this."

Datro tried to calm himself, but the result was like a kettle trying to hold in its steam. "Listen to me," he seethed. "That is not possible. You do not understand what is happening. He will not allow it and he will surely kill me if I do not have results."

"That cannot be true. Supreme Bishop is a nice man. I have seen him."

"You do not know what he is now. You just do not understand. He is the reason why this whole thing started and he will not allow it to fail."

"Then let's just take some more time to make sure that the solution is perfect."

Datro sprung from the table, but was jerked immediately back by the restraints. Alexia jumped back in fright and nearly dropped the vial of solution in her hand. Datro growled, glaring at the bonds that held him.

He insisted strongly, "This must be it. This is all I have left. I will not let that thing control me. This was always *my* research, so I will complete it my own way. This is the reason why you are still here; this moment."

"You mean you have only kept me around this whole time so that one day I would give you the solution?"

"Did you think that you were here because I valued your assistance? Don't be naïve. I could have done everything myself." Datro now just stared up at her as if trying to force her towards him with his mind.

She took a deep breath.

"Alright, Sir," she said as she stepped forward. "But, I just want to make sure, if anything does happen to you, that you do not think me responsible. I do not want to give this to you."

"I do not care what you want or think, Alexia. I never have. Just give me the damn solution."

That was enough for her to wipe away any concern. If he did not care enough to forgive her, then she would not need to care about any unwelcome regret.

Datro, noticing her final acceptance, smiled and leaned back on to the table. "Alright, let us get on with it then."

Alexia let out another deep breath in a final release of uncertainty. She then reached down and strapped Datro's head down to the table to make sure his entire body was secure.

"Just remember, Sir..."

"I know what I am doing. Just get on with it."

She leaned forward and put the vial up to his lips. Carefully, she started to pour the minty white liquid into his mouth, careful not to pour too fast and cause him to choke. When the solution was gone, she wiped away the small bit that dripped down his face and stepped back.

Hesitantly, Datro swallowed and then tensely stared up at the ceiling.

For what seemed like ages, nothing happened. The room was so silent, that even the flicker of the glow lights seemed to make faint sounds. Alexia just waited for what she assumed would be another painful and excruciating death. Then, it finally started. Datro felt his body begin to warm and sweat started to bead on his forehead. Instinctively, he tensed up his muscles, as if waiting for an impact. His heart started to race and his blood now felt like it was about to boil. He did what he could do to prevent himself from convulsing, but his body shook violently. The veins in his arms and legs bulged out as he struggled against the restraints.

His body continued to heat up, but he could not understand where all of that energy came from. It was almost like he was drawing it from his surroundings. Part of him was sure that at any moment he would burst into flames. He had contained any screams up till this point, replacing them with pain filled groans, but soon one would escape. Just when he felt like he could no longer endure the pain, he felt a sensation like that of a cool breeze flow through him. The feeling made him immediately relax.

Alexia noticed his release and her eyes grew with concern. She had seen this moment before. She jumped up to the table.

"Sir?"

His eyes just stared blankly and unblinking up at the ceiling. He still breathed, but nothing else. She placed her ear to his chest to listen to his heart, but it beat normally. He was now slightly cold to the touch, but otherwise seemed perfectly fine.

As she continued to examine him, she noticed a flicker out of the corner of her eye and turned. She was not sure, but it seemed as though the light from the glow lights was fading. Assuming it was just her imagination, she turned back to her work. Then it became obvious. The light in the room was clearly dimming for no discernible reason. As the light faded more, she noticed a faint glow coming from Datro's body.

Is he absorbing the light? she thought in shock.

Alexia raced around to find a candle, which she lit, but somehow when the flame appeared it instantly dimmed as well. The room was becoming so dark now that she could barely find her way around. As the room became darker, Datro glowed brighter. Actually, it was not so much that his body glowed, but that there was a curtain of light that surrounded him.

She stared at it in awe. Then the light began to recede, flowing directly into Datro's body itself. As it did, Datro's body began to shake again. Alexia put her hands to his chest to try to feel what has happening inside of him. Soon though, all the light in the room was gone and she could see nothing. His shaking continued to intensify and her concern grew.

Backing away, she bumped into the table behind her and felt a slight warmth touch her back. It was the candle. Incredibly, the flame was still present, but it gave off no light. The warmth gave her reassurance, so she turned around and reached out her hand to move it closer but, as she did, an intensely bright flash erupted from behind her.

She quickly turned, but had to cover her eyes. In that instant, she could see the silhouette of Datro's body lying at the center of the flash. Then the blast hit her. A concussive force erupted outwards from Datro and threw her back. Everything in the room flew backwards into the walls and Alexia struck the table behind her. She fell to the floor amidst the commotion. Glass shattered, wood splintered and a wave of heat hit her face.

When she went to the ground, her head struck the floor hard and her vision blacked out for a moment. It came back, but only in blurry images. She heard the sound of shelves crashing to the ground and papers fluttering around in the air. Try as she might, she could not move. A sharp pain shot through her neck. She lay there, motionless and helpless. On the far side of the room she could see an orange glow growing on the floor amidst the rubble.

Fire!

The sight of it caused her panic and, again, she tried to move. She could not even roll to her side. She could move her arms and legs slightly, but could not force herself up. She had lost all strength. With no other options, she started to scream.

"Help. Help! Sir?! Are you there?" she pleaded.

Alexia listened for a response and when nothing came, her heart sank. But, then she heard the sound of feet hitting the floor. She managed to turn her head and saw the blurred image of legs standing in the middle of the room.

"Sir?" There was no answer. "Sir is that you?" With what little strength she had, she managed to roll onto her side and look up at the body. It was Datro, she was sure. His dark, wavy hair was distinctive even with her blurred vision. He just stood there, looking down at himself.

"Sir," she again pleaded. He finally looked down at her. "Help me, Sir. I cannot move."

Datro walked up to her and bent down to her level. He looked her over without saying a word. Finally, he said coldly, "Do you remember what I told you, Alexia?" She did not know how to respond. "You have done well, but now you are no longer needed."

She again began to panic. "Sir, wait. Help me, please."

Glass crunched under Datro's feet as he walked away and out of the room, not even bothering to look back. Tears began to flow from Alexia's eyes; tears that had been absent for so long. There was no point in yelling again. She knew that he would not return. She was now alone. She was always alone.

Letting her arms go, she rested back onto the ground. She could never fathom why she stayed with Datro, even though she always knew that he did not really care about her, or her work. Now, she finally knew why. He was the only one. Even though he was so cruel to her, he was all that she had. The orange glow continued to grow on the far side of the room and she could feel the heat start to hit her face as she finally closed her eyes.

The night felt just the same as last time. They only hoped that the results of the night would not be. It was clear and not a cloud in the sky. The sun was set, but some light still stretched upwards, giving the heavens a yellowish-pink hue near the horizon. The state district was deserted, as always at this time of night, and Coal, Kaine and Syd were happy for it.

They slipped their way through the back alleys, making little more than a rustle as their cloaks fluttered behind them. Coal led the way, with Kaine and then Syd bringing up the rear. Each carried their usual lot of armaments. Coal had his halmon and kidon, Kaine had his single-edged feryl and bow, and Syd carried his massive rangon blade on his back. A smaller blade was sheathed at his side in case the rangon proved too much for his broken arm. Coal had insisted upon it, despite Syd's assertion that he could handle the pain.

All three were equally energetic about finally getting a chance to move. They had been confined to Reme's and Dash's hideout for two days, while Reme scouted out a safe route to the Valorian Science Society. It was a long two days. Each one of them found it intensely difficult to just sit and wait, when they knew that so much was happening around them. It was imperative, though, that they did not leave, because nearly the entire city was after them and they could not chance being found before they could even mount an assault.

While none of them wanted to admit it, it was good for them to rest a bit and let their wounds heal. Syd's arm would take quite some time to fully heal but, once he had braced it solidly, he refused to admit it was an issue. It was clear though, especially with his large, two-handed sword, that it would hinder him to a certain degree. Coal's leg was nothing more than a scratch now and he made it a point to not even mention it.

Reme had returned in the late afternoon that day with the good news that he had found a nice path for them. It would take them through back roads, alleys and even vacant buildings. It was a route where no normal citizen or Tellurian would go. Despite Reme's enthusiasm and willingness, they refused to let him accompany them on the mission, but thanked him for the help.

Once the sun had set, they left the hideout. The path was far from a straight shot to the state district. Circumventing Seduke, which was the only district in the city that would be active during the night, was imperative. Coal did not care how far they went, as long as they were not seen on the way.

They were getting close now, as they started to see the distinctive architecture of the state district. So far, their path was unhindered, but they had not gotten to their destination yet. The last stretch would clearly be the most treacherous.

Coal came to a sliding stop at the edge of a building, resting his back against the side. Kaine and Syd stopped next to him. He inched his head around the corner and examined his surroundings. There was an open street in front of them that they would need to cross to get to the next alley and it was uncomfortably open for Coal's taste.

A small, black bird landed on a rooftop nearby and Coal held up a cautious hand.

"What is it, Sir?" Kaine whispered.

"A bird. Hold here."

He crouched silently, his eyes fixated on the small creature. It looked to be an ordinary bird but, of course, that was the purpose behind the Tellurian's camouflage. It pecked lightly at the rooftop before lifting off and flying away. Coal looked around once more before signaling to his men.

"Alright, let's go."

They darted quickly across the road with their heads down, disappearing into the alley on the other side. It was now just a straight shot to the Science Society. Once there, they would enter through a small door at the back of the building used for loading and unloading supplies to the labs below. The stairs would lead almost directly to Datro's lab.

Coal looked up and could see the glass dome of the building ahead. He felt a flurry of anticipation well up inside of him. He would finally be able to strike a blow against the detestable creatures.

The alley led right to the side of the building and they inched their way around to the back. The alley opened up into a larger courtyard in the back and Coal hesitated. Reme had not mentioned this.

"I do not see anything, Sir."

Making sure of their solitude, Coal responded, "Let us hope that is the case."

He moved ahead and settled up next to the back door. He reached for the handle and tried to open it, but it was locked.

"Reme said it would be open, dammit," growled Syd.

Coal tugged a few more times but it would not budge. He examined the edges of the door and put his shoulder into it to test its strength.

"It looks pretty solid, Sir. I don't think we'll be able to break in."

Coal grimaced. "Someone must have locked it since Reme was here."

"Such is our luck these days."

"What do we do now?" asked Syd.

Despite all of their planning and strategizing, Coal overlooked this simple situation. He had planned for many eventualities and circumstances, but this one had slipped his mind.

"Are there any other entrances?" he asked.

"From what Reme said, the only other door is the front door. I suppose the scientists like their privacy."

Coal did not like the idea of opening themselves up so easily. The front of the building was adjacent to the main district square and the entire front side was made of glass, so anyone inside could easily see them entering. He knew there was a good chance that something was waiting for them in the atrium, which was why the small backdoor entrance was so appealing. Unfortunately, there seemed to be no other way.

"Then we must go to the front. Let us hope that the Tellurians are napping on their watch duties," Coal joked, trying to hide his concern. They turned and started to make their way towards the front, keeping themselves as close to the side of the building as possible.

The entranceway of the building stretched up three floors with two pillars holding up the pyramidal overhang. The entry was also entirely made of geometric, glass sections, so it was sometimes difficult to even find the door. Inside, the décor emphasized sharpness. It seemed as though everything had an edge and it formed distinct shadows in the low light. The ceiling of the open antechamber was also a glass dome made of various geometric shapes, which, in the day time, redirected the light from the sun to illuminate the entire room, no matter where the sun was in the sky.

The sky was becoming darker as the sun set further below the horizon, but soon the Guardians would begin to rise and light up the city even more than the setting glow of the sun. They needed to move quickly. They came to the front of the building and stopped. Coal looked around, but could see nothing. There were hundreds of places for the Tellurians to hide now, so the fact that he could not see any did not at all mean that they were not out there.

"The atrium is a death trap if they are waiting for us, so once we get inside we must immediately make for cover. Follow behind me and do not separate. Are we clear?"

They both nodded.

"Alright, let's go."

They hurried around the corner and raced towards the door. When they got there, Kaine pulled it open quietly and Coal squeezed through. Once inside, he raced across the open floor towards a large statue in the middle. Kaine and Syd followed close behind.

All three rested up against it. "Now what?"

Coal turned around and looked over the top of the statue's base. There were two hallways that went further into the building, but there was no way of telling where either one led. He sank back down behind the statue. No unexpected visitors had shown themselves yet, so it was unlikely that they would run into any unless they were in the lab itself. His concern was not yet abated.

"Well, men, what do you think; left or right?"

Syd responded, "I'm always partial to right."

Coal turned to Kaine, who only shrugged.

"Well then right it is," sighed Coal. "Keep up your guard. They could be lurking just about anywhere."

He inched his way to the side of the statue and looked around once more. When he was satisfied that it was clear, he started to run towards the hallway. He heard Kaine and Syd's footsteps behind him. As he neared the opening, a bright flash erupted from the darkness. He barely had enough time to throw up his arm to block the light. He turned his head quickly as he skidded to a stop. They all shouted in shock.

The light came out of the hallway like a cannon and, when it entered the atrium, it spread out in a flash. Outside the building, beams of whiteness exploded from the windowed façade and dome. The light carried so far that even farmers outside the city in the plains would be able to see it.

Even after the light dissipated, Coal, Kaine and Syd kept their eyes covered. It was impossible to tell if the light was gone. The first flash, before they could cover their eyes, managed to throw colorful blotches into their vision. Only when the shaking started, did they finally look around.

A few seconds later, the entire building shook violently. It was like an intense shock that sent a quick vibration through the ground. They all held out their arms and crouched down to balance themselves, but quickly realized that standing where they were was not the best plan.

They heard cracking and looked over to see the glass façade shatter. The entire wall started to crumble into a glass heap.

"Run," shouted Kaine.

Coal then looked up and watched as the glass dome shattered as well and shards started to pour down towards them. All three of them bolted for the hallway. If they were caught in that deadly rain they would surely be shredded to pieces. The hallway was still dozens of feet ahead of them and they sprinted like madmen. Coal felt a few small pieces hit his back as they dove for cover and slid safely into the hall. The almost peaceful and melodic sound of thousands of pieces of glass hitting the floor echoed behind them.

The glass continued to fall for several more minutes as more and more of the dome crumbled. The three men groaned as they got to their feet. Syd flexed his broken arm a few times to check that it was okay and cringed slightly as he did so.

A chilly breeze blew in towards them from the, now wide open, front wall.

"Are you alright, Syd?" asked Kaine as he brushed himself off.

"Of course. What? Do you think a giant ceiling of glass is going to stop me? It never had a chance."

Kaine chuckled.

"Enough of the jokes, you two," said Coal. That was far too close for comfort. I, for one, would like to know what on Paks that was."

Kaine continued to try to brush off the light dusting of glass flakes covering his cloak. "It felt like it came from below us, from one of the labs. It could be Datro's."

Syd asked, "You mean, that psychotic fool is down there right now?"

"There is that possibility." Kaine turned to Coal. "If he is down there, Sir, then our luck may be changing."

Coal shook his head. "I am not so sure. Every creature within a hundred miles saw that light. If he is down there, then he is the cause of it. That was no ordinary reaction. Something has happened and we need to find out quickly. The Tellurians will be coming."

They ran off down the hallway.

When they got to the lab, everything was ablaze. Flames licked up towards Coal's face when he reached the bottom of the stairs. He shielded his eyes as the heat buffeted against him.

The lab itself was like a small oven. The room was windowless, confined and walled in with stone, so the tables, book shelves, papers, scrolls and flammable liquids burned happily. There was not a thing in the room that did not want to burn.

Coal stood at the bottom of the stairs and tried to look around, but the heat prevented him from keeping his eyes up for too long.

"Do you see anything, Sir?" shouted Kaine from behind him. Both Kaine and Syd stood back from the entrance.

"It is hard to say. I do not see anyone, so either they escaped or they are dead. We need to find something before it all burns. I will not leave here with nothing."

"But, Sir." A bookshelf crashed down nearby as the fire ate away at the base. "I do not think it would be wise to go in there."

Coal spun around and flashed him a stern glare. "I said I will not leave here with nothing, Captain. We are going in there, am I clear?"

Kaine quickly nodded. "Of course, Sir."

Coal again scanned the room. "Syd I want you to check over by those shelves to the left. The fire has not spread that far. Kaine, examine that table in the middle. It seems to be a central focus of the room. I will go to the tables in the back." He turned back again. "Do you understand?"

They both nodded.

"Good. Work quickly."

He pulled his cloak up and over his head and, hesitating, leapt off the bottom stair and into the fire.

"There is no way I am going into that room," blurted Syd. "The Commander is crazy." He stepped down to the last step and looked out at the room apprehensively.

Kaine pushed him aside. "Well then, wait here. I, for one, would rather face the wrath of this fire than the wrath of the Commander any day." He covered his head and raced quickly into the room.

Syd groaned and rolled his eyes. "Why does he have to always be right?" He backed up the stairs and took a few deep breaths. "This is not what I signed up for," he said as he jumped in.

Inside the room, it was close to unbearable. Even with their thick cloaks around them, the heat easily penetrated to their bodies. Flames lapped up and burned their ankles where the cloaks did not cover.

Coal reached the line of tables on the back wall and started to frantically sift through what he found. It was mostly beakers, jars and test tubes filled with all kinds of unidentifiable things. He tossed most of it to the side. He did not know what he was looking for, but he would know if he found it.

On the far side of the table, the flames were beginning to eat their way towards him. He saw a large glass beaker resting atop a heating plate and snatched it quickly before the fire could reach it. It was scalding and he nearly dropped it. There were still some remnants of a liquid substance in the bottom. He held it up to his nose and smelled a strong minty aroma.

Syd picked his way over to the shelves lining the west wall. He was relieved that the fire had indeed not become too intense that far across the room, but he could still feel the heat from the main blaze. Some of their more delicate scrolls and books had begun to burn due to small embers floated their way across the room, but most of the texts were untouched. He began shifting through the titles, looking for anything that might relate to Datro's experiment.

Kaine quickly jumped to the side, as another shelf came crashing down in front of him. He was finding it difficult to find his way towards the center of the room. The blaze along the east wall was the most severe and it was quickly engulfing the middle as well. He jumped over an upturned table, nearly falling as his foot landed on a stray piece of wood. After much maneuvering, he made his way to the table in the center.

It was a solidly built table. The base was made of thick hardened wood and the surface covered with iron. There were restraints attached to the top and he noticed blood stains splattered across it.

What was he doing here?

Looking around, he found it odd that the rest of the lab was in complete disarray, while this table in the middle seemed untouched. It was not anchored to the ground, yet it did not seem to have moved.

Is this the source of the explosion? Was there something here that caused it?

The straps were clearly intended to hold something down and, based on their positioning, it was most likely a body. Even with the fire scorching around him, he was lost in thought. He was only finding more questions, not answers. A faint groan broke him from his trance.

He shot his head around to find its source. He heard it again and turned his head towards the sound. A small hand was sticking out from beneath a fallen table. Racing over, he lifted the table up to reveal Alexia's beaten body.

Kaine knelt down and turned her over. She moaned as he moved her.

"Sir, there is someone here. She is still alive," he shouted over the commotion. He brushed her hair away from her face. She was dirtied and bruised, but not burned. Her clothes were singed around the edges at some parts, but it seemed like the fallen table had protected her from the brunt of the fire. He felt a bump on her head and then noticed blood soaked into her hair.

Coal raced over and knelt down next to Kaine.

"We need to get her out of here quickly, Sir. She is weak."

"Alright, pick her up." He turned and shouted to the other side of the room.

"We are out of here, Syd."

Kaine put his arms underneath Alexia and lifted her up. Her head fell lifelessly backwards, so he tried to support it against his shoulder. Coal raced off towards the stairs and Kaine followed.

As they ran up the stairs, the fire continued to spread through the lab, destroying all evidence of the gruesome experiment; the experiment to create the ultimate weapon that would win the war. The only information that now remained was in the minds of two people. One of them was clinging to life by a weak thread.

47

The Valorian Science Society was a spectacle of activity. Soldiers, councilmen, scientists, and ordinary Valorian citizens crowded around the ostentatious building to try to get a view of its destruction. Patrolmen did the best they could to hold back the throngs as the event was investigated.

Word had spread quickly through the city. There were stories of a brilliant light and an earth shaking explosion. Luckily, the first ones to arrive at the scene the night before were patrolmen from the front gate. It was hard to seal off a building that no longer had a façade, but they did the best they could before anyone else could arrive.

It was now late morning and it was a clear, but chilly, day. While some soldiers kept the crowds at bay, there were a few sifting through the rubble of the basement lab and others milling about the atrium, trying not to cut their feet on the carpet of glass.

None of them were at all sure what had happened, but none of them wanted to admit that fact either. They continued to wander around to give off the image that they were indeed making some sort of progress. The raucous crowd suddenly hushed and the soldiers in the atrium turned to see the cause of it.

The Grand Master strode purposefully up the stone stairs to the building. The crowd quickly moved out of the way to make a path. Two Forces soldiers walked behind him, trying to keep pace. When he reached the top of the stairs, one of the patrolmen stepped forward to say something, but the Grand Master walked immediately past him without even a hesitation. As he went through the atrium, he did not even alter his stride, dispassionately stepping onto the glass covered floor. The glass crunched under his decisive footsteps. He went immediately down the right hallway and towards the basement lab.

As he walked down the stairs, he started to see the black ash coating the walls. It stretched far up the stairway, with only small hints of residue at the very top, but it thickened considerably as he descended. Ash kicked up from the floor as he walked into the lab. Black coated almost everything. The only bare spots were from where an object was recently moved. Everything that could have burned, had burned, and even objects that were normally inflammable had started to melt under the intense heat. The large testing table was a heap of coals and half melted metal. Clear blobs of melted glass dotted the area as well and stuck out from the uniform darkness.

Two soldiers, who had been looking through the wreckage, turned and quickly saluted as the Grand Master arrived. "Your Highness."

He callously ignored them.

Walking past the soldiers' down-turned heads, he looked around the room. There was nothing left to speak of; nothing that anyone could recognize as what it once was.

One of the patrolmen started, "We believe, Your Highness, that the fire started..."

"Leave," he said, unemotionally.

The man froze, his arm still pointing towards the far side of the room. He looked like he was considering finished his sentence, but wisely decided to let it go. They saluted again and started to walk from the room. The two Forces soldiers followed quickly behind.

The Grand Master continued to quietly observe the room, walking carefully around the piles of ash that neatly clung to the cuffs of his pants. He stopped above the spot where the testing table once stood.

"What happened here? What was the cause of this?" he asked aloud.

A small, black cat paced into the room with a silent gait. It emerged from the stairway, where it had evidently been hiding for some time. It quickly transformed into its Tellurian form and stopped next to the Grand Master.

"I do not know the exact details of what occurred, but I believe that this particular accident was a result, not of failure, but of success."

The Grand Master's curiosity peaked.

"What makes you say that?"

"When I first arrived last night, there was a definite disturbance in the flow of natural energy. The manipulation was unlike anything I have ever encountered and powerful at that."

"I felt it as well when I entered, but I could not place it," the Grand Master pondered. "So, you think that he has succeeded then?"

"It seems that way, Master."

"Any sign of him?"

"Not a trace. There are no remains or signs of his departure. The ash has covered everything. Either he was destroyed completely or he escaped beforehand."

The Grand Master meticulously pushed the melted remnant of the metal table top to the side with his foot.

"You said the explosion was felt outside the building. And it was powerful enough to shatter the glass front of the building as well." The Tellurian nodded as the Grand Master paced. "It makes me believe that anyone in the room would have been killed, or at the very least significantly injured and engulfed in the flame. How is it then that Datro escaped, I wonder?"

"I do not know, Grand Master."

The Tellurian bowed apologetically. It sensed that the Grand Master had made a quick conclusion, and an undesirable one at that. It did not want to interrupt the Grand Master's thoughts.

"It seems to me, that the only place that would have been safe..." He paused. His anger was beginning to grow. "...would have been the center of the explosion," he bellowed as he threw the charred remains of the test table against the far fall.

The Tellurian took a step back. "Are you implying, Master, that..."

"The bastard took it himself! He has betrayed me." The ground began to shake as the Grand Master roared with clenched fists. What little remained in the room came crashing to the floor and black ash plumed up all around them.

Somewhere in the city, Datro Cervon felt the deep rumble beneath his feet and he smiled amusingly to himself. "How does it feel, creature? How does it feel to be tricked by a poor, pathetic human?"

48

Farren clung tightly to the cloak around his shoulders as the wind tried to free it from his grip. Clouds were beginning to dot the sky above and, at that moment, the sun was hiding itself behind one. It was beginning to cool down considerably as the day stretched on and as they trekked further up the plateau.

Farren's muscles were beginning to ache; muscles that he had not even realized he had. His feet were sore from tripping on so many roots and cracks in the rock, and his clothes stunk from layers of sweat and dirt. Despite all of this, he continued up the mountain with slowly draining energy.

The three of them, Kyte, Kaleb and himself, were now on their second day of their journey up the Setting Plateau. After making it a reasonable distance during the first day, they made camp and rested the night. Kyte had assured them that there was no worry of Tellurians any longer, so they were able to start a fire and have a comfortable night's sleep.

It was a pleasant evening, as they all chatted away by the fire for a short time, exchanging stories and adventures. Much to the chagrin of Farren, the self-proclaimed marauder of Valoria, his exploits did not even compare to some that Kyte was willing to tell. While Farren's pride had been slightly wounded, his desire for adventure was greatly heightened. There was much more in the world that he had not yet seen.

Kaleb, too, was astonished by some of the stories that were told, mainly because he had rarely left the city of Valoria. He had not ventured far, but when he did, it was for a mission, thus he did not have an opportunity to enjoy his surroundings. He had spent most of his youth under the tutelage of Guy, either studying or training, so he had very few opportunities for adventure. He did not resent Guy for this but, instead, was grateful for what he was given. That did not mean, though, that he did not dream of what else was out there.

They went to sleep early and woke before dawn. Even with the sun still set, the morning had pleasant warmth to it; something that quickly disappeared during the day.

It was getting towards the late afternoon and they had made good progress. The top of the ridge could be seen now, but it looked like the final leg would be a near vertical climb. Up to this point, they had successfully avoided the most treacherous terrain and stuck to an exhausting, but reasonable, path. The choice had added a little to their overall time, but that was of little concern.

Farren's and Kaleb's injuries were still far from healed, but luckily they had not been a problem so far. If they had reinjured them, however, it would have been much worse than the extra time they were currently incurring. Farren looked at the final climb and grabbed his side in concern. He was not sure how it would hold up.

Kyte pushed himself up over a large embankment and turned to help the two boys up. Kaleb grabbed Kyte's hand and, putting his feet up against the ridge, he walked his way up the side. Farren followed suit.

"That climb does not look reassuring, does it?" pointed Kaleb, as they stopped to catch their breath at the top of the ridge.

"We will be fine. Besides, we have Kyte to catch us if we fall, right?" Farren said, as he gave Kyte a friendly pat on the back.

They continued on, but it seemed as though the end of their climb was not nearing. Farren was not sure if he had just misjudged how close they originally were, or they had slowed their pace. He had done his best to make sure their pace was steady, though. There was something strange happening, but he could not quite put his finger on it. He shrugged off the thought for now.

We have probably just slowed. I am getting a little tired.

With more climb to come and little else to do, Farren decided to try to pass the time with a little conversation.

"Kyte, what was that story you were going to tell us last night before we fell asleep. You were saying something about The Almighty and the story of his demise. There was someone else, but I do not remember the name."

"Do you mean about Balin, Prince Farren?"

"I think so. That does sound familiar. Is Balin a man?"

"He was once one, yes. It is not something that I like to discuss, but I do not blame you for being interested. It is a belief among the Magi that was always greatly rejected by the humans, which I always found rather odd."

"What do you mean?"

"Well, to humans, The Almighty is considered to be all powerful. The Almighty was the creator and overseer of this world and continues to rule over it to this day. The Magi know, though, the one known as Balin now rules over Paks in place of The Almighty. He destroyed the Almighty and, as a result, became the god of Paks"

"I can see why we would be skeptical. It is crazy to think that our god could be killed by someone else. Why do you find this odd, Kyte? It seems obvious to me."

"I do not find it odd because of that. It is because Balin was said to have been a human once. It is said that Balin was a human man that gained Magi powers."

Farren stopped in surprise. "Is that even possible?"

"Anything is possible, Prince Farren. Paks is filled with many mysteries. The story of Balin is quite fascinating, actually. I was told it many times as a child. It was said that Balin was once an ordinary man that lived in the mountains south of Coroge. Coroge was not yet a great city, but rather a small village that thrived off of the great Dorian River and the abundant Pine forest. He was a Creed and, as it goes, Balin became distraught because his wife was very sick. There was no cure for her illness and he could not find a Magi that would help him. He lived during the Emerald Ages, back when Magi roamed as freely as humans do now. He prayed to The Almighty for help, but no response ever came.

In order to try to save her life, Balin found an old Ignati that had been shunned from his clan. The Ignati was upset with The Almighty and decided to teach Balin to control natural energy; the force that gives Magi their powers. To teach others to learn the art of magic was taboo among Ignati, who were known as the very first of the Magi. Magic was a privilege for only the highest of species. After years of training, Balin succeeded and gained immense powers. But, it was too late and his wife had died while he was away. He fell into despair and blamed The Almighty for her death. The Almighty felt pity for him, so he came to Balin to console him, but instead Balin used his new powers to surprise and kill The Almighty. When that happened, Balin became the ruler of Paks."

"But, how could The Almighty be killed? Wasn't he immortal?"

"That is one of the myths that most humans believe. The Almighty was actually a Magi; the first, in fact. He was an Ignati, thus he did not age. But, he was not immortal."

"How could a Magi create the world? I know the Magi are powerful, but the power to create a world is beyond belief," asked Farren.

Kyte showed his trademark welcoming smile. "The story goes that The Almighty created the world but, to the truth of the story, I cannot say for sure. What the stories say and what I believe are two completely different things."

"So, you do not believe it then? What do you believe?"

"I believe, Prince Farren, that we are not meant to know such things. All we need to know is that it happened, and we are here now. Faith guides me more than truth."

Farren considered the thought, and understood the reasoning, but could not make himself completely agree with it. He wanted to know the truth.

While Farren was deep in thought, Kaleb asked, "But, you believe that this man named Balin killed the Almighty?"

"Oh, yes. That story is not a myth, it is an account passed down through our generations. Our elders experienced the moment when it occurred. They experienced the turmoil that transpired in the world after it happened. There were wars for many years among Magi. The Magi were split between those that worshiped the Almighty and those that bent their knee to Balin. The worshipers of

Balin consisted mostly of Tellurians and a few clans of renegade Aerii. They have always despised the Ignati, so they rejoiced in their demise. Most Aerii consider him to be a devil rather than a god, but some do worship him. Considering that The Almighty was an Ignati and that all Ignati served him willingly, it is obvious to say that the Ignati despise Balin. To make matters worse, the Ignati are bound to serve the one that rules over Paks, thus they were forced to serve Balin as well." He paused. "I myself worship the Almighty, as my clan did."

"It sounds a little unbelievable to me. I cannot image that a Magi could be a god, or that a man could gain magical powers to kill him," said Kaleb.

"There are many things in this world that are beyond belief, Young Kaleb, but that does not mean they are not true. Take, for instance, the existence of the Magi. Until a few weeks ago, you probably did not believe that I existed."

Kaleb chuckled. "Good point," he said.

As they walked, Farren kept quiet. He was clearly still fretting over the story he was just told. His concern was not over the validity of the story; he believed Kyte. Despite the grandeur of the story, after the last few days there was little that he would not believe. Farren still could not accept that what he believed before was false, or in this case, an incomplete truth. He walked in an absorbed daze, oblivious to his surroundings.

"I've seen this before," commented Kaleb as he pointed to a small bush near his right foot. He stopped and looked around at their surroundings. "I have a feeling that we have been here before. Is it possible we have circled?" There was not much variation from rocks, bushes and trees on the plateau, but something seemed oddly familiar to Kaleb.

"Yes, I know, Young Kaleb, I have noticed it myself," said Kyte.

Farren finally broke loose from his thoughts and looked around as well. He stared up at the ridge ahead and again noticed that it did not seem like they were getting any closer. "What is happening? It is like we have gone nowhere."

Kyte reached his hand up into to the air. He probed the area consciously to feel for any disturbances. The two boys looked at him curiously. They had already seen their Magi friend do some amazing things, so nothing really surprised them anymore, but they still found it all fascinating.

"I believe that we are caught in a trap," Kyte finally said.

"A trap?" Farren asked, alarmingly. "What do you mean?"

"Our path has been too easy. From the beginning I assumed that the plateau would try to test us in some way because we had taken an easier path, but I had not sensed anything up until now." He again probed around the air with his hand. Closing his eyes, he focused his mind. "But, this I did not expect."

"What is it, Kyte?"

He sent out a burst of air and the vision of the land ahead of them shimmered like the barrier before. This time, though, not only did it seem like the air was shimmering, but the image of what lay ahead did as well. The world around them turned into the rippling surface of a pond.

"It is what is known as the Hall of Mirrors barrier. Once you are trapped inside, it makes you believe that you are traveling forward, but really you have gone nowhere. It creates a hallucination of sorts. The vision we see ahead of us is most likely not even what lies beyond the barrier."

"You have got to be joking. How long have we been trapped?"

"It is impossible to tell. We could have been trapped in it since we took this path. That is the plateau's test for those who decide to take the easy way. We could be much further from the top then we thought."

Farren's concern was beginning to grow. "You know how to get us through, though, right? All you have to do is use your magic. How do we get through?"

Kyte, at first, did not seem to have an answer, but then he spoke with an unsure tone. "It is said that in order to see through the mirror you must first be able to see clearly through yourself."

"What on Paks does that mean?" asked Kaleb.

Kyte took a deep breath as he looked forward towards the false image. He then turned and said with a grave expression, "I do not know."

At the base of the Setting Plateau, Astero stood examining the barrier in front of him. He had arrived some time before, flying quickly on the stiff breeze over the Central Plain. He had been able to follow the slight disturbances in the flow of natural energy; disturbances that all Magi produced whether they used magic or not. Over the plain, there was a moment where he thought he had lost the trail, but he was able to pick it up quickly.

He was certain he would soon catch up to them, but then he ran into a problem. When he encountered the barrier earlier that day he was immediately repelled by it with excessive force. It did not help that his animal form was so light and fragile, but it was clear to him that this barrier was nothing he had encountered before.

For hours, he had been standing and examining it, trying to uncover its secrets. Most magic could be deciphered and unlocked, one just needed the key. Astero was a master tracker and his ability to sense magic was unparalleled, so if there was a Tellurian who could make it through the barrier, it would be him.

Much to his annoyance, though, the barrier was proving to be unbreakable. It was an ancient magic, and there were few left in the world that understood such archaic enchantments. To make matters worse, Astero could not get too close, otherwise he would be repelled away, so examinations needed to be done from a distance.

He crouched down in his true form and tried to feel the barrier with his hands. Closing his eyes, he focused his mind to try to sense the flowing of energy. The barrier formed in his mind as a constant circulation and current of that energy. Now that he could see it, he again probed towards the flow, trying to sense its contents. What he searched for were the rules that governed the barrier. Once he knew those rules, he could begin to find a way through. His mind slowly stretched itself outward, making sure not to get too close.

A rush flowed through his mind like a cold breeze and he could feel the barrier's energy. He searched through the current, looking for answers. Suddenly, just as he thought he might have found what he was looking for, the flow became rapid and his mind could not handle it. He tried to pull free, but it would not let him. He began to panic, and then the barrier rejected him with a forceful blow, sending him flying backwards.

Astero hit the ground, sending dirt flying up around him. He tried to shake away the chaotic sensations in his head. It felt like someone had shocked his mind with a cold charge of power. Once he settled himself, he snarled and ran at the barrier. He pounded a fist on it and was quickly blown backwards. Undeterred, he continued to pummel the invisible field.

"It seems like you are having difficulties," said a voice from behind him.

Astero spun around sharply and rested his frantic eyes on the massive form of Pardos, who stood calmly with an almost piqued look on his face.

"What took you so long?"

Pardos walked up to Astero and glared down at him. He stood almost two feet taller than Astero, who was the smallest of the Grand Master's guard. He was always aware of Astero's unease in his presence. "I am not capable of being flung around on a slight breeze like you Astero. I am no insect."

Astero tried his best not to show his discomfort, so he grunted and turned away. "It does not matter." He pounded at the barrier again. "We cannot go any further anyway. This barrier is like nothing I have ever seen."

"You cannot dismantle it?"

"If I do not know its laws, I cannot circumvent them. This barrier prevents anything from even coming close to it. I cannot find its secrets."

Pardos looked up the side of the plateau. "Then whatever is on the other side of the barrier must be of great importance."

"It has been here for centuries, that is clear. Whatever it protects much be ancient as well. This could be where the Aerii have been hiding. It could be their last village we have been searching for atop that plateau."

Pardos had despised the Aerii for centuries. Even before joining with the Grand Master, he had made it his life's purpose to hunt down the last remaining clans and destroy them. It was this hatred that the Grand Master used to control Pardos, who was, in fact, just as powerful as the Grand Master himself. Pardos did not care about taking control of Paks, though. The Grand Master' plan was a fleeting thought to the monstrous Magi. The only thing that mattered to him was finding the last of the Aerii.

"Could this finally be it? Could this be the last of them?" Pardos whispered under his breath. His expression sharpened. "I will not let him reach the top and find reinforcements. I will cut him down like a bird from the sky and watch him fall. He will not escape!" He raced forward, pushing Astero aside.

"No, Pardos. You must not touch the barrier. It could destroy even you," screeched Astero.

Words could not reach through the rage in the beastly Tellurian's mind. He roared as he swung a mighty fist towards the invisible field. A bright light and forceful wind exploded out around them.

49

"Incredible," Seno gawked, as he stared up towards the ceiling of the Corogean Palace entrance. The lights seemed dim in the afternoon sun and they could not even see the point of the conical shaped hall. "I would never have thought it possible."

The sun shone directly into the main doors and windows, giving the main hall an unusual brightness. The peak of the ceiling was still shrouded in shadow, but that only made the room larger. You did not know where it ended. The glow lights cast eerie shadows across the bare, jagged mountain rock, which added to the grand mystery of the place. Seno continued to smile as he knelt down and ran his hand against the engraved Creed crest on the floor; three swords pointing towards the three guardians.

"Have you never been to Coroge, Seno?"

"Of course I have, Anton, but not in the palace itself. I have limited my visits to their archives, which are stored in a separate location. The Creed document history much more accurately than we do. Their archives dwarf ours in every way."

They both stood patiently, waiting for permission to see the Minor. They had ridden almost non-stop from Valoria and, much to their relief, with no incident. Anton assumed correctly that the Tellurians now saw him as no threat, so there was no reason to watch him. Once they made it through the Shroud, the trip was little trouble. Anton had made the journey many times, so he knew the way like the back of his hand.

They were stopped by guards in the Pine and escorted to the city. Anton was a familiar face to most Creed, so they knew his importance. Luckily for Anton, the Creed were not up to speed on current Valorian politics. The impending war had clearly put the guards on edge, but they still were treating them as welcome dignitaries.

When they made it to the city, Anton and Seno were astonished by the efficiency of the Creed war time machine. The flatland in front of the city was covered with wooden spikes, ditches and pools of oil. There were dozens of trebuchets and ballista lined up behind and atop the city walls. Hundreds of bundles of arrows were laid out along the top of the wall for the archers and buckets of oil and torches were spread out to light fires.

Every man, woman and child was hard at work preparing the city for war. It almost seemed like they enjoyed the thought of battle, working with a passionate energy. Even the children skipped around, bringing food to the other workers and hauling materials from site to site.

In a strange way, Seno felt most scared of the children. They stared at him with powerful, yet oddly innocent, eyes. It was their unpredictableness that scared him most. He knew what a Creed soldier could do, but what about a child? The Creed citizens were dirty, sweat-covered and battered, but they still worked with their heads held high. Both Anton and Seno could not help but admire their tenacity. Admire, but still fear.

The soldier that had escorted them once they entered the city was named Pion, and Anton had guessed that he was a Captain. Anton was not exactly an expert on Creed military hierarchy, especially the visual representation of rank, but from the man's mannerisms, Anton was sure he was of some importance. He had left them to wait in the antechamber as he went to announce their arrival. It had been some time and they were getting a bit impatient.

"Well, they do not seem to be in much of a hurry, do they?"

"Quiet, Seno. Voices tend to travel in an open space like this and the Creed do not find sarcasm as entertaining as we do. I would prefer to avoid confrontation."

Seno just scoffed.

After a few more minutes they could hear the echoing sound of footsteps coming towards them from the main hallway straight ahead. Pion appeared at the top of the stairs in front of them.

"Alright," he shouted. "The Minor will see you."

Without waiting for a reaction, he turned and started to walk back down the hallway.

"Are we supposed to follow him?" Seno asked, as he turned to Anton.

"Yes. Do not expect much courtesy here, Seno. They will talk simply and to the point. I suggest you do so, as well. I know how much you love to tell a story," said Anton as he quickly followed after Pion.

The hallway was long and stark. They were not sure when it was going to end, if ever. Seno was even convinced they were going to come out the other side of the mountain at some point. They passed by a few other soldiers, who saluted to Pion as they walked.

It was not until they reached the long stairway that Pion said anything. "I do not know why you are here, but I would suggest that you speak to the Minor as you would your own Regis. This war that you have started has put our Minor in a displeased mood."

"It is not our intention to anger him. In fact it is the exact opposite. We wish to…"

"Save it for the Minor," Pion interrupted. "It is not my place to meddle in the affairs of politicians. Nor, do I want to."

"You and me both," groaned Seno.

Pion's face held expressionless. Seno briefly considered trying to tell a joke to get him to smile, but correctly decided against it. It was not worth the trouble. The rest of the walk was an awkward silence.

When they reached the door, Pion knocked loudly and turned to them. "The Minor will be the first to speak," he said plainly.

The doors started to creak open. Seno and Anton shielded their eyes from the bright light that erupted from the doorway. Slowly, they raised their heads and looked in.

The room was surprisingly small; at least smaller than they were expecting. There was little uniformity to it. It was a natural cave that occurred in the mountain, which the Minor had decided to use as his chamber. The walls and ceiling were the bare mountain rock and there were columns of rock stretching upwards in various places. The light came from a large opening in the ceiling towards the back.

The décor was rustic and homely. The chairs were made of natural brown leather and all wood seemed to be carved by hand. There was a large fireplace near the back wall where the opening occurred, but there was no fire lit. A small side chamber was visible and Anton assumed it was where the Minor slept. He could see the edge of a large bed around the corner.

After examining their surroundings, the two men's eyes fell on a man standing towards the far end of the room. He was facing away from them, looking up at the sunlight from the break in the ceiling. Anton and Seno heeded Pion's instructions and waited for the man to speak first.

"Welcome, Gentlemen," he said.

He turned and both Seno and Anton bowed respectfully.

"I normally enjoy visits from outsiders but, under the circumstances, I am unsure how to feel. I hope you understand. There is much happening in Paks these days and very little of it is good."

"Of course, Your Highness. These are troubling times," responded Anton.

"Troubling indeed. Let us try to make the best of this visit though, Chief Council, as we always do."

Anton allowed himself to smile gently, "That is all I wish for, Your Highness."

Minor Leo walked over to them both. "And, who might you be?" he asked Seno, extending his hand. "You have a familiar face, but I cannot seem to find a name for it."

Seno extended his as well, grasping Leo's forearm in the traditional Verturian greeting. He was surprised by the elderly man's strength. "My name is Seno Pierson, Your Highness."

Minor Leo was indeed far along in age and showed it. His hair was almost pure white and greatly thinned. His skin was wrinkled and showed blotches of discoloration, and he wore a stately robe, not unlike the one that Anton wore in council. Despite all of this, he walked upright and with prominence. Some of his youthful strength still remained and he had added an aura of wisdom around him as well.

"Ah, the historian. I have heard much about you. I have met your father, as well. You come from a storied family; quite literally."

"I know. My father used to speak of his meeting with you fondly."

"He was a good man; quick with a joke and long with a story. He had an air about him that made you gravitate to him. Smartest man I ever knew." said Leo. He turned and gestured to some chairs in the middle of the room. "Shall we sit?"

Anton and Seno nodded and they all walked over to the chairs. When they sat, Anton and Seno found the chairs remarkably comfortable and warm. In fact, the room as a whole was very welcoming.

"I am curious, Seno, have you had an opportunity to examine our archives before?"

"I have. They are quite extensive, Your Highness. I was pleasantly surprised, the first time I came, if you do not mind me saying."

"It is a common misconception that we are a barbaric people. Not a misconception based on hatred, but on distorted facts. It is a shame that we see each other so differently," he said, sadly. "We cherish our history above all else and honor what our ancestors have done."

"A noble pursuit," Seno agreed. "I believe that the kingdom would be a better place if everyone knew a bit more of its history. You can learn a lot about the present by knowing the past."

"Well said. I could not agree more."

The Minor was not like Seno had imagined him. For years he assumed there was much more to the Creed than most people imagined, but Minor Leo far exceeded his expectations. He was wise and comforting. He did not smile, but he did not need to. Seno felt reassured and protected, not fearful, in his presence.

"I do not mean to be impolite, Your Highness, but there is a very important reason why we are here," pressed Anton.

"Yes, of course. I forget sometimes how much you politicians like to get to the point. We Creed are much the same, but I find myself growing long in verse in my old age." There was a lighthearted tone to the comment, but, again, Leo did not smile. "That is why it was such a pleasure to speak with your Aerious friend."

Anton raised a brow in confusion. "Aerious?" He turned to Seno expecting a response, but got none.

Seno shrugged. "I know nothing of an Aerious."

"You are not allied with the good Commander? It was my assumption that you were here on his behalf."

"We are," assured Anton. "But, not with his knowledge. There has been a development in the capital and we are unable to contact Commander Coal, or his men. We have come here as a last resort."

"And, you do not know of this Aerious?"

Again, Anton turned to Seno.

"They never did mention an Aerious, but they came to me some time ago. He could have been a recent ally."

"What did this Aerious tell you?"

"Everything," said Leo. "He told me that you were under attack by the Tellurians and that Regis Bishop is not himself. He also told me that this new foe intends to attack us as well. A foolish idea, but you can never underestimate a Magi. We are preparing ourselves."

"You did not send help?" blurted Seno.

Anton gave him a disapproving glare.

"I wish it were that simple, Seno. I would have helped you if I could. We sent scouts to keep our eye on the creatures, but none have returned."

Seno continued the verbal assault. "What do you mean you could not help? You are the Minor."

Anton held out a warning hand in front of him.

Leo raised a hand to tell him he was not upset. "It is alright, Anton. He is quite right." He turned back to Seno. "Unfortunately, as I said, it is not that simple. There are many officials that do not share my same sentiment towards peace. My grandson is among them. I am ashamed to say that I have been unable to sway their hatred."

"You mean General Lockhart," Anton stated.

Leo nodded. "He refused to send aid and instead focused our military's efforts on boosting our defenses."

"You could do nothing to sway him? Surely you have more power than that."

Minor Leo got up from his seat and started to walk to the back of the room. "War is a young man's game, gentlemen. When it comes down to affairs of battle, it is Weston who makes the decisions. I am but a figurehead in my old age."

"But, how could you let something like this happen?" continued Seno.

"Because, I trust my grandson. I know that, in the end, he will make the correct decision for our people."

Seno was going to continue his argument but Anton stopped him. "I understand your feelings, Your Highness, but you do not have all of the facts. Things have changed."

Leo turned his head, his curiosity peaked. "You have come to *us* with new information? Why not your own people?"

"As I said before, we did not have a choice."

Silence fell on the room for a few moments.

"What has happened to the Commander? From what the Aerious told me, he was the one leading the counter attack against the Tellurians."

"We are unsure exactly what has happened, but Coal and his men have been banished from the city. What the people have been told is that they kidnapped the Prince and attacked Lady Kara. Of course, that is completely false, but the real story is uncertain."

Minor Leo raised a brow in concern. "Do you believe he is dead?"

"No, but no one has seen or heard from him since then. His influence is greatly diminished. I do not see how he could do anything on his own, especially now that the Davati have joined with the Tellurians."

"The Davati? Truly?" Leo groaned. "Fanix, that fool. The Tellurians cannot be trusted. What does he expect to gain from joining with them? He cannot possibly think that the Tellurians will leave them alone after they are finished. It must be a defensive move. Ignorant, but he may think it necessary. The Minor always was a coward."

"The situation has become even worse than that. We need your help more than ever," Anton urged.

Leo thought quietly to himself. Finally, he responded coldly, "I sympathize with your plight, but what has happened does not change the situation. If anything, this new development gives us more of a reason to stay here and solidify our position. A Davati assault requires specialized defenses. I know that my son would agree as well," he added.

Both Anton and Seno were stunned by the Minor's response. They were beginning to believe that he was a reasonable man; that he would come to their aid. It seemed that they mistook him for something he was not.

"So, you will let our people die as you sit behind your walls and cower," shouted Seno.

Leo's eyes widened and a deep growl rumbled in his chest. He held himself in control, but it was with much effort. "Watch what you say, historian. I am an old man, but my temper has not aged and neither has my strength. It is not wise to judge the honor of a Creed," he advised. "If I was a younger man I may have already thrust a sword through your chest. You should feel lucky that I am now much older and wiser, and have managed to develop a modicum of control. That being said, this is no ordinary battle that is about to be fought. If we attack now, we will surely lose, and then there will be no one left to stop them. Behind our walls, we are unbeatable. If I believe there was something we could actually do to help you, then I would. But I must look to the safety of my people before anyone else," he stated strongly. It took him a few moments to regain his regal composure, but when he finally did he said, "I am sorry. There is nothing I can do."

Anton was upset by the situation, but still in control of his emotions, unlike his companion. He had met the Minor many times over the years and had been confident that he would assist them. Things had changed, it seemed. It may be the grandson that he would need to convince. First, he needed to mitigate the situation. "My friend apologizes for his brashness, Your Highness. He has lost his stately control over the past few years," he said with a lighthearted tone.

It took a moment for the comment to sink its way in. "It is alright Chief Council, these are emotional times. Even I find it hard to keep control." He turned to Seno and gave him a respectful nod. Seno, after letting out a deep breath, returned it in kind.

"Despite what we have told you, though," added Anton. "These new developments are not the ultimate reason why we are here. There is something else that has come to our attention."

Minor Leo walked over and sat back down in his chair. "Nothing seems to be well in the capital these days."

"I am afraid not," agreed Anton. He turned to Seno.

Seno was still trying to calm himself but, now that it was up to him to try to show the importance of the situation, he pulled forward his old scholarly persona. "Are you familiar with the stories of the Magi Wars, Your Highness?" Seno asked.

"Of course," Leo responded, a bit perturbed by the insinuation that he may not be familiar with such important history.

"There was an event in Herous, towards the end of the war. A group of Tellurians attacked the city, but we managed to stop them before they could complete their goal."

"I am unfamiliar with the story."

"That is because it is a closely guarded secret. Very few know of it."

Leo leaned back in his chair and crossed his legs, intrigued by the thought that there was a historical event that he had not heard of.

"What was their goal? There was nothing in Herous at that time of any importance."

"That anyone knew of," Seno added, quickly. "At that time, it was just a simple fishing village; one of the larger ports on Paks, but still quite inconsequential. In truth, though, there was a secret lab hidden in the city which was researching the building of a weapon."

"Do you mean The Hand of the Almighty?" Leo responded in surprise.

"You know of it?"

"Only from stories. There was rumor in Vertura during those times that the Brivans were developing a weapon, but it was nothing more than hearsay."

"It is indeed true, Your Highness. We were developing a weapon to protect us from the war and fight back. Unfortunately, it was never completed, which is why it disappeared into history."

"That is as the stories go, but no stories ever speak of what it was. What was this weapon?" asked Leo.

"Until just recently, I did not know. It was the most closely guarded secret in our history. But, when Coal's men came to me for information, we concluded that the reason the Tellurians had returned was to try to steal the weapon again. So, I went back through every text I knew of to try to discover what it was."

Minor Leo was not the sort that enjoyed being left waiting. "And?"

"It is not a weapon of the regular sort. It is not iron or wood or stone. You cannot wield it, fire it, or kill with it. It is, in fact, a solution. An alchemical potion that, when ingested, gives humans the ability to control natural energy."

Minor Leo was speechless. He had spent much of his life dedicating himself to studying the history of Paks. He had heard of every story and every battle, and knew of every famous figure and every failed conqueror. There was little that ever surprised him, but this was not something that he ever thought possible.

"Magic?" Leo whispered aloud.

"Yes."

"You are sure?" he asked again.

Seno only nodded.

Leo lowered his head in contemplation. It was unclear if he was concerned or excited by the idea. Either way, the Minor's thoughts were clearly conflicted. "I must speak with my grandson," Minor Leo finally said firmly.

50

Alexia woke with a groan and her eyes slowly pried themselves open. At first she did not feel much pain, but when she tried to move her head, the dull ache became apparent. She decided that getting up was not the best idea, and rolled carefully onto her back.

She was in a large room; large, but with little to fill it. There was the cot that she was laying on, a few raggedy couches and a table. As she stared at the ceiling, she noticed how old and neglected the room was.

Where am I?

She tried to move again, but more slowly. Her head still hurt, but she pushed through it. It wasn't until she started to try to sit up, that she realized how stiff her body was. She slumped back into the cot, defeated.

"Good idea. No point in hurting yourself more," said a voice.

The voice startled her and she spun her head around. She winced as a pain shot through her neck and head.

"Sorry about that. I did not mean to startle you."

After the ache subsided, she looked over and saw a man leaning up again the far wall, peering out of one of the windows. He was tall, with shoulder-length, dark brown hair that was wavy and unkempt. Alexia's eyes immediately moved down to the sword sheathed at his side.

"How are you feeling?" he asked again, still keeping his eyes trained out the window.

She did not hear the question. The sword worried her. The last thing she could remember was being in the lab, helping Datro with his experiment. Datro had asked her to give him the solution.

Did I give it to him? Did it work?

"Well?" the man asked again.

Alexia shook herself from her daze. The man was now standing right next to her bed. She almost shrieked in surprise, but held it to a stifled inhale. She still could not respond.

The man knelt down next to the cot and smiled at her. "No need to worry. You are with friends." He reached out his hand. "My name is Kaine."

She stared at the hand for a moment, then looked back at his smiling face. Apprehensively, she reached out and shook his hand. "Alexia," she said feebly.

Kaine chuckled. "It is nice to meet you, Alexia. Now that we have dispensed with the introductions, my original question still stands. How are you feeling?"

"Sore, but ok, I guess." She noticed some bandages on her arms and reached her hands up to feel one on the right side of her face.

"That is good. You are lucky to be alive."

"What happened?" she asked quickly.

Kaine got back to his feet. "That is exactly what we were going to ask you." He walked back over to the window. "You do not remember anything?"

"No." She lied.

"That is what we were afraid of," Kaine responded with a dejected tone.

Alexia shifted around to get into a more comfortable position. Now that she was sitting up, she reexamined the room. "How did I get here?" she asked.

"We brought you here," he stated. His voice was no longer as friendly as it was before. His eyes were fixed out the window.

"Who are you?"

Kaine did not answer. After a few seconds he just turned and walked down a set of stairs in the floor. Alexia was confused. She thought about shouting after him, but her voice stayed silent. When Kaine did not return after a few minutes, she got up. It was painful at first but, once she got to her feet, she felt better. She tiptoed over to the stairs and looked down. She heard talking, but could not make out what they were saying. She then went over to the window and looked out.

She was on the second floor and somewhere in the bazaar. A cold breeze forced her to fold in her arms. It must have been pretty early in the morning, because there were not that many people walking around yet and some of the merchants were still setting up their stands.

She looked down just below her to see if there was any way for her to escape. It was a far drop and there were no ledges or places for her to get a foothold on the way down. A merchant had already set up a stand just below the window and was selling handmade textiles. It would be foolish to jump. Besides, she did not yet know if these men were really dangerous, or friends, as they claimed.

"I would not do that if I were you."

Alexia jumped at the voice. She had not heard any noise to warn her that someone had come up the stairs. Turning slowly, she tried to wipe the guilty look from her face.

"I wasn't going to do anything."

She was expecting to see Kaine, but this man was different. He was just as tall, maybe a few inches taller, but with a stronger build. He had short cut, dark brown hair and a firm jaw. He wore similar, ragged clothing that looked to be thrown together from a mish-mash of selections. The only weapon he was holding was a short sword, sheathed horizontally in the small of his back, and his expression was much sterner than Kaine's. Something about him looked familiar. He was someone of importance, but she could not put her finger on it.

"I should hope not. As Kaine has already informed you, we are friends. We have no intention of harming you. In fact, if it was not for us, you would be dead."

The man's bluntness was a bit harsh and she was beginning to wish that Kaine had not left. At least Kaine's attitude was analogous to what he was trying to tell her. This man did not seem friendly, nor did he seem dangerous. Although, that is what Alexia always thought of men. Often times she was wrong. A moment later, Kaine appeared behind him from the stairs. He whispered something into the other man's ear before they both turned and looked at her.

Finally, it occurred to her. She had seen the man many times before. She did not recognize him at first because of disheveled appearance. Normally, he was perfectly groomed and walking strongly in his uniform. "You are Commander Lucer," she said before they could speak. She looked over to Kaine. "I remember seeing you when Datro was arrested. You are the traitors that rebelled against the Supreme Regis. I heard his speech."

"It seems your memory is clear, but mistaken. You are correct when you say I am Coal Lucer, but we are not traitors, girl," responded Coal. "What you have been told is untrue."

"Why should I believe you? The Supreme Regis said you attacked Lady Kara and kidnapped the Prince. Of course you would deny it. I would rather believe my Regis than a traitor," she said with attitude.

"Why would I attack my own baby sister?" Coal shouted back. "Why would I betray my friend? Bishop was my best friend. I would never do such a thing."

"If he was your friend, why would he lie about it at all?"

Coal masked his sadness with anger. "Because he is not himself!" he shouted. After calming slightly, Coal continued. "He is not himself, and that is all you need to know. We are innocent and the truth is far different from what you have been told. Now tell me. Who are you?" he asked brusquely. "What were you doing in Datro Cervon's lab? You said you remember me from when Datro was arrested. Do you know him?"

She had an uneasy feeling. Coal clearly wanted something and she sensed that he would do anything for it. She never quite believed that the Commander would rebel like they said. He was known as a very heroic and courageous man. This man in front of her, though, was much different than the one she had heard about.

What should I do?

Kaine stepped forward. "Alexia, please. We need your help. What were you doing down in the lab? Do you know what happened?"

"I..." she stuttered. Emotions were beginning to well up inside her. She could not say anything more.

"What happened?!" Coal shouted.

Kaine held up a hand to calm him. "Sir." He turned back to Alexia and grabbed her by the shoulder reassuringly.

After the outburst by Coal, Alexia now had tears flowing down her face.

"It is all right if you do not remember what happened in the lab. You were in rough condition when we found you, so there is nothing to be ashamed of. But, can you tell us why you were there? Do you work with Datro?"

Alexia sniffed, wiping away some of her tears with her sleeve. It took her a few more moments before she could speak. Coal was clearly getting restless. She nodded. "Yes, I am his assistant."

Coal's eyes widened. He stepped forward but Kaine held him back with a glance.

"So, then you must know what he has been working on. Were you working on it with him?" Kaine asked.

She was in a dilemma. Datro had told her to never tell anyone about what they were doing. Up until now, she had kept that promise. She never really liked Datro that much, but she respected him. She told herself that she should not tell these men, but Kaine's look was reassuring and, while Coal did not seem friendly, he did not have the look of a bad man.

"I was ordered never to tell," she said.

"You do not understand what is at stake, girl," Coal insisted strongly. Kaine tried to stop him as he came forward, but he just pushed him to the side. Alexia tried to back away, but she ran into the wall behind her. Inches away from her, Coal continued to rant. "If you have been working with him, then you must know what it is he was working on."

"No, I assure you I don't," she pleaded. "He never told me anything."

"But, you must have had a feeling that what you were doing was wrong. You had doubts, did you not?"

"Well..." she stammered.

"He is not a moral man. Everything he does is for his own selfish goals."

Alexia began to sob. "No, he is a visionary. He is a genius,"

"He is a murderer."

Visions of the dead bodies, lying limp on the testing table started to flash into her memory. She remembered the weight of their lifeless bodies as she was forced to drag them out of the lab. She could not take it; the revolting stench, the look that was frozen on their faces. The emotions that she did not shed then, were beginning to arise.

She fell onto her bed and sobbed. "No."

"He left you for dead in the lab. If it were not for us, the flames would have burned you alive."

She could feel the heat on her face. She could see the look in Datro's eyes as he walked away from her through the flames. He did not care about her. He *never* did. She was a fool to ever believe him.

Remarkably, her sobs started to subside, but they were replaced by shame. She just stared blankly in front of her as her memories returned, one after another.

Kaine put a hand on Coal's shoulder, but he shrugged it off. "Not yet," he said.

It took some time for Alexia to work through her thoughts and emotions, but eventually her strength returned. She finally looked up at Coal, her eyes red, but full of determination.

"Do you remember?" he asked.

"Yes."

"What happened?"

She sat up a bit and sniffed, her tears not completely gone. "There was an explosion. A fire started in the lab. I was knocked back and hit my head, I think. I couldn't move."

"What caused the explosion?"

"He took it himself. I told him not to, but he insisted. I could not stop him."

"Who?"

"Datro. He was mad. He kept saying there was no choice. He said that the Supreme Regis was going to stop the research."

Coal looked back at Kaine; worried. "What did he take?"

"The solution. It was what we were working on." She seemed confused. "You did not know about it?"

"We knew that you were working on building a weapon, but we did not know what it was."

"It is not a weapon, it is a solution; a potion."

"A solution for what?"

She stared down at the bed and shook her head guiltily. "I do not know. He never told me what it was for."

"What do you think it was for? You must know something."

Alexia had made assumptions and guesses of what it was. Datro was so obsessed with it, that it must have been important.

"Please, Alexia," said Kaine.

She was still reluctant to say. "It is only a guess. I do not know for sure."

Kaine insisted. "Anything you can tell us. Anything at all."

She did not realize it would be this hard to say it. For some time now, she had realized what it was, but no one had asked her. It never occurred to her she would have to tell someone.

After rolling it over in her mind, she said, "It is a potion that changes the person that drinks it. At first I thought it was to just make them stronger." She added with a flex of her arm, "Physically." Images of the testing process flashed into her mind.

She shook her head. "But, soon I realized I was wrong. The solution was not working correctly. It was too volatile and unstable. Datro went to retrieve some information that revealed to him what we were missing. It was some plant that he found in the Shroud. I was able to identify it as something called the Haze Creeper. Are you familiar with it?"

They both shook their heads.

"From what I read, Magi once used it to enhance their magical abilities. It allows for better control over the flow of natural energy."

"So what? What does that have to do with anything?" Coal asked.

"Don't you see?" she asked them. "The potion does not make you stronger. It gives you the ability to use magic."

Kaine and the other man just stood dumbfounded. This was not what they had expected. It was supposed to be a weapon.

"A human…" Coal muttered. "…using magic?"

Alexia just nodded.

"That is absurd."

"I can assure you it is not. I saw the reactions that the potion had in our tests. The subjects gave off massive amounts of energy. I did not want to believe it either, but that is what it does."

Coal was having a hard time accepting what Alexia was saying. He gritted his teeth and tried to shake away the thoughts.

"Sir, it makes sense," Kaine said to him. "This is what they were after from the very beginning. We did not believe that there was anything we had that they wanted, but this is something truly powerful. With it, they could create a larger and more powerful army."

"Who are you talking about?" Alexia asked. "Who wants to create an army?"

Kaine looked back at her, but said nothing. Turning back to Coal, he said, "Sir, you know she is right."

"Of course I know," he snapped. "But, what can we do? This is something that is beyond our capabilities."

"You do not know that for sure, Sir. There could be a way to stop them. We must keep looking," Kaine urged.

Coal let out his rage with a hard fist into the wall. His shoulders heaved as he breathed heavily. Kaine just stood there. He felt Coal's frustration, but he was much better at controlling it.

"Stop ignoring me. I am not a child," yelled Alexia. Kaine and Coal spun around in surprise. "I demand you tell me what is going on," she said.

Alexia was standing, rigid and determined. Neither Kaine nor Coal had expected this timid girl to be quite so difficult. It had taken so much just to get her to talk and now she was demanding information.

Kaine looked to Coal. "She has helped us, Sir. I do not think it would hurt for us to tell her. She poses no threat. Besides, it is not like she is the only other person now that knows."

Coal shook his head, annoyed. "Do not remind me, Captain. The fact that you have blurted out this secret to half the city already does not please me." He groaned loudly. "But, you are correct. I suppose there is no harm in it. You have helped us, so it is only fair that we help you in return." He walked back over towards her. "But, you must agree to tell us everything you know if I tell you. You will answer all of our questions. Agreed?"

She nodded.

"Alright." He pulled over a chair. "You may want to sit down for this."

Datro Cervon sat silently in the darkness. The building was abandoned and clearly pilfered for all of its possessions. It was in the bazaar, just like most abandoned buildings were. In the past, the bazaar had been an extension of the high end shopping district, but now it was just a haven for traveling merchants and bartering citizens. Most of the solid structures were abandoned. Only their façades were used for temporary displays.

There was no way he could have gone back to his own house, or any place that he normally frequented. Most likely the Grand Master now knew what he had done and he would be searching for him. As long as Datro stayed here, he would be safe. At least until he decided to make his move.

Datro was in the basement, sitting on the remnants of an old wooden crate. It was likely once used to hold some form of fruit, as evidenced by the smell of rotting citrus. All that was left in the room were crates and broken glass.

He had swiped a glow light from a merchant's stand before he entered the building and it sat on a crate a few feet away. In the faint orange glow he examined himself. His usual emaciated physique had changed. Lean muscles now stretched across his previously withered limbs. While his clothing had burned from the flame, his skin seemed unaffected. Either that, or his wounds had healed. He could not remember during the excitement of the moment.

There was a complete sense of confidence flowing through him. He felt like he was indestructible. Energy was pumping through him and it felt exhilarating. It would take some time for him to be able to control this new power but, when that happened, there was no one that could stop him. He knew the power that he could now harness. According to the notes from the tests done during the Magi Wars, human magic was considered more powerful than all others. The specific form of the magic itself came from the will of the person's soul. The form and intensity were different for every person. The stronger the will of the human, the stronger the magic.

Datro got to his feet. He had not yet been able to determine the form of his magic, but the flow of energy through him had also increased his physical abilities. He flexed his arms and threw a few punches out into the air. He grinned contentedly. Spinning around quickly, he kicked out his leg in a sweeping motion and then jumped and kicked out forward. He landed neatly on his toes. His smile evolved into a haughty chuckle.

He picked up one of the crates and bounced it up and down in one of his hands. In a flash he tossed it up in the air, spun around and destroyed it with one kick. It burst apart into indistinguishable shards of wood. Seeing the extent of the destruction, he started to laugh wildly. He picked up another crate, threw it up and destroyed it with a punch. He continued to destroy each crate, one at a time. His enjoyment could almost be felt in the air.

Suddenly, one of the destroyed crates flew into the glow light and knocked it from its perch. The room darkened. He walked over and picked it up and when he did, the light started to intensify. It did not become any hotter, but the light was much stronger. He held it up closer to his face. He stared at it, concentrating on the warm glow. As he focused, the light continued to get brighter. Soon, the light was so intense that he could not bear to look right at it. He moved it away from his face, but eventually he had to look away and shield his eyes. The light filled the room so completely that there weren't even any shadows from the destroyed crates. A burst of heat erupted from the light and he dropped it in surprise. Before it even touched the ground, the light exploded intensely and then disappeared in a flash.

Warily, Datro unshielded his eyes and looked back in front of him. He could see nothing. There was not a speck of light left in the room. In the darkness, he could hear his excited breathing. He held his hands up to his face but, even inches away, he could not see them. He was not scared, though. A light laugh started to replace his heavy breathing. It was fantastic. He did not know what had just happened, but it made his skin crawl with excitement. His laugh echoed through the room. It did not matter if anyone could hear him outside. He collapsed to his knees and continued to laugh.

If the anticipation of meeting the Minor of Vertura could be described as exciting, then the only word to describe how Seno was feeling now was euphoric. To be a non-military citizen involved in a Verturian war council was uncommon, but to be a Brivan diplomat involved in one was, unheard of. He knew the historical significance of the event and he reveled in it.

After hearing the news of Valoria's secret weapon, Minor Leo had called an immediate meeting. Leo understood how dangerous this new state of affairs could become and needed the advice of counsel. The Creed, it seemed, took their history quite seriously. News of a Magi attack had put them on the defensive, but now it seemed that defensive tactics might not be enough. This was an attack from an old enemy, but with new and powerful allies.

The room that they all met in was a stark room but, of course, that was the point of it. There was a large, rectangular, wooden table sitting in the middle, with chairs surrounding it and a cast iron chandelier hanging just above. Aside from the chandelier, there were two glow lights on each wall, producing just enough light to be able to read comfortably. The only décor was a large mural depicting a battle on one wall and a coat of arms on the opposite.

There were three other men sitting around the table and it was painfully obvious that they did not find Anton and Seno's company enjoyable. Their scornful stares did not seem to abate Seno's enjoyment of the situation, though. It had been awkwardly quiet since the other three men had entered and sat down without a word. They had exchanged wary glances between one another, but had said nothing to Seno or Anton. They all quietly waited for the Minor to arrive.

A few minutes later, the large door to the room creaked open and the aged ruler entered. He had removed his stately robe and was now dressed in military uniform. Leo looked much more dominating and much less approachable in the black and grey attire. He took his seat at the head of the table.

"I see that you all have been getting to know each other," he said. It was clearly meant to be a joke, but he did not laugh. Seno smirked slightly before forcing the amusement away. "I understand that there is very little love felt between our people, but let us try to at least be civil." He turned and gave his grandson Weston a serious look. "We are both facing a common enemy."

"We do not need their assistance, nor do we desire to give them ours," Weston responded quickly. "The self-proclaimed rulers of Paks should be able to handle their own problems." he continued, turning to Anton.

"Weston!" barked Leo, as Anton and Weston glared at each other. "I said we will be civil."

As much as Weston hated the idea of sitting amicably with these Brivans, he nodded solemnly. His enormous stature stood out amongst the group, but neither Seno nor Anton was intimidated.

"Who is this?" asked Weston, looking at Seno. "I know of the Chief Council from his many visits, but this one is unfamiliar to me."

"This is Seno Pierson," answered Leo. "He is a historian of Valoria. A very prominent one at that."

"What is a historian doing here during a time of war? This is no place for such people. It is even absurd that the Chief Council is here."

"If you would control your temper and allow me to speak, Weston, then maybe you would find out these things."

Weston grunted his disapproval but quieted nonetheless. Minor Leo turned back to the rest of the table.

"Well then. Before we begin, I believe that complete introductions are necessary," said Leo. "Our visitors, as you now know, are Chief Council Anton Grey and Historian Seno Pierson, both of Valoria." He gave them both respectful nods. "And you all know my grandson, Weston, General of The Order." He gestured towards the other two with a hand. "These are his two top captains, Pion and Rouse. I believe you have already met Pion."

"Yes," responded Anton.

Pion and Rouse were both large and strongly built, but neither as large, nor as dominating as Weston. Rouse was a bit shorter and had a stockier look, while Pion was leaner. Rouse's head was shaved bald and Pion had a long stretch of dark, black hair firmly braided down his back. They could not have looked more different, but it was evident that their attitudes were much the same. After a round of courteous, but forced, nods and acknowledgements, Leo continued.

"Let us begin then. I understand, Gentlemen, that this is unorthodox and none of you are happy to be here, but these are troubling times. Seno and the Chief Council have brought me some disturbing news from Valoria that may change our current strategy."

"Valorian lies will not change my decisions," stated Weston. "They can say what they want, but nothing will change."

Leo ignored the comment and raised his voice as he continued. "They have come at great risk to their own lives to bring us this news and ask us for aid. As men of character, we will listen to their words."

Leo turned to Anton. Anton pushed out his chair and rose to his feet.

"Thank you, Your Highness." He cleared his throat. "As all of you have been previously informed, Valoria is under attack from Tellurians. The Supreme Regis has been killed and supplanted by a Tellurian that mimics his appearance. Up until now, Commander Coal Lucer and his men were the only ones that knew of this and have been attempting to stage a counterattack against the creatures. Unfortunately, it seems that an attack has failed and Coal has been branded a traitor and banished from the city."

"Is he alive?" asked Pion.

"We assume so, but we cannot confirm it."

"What makes you so sure?"

"It seems that this Tellurian has grown a distinct hatred for the Commander and if he has killed him, he would surely announce it. Display the death, in fact."

Weston asked, "Then, where is the Commander now?"

"We do not know. I was not in contact with him when this happened and there has been no word from him at all. I can only assume that he is in hiding, creating some sort of plan."

"You make many assumptions, Chief Council. Isn't it just as likely that he has fled the city? It is a logical choice, given the circumstances."

"You know Commander Coal well, General. What do you believe?" Anton jabbed back at him. "Do you believe he would run?"

Anton was not a man that backed down when challenged. Weston was clearly the stronger man, but there were few that could turn a phrase as well as the Chief Council. They stared each other down.

"Of course not," Weston finally responded. "The Commander is an honorable man. That does not lessen the severity of his circumstances, though. There is little he can do, so whatever he plans to attempt is suicide."

"My point exactly. With Coal seemingly out of the picture, there is little to stop the Tellurian from his plans. To make matters worse, the Davati have joined forces with them in an attempt to attack Coroge."

Weston turned to his Captains. "Have we set defenses for an aerial assault?"

"To a degree," responded Rouse. "But not enough for a full Davati attack. It will take some time, but even then..." he trailed off.

"Do they bring the *Fionetta*?" he asked Anton.

Anton nods. "It arrived in the capital about a week ago."

He contemplated for a moment before responding. "This complicates things, but we have fought those cowards before. Our defenses will withstand it," he said unconvincingly.

"Maybe, but the Davati are just a pretext to cover the real danger," Seno chimed in. He had been sitting studiously the whole time, absorbing the conversation, but now he felt it was time to contribute.

Weston turned to him. "Explain."

"I have not concluded why the Tellurian is even using the Davati. They could be a ruse, or maybe a contingency. All I do know, is that they are not the real threat."

"Then what is, Historian?"

For once Seno did not feel the urge to drag out his explanation into a fanciful story. It was too much work, so he just said it plainly. "The Hand of the Almighty."

It took a second for the comment to sink in, but when it did, all Weston did was laugh. It started out as a snicker but quickly exploded into a boisterous guffaw he could barely hold in. Pion and Rouse were not privy to the situation, so they just sat there confused. Weston could barely stay in his chair as he threw his head back and let out his amusement.

"Weston," said Leo sternly. "Control yourself. This is highly improper. We do not laugh in the faces of our guests".

"What?" he managed to blurt out. "Did you hear what he said? It is ludicrous"

"Yes, I did. It is not welcome information, let alone information that warrants amusement."

"So, you believe them then?" asked Weston.

Leo was not entertained at all by his grandson's reaction and just calmly stated, "Yes, I do. You would do well to listen to them."

"You honestly believe that there exists a weapon developed by the Brivans hundreds of years ago, that is even more powerful than the Magi?"

"You have read the history behind it, Weston."

"To read it is one thing. To believe it, is completely different."

"I can assure you that it is real," said Seno. Weston spun around and glared at him, clearly displeased by his interruption.

"Your assurances mean nothing to me. It is absurd to believe that the Brivans were able to develop such a thing and then never use it themselves."

"That is because it was never completed during the original research," Seno explained. "The scientists were unable to perfect it and they abandoned the project. When those men died, most of the knowledge of the project died with them."

"If it was never completed and there are no records of the experiments, then what is our issue?"

"We can only assume that the Tellurians know of a way to complete it. When they do, there will be nothing to stop them."

"More of your assumptions," Weston shouted. "Do you even have any concrete facts to prove these theories of yours?"

"If you look at the facts at hand, it is the only conclusion. The Tellurians killed the Supreme Regis and took his place. Then, just a few days later they released Datro

Cervon, Head Researcher of the Science Society, from prison. He was charged with assassinating Supreme Regis Lien."

"Since then, there have been rumors circulating that Datro has been experimenting furiously in his lab, but no one knows why. The lab has been closely guarded," Anton added.

Weston questioned, "He could be creating anything. What makes you so sure that it is the Hand of the Almighty?"

"Because the Tellurians would want nothing more from us than that. You know the history. Tellurians think of us as inferior animals. They would never suggest that there is something we have that they want, unless it is truly powerful. Plus, they have tried to steal the weapon before during the Magi Wars. They know that we have it and where to find it."

Weston rose to his feet. He stood there for moment before pushing away his chair and starting to pace up and down the room. It was evident that he understood the circumstances, but did not want to believe them. No one dared to say a word as he a fought with his conscience.

"What is this weapon? Is it as powerful as the stories foretell?" he finally said. "And do not tell me what you assume!"

Seno stood slowly, not sure how to voice what he wanted to say, so he just said it. "It is just as powerful, but it is not a weapon. It is, in fact, a solution. A solution that gives the user the ability to control natural energy."

Weston asked in surprise, "What good is that to the Tellurians? They already have that ability."

"The Tellurians did not create it, Weston," added Leo.

It took a moment for the comment to sink in for the General. "You cannot mean...?" he muttered.

"It gives anyone the ability... even humans."

Weston's eyes widened.

"That's ridiculous," shouted Rouse. "Humans cannot sense, let alone control natural energy."

"He is correct," said Weston. "Our people have tried it in the past. It cannot be done."

"I promise you, it can. I do not know how the substance works, but that is its intended purpose."

Rouse got to his feet and started shouting. "You expect us to believe such lunacy? You have surely concocted this fantasy to convince us to help you. Do not think for a second that..."

"Rouse!" Weston bellowed. His glare was enough to quiet the Captain instantly. "That is enough."

Weston turned back to Seno. "Is this all true, or is Rouse correct? Are you trying to deceive us into helping you in your fight?"

Anton decided to break back into the conversation. "You understand, don't you? With this substance the Tellurians can create an army of Magi that are under their control. You will not be able to stop such a force, even with your great walls. It will be the end of us all."

Weston imagined the devastation that would ensue if such a force was created. It would be like the Magi Wars once again, but with only them to defend against the enemy. If Coroge were to fall, then there would truly be no one left to stop them. He would not be the one that let such a future occur. Weston looked over to his grandfather, who stared back at him with understanding, yet determined, eyes.

"The weapon has yet to be completed?"

"The Tellurian waits. He has not sent his army. The only reason would be that he wants to have the weapon first. Either it has not been completed, or they are waiting to create a large enough force."

Weston had spent his entire life ensuring that he was the strongest. It was his mission to make his men into the greatest fighters in all of Paks. He would do anything to protect his people, but now he faced a dilemma.

For Paks, or for Vertura?

He despised the Brivans, but they were human. Against the Tellurians, they were not his enemy. He looked back at his grandfather. It had been some time since he looked to Leo for counsel. He had begun to believe that the old man had started to lose his pride over the years. He never realized that it was not pride that was most important. It was duty. His anger had blinded him from the truth. Leo just looked at him with a comforting expression and nodded. His grandfather knew. He did not need to say anything.

"Alert the men," he ordered Pion and Rouse. He turned around, and with a renewed vigor, he said, "We are going to Valoria."

52

Kyte had seen nothing like it before. He had been taught the art of defensive magic and barriers since birth, but this was not conceivable. The Hall of Mirrors barrier was known in his clan, but Kyte had not heard of anyone with the ability to cast it. Every Aerious knew how to cast, detect and dispel, if possible, almost every type of defensive magic. It was how they had managed to conceal themselves for hundreds of years. But the Hall of Mirrors was an ancient and powerful magic, used by only the strongest Magi. Even knowing that, he had never heard of one of such magnitude.

It had taken time, but Kyte was able to detect the edges of the barrier and he was astounded by what he found. Normal Hall of Mirror barriers were erected around small areas such as buildings or small villages. This one was encompassing the entire plateau itself. He had underestimated the extent of the magic in this place. It was clear that whatever was atop this plateau was not meant to be found.

The Hall of Mirrors was a combination of force, visual and mental barrier magic. Not only did it cast a visual illusion, it forcibly kept the enemy within its borders and altered their mental state to make them believe there was nothing wrong. Men had been known to wither and die while trapped inside, while not even realizing what was happening to them.

Kaleb lay on the ground nearby, his head rested up against his pack and his feet up on a large rock. His eyes were closed, but he had not been able to sleep for some time. Unlike Farren, he was calm and relaxed. He had realized some time ago that he was not going to be any help, so worrying himself would not do any good.

Farren, on the other hand, was in complete hysteria. He flung his hands around as he paced back and forth, making incoherent noises. Kyte was sitting on a rock in front of him, deep in contemplation.

"So, you said that there is no way for us to force our way through?" Farren asked.

Kyte shook his head. "It is not possible. The Hall of Mirrors is one of the strongest force barriers. There are only three ways through it. You must know the incantation that releases it, the one who cast it dies, or you are allowed to pass through by the laws of the barrier."

"Laws? What laws?"

"All barriers are built with a set of governing laws. They are made to do a specific thing. For instance, keep out all who are not Aerii. In that case, an Aerious could pass right through, but anyone else would be rejected."

The sun was setting and darkness was approaching. They were high up on the plateau, so the air was much cooler. Farren clung to his cloak tightly.

"How on Paks are we supposed to know the laws of a barrier created a thousand years ago?"

"You have to have been told them, or luckily fall within them. There is no way to tell the laws, even by examining the barrier. That is another one of the strengths of the Hall of Mirrors."

Farren shouted in frustration. With the cold creeping in, he started to rub his hands together and blew some warm air into his cupped fingers. Kyte, who seemed to be unfazed by the cold, smiled at Farren and got to his feet.

"Young Kaleb?" he said.

Kaleb turned his head to the side and peered over to Kyte. "What is it?"

"If you are not busy, would you mind collecting some wood for a fire? It seems like we will need to spend the night and it will only continue to get colder."

Kaleb leapt to his feet. "Of course. It would be nice to have a little warmth for once. Besides, I do not like just sitting around this place."

After Kaleb disappeared down the path, Kyte turned back to Farren. "Do not worry yourself, Prince Farren. We will find a way through. It will just take time."

"But, we do not have time, Kyte. We don't even know what has been happening since we have been gone. The Tellurians could have already won. We could be doing all of this for nothing."

"That is why you must have faith," Kyte said as he placed a hand on Farren's shoulder. "I know in my heart that the Commander will do everything in his power to defend Valoria. I know that, somehow, the Tellurians will be defeated. I do not know how, but I have faith that it will happen. We must keep on going forward and believe that our friends will do the same."

Farren looked up at Kyte, who seemed to glow with calm reassurance. Kyte's smile reminded him of his brother's. It was the smile that told him that Bishop would always be there for him, no matter what. The memories formed an ache in his chest.

Brother. I wish you were here with me.

Farren forced a smile back up to Kyte. He nodded. "Faith, you say?"

"It is a remarkable thing. I know that humans have lost much of their faith over the years, but that does not mean you cannot still find it."

"I have faith that my brother is watching over me. I have faith that he will not let me fail."

"Then you won't," smiled Kyte.

The sun was now starting to disappear over the horizon and the sky was turning a dark red. The temperature was dropping and Farren was beginning to realize how cold it was going to be. If they could not get a fire going, they may very well freeze to death overnight.

"Kyte, did you say that the barrier would break down if the one that cast it died?" Farren asked as he continued to unpack.

"Normally, yes."

"Is it really possible that the one who cast it is still alive?"

"If the barrier was created during the Emerald Ages, as I believe, I do not think so. We Aerii live long lives, but not that long. It could have been cast by an Ignati, but this is considered Aerii holy ground, so it is unlikely. The reason that the barrier still stands is probably because it was created by multiple Aerii. If that is the case, then their combined magic could conceivably create an eternal barrier."

"A barrier that would last forever?"

"Yes. There are many barriers that do, but I did not think it was possible to create an eternal Hall of Mirrors. It would take incredible magical power and control."

Their conversation was interrupted as Kaleb came stumbling back into their small camp. A large bundle of sticks and branches was haphazardly clung under his right arm and he was dragging a large, dead bush with his left. He dropped them in the middle of the camp.

"It isn't the most ideal wood to burn, but it is all I could find. It is getting colder by the second," he said, blowing warmth into his bare hands. "I found the wood, now it is one of your turns to make the fire. I cannot feel my hands."

Farren and Kyte shared amused looks, but tried not to laugh. Kyte went over and started to form the sticks into a fire and stoked it until it was ablaze and warm. The night sky inside the barrier was breathtaking. It was hard to imagine that it was all just an illusion. Not even magic could creature such a spectacular view of the starry night sky, with the warm glow from the guardians and bands of pink and yellow that stretched through the sky on the darkest of nights.

"Get some sleep, Prince Farren. Tomorrow we will find a way through and then our journey will continue."

Farren's hope was now returning. They would complete their quest no matter what. He knew that Coal was continuing to fight, so he would as well. He could not let his brother down. With a genuine smile, he nodded to Kyte. "I have faith," he said as he laid back and soaked in the beauty above him.

When Farren opened his eyes, he immediately felt an intense heat. The plateau was gone and he was standing in a vast, barren landscape. It was dark, but not because it was night. He could see the glow of the sun above him, but there was a dense cloud of ash all around him. The only sign of life was the husk of a burnt tree a short distance away to his left. Everything else was reduced to a sheet of ash that carpeted the ground.

His heart was racing so fast he thought he was going to pass out. He could see the sweat dripping from his body as he bent over panting. His breathing was frantic, but he could not seem to control it. In fact, he could not control his body at all. Farren had felt this sensation before.

I am dreaming again.

It was the same as last time. He could see everything that was going on, but he had no control over himself. It was as if he was seeing through someone else's eyes; feeling what that person felt.

"Again," shouted a loud voice.

Farren's head raised enough to look forward. In the darkness he could see the silhouette of a figure. With the little energy he had left, he shook his head in refusal. "I can't," he shouted back.

"You do not yet have control. It is not enough," the man urged.

Farren's body continued to heave as he tried to catch his breath. Footsteps started to approach. He lifted his head to see the other figure approaching. All that was visible were the man's feet and the marks Farren's sweat made in the ash.

When he got close enough, Farren could make out his appearance. The man looked very similar to the one he had seen in his last dream. His hair was long, straight and a very deep black. He was larger than the other man and just as well built. Like the last man, he wore black, but not the same type of clothing. This man wore a long cloak that was fitted tightly to his chest and upper body. A leather vest, inlayed with black metal, was also tight around his chest. There was something engraved into the vest, but Farren could not make it out. The man walked quickly, but gracefully, and always with his hands behind his back.

"I know," said Farren. "But, I cannot continue. I need rest."

"You will rest when I say you can rest," the man ordered.

Farren tried to rise, but his body gave out and he slumped back down.

The man kicked Farren in the shoulder and his body fell back onto the ground. Ash kicked up all around him and then started to settle back down, clinging to Farren's sweaty skin. The man loomed over top of him.

"We had a deal. In exchange for your life, you agreed to do what I told you until that fateful day," the man growled.

"I know. I just cannot keep going right now. I do not have the strength. This is too much. I need to rest."

"I said you will rest when I say so," the man bellowed. He held one of his arms out in front him.

Farren's heart started to race even faster and he felt his eyes widen in fear. He tried to move but he went nowhere. Suddenly, the man's palm started to glow red and a massive ball of flames erupted towards Farren. The pain was excruciating. The heat seared deep into his skin and he seemed to burn from the inside out. The little energy Farren had left was channeled into an ear-piercing howl as he felt his flesh melting from his body.

Farren jolted up from the ground. He could still feel the fire tearing into his flesh, so he started too furiously rip the clothes from his body. His fingers dug into his skin, but that pain was nothing compared to what he had already felt.

"Farren stop," a voice shouted.

It was a friendly voice; not the menacing voice of the black haired man. He did not know what to think. We could still feel the fire burning him, but something was different. It was difficult to think with the pain clouding his mind. Then, two sets of hands grabbed onto his arms and legs and started to pin them to the ground. He continued to struggle.

"It's us, Farren. Stop. It's us."

It was dark, but his eyes started to adjust. It was not the same darkness as before. This was a nighttime darkness. Then he felt a cool breeze against his skin. His body twitched in reaction, almost fearful of it. Two faces started to form out of the night. It was Kyte and Kaleb. Their expressions were filled with confusion and concern.

"Calm down, Farren. We are friends. You are awake now," said Kaleb.

Farren's heart started to settle and his muscles relaxed. It took a few more minutes, but his body finally calmed completely. The heat was dissipating and the cool breeze of the night returned to his skin. His mind was still rattled, but his body was now under his control. Kyte and Kaleb released him.

"Are you alright?" Kaleb asked. "You just started to scream and thrash around for no reason. We were afraid you were going to tear your skin right off."

Farren looked around, making sure he was where he thought he was. This dream was far worse than the others. It was so much more real. The affect lingered, even after he woke.

What is happening to me?

"Prince Farren?"

Farren shook away his daze.

"Yes," he managed to mutter. "I am alright."

"Another dream?"

"It was so real, Kyte. I thought I was going to die and I could do nothing about it." His voice was becoming hysterical. "I could still feel it, after I woke up. I could feel the heat."

Kyte's concern was growing. "Heat? Were there flames in your dream? What was happening?"

Farren shook his head. He could not repeat it. It was far too painful to even describe. He tried to swallow, but he found his mouth dry as a bone. He coughed in reaction.

Kyte turned to Kaleb. "Get some water for him."

Kaleb raced over to his pack to find his canteen. When Kaleb moved from his view, Farren saw something. His mind was in such turmoil he did not notice at first.

The entire landscape in front of him was shimmering. The faint light stretched up towards the sky and then back around him.

The barrier?

His eyes darted around, and in all directions he could see it. It was fainter as it extended down towards the base of the plateau, but it ended not twenty yards in front of him. It was a solid wall of light. As he peered around, the light started to fade. Farren looked to Kyte, but he did not seem to notice at all.

Am I the only one that is seeing it?

The light was fading fast, but Farren did not know what to do. He did not even know what was going on. He struggled to his feet.

Kyte tried to hold him down. "Farren, what's wrong? What are you doing?"

Farren ran forward, passing a confused Kaleb who held out his canteen. "You don't see it?" Farren asked.

"See what?"

"The barrier. It is glowing." Farren pulled himself up onto a rocky ledge. There was a bright ball of light, nestled in the fading wall of the barrier. Farren did not know what it was, but he was going to reach it. It was as if he was drawn towards it. He pushed himself through the thick brush, not caring that his arms and legs where getting scratched by the dry wood.

"Farren stop," shouted Kyte. "You must not touch the barrier. It could kill you."

Farren could hear Kaleb and Kyte scrambling after him; confused about what was going on. Farren did not care though. He must reach the light before it faded away. The wall was disappearing fast and he could barely still see it, but the ball of light was still visible.

The barrier finally disappeared completely, but he pulled himself up one final ledge. The faint light of the bright ball was floating right in front of him. He stared at it, mesmerized. He could feel a strange energy emanating from it. It was like it was calling for him. Slowly, he reached his hand towards it.

"You mustn't Farren, no. It is too dangerous," yelled Kyte. He tried to shoot a gust of air towards the young Prince, but the barrier seemed to reach out and reject it.

When Farren's fingers touched the light, the glow intensified and then exploded outward. Kaleb and Kyte shielded their eyes in shock. The light seemed to come from nowhere and scattered out across the invisible barrier and out into the night. When it seemed as if it would continue to stretch all the way to the stars, it stopped and raced back towards the singular point in the blink of an eye. As the points of light returned, the intensity was too great and they all turned away, covering their eyes.

After a few seconds, they all opened their eyes again and looked back. In front of Farren hovered a glowing set of markings. Farren could not read it, but it was clearly some sort of writing. He stood staring at it in awe, before turning to Kyte.

Both Kyte and Kaleb were staring at the strange text as well. They were baffled, especially Kaleb, who looked as if he was going to faint from utter confusion.

"Do you know what it says, Kyte?" yelled Farren.

Kyte had seen much in his life, but this was beyond even his reckonings. He had never seen, or heard, of such an occurrence.

"I believe so," he returned. He made his way up to the ledge where Farren stood. After brushing himself off, he looked back at the writing. "It is an ancient Aerii language. I was taught it by my father." He stretched his hand out and started to make sense of the writing.

Kaleb groaned as he pulled himself up onto the rock. Farren reached out and gave him a helping hand.

"What is going on?" Kaleb asked. "What did you do?"

"I don't really know. When I woke up, I could see this glow." He shrugged. "Something was drawing me to it. I had this rush of energy and there was a part of me that knew I had to reach the glow."

"A rush of energy? You just knew?" Kaleb asked, skeptical. Farren shrugged and nodded. Kaleb just sighed and said, "Well, I can't argue with results. I do not know what happened, but you clearly did something."

They both turned to Kyte. "So, what does it say?" Farren asked.

"It is a poem." Kyte took a few steps back to get a better look. "It says, those pure of heart need never fear, nor hide behind their pain. For centuries I've fought evil here, forever I will remain."

As Kyte finished the last word, the letters started to glow brighter. The letters scrambled and formed back into the solid glowing ball. The orb started to stretch open, creating a doorway through the barrier. When it stopped, there was a rectangular opening, lined with glowing light. What was on the other side looked exactly the same as before, but it felt much different. All three of the men, even Kyte, stood dumbfounded as this all occurred.

Kyte turned back to the other two. "Quick, get our things. We do not know how long this doorway will stay open."

They all rushed back to their camp and started to pack up their gear. In a matter of minutes they were climbing back up to the ledge. When they got back to the doorway, Farren stepped slowly up to it. It was clearly an opening, but he was still wary of going through. Slowly, he reached out his hand. When it broke the invisible plane of where the barrier once stood, he naturally tensed his hand, expecting a reaction, but nothing happened. It was just an open doorway. Feeling reassured, he lead with one leg and slowly stepped through. Kyte followed quickly, then Kaleb a few seconds later.

Farren was not sure exactly what he was expecting, but this was not it. Nothing was different. The image that was projected on the barrier was the same as what they now saw. They were still on the side of the rocky, shrub-covered plateau. This did not seem like a magic world that needed ultimate protection. The only thing that was different, was the wind. The cold, buffeting wind was gone and it was much warmer without it. Otherwise, Farren was not impressed.

"Are you sure we went through the barrier?" asked Kaleb.

Kyte responded, "Of course. That was clearly the edge of the barrier and we have passed through it. That writing must have been the incantation to release the magic."

"Then why is nothing different?"

Kyte examined their surroundings, looking for an answer. Off in the distance, towards the top of the plateau he noticed a faint glow that stretched across the entire summit. "Look," he said, pointing. "We have not yet reached the top. We are still exactly where we were, but the forest at the peak has been revealed. We are free of the Hall of Mirrors, but we are not yet at our destination."

"What is that glow?" said Farren.

"The Forest of Twilight is said to be eternally radiant. All that lives in the forest glows with natural energy."

Farren smiled as he pictured it. He imagined the rivers sparkling, the leaves glowing and the insects buzzing around like shooting stars. It was surely an amazing sight to behold. He wanted nothing more than to see such a place. He adjusted the pack on his back and started to trek up the path. Kyte and Kaleb quickly followed; their excitement palpable.

It was indeed beyond description. Even Kaleb started to get excited as they got closer to the top. They could see the tips of the trees and the living fluorescence became more apparent. When they did finally pull themselves up the final ridge, the complete landscape was visible.

Even at the edge of the tree line, looking in, it was astounding. Mammoth Everwoods erupted up from the earth throughout the forest; their trunks almost perfectly vertical. The bases of the trees disappeared neatly into the ground, making little more than a ripple on the forest floor. The Everwoods were the only trees in the forest and they dominated the landscape.

High in the canopy, the Everwood's foliage created a brilliant, whitish- green ceiling of light. The ground was carpeted with low growing grass and mosses, all of which glowed in their own distinct hue. Vines spiraled up the trunks of some of the Everwoods, but restricted themselves to the bases, since it was far too difficult to grow up the entire length.

The contrast between the towering Everwoods and the rest of the low growing plant life was peculiar, but made the forest seem all the more magical. It was odd that a soil that could produce such monstrous trees would grow little else. The ground was remarkably flat, so they could see deep in to the woods. It did not seem to change.

"Wow," gasped Farren.

"I could not have said it better myself," agreed Kaleb. "When you are right, you are right."

There was no movement at all. They saw no wildlife, no rodents scurrying in the groundcover, no birds fluttering amongst the pillars. There wasn't even the buzzing of insects to break up the tranquility. Farren could not decide if it was peaceful, or disquieting. It made it seem like the forest was theirs and theirs alone. It was almost as if it was placed there, waiting for them to arrive.

Farren walked up to one of the massive trees. "Are these Everwoods? I thought they were nearly extinct, aside from those in the palace ground in Valoria. How is there an entire forest of them in this place? They are so much larger here."

Kyte, even as an Aerious, was equally awed by the sight. From the stories he had been told as a child, he knew what to expect, but hearing it in stories could not compare to seeing it with his own eyes. He could feel the intense concentration of energy that flowed in the forest and it invigorated him. "The Everwood is able to grow to its size by absorbing natural energy. It almost died out because the flow of energy has slowed over the centuries but, in this place, it is as thick as it once was. It is like the Forest is frozen in time, five hundred years ago."

"Why has the natural energy stayed so strong here?"

"My mother once told me that under the plateau there is a spring of natural energy. It accumulates here in large concentrations. The barriers would also have kept the energy confined here; not allowing it to dissipate, as it has elsewhere," Kyte described. "Can you feel it?"

"I don't know," said Farren. He examined himself, as if he could see the energy itself. He hopped around on his toes. "I do feel lighter and the air feels..." he pondered, trying to find the word to describe it.

"...Crisper," finished Kaleb, who has bounding around the area in excitement. He swept out a couple of powerful kicks and started punching the air. Running up to a tree, he planted his feet into the side, flipped backwards and neatly landed on his feet. Without breaking stride, he continued to run around, enjoying his newfound vitality.

Farren laughed. "Yes, crisper is a good word for it," he said to Kyte. "My energy is returning and my pain is gone. Everything seems to have just lifted away."

"Natural energy will do that. Even if you cannot sense it, natural energy affects you. I have not felt such strong flow in many years. Feeling it gives me confidence that we will find what we are looking for."

Farren had almost forgotten that he still did not know what they were in search of. He trusted Kyte and knew that it was important, which was why he never questioned him, but now he was becoming curious.

"What *are* we looking for, Kyte?"

Kyte was walking up to one of the Everwoods. He placed his hand gently on the smooth bark and looked up towards its distant peak. He felt as if he was home. He could not describe it, but it felt right.

"Tomorrow, Prince Farren. For now, let us just enjoy ourselves and get some rest. This place may be beautiful, but it is just as deadly as the Shroud and in far more sinister ways. We need to have our wits about us tomorrow."

The temperature in the woods was perfect, so Farren did not even bother unpacking any of his things. He found a thick spot of moss near the base of an Everwood, rested down his head and stared up at the canopy. It seemed like the ground where he lay softened under his weight to make it more comfortable. After a few minutes, Kaleb settled down as well and they tried to get some rest. Farren did not understand how such a beautiful place could be deadly, but he trusted Kyte. Kyte knew far more than he ever would. Tomorrow would be a long day. Once he lay down, he finally realized his exhaustion. He was going to need the sleep.

Since leaving Valoria, sleep had become a luxury for Farren. Dreams had plagued his nights and allowed him little rest. Even when he did manage to close his eyes for a short moment, the sleep did little to rejuvenate his weary body. His side still ached from the battle with the Tellurian and his youthful energy had long ago been drained. He needed a restful sleep, but even the beauty of the Forest of Twilight refused to give it to him.

The natural glow of the forest seemed to seep into his mind. Even with his eyes closed, it lit up his thoughts and did not allow his mind to calm into a slumber. He got no rest and his body was starting to deteriorate from within. He did not know how much more it could take.

Kyte and Kaleb, on the other hand, had slept well. Kaleb had awoken a short time ago with an exaggerated yawn. Kyte had been awake since the sun first peaked out its glowing head. He had risen and packed up so quietly that Farren had not noticed at all, even though he was just lying awake in his makeshift bed.

Since they were still near the edge of the forest, the sunlight streamed in from the side of the trees. Farren noticed, though, that very little sunlight was able to penetrate the dense canopy above. Further in, the natural glow of the forest would probably be the only light. Even in the day, he would not be able to escape the glow. It started as beautiful, but now it was a burden. Sleep looked like it would never come.

Farren rose to his feet, his entire body aching as he moved.

"Did you not get any sleep?" Kaleb asked; noticing Farren's discomfort.

"No," Farren groaned. "I could not block out the light."

"Oh, I just covered my head with my blanket and it was fine. It was a little annoying at first, but I was exhausted. It felt good to get some sleep."

"Lucky you." Farren moved around to try to stretch away his tension, but it only provided momentary relief. He had not unpacked anything, so he just waited for Kaleb to get ready.

"Does something trouble you, Prince Farren?" Kyte asked him.

"I'm just tired, Kyte. I haven't had a good sleep since we left Valoria. I don't know how much longer I can go on like this."

"Is it the dreams? I did not hear you yell out last night."

"No, it wasn't even that." He couldn't find the words to describe it. "You know how you said there was a concentration of energy in the forest because there is some sort of spring of energy below us?"

Kyte nodded. "Yes. It flows much quicker here than anywhere else."

"Well... it's almost like that energy is affecting me somehow. I don't know how, but it feels like its flowing through me and I can't control it."

"That may be the case, Prince Farren. You do seem to have a strong connection to the natural flow; much stronger than most humans. It is possible that you are starting to feel it, but your body is not accustomed to it."

Farren was surprised. He had assumed that the concentration of energy around him was the problem, not that he could actually sense it. "But, I did not think that humans could sense natural energy."

Farren smiled. "That is a common misconception. They can, but only slightly." Kyte placed his hand out in front of him. "If a human were to practice, they could conceivably increase that ability, but humans do not realize this."

Gradually, a faint glowing orb started to appear in Kyte's palm. Farren's eyes widened.

"What is it?"

"It is energy, in its pure form. You can see it because it is concentrated at a single point. You are beginning to notice your ability because there is more energy in the forest to sense, but you have always had the ability."

The orb continued to brighten. Farren started to lean in towards it, in awe of its magnificence.

"So, you are saying that I have the ability to use magic?"

"There is a difference between sensing the energy and being able to control it. It would take hundreds of years for you to gain that control. But do not fret, Prince Farren. You have a fantastic gift. You should be proud to be able to sense the natural flow. It will open up your world."

For the first time since they had set out on their journey, Farren was happy. Through all of the pain and the sorrow, through the nightmares and his clouded mind, Farren was genuinely happy. It was a lonely speck of a light in a cavern of darkness, but it felt warm. Since it was the only light, it was all the more special.

"We must get moving," said Kyte. "The forest will have many more tests for us. We cannot waste time here," he said, purposefully ignoring Kaleb's request. "There is still a long road ahead of us. If we move quickly, we may be able to reach our destination by the end of the day."

53

"We are ready," said Minor Fanix.

He was standing in the open plain of the training grounds, which his men had been training on for nearly a week. The ground was trampled from all the activity and scattered with broken arrows, spears and other weaponry.

The Davati Airmen had been practicing their aerial maneuvers and tactics, using the smaller attack ships. In battle, the *Fionetta* would be used as well, but training with it would be impractical. Jumping from the decks of the ships, they utilized specially designed rigid wing suits to coast their way to the ground. The suits were a wing-shaped frame of light weight wood that was coated with a paste like material that dried to form a thin membrane around the frame. Each wing could be slightly adjusted up and down to add some control, but very little. Davati soldiers went through years of training to master the suits and become Airmen. Despite the training, it was still quite dangerous and many men died from little more than an unexpected breeze, or a torn suit.

The Valor Forces, on the other hand, were known for their strength, discipline and sheer numbers. The size of the Forces was nearly four times that of the Airmen, and their fighting skills were clearly superior. While Airmen spent most of their training time mastering the wing suits, the Forces soldiers practiced swordsmanship and battle maneuvers. Each soldier had a specific task in the whole of the army and they were trained to master it. There were dozens of units that employed many different weapons, each with a purpose that benefitted the whole. The Valor Forces were bred for individual strength and collective efficiency.

The *Fionetta* could be seen off in the distance. The Grand Master stood next to Fanix, a mix of anticipation and anger apparent in his expression. The Minor did not dare ask him what was bothering him. He knew, so it was not necessary.

Out in front of them, stood a massive assembly of men; the combined force of the Davati Airmen and the Valor Forces. It was an army of ten thousand men and each one stood rigid in attention. They too, were fearful of the Grand Master. To them it was the Supreme Regis, though. They all just waited quietly for their orders.

Minor Fanix had called them to attention earlier. It was the fateful day. The men were excited, but tried not to show it. Soon they would be at the gates of Coroge and then, hopefully, inside of them. The two armies stood together, but separated. There was a distinct line that split the green from the blue. Even if they wore the same uniforms, it would be clear who was who. The Valorians were physically much larger in almost every way. Many of the men had begun to form some camaraderie with their foreign brethren but, after the battle, it would quickly disappear, so trying to make solid ties was pointless. They would always be enemies, even if, at the moment, they were allies.

It had been some time since the Grand Master had arrived and he still had said nothing. He just stood silently next to Fanix, examining the army. His silence was beginning to create unease among the ranks.

Fanix turned to him again. "Do you wish to say something to the men?"

Without turning, The Grand Master said, "No, human, I will let you do the honors."

It still hit hard. The Grand Master had continued to refer to Fanix as human, despite all that he had done. It was hard enough, as a Minor, to have to put up with such demeaning talk, but to hear the Grand Master call him *human*, while he referred to Commander Lucer by his real name was infuriating. He managed a contrived bow of appreciation. "Thank you, Your Highness."

Fanix cleared his throat, then stepped forward. Some of the men, who were beginning to lose focus, snapped back to attention. It was a cold morning, but the sun was out and there was no wind, so it was bearable. Besides, the men did not feel the brisk chill through their adrenaline.

"Men!" he shouted. He paused for affect. "I should not have to tell you the significance of this event. Never, in the history of our kingdom, have two sects come together to do battle. Never, has there been an alliance of such magnitude. Today, we write history." A buzz started to travel through the ranks. "Today, we look into the eyes of the Creed and say, no more! No more will you stand above us with your iron fist and threaten our sanctity. No more will we be fearful of your battle-hungry ways. Today, we march to rid Paks of those barbarians and bring true peace to our kingdom. Death to the Creed!"

The raucous shouts that erupted were deafening. The voices of ten thousand men came together and nearly shook the earth beneath them. Their incoherent shouts began to form into a uniform chant. "Death to the Creed! Death to the Creed! Death to the Creed!"

Minor Fanix turned back to the Grand Master for approval, but the Tellurian only smirked. Fanix was not sure what he was expecting, but a smirk was not it. Annoyed, he returned his attention back to the men.

He raised his hands to settle the ranks. "We set out immediately. All Airmen report to the *Fionetta*. Valor Forces will go by land. You all know your duties."

The men saluted. Squad commanders stepped out from the crowd and began to direct the men to their assigned locations.

"Excellent speech, Human," said the Grand Master. The compliment almost seemed sincere, but Fanix knew it was foolish to think so. "The men really seem to rally to your words."

Fanix ignored the comment. "Are you sure it is wise to start this war without the weapon?"

"Wise has nothing to do with it." Talk of the Hand of the Almighty was clearly upsetting the Grand Master. "We no longer have the benefit of time. We have waited long enough. My warriors continue to dispatch of Creed scouts. They have known of this battle for some time. We cannot give the Creed any more time to prepare."

"But, what of Datro and the weapon? What will you do?"

The news of Datro's treachery was still fresh in his mind. He never did trust him completely, but never did the Grand Master imagine that Datro would betray him in such a way. The fact that he had never considered it was more upsetting than the betrayal itself. There was now another human he had underestimated.

"I will dispatch of him myself," the Grand Master growled. "If it is me he wants, then I will gladly accommodate him."

Fanix bowed his head. "I will do my best to defeat the wretched Creed in your stead, Your Highness."

"I want more than your best, Human. I want absolute victory."

Fanix bowed lower. "Or course. I will bring you nothing less."

Knowing that the Grand Master would not be joining the army excited Fanix. He would have lone control over the single largest army the humans had ever assembled. It was exhilarating. The only piece missing, was the weapon. He could still win but, against the Creed, there were no guarantees.

"I will send some of my warriors with you," said the Grand Master. "They should be more than enough to ease your weak and troubled mind. The weapon will be unnecessary. It was always just a precaution."

"You are more than kind, Your Highness."

"Now go. The faster you can arrive at Coroge, the faster it can fall."

Fanix just silently bowed once again and turned to walk away. He did not need another reason to rid himself of the Tellurian. Once they took flight, the air was his domain. That was his world.

In ten days, they would be at the gates of Coroge and the battle for the future of Paks would begin.

In Coroge, there was a similar chill, but here the sun was blotted by the clouds and there was a stiff breeze cutting across Weston's face. The cold did not bother him. He was too deep in thought as he watched his men finalize their preparations for the journey to Valoria.

"How much longer?" he asked Captain Rouse, who stood next to him.

"We should be ready to march by midday, General."

"Excellent work, Rouse. You have made the preparations quickly. I am impressed."

"It was not all my doing, Sir. The men have been ready. Since you announced the situation in Valoria, the men have been waiting for you to change your mind. They all want a chance to take on a Tellurian face-to-face and it would be difficult from behind a wall." Rouse added the last comment with a chuckle.

Weston smiled in return. "Indeed it would. I hope I did not make them wait too long."

"They had faith in you, Sir."

Weston started to walk down the central street of the city, towards the gate. Men, women and children were racing around, ensuring that every last bit of equipment was ready, every last horse was properly bridled and shod. Men were sharpening weapons and gathering bundles of arrows. The women were packing food and water.

"How many men do we have?" Weston asked.

"A little over five-thousand. Two thousand cavalry and the rest are on foot."

"What of the enemy? Do we know their numbers?"

"By our estimation, they could have as many as ten thousand, Sir."

The large number did not seem to concern the General. "It should be a good battle then," he said.

"That number includes the Airmen, as well," added Rouse.

"Oh yes, I nearly forgot those flying cowards. If we take the fight to them, their usefulness is greatly diminished. My fear is not with them, but make sure that every last man packs their shields."

"Of course," noted Rouse.

"Do we have the ballista and explosive arrow tips prepared? If they do not want to come down to us from their perch, we can always drag them down."

"They are ready."

"Then they will be nothing to concern ourselves with. It is the Valorians and the Tellurians I am worried about. Have we gathered any intelligence from Valoria yet?"

"Not yet, Sir. None of our patrols have returned."

"Do we have any intelligence on those creatures? Anything at all?"

"Only what the Aerious initially told us and what the Chief Council and the Historian have told us now, Sir. We have not been unable to get anywhere near Valoria for weeks."

"Is there anything that they told us that we can use? Do we know how many Tellurians there are? What their ultimate goal is?"

Rouse shook his head. "Nothing, Sir. The Aerious said it is almost impossible to determine the exact numbers of a Tellurian force, because of their transformation ability. There could be only a few, or there could be thousands. There is no way to tell, until the battle begins."

"That is always comforting. What are your thoughts, Rouse?" asked Weston.

"I think is wise, Sir, to assume to worst. They would not have waited so long for this kind of attack unless they had significant numbers."

They reached the gate and Weston signaled to a man at the top of the wall to let them through. The giant counterweight started to lower and the gate began to creak open.

"Yes, but if they numbered in the thousands, Rouse, they would not have needed such an elaborate plan. They would never have enlisted the help of humans unless it was absolutely needed."

"You may be right, Sir," Rouse considered. "But, we cannot assume that. We must prepare to face thousands and be grateful when only a few show their ugly faces."

They started to walk out across the bridge that traversed the moat and into the barren plain that stretched out in front of the city.

"Wise words, Captain. You may make a suitable General yet," he said. His expression quickly turned serious. "But this time, I can only assume that there will be a few."

"Why is that, Sir?"

Out on the plain, thousands of Creed were forming together their impressive wartime machine. Huge groups of horses stood waiting, clad in metal armor and packed with every weapon imaginable. Dozens of catapults and ballista were set on wheels to be pulled the hundreds of miles to the capital. The look on every man's face was that of anticipation. No person, not even the women who were seeing off their husbands, nor the children who were watching their fathers go to war, looked afraid. This was their life. This is what they were born to do.

Weston loved to see his men prepare for battle. It was an imposing sight to witness. This time, though, it felt different. When he looked out at the thousands of men that he had grown up with, trained with, and lead into battle, he felt a trace of sorrow. This battle was far different from all the others.

Looking to his good friend and Captain, he said, "I must believe that there are few, because if there are thousands, then this will be a battle we cannot win."

It was a shock to hear his General speak of failure but, in his heart, Rouse had realized this fact a long time ago. This was going to be the greatest battle that had ever been waged in Paks since the Magi Wars. Even if they did win, many of them would not survive. Paks would be forever changed.

Neither of them spoke. Despite their overwhelming strength and confidence, they were still mortal men. They knew death would come to them someday, and now it looked as if it may come sooner than expected.

After a few silent moments, a smile formed on Rouse's lips. "It's exciting, isn't it, General?"

As if thinking the very same thing, Weston smiled and nodded "I promised you a truly great fight one day. Do you remember?"

Rouse laughed. "Oh yes. I would not forget such a promise. It has kept me sane through these years of peace. I was actually beginning to think it wasn't going to happen."

"Well, here it is my friend. Are you impressed? Does it live up to your expectations?"

"I could not have imagined it any greater." Drawing his sword and pointing it out in front of him, he declared, "I intend to make my final mark on this world in the chest of a Tellurian. They will remember this battle as the day of their folly. It will be the day they thought they could challenge the Creed and live to tell about it."

"That sounds like a spectacular death; a death worthy of a Creed warrior."

"None greater, Sir."

Weston patted his Captain on the back and smiled. "Then alert the men. We do not want to make them wait any longer. Let us go make our mark."

Rouse sheathed his sword and saluted. "Yes, Sir."

They both turned and started to walk back towards the gate.

"We will take the route north of the mountains. In eleven days we will be at the gates of Valoria and we will show these Tellurians how foolish their plan truly is."

54

In the serene and glowing atmosphere of the Forest of Rising Twilight, a leaf was slowing falling to the ground. Since there was no wind in the forest, the leaf seemed to just drop straight downward, with very little drift back and forth. Its journey had begun high up in the canopy of the forest, its stem finally giving way and releasing it from the branch. Since it was no longer connected to the natural flow, its glow had diminished and it looked just like any other leaf. It had taken a long journey from the top of an Everwood, but its fall would soon be over. Suddenly, though, just before it seemed it would gently rest on the forest floor, an arrow whistled through the air and struck the leaf, pinning it against the trunk of its mother tree.

"Just like that," said Kyte. He lowered down his bow and turned to Farren, whose expression was a mix of awe and annoyance. "Did you see? My back arm was held high and steady. Just before firing you let out a deep breath to calm your body and steady your hand."

"I understood it the first time, Kyte," said Farren. "But, there is a difference between understanding and doing."

"The only difference, Prince Farren, is your faith. If you have faith that what you understand is correct, then you will always succeed in what you do."

"How is it that you always make things sound so easy?" asked Farren.

"Because they are," said Kyte, with a smile.

Farren shook his head, unconvinced. He let out a deep breath and strung an arrow into his bow. Looking down the shaft of the arrow, he targeted the pinned leaf on the tree. He held the position for a moment, and then let out a deep breath. The arrow released, and in a second it was imbedded into the tree, just a few inches from the leaf. Farren let out a big groan.

"Very good, Prince Farren. You are getting much better."

"But, I did not even hit it. You hit a leaf out of mid-air and I cannot even hit a still target."

"It will come. You must be patient. I have honed my skill over a hundred years. These things take time."

Unexpectedly, an arrow went whizzing by both of their heads and stuck itself dead center in the middle of the leaf. They heard a chuckle from behind them and turned. Kaleb was standing with a satisfied grin on his face.

"That wasn't too hard," he said.

"You are a fool, you know that right?" said Farren. He picked up his quiver of arrows and started to walk over to his bag. His annoyance was obvious.

"Come now, Farren, it is all in good fun. Why can't the teacher have a little fun with his old student? We never got around to bow training. You are holding your expectations too high. It took me months to be able to do that."

"I do not have months," said Farren. "I do not even have days. I need to learn quickly if I am to be of any use in this fight." He put his cloak back around his shoulders and threw on his backpack. "Let's go. We have delayed here long enough."

The young Prince started to walk off without waiting for an answer. Kaleb and Kyte could say nothing to sooth their companion's torment. They just picked up their things and followed after him.

It was the third day in the forest. No matter how far they walked, very little changed. The Everwoods still dominated the landscape, but now small bushes and even saplings were starting to appear amongst the towering behemoths. There were flowers, tall grasses, and ferns. The ground started to swell from its original flatness. They had passed a few small streams, which were as refreshing as they were cool. Farren had never tasted such crisp and clean water. He was not sure if it was the water, or the fact that he had not had anything descent to drink in days.

Sleep still did not come to the young Prince. The second night was the same as the first. The natural glow of the forest seemed to seep into his mind and he could not keep it out. In fact, it seemed to grow more intense as they went further into the forest. Kyte had told him that the source of the energy; the spring that ran beneath the forest, must be near its center. That is most likely why more and more flora continued to appear.

There was also very little natural light that managed to break through the dense canopy, which made it difficult to tell if it was indeed day or night. Combining that confusion with lack of sleep, Farren's mind and body could barely stay together. This was one of the dangers of the forest. This is what Kyte had warned them of. Despite the internal turmoil, the three men trudged onward.

Luckily for them, no other dangers had arisen. In fact, there was nothing in the forest at all. They had noticed the quiet when they first entered, but assumed it would change as they ventured further into the forest. They had spent most of their time talking amongst each other, so they had not noticed that nothing had changed. It was Kaleb who finally realized, after they all fell silent for a while. There was nothing alive in the forest. There were no sounds of animals or living creatures. No birds fluttered around in the tree tops and no small mammals scurried around in the underbrush. There was not even the buzzing sound of insects, or the whispers of the wind. There was nothing. The moment they all realized it, they could not keep it out of their heads. It had not taken long for the beauty and serenity of the forest to turn to agony and eeriness.

After the third day continued to roll onward, and they still came upon nothing, Kyte become quiet. Until then, he had been answering every question that Kaleb and Farren asked him. His explanations of the Aerii history fascinated the two boys and most of the second day they talked endlessly about the Emerald Ages and the different Magi clans. Kyte loved to talk about his people's history, but something was now weighing on his thoughts. Neither Farren nor Kaleb had wanted to ask him about it, but their exhaustion was beginning to overcome them. Kyte had been their anchor until now. They had not wanted to think that their anchor was wavering, but they needed to know what was going on. They could not plod on forever.

Just before the Prince could say something, Kyte stopped suddenly. The boys stopped as well and waited to see what was wrong. Kyte stood silently, staring straight ahead. It almost seemed like he was squinting to try to see something, but there was nothing ahead of them except more forest. After a few minutes a smile finally appeared on the Aerious' face.

"We are here," he said.

Farren and Kaleb were confused. "Here? What do you mean here? I see nothing," said Farren.

Kyte put out his hand and sent out a gust of air. Just like before, at the base of the plateau, the image of the forest in front of them rippled like a pool of water. "We are at our destination. This is what we have come so far to see."

With another big gust of wind, the barrier rippled furiously and then disappeared completely. What appeared behind it was far beyond what they could have imagined. It was like an imagined oasis in the middle of a vast desert. The Everwoods still towered up into the sky, but now they were more than just trees. They were the foundation for a grand treetop city that seemed to stretch as far as they could see in every direction.

"What is it?" asked Farren, awestruck.

"It is the City in the Sky," proclaimed Kyte. "The grand city of the Aerii."

Staircases spiraled up the trunks and met with tiers of white, palatial buildings and platforms. Bridges stretched from tree to tree on every level, creating a confusing maze of passages. The trio was in awe of everything that they saw. It looked as if the buildings were studded with jewels, because they sparkled like a thousand diamonds. Each building was constructed with grand archways, columns, domes, and railings. The city was massive, but it still hung up in the treetops as if it were floating on the air.

On the ground, the grass was thick and green, with a rainbow of glowing flowers carpeting everything but the walking paths. Streams intertwined and wove their way through the trees, reflecting the sparkle of the buildings. The natural glow that lit up the forest was even more intense in the city and a rainbow of colors cascaded off of every building, pathway and tree branch.

Kyte and the two boys walked slowly through the paths; mouths and eyes agape. Even though Kyte had heard descriptions of the place as a child, seeing the real thing was far different. Farren grazed his hand through the grass and the tall flowers, which were the largest he had ever seen. He needed to be sure they were even real. Kaleb quickly dashed over to one of the staircases and started to run up to one of the upper levels. Farren was too exhausted to follow, so he just collapsed into the grass and stared up at the sparkling city above him.

Kaleb shouted down from above. "It is incredible up here. I can see everything. Farren you have to come up here. Wait, is that gold?" His voice trailed off as he ran off in the other direction.

Farren had no interest in moving from his cushioned bed of grass. He was quite content. Kyte wandered off to enjoy the view as well, leaving Farren on his own. Even though light was far brighter in this place, Farren's mind was calm. He could close his eyes and feel relaxed for the first time in ages. He did not care to think about why, he just took a deep breath and drifted to sleep.

Farren wasn't sure how long he was asleep, but it could not have been too long. He was stirred awake when he heard voices. Through his cracked eyes, he saw Kyte and Kaleb conversing quietly a short distance away. Their expressions were not full of excitement as they were before, but rather concern. Farren slowly got to his feet and Kaleb noticed his movement.

"Oh good, you are awake. We did not want to wake you since you have not slept for days. You needed the rest."

"What is going on?" asked Farren, stretching as he rose.

"Well," said Kaleb. He turned back to Kyte who shrugged back. "We may have a problem."

"What do you mean problem? Is this not what we were searching for?"

"Yes and no. This is indeed what we were searching for, but…" Again, Kaleb turned back to Kyte. "I think it best that Kyte tells the rest."

"You have been asking me, Young Prince, what it is we are searching for."

"Yes, and you have been avoiding my answer for days."

"I was avoiding telling you because I thought it would be better to show you first hand." He gestured to their surroundings. "And I have. But, this is not what we came here to find."

"What do you mean, Kyte?" said Farren, his concern growing.

"I have told you much in the past few days about the Aerii and their many clans, but I have not once told you about the highest clan. It is called the Sky Clan, and it was the noblest and strongest. They are all direct descendants of the first Aerii.

They trace their lineage through the centuries. They are also the keepers of the ancient magic; powerful spells from ages long past."

"Okay. I understand that, but what does that have to do with us now?" said Farren.

"It was said that the Sky Clan lived in the great *City in the Sky*, which resided in the ancient Forest of Rising Twilight."

It did not take long for Farren to realize what Kyte was implying. "We are here to find this grand clan?"

Kyte nodded. "If there were any Aerii left on this side of the world, then it would he here in this forest. My father told me much about this place and the Sky Clan. I believed that we would find aid here." He paused. "But, look around you, Young Prince. There is no one here. The city is as deserted as the forest. At first we were in awe of the city and did not notice, just as we did not notice when we first entered the forest. Soon, though, it became apparent that the city is abandoned."

"We searched everywhere, Farren," added Kaleb. "There is nothing."

"So what are you saying Kyte; there is nothing here? Our quest was for naught?" said Farren, who was starting to get a little riled.

"That is what it seems," said Kyte. "I am sorry, Young Prince."

"But how is that possible? How is there nothing here?" Farren said, his voice growing distressed. "Even the animals, they are all gone."

Kyte took a deep breath and lowered his head in guilt. "I have a theory, Young Prince. It does not solve our problem –it will not bring the Aerii back- but it may shed light on things." He waited for Farren to respond, but the Prince said nothing and his head stayed hung, so he continued. "There is a poem that is always used when telling stories of the City in the Sky. It is a rhyme that is used to help one find their way to this place. My mother used to sing it to me to put me to sleep as a child. I remember it to this day. I will only say the final verse."

"If you are truly in need and find what you yearn, remember that if you ever leave, you may never return."

Kyte let the Farren think on it for a moment. "It was said that the City in the Sky was a sacred place for only the most worthy to live. Everything you could ever desire could be found here. That is why there was a spell put on the city. If you were to ever leave, you could never find your way back."

Farren finally responded. "If it was so perfect, why would anyone leave?"

"That is the real question. Normally no one would. There was no reason to. But, of course, there are times when certain things that are normally not necessary, become necessary. I assume that the Magi Wars forced the Sky Clan from the city. As the strongest clan, they would have been needed on the battle field. Once they left, if they survived the war, they would have been forced to find another land to live on, and thus the city was left empty."

"It explains quite a lot, Farren," said Kaleb. In the city, there is no sign of damage, no bodies. It is as if they just packed up and left."

"What about the animals? Your reasoning explains why there are no Aerii, but it does not explain why there are no animals here," said Farren.

"With the amount of energy and magic in the forest, the animals that lived here became dependent on the Aerii. When the Aerii left, there was nothing for them here. They could not stay, so they must have left as well."

Farren again turned silent.

"I told you, Young Prince, that it would not help us to know the reason. We are still where we are and with nothing to show for it. For that I am eternally sorry," said Kyte. "I believed this to be our greatest hope, but I was wrong."

"It is not your fault, Kyte," reassured Kaleb. "You could have never known they would not be here."

"It doesn't matter if it his fault or not," barked Farren. "It does not matter whose fault it is. That does not change the fact that we came all this way for nothing. There is a war happening back in Valoria and we are running around the countryside looking for imaginary Magi."

"That was not the intent Farren," responded Kaleb.

"Of course not, but that is what happened."

"This is not the end, Farren. We can still fight. Just because we did not find aid, does not mean the war is lost."

"How do you know? The war could be over already for all we know. Coal could be dead. Coroge could be taken. What can *we* do? I can't even shoot a damn leaf on a tree," said Farren, his emotions starting to seep out.

Kyte walked up to him and placed his hand on his shoulder. "There is much we can do. It does not take an army to turn a battle, just a perfectly placed sword or well fired arrow. Do not doubt yourself, Young Prince. You are one of the strongest humans I have ever met and your compassion surpasses even your strength. From the moment I met you, I knew that you would play a big role in this story. That is why I brought you with me. I know that you have seen and felt nothing but pain so far, but, Young Prince, this story is just beginning," said Kyte. "I have faith the ending will be a joyful one," he added with a smile.

$\mathcal{T}\mathcal{T}$

The last remaining member of the Aerii Shroud Clan, Kyte Valen, swung peacefully back and forth in a hammock high up in the treetops, his eyes looking up at the glow of the canopy. Much of the city was below him, sparkling brightly in its brilliance. He had picked this spot to sleep because it was as far from the distractions of the city and, more importantly, his two human companions, who did not want to stray too far from the ground.

Since admitting the failure of their mission to Farren, Kyte had felt a weight of guilt on his chest that he could not seem to remove. He had done his best to lift the Young Prince's spirits, but he was not sure anymore if he even believed the words that he told the boy. Sure, they could still fight back and join in the war, but without significant help, they would not find victory. The Tellurians were a meticulous race. They would have planned this assault down to the last detail. Only power and numbers could help them now.

Or quite a lot of luck, he thought to himself.

It had been decades, after his grandmother had died, since his faith had been shaken. She was the last of his clan to perish from the great disease. Kyte had prayed night after night for years so that she would be saved, but his prayers were never answered. For a long time after that, he had lost all faith. He spent his lonely days wandering the Shroud, looking for answers, but never found any.

One day he decided that it was time to venture from his mist covered cage and look upon the world. He had never once left the Shroud, so when he emerged from the darkness and saw the beauty of the world he realized that there was indeed a higher power. Only the Almighty could create such wonders. That was also the day that he met Drek and they spent years traveling the country side. During this time, he also first gazed upon humans and admired their ingenuity and tenacity. Looking down upon the movements of Paks, he found that there was indeed a purpose to all that happened, but there was no way to see it. You just needed to believe it was there.

He had regained his faith over those years but, once again, he was now struggling to find the purpose in what was happening. Farren and his companions were good people. They did not deserve what was happening to them.

Kyte had made Farren put his faith in him and he had let the Young Prince down. He was not sure what to do now. They had spent the night in the city, to rest and recover from their exhausting quest, with much disagreement from Farren. It was Kaleb who finally managed to calm Farren down and convince him it was the best thing to do. Farren needed rest more than any of them and the city seemed to be the only place he could find it. This night, though, it was Kyte who could not find sleep.

Kyte was sick of the silence. He was sick of being alone. There was silence in the Shroud and there was silence here in the forest. Everywhere he went, there was silence. When he was in Valoria, he basked in the jubilant action of the city. In the city he felt a part of something. It had been decades since he had felt so alive. Kyte did not want to lose that again, like he did his family. As the Aerious lay in his hammock, remembering that good feeling, something stirred on the forest floor.

"Kyte!" came a frantic shout. "Come quickly!"

Kyte nearly fell from his perch in surprise. He spun around and looked down to see what was happening, but the lights of the city obscured his view.

"Kyte!" came the shout again.

Kaleb?

Without thinking, the Aerious grabbed his sword, leapt from the hammock, and plummeted down to the earth. He used his wind magic to steer his way through the maze of branches and walkways. As he neared the ground, he spotted Kaleb crouched in a ready position, bow drawn. When he looked at where he was aiming, he saw something he did not thinking possible.

Tellurian!

Before he could react, the Tellurian looked up at him. A second later, a giant stake of wood erupted from the ground and shot towards the Aerious. With a gust of wind, Kyte was able to push himself out of the way of the stake, but it put him into a tumble. With all of his effort, Kyte was able to throw a cushion of air beneath him before hitting the ground and he came down softly.

"So, there is your little friend," barked the Tellurian. "I knew he must be somewhere close."

Kyte looked up at the enormous creature, which was in its true form. To make matters worse, it had Farren by the neck and wrapped in vines. The Young Prince struggled to free himself, but his efforts went unsuccessful. Even his shouts were muffled with vines. When Kyte realized that Farren was not injured, his focus turned back to the Tellurian. There was something about the creature that made Kyte feel uneasy.

"Who are you, Tellurian, and what are you doing in this sacred place?"

"You do not remember me, Aerious? I would have thought that I made a bigger impression when we last met. I usually stick in people's minds more clearly. Maybe I should make an even bigger impression," said the Tellurian. He pulled out a dagger of wood and pointed it against Farren's throat.

"Wait," shouted Kyte, as he made a realization. "Stop. I *do* remember you. You are the one that took the Lady Kara." It was obvious now. Kyte had never come across such a powerful and massive creature.

"You know this Tellurian, Kyte?" asked Kaleb.

"Yes. It is the same one that attacked the Young Prince outside Valoria."

"So, you do remember me Aerious," barked Pardos. "I was worried that I had lost my edge. You have made me travel far to find you, but it was worth it. Repayment is in order for your underhanded attack on me on the plain. I do not take those types of things lightly," said Pardos.

"If it is me you want, than let the Prince go and I will take his place. He is innocent in all this."

"Oh, I wish it were that easy," said Pardos. "I care nothing for the boy, but my master wants him. He needs another hostage and he quite likes this one, so I will be taking the boy. Besides, I do not trust the other little human and his arrow pointing at my chest."

Kyte turned to Kaleb, who still had his bow fixed on Pardos; his eyes unblinking.

"Kaleb," Kyte said to him. "Put down the bow."

Kaleb did not avert his gaze from the Tellurian. "No. I will not let him take the Prince."

"Do not worry, Kaleb. Farren will be safe. I will handle the Tellurian. You need to trust me on this. I know I have asked a lot from you and have given little in return, but I need you to trust me again. I will not let the Young Prince be harmed."

Kaleb turned and looked strongly at Kyte. There was anger in the boy's eyes, but also fear. Reluctantly, Kaleb slowly lowered his bow and put it on the ground. He backed away and settled himself at the base of one of the Everwoods.

"Thank you, Kaleb," said Kyte. "I will not fail you this time."

When Kyte looked back to Pardos, the Tellurian had a satisfied smile on his rough face. "Good," he said. "I would not want a pesky child to get in the way of our fun." Pardos then released Farren and pushed him to the side. The Prince fell in a heap, still tangled in vines. Suddenly, a wooden cage erupted around him and locked him in. "I would not want my master's precious package damaged either."

Pardos walked out to the center of the grassy area and stopped. He stretched out his arms and cracked his neck with obvious exaggeration. When he was done, he said with a grin, "Shall we begin?"

In the blink of an eye, Kyte thrust out his hand and sent a great gust of wind bursting towards Pardos. The wind buffeted against an earthen wall that had risen up to protect the Tellurian. Just as quickly, Kyte drew his sword and slashed a scythe of wind at the wall, cutting it in two. When nothing appeared behind the wall, Kyte quickly spun around to find the great Tellurian bearing down on him in his black panther form. Kyte sent Pardos reeling with a shield of wind that rebuffed the attack.

Pardos quickly recovered and darted off in the opposite direction. Kyte continued to send scythes of air screaming towards him but, in his panther form, he easily out-maneuvered the Aerii. Pardos also partially shielded his movements with walls of earth that he drove up from the ground all around the battlefield. It was becoming a cat and mouse game, but the mouse was closing in. Pardos had run circles around Kyte and was getting dangerously close, hiding behind the piles of earth.

Unexpectedly, another wall of dirt appeared right in front of Kyte. He stumbled backwards in surprise, but the Tellurian had played this card before; using the wall as distraction. As expected, Pardos attacked from the side and Kyte prepared to shield himself again with a gust of wind, but he felt a disturbance. With little warning, spikes of earth shot out of the earthen wall behind him. It was too close to evade, so he had to divert his magic. He sent his shield towards the wall, breaking up the spikes before they could reach him. In that second, Pardos bore down on him and pinned him to the ground with his incredible strength. The panther's claws dug deep into his forearm, which Kyte was able to put up in defense to prevent a more deadly attack.

"Kyte!" shouted Kaleb, in fear.

With a gust of wind, Kyte was able to push off the Tellurian enough to swing up his sword. Pardos leapt out of the way in time, but it gave Kyte the opportunity to regain his feet and retreat. Blood dripped from the Aerious' arm and his breathing was heavy, but he still had fight in him. Kaleb let out a sigh of relief, but his blood was still pumping fast.

Pardos changed back into his Tellurian form. He chuckled and said, "Very good, very good. You are better than I expected. It has been centuries since I have fought an Aerious. It is an exhilarating feeling to fight another Magi, don't you think? There is no better feeling. But, alas, the feeling must come to an end sometime. I am past due, as it is, to bring my master his prize. I will finish you, just as I did the last Aerious years ago."

"You will finish nothing, Tellurian. I will not allow it."

Pardos bent over laughing. His deep base voice reverberated against the Everwood trunks. "What do you intend to do, Aerious? How do you intend to defeat me when you cannot even protect these boys?"

Kyte looked over at Farren, who was still struggling to free himself from his ensnarement, and Kaleb, who looked back at him with a stern but reassuring glare. "You are right," Kyte sighed. "I have not protected these boys, but then again they do not need my protection. They are stronger than I will ever be. In fact, they have given me much more than I have given them. That is why, now, it is my turn to give back." He shouted over to Kaleb. "Get out of here, Young Kaleb. It is no longer safe."

"What will you do?" Kaleb asked.

Kyte smiled, but there was hidden guilt and fear in it. "I will bring down heaven and earth on this creature."

Kyte's unwavering expression told Kaleb that there was no arguing with him. "What about Farren?"

"The Young Prince will be safe. The Tellurian will not let his master's prize be harmed. *I* will not let him be harmed."

Kaleb picked up his bow and, with a final look back, he retreated off into the city. Pardos did nothing to stop him. He held his attention on Kyte.

"Well then, Aerious. We are alone at least. Let me see what you are made of. Let me see your power," said Pardos. "You have just seen the very tip of what I am capable of. Bring heaven and earth down upon me and see if it is enough."

"It will be more than enough. The extent of your power does not matter," whispered Kyte, under his breath. He thrust his arms out to each side and a sudden gust of wind emanated from him. "You brought this upon yourself," he shouted to Pardos. "My name is Kyte Valen, last remaining member of the Shroud Clan, Protectors of the Mist. My mother was Solana Valen, High Priestess of the Almighty, and my father was Typhen Valen, Chief of the Shroud Clan and keeper of our clan's ancient magic. I bring judgment upon you, Tellurian, scourge of Paks. May your sins be blown away on the wind," Kyte bellowed.

As he spoke, a great rotating wind started to appear around him. The speed gradually picked up and the intensity started to rustle even the leaves at the tops of the Everwoods. The wooden walkways and buildings started to shutter and creak, grass tore itself from the earth and the great Everwoods started to bend in the tornado. Even droplets of water started to rise up from the streams. At the sight of all of this, Pardos' confidence started to falter.

Just before it seemed like everything would come crashing down around them, Kyte pulled the rotation in towards him with a great heave and everything went calm. When the dust settled, it looked as if there was a tornado whipping around Kyte's body like a shield. Through the biting wind, you could see Kyte's cold, white eyes staring back.

Pardos brushed away the dirt and debris from his eyes and looked over at him. "Enough of these petty tricks, I am finishing this!" He threw his hand to the ground and dozens of spikes erupted up around Kyte, but as each one hit the wall of wind, it blew apart like sand against stone. Pardos growled in annoyance. He tried again, but everything that he threw at Kyte was blown away.

When Kyte was done playing with the Tellurian, he made his attack. With incredible speed, Kyte gusted forward, wind still savagely blowing around him. The speed surprised Pardos and he tried to throw up a wall for protection, but it exploded apart as Kyte smashed into it. The blast sent Pardos flying backwards and onto his back. The Tellurian quickly regained his footing, but it was not quick enough. Kyte smashed Pardos in the side with a monstrous kick. He managed to lessen the blow, but it still sent him reeling to the ground. Before Pardos could even react, Kyte was upon him again, and with one mighty blow, Kyte ended everything. His fist drove into Pardos' stomach and an eruption of wind energy blew a crater ten feet wide into the earth. After an ear-piercing roar filled with spit and blood, Pardos fell limp and unconscious.

Time seemed to stand still and the world went quiet as the dust settled. When Pardos fell unconscious, the vines and cage binding Farren fell free and turned to dirt. After catching his breath, Farren got to his feet and examined the wreckage. The once grass and flower covered earth was just a pile of dirt and rubble. The blast had also brought down many of the walkways from the city above and drained water from the sparkling rivers. In the very center stood Kyte, whose shield of wind had died away, leaving him bare. He was looking down at Pardos, almost with an apologetic expression. After a moment, he turned and started to walk away.

It took a few seconds for Farren to register what had just happened. He had never seen such power and ferocity come from his Aerious friend. Kyte was like a completely different person. Then he looked over at Pardos and his mind returned to reality. There lay the limp form of the creature that had haunted his dreams ever since that fateful day. There was the creature that took Kara from him. Rage began to build up inside of him and, with an angry roar, he ran at the Tellurian with swords drawn.

Kyte heard the roar and turned. "Farren, no!" he shouted. He was too far away to stop him. With a last ditch effort he used his magic. A barrier went up around the Tellurian just before Farren was upon him. The boy hit the barrier and was thrown backwards. He quickly got back to his feet and tried again, but he was repelled once more.

"Farren, stop!" said Kyte again.

Farren continued to pound on the barrier with his fists and sword, ignoring Kyte's pleas. When it was obvious that he would not break through, Farren collapsed and started to weep. Kyte rushed over to him.

"It is okay, Young Prince. It is okay."

"But, why?" Farren asked. "Why did you stop me? It is him! He is the one that took her!"

Kyte took Farren in his arms. "I know, Young Prince. I knew him the moment I laid eyes on him. But there is something going on here you are unaware of. We need him alive. He has a part to play in our quest."

They both heard the Tellurian stir inside the barrier. Pardos groaned loudly and tried to get to his feet but he could not. When he realized he was caught in a barrier, he tried to use his magic, but nothing happened.

"It is no use," said Kyte. "You are in a magic barrier. You are cut off from the natural flow. Your magic will not work." Pardos then started to pound on the side of the barrier, but it did nothing. "Stop, you fool. You will only hurt yourself even further," said Kyte.

"Do not tell me what to do, Aerious. I will break free of this barrier eventually, just like I broke through the barrier to the plateau. It is only a matter of time."

"You did not break through anything, Tellurian. The barrier allowed you to pass. The barrier around the plateau is impregnable. The only way through the barrier is if you know the incantation, or it allows you to pass through by the laws," explained Kyte.

"Are you trying to say that an Aerii barrier allowed a Tellurian to pass through? Ha! You are a fool. That is the most absurd thing I have ever heard. I forced my way through that barrier."

"You are not as strong as you like to think, Tellurian," said Kyte, as Pardos cringed trying to get to his feet. "The result of our fight proves that."

Pardos growled at him. "You got lucky, Aerious. I did not expect you to carry such magic. Fight me again and we shall see who wins."

"Shut up and listen to me," barked Kyte. "Ever since I saw you in the city I have been troubled by one thought. How is it that you are here? How did you make it through the barrier? It did not make any sense to me. It should not be possible. But, then it hit me. The barrier allowed you through because you do not truly wish us any harm. You came after us because you were ordered to, but there is something deep down inside of you that did not want to."

"Ha!" cackled Pardos. "And you call me a fool? I came here to kill you, Aerious. I want nothing more in this world right now than to rip out your throat."

"Listen to him," said Farren. "He is a monster. He came here to kill us, just like he came after us before. We should kill him now."

"No. You are wrong. He did not come here to kill us. He came here only to prove his strength. Like any warrior, his pride was hurt when I attacked him before and, like any warrior, he wanted to prove himself again. In that respect, he is not different from any of us," said Kyte.

Pardos threw himself again the barrier again. "Let me out of here and I will show you my strength, Aerious."

"Save your threats, Tellurian. All I am interested in now is information. You will tell me what your master is planning."

"Don't be ridiculous," said Pardos. "I will never betray my master and my comrades. You will never get anything from me."

"An honorable sentiment. I respect your devotion to your people, but I know that there is also something inside you that does not believe in what they are doing. Your faith in your master is strained."

"You will not sway me, Aerious. My loyalty to my people is far stronger than your words," said Pardos.

"Yes, but is your master's loyalty that strong? Does he show such dedication to your people? Would he give his life to protect you?"

"Quiet!" shouted Pardos. He started to pound violently on the barrier to try to drown out Kyte's words. He continued to pound until he collapsed in exhaustion.

"I know how you feel. I know what you fight for," said Kyte. "I have wanted it myself for decades. All you want is to not have to hide anymore. You want to be able to be free once again. I understand that, but that freedom does not have to come at the expense of the humans. We can all live together. Your master wants to plunge Paks into another war. That will do nothing but return us to the same state we were in hundreds of years ago. This is a new age. If you want freedom, than make peace and live freely with everyone else."

Pardos groaned. "Peace. There is no such thing as peace."

"Of course there is, it is just harder to comprehend than war. War is easy. Peace is the difficult one."

"You speak of peace, but the Aerii are no better than we are. You killed thousands of Tellurians, many of whom were innocent."

"Most everybody is innocent in war," said Kyte. "It does not matter who fired the first arrow, or killed the first man. Sometimes, all it takes is one guilty man to start a war that kills thousands."

"And you claim that it was a Tellurian, don't you?"

"I do not deny it. The histories say that the Grand Master was the one that started the war. But, I was not there, so I cannot say for sure," said Kyte. "That does not matter, though. What matters is that most of the other Magi that fought were innocent. They did not want the war. To seek vengeance against those who never hurt you, or wanted to hurt you, is foolishness. You would spend a lifetime killing and still never quench that thirst."

"Don't claim to know my pain, Aerii. You know nothing of it," barked Pardos.

"You are right. I do not know your pain. How could I? I can sense that you have held onto that pain for many years. You are wrong, though, if you think I know nothing of it. I too am alone. I too have felt pain and anger, and I too have seen death. What makes me different is that I do not hold onto that anger, nor do I direct it at those who do not deserve its attention," said Kyte.

"All Aerii deserve my anger," shouted Pardos.

"Why?" asked Kyte, simply.

Pardos stared back at Kyte with hate-filled eyes, but he could say nothing. He growled loudly instead and smashed his arms against the barrier once again. "Stop meddling with my head, Aerious. You will not change it. I have held onto this anger for centuries and there is nothing you can do to relieve me of it. You would have to kill me to quell that anger."

"Your anger is as misplaced as your loyalty, Tellurian. I sense great loyalty in you; loyalty that is not reciprocated by your master."

"Quiet!" bellowed Pardos.

"Your master betrays all that you believe in. I can see it in your eyes. This plan of his will not bring peace or power to Tellurians. It will only bring more pain. It will only bring more loneliness."

"Shut up!" screamed Pardos again. His rage overwhelmed him and he beat unrelentingly against the barrier. "You know nothing!"

With every hit, the barrier sapped the monstrous Tellurian of his strength, but that did not stop him. He was keen on either smashing his way through or dying in the process. Kyte just stood and watched silently. It did not take long until Pardos finally collapsed. His body lay limp on the ground with only the faintest sign of breathing.

"Is he dead?" asked Farren.

"No, he is not. He is very much alive. What you see now is the remains of a Magi who fought against his consciousness. He has questioned who he is and what his life has meant."

"Shut up, Aerious," groaned Pardos. "Will you just shut up?" The massive Tellurian managed to turn himself over and sit up. His discomfort was obvious, but it did not seem to matter to him.

"Do you deny it?"

"I do not deny your words, Aerious," Pardos finally said after a brief silence. "But, that changes nothing. I may not love my master or believe in what he is doing, but I do love my other brethren and I will not betray them to you."

"If you help me, I will do my best to spare as many Tellurians as I can."

Pardos' loyalty ran deep, but he was not sure now what was truly loyal. If the war happened, hundreds would die, but if it was stopped… he never wanted a war. He just wanted freedom. "What is it you want to know, Aerious?" he finally asked.

Kyte smiled. He was correct to put faith in this Tellurian. "Is the weapon completed?"

"Since I left the city, no. My master grows agitated. He does not want to start the war without it."

"But, would he?"

"I believe so. He does not want to give the Creed enough time to prepare. At some point, he will be forced to attack Coroge whether or not the weapon is complete."

"Do you know when that would be?"

"Not for certain. It could be any day now, or it could have happened already. My master is short of patience and his rage can get the best of him. Even without the weapon, Coroge will surely fall. With the Davati warship, the city's walls will be worth nothing."

"The *Fionetta*? They have brought it from its perch?" His expression turned grave. "These are ill-tidings. I did not expect an air battle. If I could have found aid from more Aerii, we could have leveled the playing field. I do not think I can take on the warship on my own."

"The battle is lost no matter what you do, Aerious. My master has been planning this for decades. You will need a lot more than the three of you to turn this battle. I do not think there is enough magic left in the world to help you."

Kyte's heart sank. The Tellurian was right. This fight was beyond their power. He had convinced himself that there was still a chance, but with the Davati against them as well, his wind magic would not be enough. They needed help, but there was none. With the Aerii gone, there was nowhere else to look.

When all hope seemed lost, Kyte felt something he had not felt ever since entering the forest. He felt a breeze. He looked around to find its source, but saw nothing. Then the breeze came again, but this time it was stronger. It continued to grow in intensity until Kyte realized that it was not a breeze at all. It was coming from above them. He looked up, but his vision was blinded by a bright light.

Both Kyte and Farren shielded their eyes from the light and the dust that was kicked up by the sudden gale. Then the distinct sound of beating wings came to Kyte's ears, and a loud screech echoed through the city.

56

With the Forces gone to Coroge, the palace guard was lax. The few that were left were the unlucky ones who were forced to stay behind. There always needed to be someone to guard the palace. Without the army around, these guards should have been more attentive, but their discontent with being the abandoned few outweighed their responsibilities. They stood at their posts, but their attention was elsewhere.

Unaware of the approaching figure, the gate guard stood in a daze. The figure ascended the great stairway silently, their feet making little more than a shuffle. It was not until the figure was only a handful of feet away that the guard finally game to his senses. His eyes focused on the figure and his expression showed disbelief.

"I had heard that you were dead."

"Funny thing about rumors," said the man. "They are notoriously unreliable."

The guard drew his sword and pointed at the man. The man stopped. "You cannot enter here, Datro. The Supreme Regis has put a bounty on your head."

Datro smirked. Even with a sword point at his chest, he did not show concern. He almost seemed to enjoy it. "I was under the impression he thought I was dead. Why would there be a bounty on the head of a dead man?"

Datro's uncaring demeanor put caution into the guard's thoughts. There was something different about Datro, and the guard was anxious. His sword arm started to tremble. "The Supreme Regis believes you are alive, but most everyone assumed you dead."

"Interesting that our great ruler would have such insight. How do you think it is that he knew the truth, while everyone else believed to the contrary?"

Datro took a step forward, forcing the point of the man's blade to press against his chest. The guard stepped back. His courage was waning. Datro suddenly grabbed the blade of the sword, gripping it tightly. The guard was so surprised, he tried to wrench it free, but it did not budge. Blood started to trickle from Datro's hand, but he still held firmly.

"Oh no, my friend. You are not going anywhere. This party is just beginning," hissed Datro.

The guard's eyes widened and he quickly released his sword and turned to run. He only made it a few feet before Datro thrust out his hand. The man stumbled, as if hit by a strong wind and fell to his knees.

He let out a shriek. "What is happening?!" he said as he pawed at his eyes. "What did you do to me?" The guard started to feel around on the ground, flashing his hands in front of his face. "I cannot see anything. What have you done to me, Datro?"

The man's mind was filled with fear and confusion. He could no longer see, but he felt no pain. It was only darkness. He continued to grope around on the ground, searching for anything that was recognizable. His hands finally reached the base of the wall and he made his way to his feet.

"Help! Is there anyone there? Anyone, please."

He banged away at the wall, but there was no response. His fists made only muted thuds. Footsteps started to crunch along the ground behind him.

"Why do you run?" said Datro. "You asked a question, but you don't stay around to hear the answer?"

The guard spun around and tried to find where Datro was approaching from.

"What I have done is take away your light," Datro continued. "You see, my ignorant friend, without light, you cannot see. All you have now is darkness and we are not meant to live in darkness. This is all you will see for the rest of your miserable life."

Datro's sword point touched the man on the forehead. The sudden feeling made the man jump, but his body would not move. He was frozen. With the wall to his back and a sword point to his front, he had nowhere to go.

"Are you afraid?" said Datro, whispering into the man's ear. "Do you want it all to end?"

The guard could not speak and only nodded his head slowly.

"Then I want you to tell the guard on the other side to open the gate."

"But, why? Why do you want to get into the palace?"

Datro pressed harder with his sword and blood started to drip from the man's forehead.

"Ok, ok," he shrieked. "But, what should I say? There needs to be a reason for them to open it."

"Tell them the truth, of course. Tell them that I have been found and that I wish to speak to the Regis."

The guard swallowed down his fear. "Okay." He took a deep breath and shouted. "Open the gate. The fugitive Datro Cervon has been found. He wishes to be brought to the Supreme Regis."

For a moment there was only silence. Then, suddenly, there was a loud click and the immense gate started to creak open.

Datro grinned. "Thank you." With one quick motion he thrust his sword through the man's neck.

For only a second, the man's vision flashed back to him, showing the smiling face of Datro Cervon standing in front of him.

"It is all over now," said Datro.

Then it all went black again and he crumbled to the ground. Datro wiped the blood from his blade and returned it to his sheath.

As the gate opened, a voice shouted to Datro from the other side. "Did you say that Datro Cervon has been captured? I thought he was dead. Are you sure it is him?"

When the gate opened up enough, Datro strode through. The guard on the other side froze in surprise. He reached for his sword, but Datro quickly waved out his hand, whisking away the man's light. That guard dropped his sword.

"What happened?!"

Before he could react, Datro kicked him to the ground and silenced him with one thrust of his sword. He then continued on to the small stables nearby, picked out a horse and started to ride toward the palace.

The sky was darkening up above. It looked like rain was coming.

"Our luck might finally be returning," said Syd, as he stared at the rain coming down outside the second floor window of the *Kaisers'* bazaar hideout. It had started as a trickle, but was now thick enough to send most citizens running for cover. All of the stand owners on the street below were frantically packing away their things as well. There was no break in sight, so there was no point in them staying and ruining their wares.

"It looks like we might have a nice clear road to the palace," Syd added.

He turned back into the room. Kaine was finished getting ready. He had his feryl sheathed across his lower back and his quiver across his shoulders. There was an additional belt of small throwing knives around his waist. Because of the large cloak he had on, he had to carry his bow in his hands.

"The Almighty is looking upon us today," responded Kaine. "I have never been quite so excited to see rain."

They both turned to the stairs when they heard footsteps. Coal emerged quickly. "Are we ready?"

"Just about, Sir"

"Good. There is no time to waste. I do not know how long this rain will last, but it is our best hope to make it into the palace undetected, so we must hurry."

"Exactly our thought too, Sir. It will be excellent cover."

Kaine finished putting on some ratty leather gloves and pounded his fists together. "Ready when you are, Sir."

All three of the men were well-armed, but disguised. The only weapons they were showing were Kaine's bow and the hilt of Syd's giant rangon strapped to his back. Everything else was hidden. Syd's broken arm was splinted around a straight piece of steel and wrapped tightly with leather. He had confidence he could still wield his blade, but Coal was not as assured. The Commander made him bring a smaller blade as well, in case the pain over-whelmed him. Their clothes were ratty and worn; as they were made to look like beggars on the street. They were not the best disguises, but they would have to do.

"Where is the girl?" asked Kaine.

"She is downstairs with Reme and Dash. Asleep, I think. She is still very tired from her ordeal."

"We worked her pretty hard."

"She will be fine, Captain. She is a tough girl. All she needs is some rest."

"I hope you are right, Sir."

Coal put up his hood. "Let's go."

As they reached the bottom of the stairs, Reme ran up to them.

"Commander, wait. Are you about to leave?"

Coal nodded.

"You should be clear to the palace right now. The guards run for cover as quickly as the citizens when it rains. You won't have to worry about them. Make sure to take the short cut I showed you."

"Of course," said Coal. "And thank you for everything. I do not know what we would have done without you."

"No need to worry, Commander. You would have done the same for us. Besides, any friend of the Boss is a friend of ours."

Coal smiled at the young boy and shook his hand. These boys were growing up so quickly. It seemed like just the other day when he would have to scold Farren and them multiple times a week for wreaking havoc in the city.

Has Farren grown as well? Have I been so blind as to not notice? He brushed the thought aside.

"We will watch Miss Alexia while you are gone. You don't have to worry about that. Just make sure to kill some Tellurians for us, will you?" Reme grinned.

"Of course, Reme," shouted Syd.

"Commander, wait!" shouted Alexia, who had emerged from the stairs to the second floor.

"What are you doing awake? You need your rest," said Coal.

"I have slept enough, Commander. Besides, I do not think that I will be able to sleep knowing what you are about to face." Her face reddened. "I have come to wish you luck and tell you that I will be praying for you."

"Thank you, Alexia. Do not worry yourself. We are tough men to kill," he said reassuringly. Unfortunately, he did not have the same confidence he was displaying. They had never faced an enemy like this. Her prayers would be greatly needed.

"I want you to destroy him," Alexia added with conviction. "Datro is a vile man and he needs to be stopped."

"We will do all we can. I know his wickedness well. He should have been silenced years ago. You do not have to worry," said Coal with a reassuring smile.

And, with that, the three men turned and disappeared out into the curtain of rain. Alexia watched despondently as they faded quickly into the city. Over the past few days she had grown to like the three men. They were hard men, but men with honor and decency. She had not felt compassion from a man since her father died and now these men were racing off to certain death. They had saved her life, but she could do nothing to save theirs.

Reme walked up behind her and patted her on the shoulder. He looked at her with a smile. "Do not worry about those three. You should never count them out. Trust me. I have learned from experience."

The three Gallant's pace was quick and they found no resistance. The rain was like a veil of invisibility. Even if there were any patrolmen still on guard in the city, they did not pay much attention to them. They were just three homeless citizens, trying to find shelter from the rain. Their clothes were soaked from head to toe, which nearly doubled their weight and made it harder to move. They were soldiers though, so it did little to slow them down. Their blood was pumping with excitement. They had been sitting in the dark for too long. It was now time to fight.

They kept to the alleys just to be certain they weren't detected. Water was starting to build up in the streets from the rain and their feet splashed in the pools. The sky was only getting darker and there was lightning in the distance. The plan was to sneak into the palace and confront the Grand Master. It was their only course of action. They needed to stop him before he could get his hands on the solution and build another army. If that were to happen, there would be little they could do by themselves.

There were only a few guards left since the Force marched so, once inside, they shouldn't have too much trouble. Getting into the grounds was going to be the difficulty. They were fugitives now. No one was going to just open the gates for them. They would need to find another way in. And, of course, there was Datro. His betrayal of the Grand Master threw a wild card into all of their plans. They did not know what the scientist would do, or how powerful he had become. No one had seen or heard from him since the disaster in the lab. Knowing Datro, he had some sort of plan in mind and it could spell disaster for everyone. If he did show himself, though, Coal would destroy him once and for all. Ever since the assassination of

Bishop's parents, Coal had been waiting for the day he could put his sword through that coward's chest

The city square was up ahead. From there, it was a straight shot to the palace stairs. Coal stopped his two Captains in the alley. It would be impossible for them to make it across the square without showing themselves, so Coal wanted to make sure that there no patrols around. He inched his head around the corner of the building and scanned the area. There was a patrolman by the fountain in the center and another pacing back and forth by the path to the palace.

"What does it look like, Commander?" asked Syd.

"Two guards."

"Is there any way around them without being seen?"

"It does not seem so. The guards are not moving from their posts. Apparently the Tellurian does not care about finding us, as long as we do not approach the palace."

Kaine moved up next to Coal and looked around the corner. "That means he is scared. He knows he is vulnerable."

"Possibly," considered Coal. "But, that does not change our situation. We need to get through the square."

"Is there another way?"

"Only a few, but they would take us out of the way and there is no way to tell if there will be patrols there as well."

Syd was getting impatient. "Let me take care of it, Sir. It would be only a moment."

"No," ordered Coal. "They are only pawns in this fight. We cannot kill them. They are still one of us."

"I will do it then," whispered Kaine. It will be silent and I will not kill them."

Coal looked back out into the square. The other streets looped far out to the sides. It would take hours to go around. There was no other way. The rain was still coming down hard, so it would be excellent cover. They would never see Kaine approaching. Coal nodded to Kaine.

The slender warrior crept out into the square. The patrolman by the fountain stood with his back to him and the one on the far side could never see him in the downpour, even if he knew to look. Kaine was trained in the art of silent killing. There was no one better in the Sect at not being seen. He moved swiftly and, even on the water drenched stone, his footsteps did not make a sound. Within seconds, he was behind the first patrolmen. With a swift motion, the guard was on the ground, unconscious.

He peered around the fountain at the final guard. The man looked tired. His feet dragged and his head drooped. Clearly the Grand Master was over-working him. Kaine darted over to a building on the near side of the square. He hid behind a pillar on the building's façade. He waited for the patrolman to turn and then he raced towards him. The man never saw him coming, but there was something that did.

When Kaine was just feet from him, a vine shot up from the ground and snagged him by the leg. He lost his footing and fell to the ground. The patrolman spun around. When he saw Kaine on the ground he drew his sword.

"Who are you?!"

Another vine shot up and latched around Kaine's arm, preventing him from grabbing his sword again. Kaine struggled to rip free. The guard did know what to do. He did not know what was happening. A strange man had appeared out of nowhere with a weapon, but he was under attack by something. In his confusion, the patrolman did the only thing that made sense to him. He unsheathed his sword and started to help Kaine break free.

"What are these things?" he screeched as he hacked away at the vines.

Kaine yelled back at the man. "Stop! Leave me. You need to get out of here. You are in danger as well."

Before the guard could react, a stake of wood drove upwards from between the stone pavement straight into his chest. He gasped, as the air from his lungs escaped him. Kaine's eyes widened. The guard struggled, but a few seconds later his body went limp. A mix of rage and fear pumped through Kaine's body.

He shouted out across the square. "Commander!"

Ripping an arm free, he grabbed up his sword and cut away the vines. He got to his feet as Coal and Syd came running up. They looked down at the dead guard on the stake and the shredded remains of vines scattered around.

"What happened here?"

Kaine struggled to catch his breath. "There is a Tellurian nearby. The guard tried to aid me and it killed him."

"Damn creatures," muttered Coal.

Syd instantly threw off his cloak and drew his rangon. He scanned the area for movement. "Did you see it?"

"No. It is staying hidden."

For what seemed like eternity, the square was nearly silent; nothing but the sound of rain against stone. The three men stood ready for anything, but nothing came.

"Has it gone?" asked Syd.

"I doubt it." Coal responded.

A loud crack of lightning flashed above them, followed by the rumble of thunder. The rumbling continued, growing in intensity. The ground started to shake beneath them.

"Oh Almighty, what is it this time?" groaned Kaine.

"It cannot be worse than what we have already seen," said Syd.

The rumbling stopped. They all stood ready. A loud blast shook the ground behind them. They all spun around and saw a monstrous creature towering over the buildings.

"I take that back. This is new," groaned Syd.

It stood almost twice the height of the tallest building and its body was made of vines and earth. It swung its arms around without care or worry. It hammered into the side of a store, throwing stone out into the square. The three men jumped out of the way as a piece rolled past them. Kaine strung an arrow and fired it at the behemoth. It disappeared into the tangle of vines with no effect.

"It was worth a try," remarked Coal. "But I think that we need something bigger."

"What do you suggest then, Commander?"

They dove to the side again as the creature continued to toss chunks of builds and brick at them. All they could do was dodge to avoid being crushed. It started to cross the square towards them, spanning thirty feet with every step.

"We run," said Coal. "Make for the palace."

"We won't make it."

Coal stared up at the beast as it approached. "We must try," he muttered.

They turned and sprinted down the street towards the palace. The giant creature quickly followed. Its movements were slow, but it made up for it in size. Its stride would quickly close the gap between it and Coal. As the creature passed by the fountain, it ripped off the stone figure in the center. With a giant heave, it threw it towards them. Its aim was off and it crashed into a building to their right. The resulting tremor nearly felled them, but they kept running.

The creature was gaining on them, but they tried not to look back. They did not need to see it. They could feel it approaching. Their bodies were put to the test, sprinting with every last bit of energy they could muster. The palace stairway was in sight. If only they could make it. The beast was just above them now, its shadow casting down on top of them. Coal managed a quick look back. The creature's giant arm was reared back for a deadly swing.

Suddenly, a loud screeching sound erupted from the sky and a giant eagle collided with the earthen monstrosity. The force of the hit caused the creature to stumble backwards and fall. The ground shook and the eagle proceeded to peck and claw viciously at the vines and earth, ripping it apart. The giant creature managed to swat away the bird a few times, but it kept attacking. Coal and the others were frozen with confusion. Then they heard a voice shout at them from behind.

"Commander! This is your chance. We must go!"

When they turned, they saw Farren standing in the street, not more than twenty yards ahead. His cloak was wet and tattered, covering most of his face, but it was clearly the Prince. There was something different about him. He seemed stronger, but that was not it. It was his eyes. They were stern and filled with passion. He waved for them to follow.

Coal turned back and looked at the battle between the two giant creatures. It was clear that the eagle did not stand a chance, but it fought valiantly. He looked to his Captains.

No words were needed. They both knew what had to be done. "Leave it to us, Sir," said Kaine.

Coal smiled. It was not a happy smile, but a smile that exuded appreciation and also sadness. "Give it hell, you two," said Coal.

They both returned the same smiles, before Coal quickly turned and ran off towards Farren and the palace. Farren saw that Kaine and Syd were staying behind and instantly realized what was happening. Just before he turned to run off towards the palace with Coal, he shouted out to them. "The master must be in contact with the puppet to control it. Destroy the master and the puppet will fall."

Kaine looked over at the creature, examining its bulk. At the top, near the base of what was the creature's head, he thought he spied a small bird perched amongst the vines. Kaine smiled to Syd. "Let us see if this creature bleeds, shall we, good friend?"

"As usual, you took the words right out of my mouth."

Having thrown off their drenched and heavy cloaks, the two Captains faced the giant creature. The eagle had finally flown away, having done its job, and the behemoth was gaining its feet once again. The two men charged. Their gallant shouts echoed through the streets.

Before the creature could fully stand, both of them had leapt onto it, grasping the tangled vines. When they found their footing, they started to climb. Vines were breaking and dirt and earth crumbled down on their heads, which made it a difficult climb. Every time the creature made a sudden movement, they would be forced to cling tightly to prevent themselves from falling.

At first it was unaware of their presence, but when Kaine was nearing the top, the creature noticed him. The small bird perched atop the creature's frame turned towards him and, in a matter of seconds, it reacted. The vines that made up the bulk of the creature came alive and started to attack Kaine. He quickly drew his short sword and cut himself free, continuing his climb. The creature swung his arm to swat away the pesky human, but Kaine managed to leap onto its other arm, to avoid the blow.

He clung by his fingertips, swinging frantically back and forth as the creature tried to shake him free. The rain was making it extremely difficult to hold onto the smooth vines, but he held on with all his strength. Finally, the creature spun and swept its arm towards the side of a building. Just before the mess of vines collided with the stone store front, Kaine managed to gain his grip. The blow tore through the building, exploding in a cloud of dust, stone and wood. Kaine slipped.

When he fell, it felt like he was falling through water. It all happened so slowly. He reached out to grab onto something, but he grasped only air. He heard Syd's frantic shouts.

"No!!"

Kaine looked over as he fell and saw his friend staring back at him. Syd still held tightly to the side of the creature, but he looked as if he would jump off after Kaine without a second thought. His face showed a mix of fear, anger and disbelief.

Kaine's body fell amid the debris and destruction. The instant he hit, his body went limp and draped silently across the rubble. For a moment, there was silence. Syd's face was blank. His lifelong friend lay unmoving on the ground below him. There were no words to express what he felt in that moment.

He let out a piercing roar, like a bear that had just lost its cub. It echoed far out into the city. The rain seemed to stop in that second. The Tellurian turned towards him. He returned the look with a glare of such intense hatred that you could feel the shiver that ran through the tiny bird's body.

Syd dug his fists into the vines and earth and started to tear up the side of the mammoth creature. He ripped through everything that the Tellurian sent at him like a sword through silk. His anger was palpable in the air. The Tellurian started to back away, but it had nowhere to go. It transformed into its true form as Syd reached the top.

Weaponless, and unable to use magic while its puppet spell was cast, the Tellurian faced down the Gallant. Syd drew his rangon and charged. There was no hesitation, no strategy to his attack. This was the strength and viciousness of the Gallant Captain Syd Rayaz, the Lion of Briva. He wielded the blade with the precision and speed of the greatest swordsmen. It was unfathomable how easily he could manipulate such a large weapon.

The Tellurian was pushed back; barely able to evade Syd's onslaught. Its acrobatic movements allowed it to stay just one step ahead of Syd's blade, but it could not run away forever. Sooner or later, Syd would find his mark. Suddenly, the giant vine puppet began to move once again. Syd was caught off guard, and stopped to find his footing. In that moment, the Tellurian pounced. It kicked Syd back off the giant creature's shoulder. Syd dropped his blade as he stumbled and he watched it plummet to the ground. He fell, but caught himself on some vines. A sharp pain shot through his arm, but he mustered the strength to hold on.

The Tellurian did not let up. Vines immediately started to entangle Syd. He fought against them savagely, ripping them apart as they tried to strangle him. Soon, though, he was overwhelmed. The vines had him completely contained, even strangled him around the neck. The Tellurian walked over to him and knelt down. Slowly, a sharp spike of earth emerged from amongst the vines, pointing at Syd's neck. It did not seem to bother the Gallant. He stared back at the Tellurian defiantly.

In a sharp, raspy voice, the Tellurian said, "You are weak, human. It was foolish to even try to fight. You overestimated your ability."

Syd was still fighting to free himself as the creature spoke. Finally he stopped and managed to force out words under the pressure of the vines. "Maybe we did, creature. But you have also underestimated our resolve. A Gallant never stops fighting until his heart stops beating." A wry smile formed on his face. "Isn't that right, good friend?!" he shouted.

It took a moment for the Tellurian to realize what he meant but, when it did, a sensation of fear ran through it. It quickly turned and looked to the ground below. Lying amongst the rubble was Kaine, with an arrow pointed at its chest. When the arrow released, the Tellurian tried to move out of the way, but it couldn't. Syd had ripped an arm free of the vines and was gripping the Tellurian's ankle. A second later, an arrow was protruding from the creature's throat.

It gasped for air and fell to its knees, starting to convulse. The giant puppet started to lose control. The magic that held the creature together was breaking down. As the Tellurian's life ebbed away, so did the puppet's life.

When the creature started to break apart, the vines that held Kaine down fell lose. He did not even try to rise. His strength was drained. He had nothing left. Slowly, he started to slip down the side of the creatures back. When he finally fell, he hit hard onto the earth and vines that were beginning to pollute the street. The blow nearly killed him, but he stubbornly clung to life. Above him, the giant creature continued to rampage around as if it refused to give in. Chunks of its body rained down around him. A moment later, he saw the Tellurian's wretched form collapse and fall from its shoulders. When that happened, the puppet finally burst apart and lost all form.

When the dust finally settled, there was little left of the street and square. It was as if a tornado had ripped through the city. Stone, wood and earth littered the area like bodies on a great battlefield. There was not a building left standing. The destruction was total.

Syd managed to turn his broken body over onto his back and stare up at the sky. The cold rain felt good again his wounds. His body tingled.

Through all the pain, he let out a smile. "Nice shot," he said aloud.

Kaine responded from a short distance away. He too was lying on his back, taking in the cloudy sky. "Thanks, good friend. I am glad you are impressed."

"I did have to hold him still for you, though."

"Much appreciated. I couldn't really get the power behind it I wanted. I think I am getting weak," Kaine joked.

"Who are you kidding? You were never that strong to begin with."

Kaine's body hurt all over as he tried to contain a laugh. He could hear Syd's pain-filled guffaw as well. Syd groaned in obvious discomfort. After their laughs subsided, there was a peaceful silence as the two men smiled up at the heavens.

They had been together for longer than either could remember. Orphaned during the War of Paksian rule, they grew up as brothers. They both enlisted into the Forces and fought their way up the ranks. Despite their clear differences in personality and fighting style, they were still the greatest fighting duo in the kingdom. They had lived together and fought together. It seemed only right that they would die together.

"I'm feeling a little guilty," said Syd.

"You, guilty? I did not even realize you knew what the word meant. You have never felt guilty about anything you have ever done, Syd."

Syd chuckled to himself. "You are right about that. Fight hard, love hard, live hard, and have no regrets. That's what we always used to say when we were new recruits."

"Crazy fools, that is what we were," said Kaine. "I am still surprised we survived all those years. Then again, those were good times."

"The best," smirked Syd. "And no matter what happened, we never looked back. Guilt was for the losers."

"And we never lost," smiled Kaine. "Are you starting to feel some guilt about what happened back then? Someone you killed? Something you did?"

Syd's smile faded. "No, it is not that. I have put that all past me."

"What is it then?" probed Kaine.

Syd let out a big sigh and stared up at the clouded sky. "We never went back to pay our tab at *Ana's*."

Kaine laughed aloud. "You are such a fool. Of all things, you are guilty about that? That is what you are thinking about as you stare death in the face?"

"What else is there to think about? That Ana was one beautiful woman, wasn't she?" Syd reminisced, ignoring Kaine's jab. "I am sure going to miss her."

Kaine could not help but smile at his lifelong friend. No matter how harrowing the situation, his mind was always on one thing; women. It made him quite reliable. Kaine loved him for that. "You say that about every girl you meet in Seduke, Syd."

"Yes, but she was different. She had a maturity about her that was just intoxicating,"

Kaine rolled his eyes. He had heard this many times before.

"I saw that," shouted Syd with a smirk on his face. "Do not act like you have never thought about it, Kaine. I seem to remember a certain shy, cute girl that fawned all over you."

"It wasn't like that. She was a nice girl, but…"

"Don't lie to me, Kaine. You have never been good at it anyway. That girl was smitten with you and you could not have loved it more."

It was true. Kaine remembered her vividly. He had not been able to stop thinking about her since that day. There had never been a girl that got to him the way she did, with her coy smile and innocent eyes. And now he would never get to see her again. *I never was good with timing.*

"Her name was Neesa," he finally said.

"That's right. She was a cute one."

"She was."

"You will see her again, good friend. This is not the end of us."

The rain had stopped and the clouds were dispersing. The sun started to brighten up the sky. They could both hear the sounds of people starting to fill the streets. Their handiwork had caught the attention of the entire city.

"Yes, but that will not be for a long time. She will live a peaceful and full life. Until then, the Almighty will have to deal with just the two of us."

"I wouldn't have it any other way, good friend."

The commotion in the streets continued to grow as the sun shined brighter and people flooded in. Confusion was the common emotion. Shouts of shock and despair echoed against the stone, as store owners found the remains of their shops. Questions and accusations were shouted around, but no answers were returned. Despite the growing crowds, nobody seemed to notice the two bodies of Syd Rayaz and Kaine Ducale laying peacefully amongst the debris, Captains of the Gallants; saviors of the city.

57

The chaos in the palace continued to escalate as every servant and guard scrambled around frantically, searching for the light. They bumped into walls and tripped over chairs and tables. Their shouts of fear went on deaf ears and only succeeded in covering up the footsteps of the one man who could save them from their darkness.

Datro walked casually through the halls, watching in amusement as his magic went to work. He felt a rush of satisfaction well up inside of him, seeing their fear and confusion as the light was taken from each of their eyes. One of the guards bumped into him and he quickly blew him to the side with a vicious kick. No one was going to get in the way of him and his revenge.

He passed quickly down the hallway towards the stairs that would lead to the top floor and the throne room. There awaited the Grand Master. He could sense him; a strong confluence of energy among the network of small streams. There awaited the creature that had thought that he could use Datro for his own greedy devices. The Grand Master would soon find out who was using who.

The upper floors were empty. The Grand Master had forbidden any servant or guard from bothering him, and everyone gladly obliged. Datro walked up to the large doors to the throne room. Just like the giant doors that barred entrants to the palace grounds, these doors were large and held the symbol of the Everwood. In fact, the doors themselves were made of the great tree; one of the last remaining structures in Briva made of its wood. With one great heave, he pushed them open.

The room was dark. Windows lined every wall, but the gray and overcast day produced little light to brighten the vast room. Arches of dark stained wood stretched across the ceiling, meeting the stone at the top of the walls. Large drapes of colored silk hung freely, pulled away to the sides of the windows. They were green and gray; the colors of the Kaiser crest.

At the far end of the room, the throne sat atop a raised, stone stage. Just like the door that barred entrance to the room, the throne was made of wood from an Everwood tree. It was one solid piece of wood, carved meticulously over many years by the greatest craftsman of Briva after the Magi Wars. A Hym'Shailan Dragon was engraved on the back of the throne; one armrest formed by its tail and the other a long breathe of fire erupting from its mouth. The wood was aged, but solid as stone. It had seen the passing of many generations of Supreme Regii.

Datro's eyes moved towards the throne. Sitting in the seat, as if he truly belonged there, back straight and head held high, was the Grand Master. He was clad in full regal attire and held an emotionless expression on Bishop's false face. Datro walked calmly up to the foot of the stair.

"Have you come for some sort of revenge? Do you feel as if I have slighted you, Human?" said the Grand Master, indifferently. "I gave you the opportunity to be a part of our new world. I gave you the chance to have power and life."

Datro thrust a glowing hand out towards the false Bishop. "I have power! I took it, rather than beg for it from your wretched hands."

"You only think you have power. This new energy you have is worth nothing compared to the power that has been flowing through me for centuries; power that I have been honing and training. You are an ant among giants, Human, and I will crush you like one."

"Looking down on humans has been your downfall, creature," said Datro, taking a strong step forward. "You saw me as a tool, but it was you that was being used. You never controlled me. I researched the weapon for one purpose; to take it for my own. I was never going to give you the weapon."

The Grand Master gritted his teeth, digging his fingers into the wood of the armrests. It took all of his strength to restrain himself. It was insolence, a human talking to him in such a way.

Datro continued. "You have lost. You showed your hand and it was not strong enough. All of your years of planning and you were beaten again, by the same humans that you claim are so weak. You are the weak one, creature."

With as little warning as an arrow in the dark, a spike of earth erupted from the floor below Datro. In a flash, the tip of the spike was at Datro's throat, but it stopped. A warning shot from the Grand Master. He did not get the reaction he wanted, though. Datro did not move. His gaze stayed fixed on the throne.

Datro smirked and said, "I see through your malice and hate. I see through your actions. You are afraid." With one swipe of his hand he broke through the spike, sending the crumbled earth to the ground.

With a rage-filled shout the Grand Master jumped up from the throne. The anger rippled through him, causing his transformation to waver and bits of his true form to appear. He placed his hand out in front of himself and slowly a long wooden rod grew up from the ground. When it reached eye level, he snapped it off at the base. With weapon in hand, he rushed forward and leapt from the top of the stairs.

Datro drew his sword and blocked the Grand Master's vicious blow. The force of the attack sent shockwaves through the ground, fracturing the stone. Datro pushed the Grand Master back. The Tellurian was surprised by his strength. Datro quickly retaliated, thrusting forward, trying to catch the Grand Master off guard.

Steel clashed against wood. They fought back and forth, neither able to land a serious blow.

With his new strength and energy, Datro fought like a savage. His technique was crude and unrefined, but he made up for it with tenacity. He swung and thrust wildly. Against any other foe, he would have destroyed them easily, but the Grand Master was a Magi. Century's worth of battles and training prepared the Tellurian for anything. He would not let some maverick human overpower him.

"Where is this impressive magic you boast so much about, human?" goaded the Grand Master, as he pushed back strongly. "Do you fear to use it? Is it too much for you?"

Datro's sword sliced through the Grand Master's rod and he kicked the creature hard in the chest, sending him reeling. "I do not use it because I do not need it to destroy you."

The Grand Master growled. He tossed the two halves of his rod to the side. "Enough of this," he said before ripping the royal cloak from his back and transforming. The remaining clothes on his body shredded to pieces as his body expanded and his skin turned to rough scales.

"That is it, you freak. Show me your true self. Show me the power of a Magi, so I can see it for my own eyes before I thrust my sword into it," shouted Datro, excitedly.

When the transformation was complete, the Grand Master slammed his palms onto the ground. Everything started to shake. Datro quickly sheathed his sword and, just before the first spike erupted from the ground, he flipped backwards out of its path. Nimbly, he managed to avoid each and every spike as they continued to shoot up from the ground, as if he knew where they would appear. When he finally came to a stop, the room looked like the depths of a great cave, with dozens of stalagmites littering the ground.

Datro started to laugh. "You fool. Do you not get it? I can sense everything. I can feel how you manipulate the flow and I can feel where the energy gathers and where it will erupt from. I see all that you are. It is useless."

The Grand Master grew a long wooden spear from the ground and, with a roar, rushed at the scientist once again. This time, the Tellurian combined his magic with his attacks. A vine snagged Datro around the leg, but he ripped himself free quickly enough to avoid the attack. He rolled back to his feet, but had to jump again to the side to escape from a spike. The Grand Master did not let up. Hidden attacks came from below and above while he thrust and cut with his spear. Datro still managed to stay one step ahead of every attack, but he was beginning to tire and his body was bruised from constantly having to throw himself to the ground.

The Grand Master thrust forward with his spear, but it fell short of Datro, who retreated back with a step. His foot caught on debris and he staggered. In that that brief window, the Grand Master surged his energy through the spear and it extended forward, piercing Datro in the shoulder. He gasped in surprise and his vision blurred for a moment. The scientist then regained himself and sent a shockwave of energy at the Grand Master.

The Grand Master was blown back a few steps and the concussive force caused him to drop his spear. Datro pulled the spear from his shoulder and took the chance to attack. Just before connecting with the point of his sword, a wall of earth shot up from the ground and the blade buried deep into it. He could not wrench it free, so he left it and retreated backwards.

For the first time since the moment Datro stepped into the room, everything was silent. Datro was breathing heavily and blood was streaming down his side. The Grand Master was standing alone in the middle of the debris-ridden room, the protective wall collapsed in front of him. He had his hand out in front of him and showed a confused expression on his hideous face.

"So, is this your power?" he said. "You have taken the light from my eyes?"

Datro swallowed his exhaustion and responded, "I control all light. I can make it bright as the sun or as dark as the deepest cave."

"Interesting," the Tellurian smiled. "I have seen nothing like it before. I underestimated you, Datro. I would not have guessed that you had such an interesting power up your sleeve." He walked over and picked up his spear, as if he knew exactly where it was.

"You have underestimated me this entire time, Tellurian, and I am sick of it. This power I have is the ultimate power. I control the light and the dark."

"What can darkness do to me, Human? Nobody was ever killed by darkness."

"No, but they are killed by the things that linger in darkness. Death lingers in darkness. Everybody is afraid of what they cannot see."

The Grand Master started to laugh. "Afraid? You think I am afraid of you, human? It does not matter if I can see you or not. You do no scare me."

Datro was incensed by the Grand Master's dismissive attitude. "Without light you cannot see, Tellurian," yelled Datro. "If you cannot see me you cannot lay a finger on me, let alone kill me. I could dance circles around you and you could do nothing about it. Your death will be slow and agonizing and you will never even know what is happening.

The Grand Master continued to laugh, ignoring the raging Datro. It took a few moments before his amusement subsided. After shaking away the final chuckle, he smirked and said, "I would like to see you try."

That was the final straw. Datro picked up his blade from the ground and rushed at the Grand Master with an incensed roar, swinging wildly. Even with his spear in hand, the Grand Master did not use it. He dodged, ducked and sidestepped every attack that Datro threw at him. Datro's anger was so thick that he did not seem to notice and he just continued to attack. Finally, after minutes of unsuccessful blows, the Grand Master decided it was enough. He parried Datro's attack and sent his sword flying from his grip.

Datro fell to his knees in exhaustion. "How?" he forced out with what little breath he had left.

The Grand Master chuckled. "Oh Datro, Datro. You are the smart scientist. Can you not figure it out? Can you not comprehend it?"

"Tell me!" screamed Datro as he rose up from his feet. A pulse of energy fired out from him which blew the Grand Master backwards. The Grand Master kept his footing, though, and did not lose his devilish grin. "Tell me how you can still see," added Datro.

"I cannot see, Human," said the Grand Master. "You took away my light, remember?" The Grand Master's smirk turned to a scowl, and he shouted, "What you have failed to realize, is that I do not need to see you to know exactly where you are!"

Suddenly, the ground rumbled again. Datro looked to the ground in fear of another spike or vine, but none came. Instead, every shredded and splintered piece of wood around Datro slowly rose up from the ground. It looked as if a swarm of insects was surrounding the stunned scientist.

"What is this?" he shrieked.

The swarm hovered there for only a moment and, then, after a malicious laugh from the Grand Master, they fired in towards Datro. There was nowhere to run. He was completely surrounded. As the cloud of shrapnel closed in around him, he realized there was only one thing to do. With a ferocious yell, he expelled an enormous pulse of energy from his body. The attack hit the wave and all of the wood disintegrated to dust. Datro seemed to have averted a disaster, but under the haze of wooden dust a second attack from the Grand Master found its mark. When everything settled, the body of Datro Cervon stood skewered by a dozen wooden spears erupting from the earth; his eyes still widened in shock.

The Grand Master walked up to the scientist's body, which almost seemed to be propped up on display. His body was not even allowed to relax and fall to the ground. Every limb was held up by a wooden spear. Datro almost looked like a stone statue of incredible reality.

"I have waited centuries for this day, Human," said the Grand Master "I have put myself through torture and pain to make certain that I had the strength to see it to the end. I would have destroyed this whole palace and everyone in it before I allowed the likes of you to get in my way."

Slowly, the Grand Master's sight started to return. When he saw Datro's body, all he did was smile. He enjoyed the look of his new prize. If his plan was to fail, he would enjoy killing everyone who had tried to stop him. Turning, he walked back up to the throne and sat down to wait for his next visitor. Two of them were entering the castle at that very moment. The Grand Master hoped that they would at least be a little more amusing than his first. Maybe the sight of his first victim would make them realize the futility of their plight. They were rushing quickly up to him.

Foolish humans.

58

General Weston trotted along slowly on his horse. The crisp, cool air of the Waning Highlands could be seen on his breath. It was a colder day than it had been for the first few days of their trek and it was causing frustration to build up in the great General. They could only go as fast as the oxen could pull the catapults and ballista, and the cold weather and rolling hills were slowing them considerably. It seemed they may be put behind by almost a day.

This slow-down was beginning to wear on the men as well, who all were boiling with energy to fight. They should have been free of the Highlands and well into the Central Plain by this time, but there were still many miles of hills ahead of them. At least the sun was out and the sky was clear. Snow or rain would put a complete halt to their progress.

Weston turned to his captain. "Where is your scout, Pion? He should have returned by midday."

"I do not know, Sir. These hills are far more treacherous than they seem and the horses exhaust easily in this cold. It may be just that he has stopped to give rest to the horse."

"Let us hope that is all it is. If we have given up our strategy already, we are as good as dead."

He quickly covered his face back up with a fur mask, as a cool gust of wind passed through. The wind had abated as they had entered a more wooded area, but occasional gusts manage to pass through when they reached the peaks of hills. They had not seen any sign of wildlife for some time, as well. Clearly, their presence was well known in the area by now and all animals knew well to avoid them.

For another half an hour, the large force slowly trudged through the hills. Discontented voices were beginning to grow louder amongst the men. Weston chose to ignore them for now. He, too, was frustrated. Then there came a shout from the left flank.

"Scout!"

Everyone turned to see the faint form of a rider coming over the next hill. It slowed for a moment but, when it spotted the large army, it started towards them at lightning speed. Something was wrong.

"What do you think it is?" Pion asked his General.

"I do not know," Weston responded with concern. "But, it is nothing good. Alert the men to prepare for battle."

Rouse heard the order as well, and they both quickly galloped off in opposite directions to alert the men. Excitement began to stir. The rider skidded to a stop in front of Weston. He could not speak through his panting breaths.

"Calm yourself, soldier. Catch your breath. What is it you have to report?"

"The Brivan Army is approaching. They are no more than a half hour ride from here."

"Did they see you? Were you followed?" questioned Weston. "Did they show any indication of knowing we are here?"

The man brushed sweat away from his face. "I do not believe so. I kept close to the tree line and out of sight. Their troop movements were slow and did not change as I made my retreat."

Weston turned to a soldier behind him. "Lieutenant, take a patrol and scour the area for any scouts. Kill anything that moves; every human, animal or insect. I want nothing left alive."

"Yes, Sir." He rode off with a dozen men.

"You did well, soldier," he said to the scout. "It is difficult to go unseen by a Tellurian force. How many were in their army?"

"Nearly eight thousand, from what I could see. They were moving quickly."

"Alright, then. Return to your post. And see to it that you get food and water. You will need your strength."

So, we were too late. The Tellurian has already made his move. I did not plan for this. Does this mean he has gotten his weapon?

The General rode out in front of his army. Every man was now aware of what was happening. Excitement was building. He unsheathed his sword and raised it up as he shouted.

"The time has come, men. The Tellurian has chosen to meet us in the field rather than hide behind his walls. He has chosen the honorable path. He has proven that he is a worthy adversary. Unfortunately, today he will find that there are humans in this world that he cannot control. There are humans that will stand against even the slimmest of odds. Today we fight against the scourge that once tried to take over this world. They failed before and they will fail again. They will crash against our wood and steel and they will perish. Today we will prove that Magi do indeed bleed and that Paks is the now the kingdom of men."

A giant roar erupted from the crowd.

"Let us march!"

The scout was right. It did not take long until the sounds of a marching army could be heard on the wind. Weston ordered his men to stop and then rode up to the top of the hill in front of them with his two captains, Pion and Rouse. At the top of the hill they could see all that stretched before them. The Brivan Army stood in formation across a large flatland below them. A lone horseman was waiting out front of the large force.

"It seems that Haron's estimate was correct. That is a force of about eight thousand, Sir. They are mostly foot soldiers, some cavalry as well," observed Pion.

"Sir, they do not travel with any siege weapons or ladders. It seems they were not ever intending to attack the city. Did they know our plan the moment we concocted it?"

"No, Rouse," said Weston. "They do not need siege weapons to enter our city. Remember that we also fight against the Davati. They are the greatest siege weapon of all."

"Yes, but I do not see them. Those men are all Brivan soldiers. Where is the great Davati warship?"

All three men looked up at the cloud covered sky. A gloom was beginning to set in and it was difficult to see anything amongst the grayness.

"In the clouds," responded Weston. "That is where I would hide if I were a cowardly rat."

"So then, they knew we were coming?"

Weston pointed down at the lone horseman seemingly waiting for them out on the flatland. "It seems so."

"What do we do?" asked Pion.

"Rouse, I want you to take half of the force and march them to the top of this hill. Take the ballista with you. Get them primed and ready. I want the archers split as well; half to attack the ground forces from the top of the hill and the other half in the rear to defend against an aerial assault from above."

Rouse nodded and quickly rode off.

"Pion, I want you to stay with the rear guard. Keep your eyes on the sky and look out for an ambush. If reinforcements are needed on the hill, use your judgment. I want archers always in the rear."

"What will you do, Sir?"

Weston turned back and stared at the large Brivan force ahead of them. "I will go and meet our lone visitor, to see what they have to say."

"Strength to you, Sir."

"And to you, Captain."

Weston galloped down the gentle slope of the hill towards the Brivan horde. Their numbers were an impressive sight. Weston had not seen a battle of this size in his entire life. The kingdom of Paks had not seen a battle of this magnitude for centuries. Not even the War of Paksian rule was fought with such numbers. Weston was confident, though, that his men would fight savagely.

As he came closer to the lone horseman, he started to make out the blue and gray coloring of the man's cloak and uniform and the bright blonde coloring of his hair. *Fanix.* He also noticed a small fox like creature pacing around the horse's feet.

The Minor had his usual stern expression on his face as Weston rode up. He was wrapped in layers of extra cloth and fur on top of his usual skin tight uniform. The cold plains of the north were no place for a jungle dwelling Davati. Despite that, he showed no visible discomfort. In fact, he almost seemed pleased.

"And the savage leader finally arrives," Fanix sneered.

Weston brushed off the backhanded insult. "I hope I have not kept you waiting long. I know how much you rats detest the cold. I am surprised you even made the trip. Where are the rest of your men? I do not see your safe little perch floating around anywhere."

"The *Fionetta* did not make the trip. She does not fare well in the cold weather of the north. My men have stayed in Valoria to protect the city."

"Do not play coy with me, Fanix. Your men could not defend a city from an army of children. You hide until the right moment and then attack from behind. Those are coward tactics."

"Only fools fight face to face with an enemy that has greater strength. You wish for me to send my men at yours, steel to steel? I would rather fell a man with an arrow in the back, never even knowing I was there."

"Only you would be proud of such cowardice, Fanix. So, where is your ship? Where will it attack from? Is it behind us as we speak?"

"I think you should worry about the army in front of you, Lockhardt. You have enough to fear from Briva, to be keeping one eye to your back."

"Do you see me looking back? I do not fear your men, Fanix. Let them fire at us from above. Their arrows will hit nothing. Their aim is not that precise. I fear only courageous, honorable men. And, of course, I fear the creatures that control you." He glanced down at the fox crouched near their feet. It snarled back at him.

"This creature is under my control."

"Yes, but you are here on the orders of another. You are a coward and a pawn."

Fanix quickly drew his sword. "What do you know of it?" he screeched. The fox started to snap at the legs of Weston's horse, but the horse held its place, even kicking back at it. "It does not matter how or why I am here. All that matters is that I now have the power to destroy you and your barbaric people."

"At what cost, Fanix? You will not come out of this alive, even if you do win. Tellurians cannot be trusted."

Minor Fanix's anger was growing. "How dare you stare at me with judgmental eyes, you savage? You know nothing of what I have sacrificed. All I have done, I have done for my people."

"And you believe that the Tellurian will just leave you alone if you win this war? Do you truly believe he will let you and your people live? You have doomed us all, Fanix. Your cowardice will be the end of us."

"Not before the end of you, Lockhardt!" He eyes darted quickly to his left, towards the trees. Weston noticed and turned his attention to the trees. He spotted movement amongst the foliage.

"Run and hide, you fool," cackled Fanix. "You were marching to your death the moment you left your gates."

Weston spun his horse around quickly and shouted back to his men. "It is an ambush. Look to the trees!"

As he finished his shout, a volley of arrows shot out from the forest. He heard the shouts of his captains and shields were raised. Suddenly, the Tellurian fox leapt at the General and clamped its jaws around his forearm. Weston tried to shake it free, but its bite was strong. He quickly drew a dagger and stabbed the beast. It lost its grip, but the General refused to let his prey get away. He grabbed him around the scruff of the neck and stabbed again. The fox barked in pain and scratched and clawed to get away, but Weston would not release it. One final stab and the fox was silenced. Weston tossed it to the side like a doll. Blood was streaming down his arm, but he didn't care.

He turned back to Minor Fanix and gave him a threatening glare. "By the end of this battle, rat, I will kill you as I just killed that beast. That is the kind of death you are worthy of."

"You will not last long enough to have the pleasure."

Weston raced off towards his men. Arrows were now flying back and forth between the Creed and the hidden forces in the trees. The Creed catapults launched their large stones, which crashed against the trees and rained wood down on the Brivans' heads.

"Set them ablaze," shouted Weston as he raced back towards his men. "Smoke them from their hiding place."

Arrow tips were lit and catapult stones doused in oil. When the order was given, a massive stream of red flames fired towards the tree line. In the cold chill, the small flames of the arrows took time to catch, but when the stones burst apart the trees, the loose wood set fire quickly. You could hear the panicked shouts of the soldiers as the fire quickly spread. Soon, the Brivan soldiers started to run out from the trees and into the open plane. The Creed soldiers strung up another volley of arrows, but an order was shouted from Rouse.

"Volley to the front. The main force is coming."

During the commotion, the main Brivan Force had started its march towards the hill. Nearly eight thousand strong, their force was more than double the force that Weston had established on the hill. The Creed quickly turned their attention forward and released their arrows on the advancing force.

"Un-sheath your swords and make ready, men!"

As the vanguard prepared for combat in the front, Pion continued to send volleys in their support. Brivan men and horses fell, one after another, as they rode swiftly towards the Creed front. Their numbers were decreasing, but not quickly enough. The two forces continued to move towards each other, but the Brivan's numbers still dwarfed the Creed's. Suddenly, the ground behind the vanguard started to shake violently. The cold earth started to crumble and a great crack appeared. In an instant, a great wall erupted from the ground, separating the two Creed forces. It stood a hundred feet tall and stretched from tree line to tree line. The Creed soldiers stood; mouth agape. Before they could regain their wits, the Valor Forces were upon them.

Men and steel crashed against one another like waves against the rocky cliffs of the Rift Mountains. The Brivan cavalry rushed through the front lines, but quickly were stopped as the Creed strengthened their defense. The power and skill of the Creed soldiers stood strong against overwhelming numbers. Weston had been on the front line, but had the wherewithal to keep his attention on the approaching forces. He easily beat off the first wave of cavalry that attacked him, but his horse took a spear to the side and he was thrown to the ground.

On the other side of the wall, Pion and the rear guard were frantic. The sudden appearance of the wall put them all into a panic. Their arrows would not reach over the wall and the catapults reached just short of the top. They could hear the battle raging on the other side, but could do nothing.

Pion made the only decision he could. "Orin, take your men and circle around the right. Talmik, take the left. Use the trees for cover."

As the force split and ran towards the trees to find their way around, the leaves came alive and packs of wolves and wild cats raced out to meet them. Some of the soldiers managed to fire a volley into the beasts before they were on top of them. They did not use their magic; only their teeth and claws. Their numbers were small, but their animal brutality ripped through the Creed.

On the other side of the wall, Weston had unsheathed his massive blade and was cutting down three men at a time with every swing. The sword had carved out a massive circle of space around him. Anyone that came near him was instantly felled. The Creed fought viciously, each one taking at least three Brivans with them. After the initial charge and the shock of the giant wall, the Creed were gaining ground, but it was difficult to tell if their numbers would hold.

The remaining Brivan that had escaped the burning forest joined the main force and were pushing the Creed back on their right flank. Rouse shouted a rallying cry and they were able to halt their advance. With the wall at their backs, there was no chance of a retreat. The only place to run was to the forest along the left flank, but the trees would slow them and they would not get far. They must make their stand, or hope that the rear guard could get to them quickly.

Then the thought occurred to Weston.

Could the wall be taken down?

Everything he had read about a Tellurian told him that they needed to be in contact with the surface they were manipulating. There was a Tellurian nearby that was casting the spell. If they could destroy it, the wall would crumble. He needed only to find the creature. His confidence returned to him, but only for a moment.

A great horn sounded on the wind. Everyone looked up and watched as the clouds parted and the *Fionetta* emerged above the battlefield. Its immensity even blotted out the sun for a moment, draping the men in darkness. It drifted over the main battle and towards the other side of the wall. From the ground, the soldiers watched as the sky around the great airship started to fill with dark specks. Hundreds of Davati Airmen launched themselves from the deck and started their descent into the battle, firing waves of death from above.

"He targets the rear guard," moaned a chagrined Weston.

Pion assumed victory when the remaining Tellurian animals turned tail and ran. The men started to cheer in exaltation, but not more than a moment later, it became apparent why the creatures had ran. The *Fionetta's* shadow cast upon them.

"Take cover!" Pion tried to shout. For many of the men, it was not soon enough. The first wave of arrows carpeted the ground around them. Nearly a third of the men fell. Many of the men had lost their shields in the battle and had nowhere to hide. The arrows continued to fall like rain. Rocks and boulders started to fall as well, crushing the men below their shields. It was endless. They could not fight back.

"We can wait them out," shouted Pion, trying to reassure the men. "Those cowards will soon land and we will take the fight back to them. On the ground, they are like ants."

The men all barked their agreement with an exalted "Oorah." They would wait them out and soon the Airmen would drift to the earth; into their territory. They needed to survive and regroup with the vanguard. Weston could not win against those numbers alone. Together, Pion was sure that victory would be theirs. Separated, they would need a miracle.

But, can we last?

The sky was getting darker and the sun would soon be set. It seemed the battle would continue all night. No matter how many men they cut down, more men would follow. The Creed soldiers were being slowly ground down to nothing. This was the last thing that Weston had wanted. His quick battle was a fleeting fantasy. Now, he could only pray for a bloody victory.

The Airmen had landed and Pion and his men had made quick work of them. Not more than moments after the last Davati had fallen, another wave had launched from the decks of the great airship and the carnage continued. Pion had ordered his men to take cover in the trees, but it would only slow the process. If you could not bring down the ship, they would never be able to regroup with the vanguard. There was one ballista still intact on the battle field. If they could reach it, they could at least damage the ship and hope for a retreat. The Davati would never put their prized war machine in danger.

Pion turned to the remnants of his men, who all huddled beneath the few remained trees that provided cover. "I need ten men with shields." Apprehensively, a handful of men stepped forward. "Are there no more?" he urged.

"There are precious few of us left, Captain. Many of us do not even have weapons, let alone shields," shouted a soldier.

It was worse than he had thought. Only a few hundred remained of the thousand he had started with, and those that remained had little life left in them.

"Fine, the six of you will do. The rest of you stay here. Cover us as best you can. When the ship is damaged, they will surely retreat. When that happens, you must take the opportunity to regroup with the General's men."

"If they do not retreat?"

"Then you shall regroup with the General none-the-less," Pion bellowed. He was sick of this battle. He wanted nothing more than to finish it and return home, but that was not possible. This battle was too important. He would not allow himself and his men to give up now. "We are Creed, men. We do not cower under the cover of trees and we do not give up until every ounce of our strength has left us. We do not fear death, especially from cowards who attack without showing their faces. Who are we?"

"We are Creed!" the men chanted.

With the men's energy returned to them, Pion organized his small force. They would make a wild dash to the ballista. They stood at the edge of the forest, waiting for the next wave of Airmen to touch down. In that moment, the remaining men sent a volley of arrows onto the battlefield and Pion made his assault. They fought through the Airmen as quickly as they could. The men in the forest continued to cover them with barrages of arrows.

They finally broke through and reached the ballista. Two men had fallen, but four remained. Pion and another defended their position as the other two loaded the giant, steel-tipped spear. Its tip was loaded with explosives and was capable of blowing a hole into the side of a city wall. Just as they were about to fire, a giant boulder came crashing down from the sky, crushing the ballista. The explosive detonated, blowing wooden shrapnel off in every direction. The two soldiers loading it were instantly killed and Pion was thrown from his feet. He lay on the battlefield, concussed and disoriented. His eyes stared up at the bleak, darkening sky.

In his blurred vision he saw another wave of Airmen launch from the decks of the *Fionetta*. There was nothing they could do now. The ship would stay up on its perch and rain death down on top of them. This was the end. With the world slowing down around him, Pion started to again notice the cold chill in the air. The breeze started to pick up and his body shivered. The Airmen drifting down towards him were now just dark shadows against a gray, twilight sky; almost like birds of prey, circling before the kill.

A shrill cry echoed on the wind and more dark shapes flew into view above him. He could not make out what was happening, but he could hear the sounds of the Davati Airmen screaming and shouting in panic. Dark shapes started to plummet to the earth. Calamity was unleashing in the sky.

A Creed soldier came running up to Pion and helped him to his feet. "Are you alright, Sir?"

Pion's head was pounding and his body ached, but something had happened, and the battle was turning. "What is going on, soldier?"

"It is a miracle, Sir. Giant eagles. They are everywhere."

59

"What happened to you? Where have you been since the Tellurians came after you?" asked Coal, as he and Farren sprinted through the palace grounds.

To their surprise, the gate to the grounds had been open and the guards lay dead. The horses in the stable had been set loose on the grounds, so they had to go on foot. Coal was sure it was the work of Datro, but it did not matter. They had to make the run no matter what. The crazed scientist had made the first move. They only hoped that they were not too late.

"Kyte, Kaleb and I went to find reinforcements to the northeast. There is much to tell, but now is not the time," urged Farren.

"Kaleb is alive?"

"Very much so. He is with Kyte now."

"What was in the northeast? There is nothing that way until you get to Layalta and lands of the Matroz?"

"We were not searching for men, Coal."

"Do you mean to tell me that you found help from Magi? There are still more of them alive in Paks?"

"We found help, yes. But, that is all I will tell you now. We need to get to the palace. This may be our only chance to destroy the Tellurian."

"How do you know so much?"

"I went to the hideout. Reme told me everything. I know about what has happened since the day I left. I know you have been on the run and I know that Kara is held captive. We need to stop this creature."

Coal could not believe that this boy that ran beside him was the same one that left only weeks ago. He was confident and serious. His demeanor was that of a warrior who had seen years of battle and death. It was clear that he had left his old days behind him.

"What happened to you out there, Farren?"

Farren turned to the Commander and smiled. He had looked up to Coal ever since he was little and he had seen that expression on his face before, when Coal used to look at Bishop with admiration and camaraderie. "More than you can imagine. I can hardly tell you assuredly that it all really happened."

"So, why have you returned now?"

"I have returned to help. We must destroy the Grand Master. His plans go deeper than you know."

"What about Kyte and Kaleb?"

"They have gone where they are needed. It is up to us now to end this."

Coal found Farren's presence boosting his confidence. What was once a sure martyr's march was now a heroic march to save a kingdom. It was a story that he could tell to his children, not one that was told over his grave.

When they burst into the throne room, they found it in complete chaos. Earth, stone and wood was strewn around the room like the remnants of a great battle. The great stained glass windows lay in shards and beams of sunlight shone through brightly. In the middle of the room was Datro's body, propped up on display by the Grand Master's stakes. His eyes were wide in shock, his skin was beginning to pale, and blood was finally washing down around the spikes that impaled him. Farren nearly retched at the sight of it.

"How do you like my new statue? I feel like it adds a little bit of flair and excitement to the room, don't you?" said the Grand Master from his perch on the throne.

Farren could not take his eyes off of the body. It was the first time he had seen death so fresh and real. The blood was pooling on the ground and Farren started to tremble at its site. Datro's blank eyes stared right through him.

Coal put a reassuring hand on his shoulder. "Do not let it get to you, Farren. Use it as motivation. Let it strengthen you."

"I am glad you finally came, Commander. I have been wondering if you were ever going to show yourself. And I see that you brought the Prince as well. Perfect. You have saved me the trouble of hunting him down. This must mean that my trusty Pardos has failed me again, though. Such a pity. I always liked him.

Coal turned to the Grand Master and stepped forward. "Why is it that you seem to enjoy killing humans so much, Tellurian? What is it that we did to you that made us deserving of your hate?"

The Grand Master was in his Tellurian form, not even trying to hide his true self. "You took what was not yours, Human. Your ruler sat in a throne that he did not have the right to sit in."

"So, you blame us for what happened centuries ago? You kill men who were not even alive then to understand the offense you are blaming them for? How do you justify killing with such logic?"

The Grand Master rose to his feet and said, "I do not need to justify anything, especially to you. I kill humans because I have the power to do so. This land rightfully belongs to us and we will take it back. You have spread your human filth upon it for too long. Now it is our time."

Coal had heard enough. He drew his sword. "This land is ours now and I am the protector of it. If you wish to take it, or harm anyone upon it, you will have to answer to me."

"Apparently, you humans never learn." With a wave of his hand, the spikes that held up Datro's body crumbled and he fell limp to the floor. The sudden movement shocked Farren back to attention. He turned and saw Coal's sword drawn. Farren quickly drew his as well.

"Stay behind me," ordered Coal. "Watch him and wait for an opening. Study his movements. Find a weakness."

"Can you handle him alone?"

"Most likely not, but we must not be hasty. I will do my best to fight him off, so find a weakness and find it quickly."

The Grand Master walked down the steps and he and Coal started to circle around each other. The Tellurian had his long wooden spear and Coal his halmon and kidon. Farren stood back and watched.

"The scientist could not defeat me, what makes you think you will fare any better. He had the benefit of power and magic. What do you have? Your skills with a sword are great, but you will need much more than that, Coal."

"My sword is all I need. You will soon see."

"If you fight with only your strength, then that is how I will kill you, as well. You take pride in your skills with a blade, but I have been training with mine for centuries," said the Tellurian. "I will destroy you and your pride with nothing but this spear."

Like a bolt of lightning, the Grand Master thrust forward with his spear. Coal expertly parried and replied with a swing of his halmon. The Grand Master ducked under the blow and caught Coal in the stomach with a swift kick. Coal recovered and sent the Tellurian retreating with a vicious double attack from both his blades.

To Farren, this series of attacks happened in an instant. He watched intently, but it was impossible to keep up. The Gallant and the Magi dueled back and forth, neither one letting up, nor able to land a decisive blow. When one thought they had an opening, the other would somehow defend with improbable swordsmanship. Even with such ferocious attacks, they barely moved from where they stood. Neither one retreated. The giant throne room seemed to shrink down to one small space around them.

Coal and the Grand Master were covered with cuts and bruises when Coal finally caught the Tellurian in the side with a thrust. The Tellurian stumbled backwards. Farren had worked his way behind the magi and, in that instant, the prince attacked. His blade thudded harmlessly into a giant spike of wood that had appeared behind the Grand Master. The Tellurian swiftly sent Farren to the ground once he regained his footing. Coal attacked again to defend the prince, but was thwarted by multiple earthen spikes. Farren managed to roll away from danger. The scene settled.

"I thought that you were going to destroy me without your magic."

"And I thought this was just between the two of us, Coal. Why put this boy in danger? Do you not think you can kill me on your own?"

Coal pulled Farren's blade from the wood and tossed it back to him. "Of course I believe that I can kill you, but this is not about me, creature. I am here to defend this city and the entire kingdom from your wretched soul. What kind of defender would I be if I put those I fought to defend in danger just to keep my pride? My pride does not matter now, only victory."

"How honorable of you to throw away your pride for such pitiful people. Do you believe they would do the same for you? They have already cast you out as a traitor. You are willing to die for them and yet they abandon you on a whim. Your honor is misplaced."

"At least I have honor. They abandon me because they have faith in their Regis. I do not blame them. I only fear for them."

The Grand Master laughed boisterously at Coal's insult. "You believe I have no honor? You do not believe that I too would do anything for my people? You are sadly mistaken, Human."

Suddenly, the doors to the room started to creak open. In walked a Tellurian with the lady Kara dragging behind him. She struggled very little, but her arms were bound and her head hung low, looking at the floor.

Coal and Farren's hearts both quickened. "Kara!" they shouted.

Kara looked up. She saw them and her energy returned quickly. "Brother! Farren!" She tried to pull away but the Tellurian hauled her back and pressed a dagger into her throat.

"Where is your honor now, Coal?" goaded the Grand Master. "Will you sacrifice your sister for the kingdom as well?"

Coal locked eyes with his sister, who still scrambled to break free. Her body was pale and gaunt and her usual joyfulness had long left her. She was an empty vessel and her eyes screamed for help even louder than her voice did. Seeing Coal made her fear for her life again, the life that she had already given up hope on. A shout made Coal spin around and he saw Farren rushing at the Grand Master in a rage.

"You bastard!"

"Farren, no!"

The prince fell upon the Grand Master like an animal. The Grand Master grinned as Farren swung wildly at him with his two swords. The Tellurian effortlessly defended each blow and quickly had Farren on his back once again. Coal took a step forward to help Farren, but the Grand Master stopped him.

"This is how it is going to be," the Grand Master stated. "If you two are able to strike me down by the time the sun sets in this window, then my warrior will leave and the girl will live. If you do not, then I will make you both watch as I slit her throat."

The sun barely still hung above the window sill and Coal knew they did not have much time. Trying to reason with the Tellurian was out of the question and he did not want to waste any time. His anger was welling up, but he knew he must control it.

"Farren, get to you feet," he barked. "I know you care for Kara as much as I do, so listen to me carefully. We will attack him together. That is the only way. Follow my motions and attack his openings."

Farren glanced back at Kara. The Tellurian now held her mouth shut and tears were flowing down her face. His eyes turned back to the Grand Master. "Lead the way," Farren growled.

This time the clash was not fought on even terms. The Grand Master threw spell after spell at the two humans as they unleashed their assault. They were constantly on the move, defending themselves from every angle and every deceitful attack from below. After so many battles with the Tellurians, both Coal and Farren knew the patterns. They could tell where the next vine would appear, or stake would emerge. The Tellurians all fought in a similar way. Despite that, the Grand Master's ferocity was on a different level. They could just avoid his attacks, but had no time to recover.

As the minutes droned on, their exhaustion grew unbearable. The sun was setting quickly and they were not getting any closer to landing a finishing blow. This was no longer a battle of honor or pride. If either Farren or Coal had the opportunity, they would have stabbed the Grand Master in the back without hesitation. If only they could create the opportunity.

With one last surge, the two warriors charged forward. Coal's halmon cut through the Grand Master's wooden spear. He tried to retreat, but Farren was ready for him from behind. The Grand Master barely got up his arms in defense, and Farren's short swords buried deep into the Tellurian's hardened wood forearms, driving him to the ground. Farren tried to pin him to the ground but he was quickly thrown to the side. Before the Grand Master could return to his feet, Coal rushed forward.

"Stay down," yelled Coal, as he stood above the Grand Master, his blade pointed at his chest.

The Grand Master froze. He had nowhere to run. He knew that Coal would not be easily thrown to the side as Farren was. He was trapped. All he could do was laugh. "Very good, Coal, very good. I did not think that you and the boy had it in you. I am impressed."

Coal's expression was stone. "Unfortunately for you, I am not."

"A shame. Dear boy, you do not quite understand your circumstances. I am defeated, yes, I admit it. You have bested me," said the Grand Master. "But you have forgotten one important detail. It has gotten a bit darker in here."

Coal darted his eyes to the stained glass. The sun had disappeared below the window sit.

"Your time is up, Coal," said the Grand Master.

Kara's scream echoed and caused Coal to spin around in fear. In that moment, a vine grabbed his wrist and he dropped his sword. More vines wrapped around his legs and arms and he was pulled to the ground. Farren too was snared as he rushed to help. They both struggled mightily, but could not break free. The Grand Master casually got back up to his feet, chuckling to himself.

"Foolish girl," he said. "If she would have just kept her mouth shut, you may have stood a chance. But alas she is weak, as you all are."

"You are a coward!" Coal barked at him.

"Did I not tell you that I would do anything for my people as well? Would you have done anything different? You should not have hesitated to kill me. It is your own weakness that was your undoing."

The Grand Master started walking over towards Kara as he talked.

"Don't you dare touch her!" screamed Farren.

"But, we had a deal." The Grand Master pointed over to the window, where the sun was now set and only a red hue could be seen across sky. "You have failed and now I will claim my prize."

"If you touch her, it will be the last thing that you ever do," Coal threatened.

The Grand Master reached out and took Kara from the clutches of his Tellurian pawn. Kara could barely form words through her shaking sobs. She screamed for help, but neither Coal nor Farren could do anything. Tears were flowing freely from her once piercingly green eyes. Her cheeks were flushed against her now pale skin. Her legs went numb and she could no longer stand. The Grand Master hauled her up with one arm and took the dagger with the other.

"You had your chance to stop me, Coal, but you were not strong enough."

Kara's eyes flashed up once more and Farren caught a final glimpse of the beautiful face of his childhood friend. There was fear and sadness in it, but there was also a smile. Then, with one swift motion of the dagger, it was gone forever.

60

ass calamity continued in the sky above the battlefield. A convocation of giant eagles, each one the size of a large horse, and their wings spanning the length of a small house, crashed into the army of Airmen. Their beaks and claws easily ripped through the men's glider wings, sending them plummeting to the earth. The Davati tried to retaliate with their arrows, but they were not used to shooting at things that attacked from above, so their arrows hit nothing but air.

The scene was sending excitement through the minds of the Creed soldiers and confusion into their enemy's. Pion had quickly recovered and returned to his men. In the confusion, they had made their way to the other side of the wall and had regrouped with Weston and the vanguard. Their numbers were small, but they were making a push. It was far from finished, though. Nearly half of the Forces' army was still intact and, despite the surprise attack by the eagles, Airmen were still landing and attacking from the rear flanks.

"Good to see you alive and well, Captain," Weston said to Pion when he had returned to the fight.

"*Well* may be a bit of an over-statement, Sir, but I am here now. I am sorry it took so long. We ran into a few barriers."

Weston smiled. "Nothing you could not handle, I hope."

"Of course not. Our new friends from above may have helped out, as well. I thank the Almighty for that."

"I do not think it was the Almighty that brought the eagles, good friend. I believe we should be thanking another one of our new Magi acquaintances."

Far above them, the battle in the night sky was raging. Kyte and Drek cut through the crisp air like a fish through water. His wind magic was wreaking havoc on the Davati and his accuracy with his bow was uncanny as ever. Kaleb also flew amongst the soaring eagles, but his gracefulness was somewhat lacking. He clung to his eagle with the grip of death and let the deadly bird create all the carnage.

It had been a long trek from the Forest of Rising Twilight. When the eagles appeared in the ruins of the Aerii city, the three adventurers' spirits had risen. Hundreds of the majestic creatures appeared from the canopy above. They were drawn back to the city by the breaking of the barrier and the massive storm of energy that was emitting from the city during Kyte and Pardos' battle. The scene of their descent was just another one of the unbelievable events in the past weeks that Farren had begun to doubt had even occurred

With a renewed purpose, the three men got a much needed rest and, what seemed to them at the time, a bountiful feast. The meeting with Pardos had at first cast doubt into Farren's mind, but that next morning he knew exactly what he must do. All three made for Valoria but, part of the way back, Kyte was informed by one of the eagles that there was a great ship flying through the Central Plains. They parted ways, with Farren continuing to the capital to find Coal, and Kyte and Kaleb heading for the highlands. They made it just in time, it seemed.

Kyte flew up next to Kaleb and shouted, "The battle on the ground is raging. If the earthen wall is destroyed, it will cast more fear into the enemy. You must find the Tellurians casting the spell and destroy them."

"Go down to land? You do not have to ask me twice," yelled Kaleb. "What will you do?"

Kyte turned and looked up at the hulking shadow of the *Fionetta*. "I will bring down the ship and end this false battle."

"I thought for a moment you were going to leave me with the difficult job," Kaleb smirked. "Good luck."

"To you as well, Young Kaleb. Send word to General Weston of our plan. He will know what to do from there."

With shared nods, they parted ways. Kaleb's eagle took a nose dive towards the ground. He circled the battle a few times, looking for Weston and keeping an eye out for any creatures that may be the Tellurians that summoned the wall. It was difficult, especially in the fading light, to spot any single man in such carnage. Luckily for Kaleb, the great general was not an ordinary man. His towering hulk stood over everyone near him.

He leaned down and spoke into the eagle's ear. "Search for the Tellurians. Alert me when you find them."

The eagle screeched loudly and then dipped down close to the battlefield. Forces soldiers scattered in all directions. No one had seen such a bird in Paks for hundreds of years and in the fading light it seemed like a demonic shadow. Kaleb leapt from its back and into the fray. Despite the calamity, Kaleb fought his way to the general quickly.

"General Weston," he shouted.

"Who are you that flies on the backs of eagles?" Weston shouted back at him.

"My name is Kaleb. I am a Gallant from Valoria and friend of Kyte Valen. I bring word from Kyte. He aims to bring down the airship."

"Is that possible?" Weston asked, in shock.

"After what I have seen, I will never doubt the words of a Magi. If he says the ship will fall, then it will fall."

"That, on its own, will not end this battle. We still have the Valor Forces to contend with. I fear we may be whittled down to nothing. We need reinforcements," responded Weston.

"The great wall that blocks your retreat; it was cast by Tellurians. If we bring it down, the enemy will no longer have the courage to fight. We must find the Tellurians that created it and kill them."

"How do we find a creature that does not want to be found and can blend into the wilderness?"

"It will be near the wall, at its base most likely. My eagle is searching. The creatures will soon be found. When they are, we must be ready. I will take the eastern edge. You take the west. Look for the eagle's signal."

Weston cleared the area again with a sweep of his blade. "I would generally kill anyone that tried to give me such orders." Weston smirked. "You are one of Coal's men indeed. I will head to the western edge. Do you need reinforcements?"

Kaleb swiftly cut down two men at once with his hand blades. "I will be fine," he smiled back. "I have fought them before."

Up in the sky, Kyte was circling the *Fionetta* looking for its weakness.

Hundreds of Davati soldiers fired at him from the deck. None of the arrows reached him. There were too many of them to try to break into the bridge and bring it down manually. He would need to do it from the outside. It was such a massive ship, so he was unsure if even his magic could damage it. He changed directions and soared up underneath the hull. The turbulence from the four giant engines made it difficult to fly. He could feel a disturbing presence in the air and looked up into the cores of the engines.

"Natural energy," he whispered. "They have somehow harnessed it in the engines. How is that possible?"

An arrow went whizzing by his face and Drek reared back in surprise. Kyte nearly lost his balance and fell. He looked back up at the ship. It was not possible. He had never heard of natural energy being used in such a way. Even if the humans were able to detect the energy, it could not be sustained outside of the natural flows within Paks. If any energy was separated from the flow, it quickly withered and disappeared. Yet, these humans were able to contain it within this machine. There was no connection to the flow.

He brushed the thought from his mind. That is not what he was here to do. He must find a way to stop the ship, or else the battle would never end. Suddenly a disturbing thought came to his mind. If the ship crashed and the energy broke containment, it could cause a catastrophic explosion. The kind of energy required to hold up such a ship could lay waste to the entire landscape.

Kyte knew that as long as the ship was in the air, it posed a threat to the Creed. He would have to bring it down slowly and away from the battlefield. There was no way into the bridge and he dared not use his magic with the chance of causing a reaction with the engines. There was only one way. The magic must be drained from the engines. If he could draw out enough, it would no longer be able to stay afloat and would drift to the ground. That amount of energy could rip him apart, though, and he was unsure of the stability of it. But, if he did nothing, his friends would perish and everything they fought for would be for naught.

Drek flew underneath the front starboard engine, flapped his wings, and hovered. Kyte stood up on the eagle's back and reached his hands above his head. He searched for the energy, grasping for it with his own. It was trapped in the manmade enclose and circulating endlessly in a loop.

They have created an artificial flow, Kyte realized.

He drew up energy from Paks and thrust it into the engine's flow, simultaneously pulling energy away. He needed to reconnect the ship's energy to that with the natural stream. But, in order for that to happen, he would need to be the conduit. He would need to feed all of the energy through his own body.

The sudden surge in energy in the core shook the ship and the bow rose up. Every Davati froze in panic. Some of the men that stood on the edge, firing their arrows down at the circling eagles, lost their balance and plummeted. They did not know what was happening. None knew how the ship flew; that there was energy in the engines. It was one of the closest guarded secrets in all of Paks. What they did know, was that if the ship crashed, it would be disastrous.

The energy was immense. What Kyte felt was extraordinary pleasure and pain all at once. His body was burning with intense fury. Kyte felt as if he could lift a mountain, but would rip to shreds if he even moved an inch. Air started to build up around him and circulate. Energy was seeping from his body. It was too much. He had been warned of putting limits on his magic. His grandparents had told him of the dangers of it, but he never listened. If this continued, there would surely be a catastrophic release and everything would be razed. Kyte focused his mind and thought back to his childhood. He pictured his friends, his grandparents, and everyone in his clan. He remembered the pain of watching the last of them die and the loneliness that followed. He would never let that happen again. There was no way in Paks that he was going to lose the ones he cared for again.

One of the eagles let out a piercing screech, which caused Kaleb to spin around quickly. It was circling above the far edge of the wall, inside the trees. It had found something. Kaleb quickly dashed off in that direction. As he moved closer, he spotted the dark form of a creature on the edge of the trees. The eagle circled lower towards it, but suddenly vines shot out from the sides of the wall and closed in around its body. It screeched in panic. Kaleb fired an arrow at the figure and it dove to the side to avoid it. That gave the eagle an opening to pull itself free and fly to a safe distance.

Kaleb approached the figure warily; his blades drawn. Without warning, the Tellurian burst from the trees and launched itself on top of the young gallant. It moved with tremendous speed and thrust a small dagger straight at Kaleb's chest. Luckily, Kaleb had just enough of an opening to bring up his arm guard in defense. The fight moved so quickly that if you blinked you may have missed it. Kaleb's hand-to-hand fighting style was able to match each of the Tellurian's fast movements. Unable to use its magic, the Tellurian was forced to fight on even ground with Kaleb. The odds were in Kaleb's favor. He now had enough experience fighting against the creatures to know how they fought. Without their magic, they were predictable and all fought in much the same fashion. It did not take long before the edge of his blade found its mark.

Weston was battling with a Tellurian on the western edge when the earth shook violently. Turning, he watched as the far end of the wall started to collapse. Weston smiled and said, "Nice job, kid." Sections of earth the size of houses crumbled to the ground and fell amongst the battle. The Tellurian panicked and smashed his hands to the ground, chanting under its breath. The deterioration of the wall slowed, but such force could not be stopped for long. Eventually, the Tellurian accepted defeat and released the spell. The whole wall began to disintegrate and crumble down onto the battlefield. Soldiers on the ground abandoned the fight and just ran for their lives. Large masses of earth crushed men as they fled.

In the confusion, Weston had taken his eyes away from his enemy. Vines grabbed him by the ankles and arms. The Tellurian then quickly darted forward and thrust its dagger into the General's side. It had missed the heart, but it had found its mark. Weston gasped. A sudden rush of adrenaline went through him. His hand struck out and grabbed the smiling Tellurian around the neck. The Tellurian squirmed under the Creed's immense strength. With an effortless squeeze of Weston's hand, the Tellurian fell silent. Weston tossed the limp body to the side just before the vines released him and he fell to the ground. The battle continued to rage all around him.

After the initial shock of the wall collapsing, the Valor Forces strengthened their line and started to push back again. The Creed's number was now less than a thousand men, but they continued to fight hard. There was a renewed vigor in the soldiers and they would not retreat. Numbers meant nothing to them. It was a battle of attrition.

A short time later, everyone was knocked flat by a sudden burst of wind that came from the direction of the *Fionetta*. The ship shook and the bow dipped violently. The glow from the front starboard engine extinguished in a bright burst of light. Then the ship started to descend and drift north, away from the battlefield. Everyone on board was frantically running around, trying to figure out the cause of their predicament but, no matter what they did, the ship continued to fall. Everyone on the ground watched as the great ship drifted off into the distant darkness.

Minor Fanix, who had sat upon his horse at the rear of the battle, watched in horror as his prized machine limped away into the night. Everything had suddenly turned for the worse; the appearance of eagles, the collapse of the wall, and now this. His prized possession was gone. Fera would surely come to ruin because of his failure. He trembled at the thought of what the Grand Master would do to him. He just sat in a daze as his men ran past him in retreat. They had thrown down their weapons in panic. It did not matter that they still had a larger force. Their two greatest weapons had failed them, so their courage failed as well. The battle was over.

"General!" bellowed Rouse. He had witnessed Weston's fight unfold from a distance and finally fought his way to him. He ran up to Weston and turned him over. Blood was beginning to soak through his uniform. "Are you alright, Sir?"

Weston coughed against the cold air. "Quit your worrying, Rouse. I have had worse injuries sparring with my nephew. I was just taking a well-deserved rest that is all."

Rouse was relieved. "The ship has been brought down. The enemy retreats. Do we follow?"

"No, Captain. There has been enough bloodshed for one day," Weston said as he slowly got to his feet. "Tend to the wounded. The Brivan wounded as well. They are no longer our enemy." He picked up his sword and straightened himself up. "And bring me the Aerious."

"The battle is over, Sir."

"For us, it is over. For others, it is just beginning."

61

The sound had drained from the room. At least that is what it seemed like to Farren. He did not hear the Grand Master cackle cheerfully. He did not hear Coal's hysterical, pleading shouts. The only sound that he heard was that of Kara's final gasps for breath. They had been repeating in his mind, over and over. The injustice of it all was what drove Farren mad. Kara had done nothing. She was innocent, yet she was the one that now lay motionless on the floor at the feet of the Grand Master. Her eyes were still open and they stared right through him.

He had come so far and fought so hard, but he still was not strong enough to protect those that he wanted to protect. He had travelled to magical lands, climbed a mountain, and fought Magi, but he was not any stronger than he was before. His mind flashed back to the day when she was taken from him. It was much the same feeling, but now he knew that there was no saving her. First it was his parents, then Bishop, now this.

Will I ever get stronger? Will I just go through life as a child, constantly being a burden on those around me?

Farren looked back into Kara's empty, green eyes. No matter how much Coal shouted and begged, those eyes no longer moved. They no longer had the same glimmer they had when she would laugh and look at you with her usual joyful smile. Coal could no longer hold in his emotions, so tears starting streaming down his face. The mixture of sadness, confusion and anger was draining him. Farren could not take it any longer either. This had to stop. *Not anymore. I will not let anyone else get hurt.*

The young Prince pulled violently against the vines that bound him. The Grand Master just looked at him and continued to laugh. No matter how much Farren tried, he could not break free, but that did not stop him. It felt as if he would pull his arms clear from his body. A few vines ripped under his strength, but the Grand Master quickly replaced them. The Tellurian would not allow this enjoyable moment to end. It seemed clear that Farren's attempt at freedom was futile but, just before it seemed as if he would collapse to the floor in exhaustion, something unexplainable happened. The vines burst into dust and drifted to the floor.

Farren went crashing forward onto the ground. After the sound of his fall faded, the room fell silent. Coal stopped his emotional rage and the Grand Master's joyful cackling ceased. They all stared down at the young prince to see what would happen next. Farren slowly got to his feet, still stunned from his sudden freedom and crash to the floor, and picked up his swords. The Grand Master, not wanting to look foolish, attempted to bind him again, but the moment the vines broke free of the floor, they disintegrated. No matter how much the Grand Master tried, his magic would not work. Farren rushed at him, swords drawn. For a moment, the Grand Master felt a hint of fear. He was weaponless and without magic. Farren was on him in a second and his blade flashed quickly towards him. In the last moments, the other Tellurian stepped in his way. Farren's sword buried deep into the creature's chest.

Taking that brief window of opportunity, the Grand Master threw them both to the side and scrambled to reach his spear. Farren pulled his sword from the dead Tellurian and got to his feet. He did not bother to chase after him. Instead, he knelt down and cradled Kara's head. Her long beautiful brown hair lay lifeless and her stunning green eyes were hidden by unmoving lids. "I'm sorry," he whispered to her. That was all he could say.

Coal's bindings had also fallen free in the confusion and he rushed over to their side. He grabbed Kara from Farren's arms and hugged her tight. His tears had dried, but his trembling voice showed his emotion. "No, no, no, please. It can't be. Kara please; no. Sister, wake up." Her body stayed still.

Looking at Coal, the protector or Valoria, Farren made a realization. It did not matter to Farren what he was, or whose duty it was to protect. He had failed to protect Kara and he would never forgive himself for it. All he could do now was make sure that it would never happen again. "Get her out of here. Do not let that bastard lay another finger on her."

"What? What do you mean?" Looking into the Prince's eyes, Coal realized what he intended to do. "I do not know what happened just a moment ago, but it does not matter. You cannot take him on your own, Farren. I cannot leave you here alone."

"Yes you can, Coal. You must get Kara out of here. I will stall him as long as I can. We are both alone now, Coal. She is all that matters. If it was my brother, you would do the same."

There was something in Farren's expression that exhumed confidence in Coal. Farren was far stronger than before, but it would not be enough. He knew that he should not leave the Prince, but he could not leave his baby sister there either. Grudgingly, he lifted Kara in his arms. "I will be back. Do not die without me, you fool. We will leave here together. Do you understand me?"

Farren nodded. "I do not intend to die here, Coal."

With that, Coal lifted Kara and sprinted out the door to find a safe place for his sister's body.

After watching Coal leave the room, Farren turned back to the Grand Master, who stood warily in the middle of the room. He was still confused from the moment before. Whatever happened, he could not explain it. Now, though, he had his spear pointed towards Farren and was beginning to get irritated by their disregard of him. "Enough of this," the Grand Master shouted. "We will finish this now. I am no longer getting any enjoyment out of this charade."

"I could not agree more. Let us end this."

The Grand Master rushed Farren with an animalistic howl. The room echoed with the sounds of their shouts and the clash of metal on spear. Farren fought with a renewed vigor and a confidence that had long slept inside him. He no longer thought about each thrust and attack, or every lesson he was taught. He just battled with intensity and instinct. Despite Farren's courage, the Grand Master seemed unscathed. Sweat dripped from his brow and his breathes were heavy, but he showed no sign of wearying.

Farren picked up the intensity. The prince was not about to let this creature walk away clean. He drove back the Tellurian and put him on his heels. With Farren's two blades he had a perfect defense, but he could not manage to land a clean blow against the Grand Master's long spear. They moved swiftly around the room, circling, parrying and bounding towards and away from one another.

The Grand Master's mind was still filled with doubt. Farren was but a child only weeks ago, yet he was somehow fighting him quite evenly. No human could go through such a change so quickly, it was not possible. And there was his magic. Somehow the boy had neutralized it. He did not dare attempt to use it in the heat of battle and take the chance it would not work again. The Grand Master would have to do without it. The sun was now completely set and there was only a slight blaze left in the sky. Glow lights illuminated the room slightly, but there was a darkness that hung over them. Soon it started to become difficult for either of them to see the other's movements. The end would come soon. In such fading light, the final blow would be thrown.

Suddenly, the chamber reverberated with the sound of the Grand Master's spear clattering to the floor. Then, there was a loud grunt, as the Grand Master drove a swift kick into Farren's stomach. The prince was momentarily stunned, but quickly chased after the Grand Master as the Tellurian scrambled to regain his spear. The Grand Master grabbed the spear and turned his head. In that moment, he knew that there was not enough time to defend himself. Farren was already on top of him. He did the only thing he could. The Tellurian thrust his magical energy into the ground and a wall of wooden bars shot up from the floor. Farren crashed into them, his sword point falling just inches short of his mark.

The sudden collision knocked Farren from his fighting focus. He tried to break his way through, but the bars would not budge. The Tellurian's magic had returned it seemed. With a renewed smirk, the Grand Master surrounded Farren with a wooden cage before the boy was able to force his way around. His blades panged uselessly off of the hardened wood. The Grand Master jabbed at him with the butt of his spear, as if he was an out of control, caged animal. Soon he started to calm his actions, but the fire in his eyes still raged on.

"This is exactly how you humans should be; in a cage, like animals," said the Grand Master with a growl. "That is what you are to us. You do not have the right to call yourself Regii, or leaders. This is not your kingdom to control. Your infection of Paks has come to an end."

Farren pressed himself up against the bars and glared back at him. "What gives *you* the right to make that decision? You are not the ruler of this land. You fought and you failed to take it centuries ago and now it is ours by conquest. You speak of rights, but you have none. You never did."

"By conquest?!" the Grand Master screamed back at him. "By conquest? You took the spoils of war without ever lifting a finger. You were like rats, picking the bones of the dead. You hid in the corner until there was no one else to fight. Do not talk to me about conquest. The Tellurians fought for centuries against the oppressive Ignati and their Aerii pets. We roamed this land long before all else even came into existence. They took the land from us in the beginning. Now you dare to stake your claim without even knowing its true worth."

"I do not care about the land. I only care about the ones I love that tread upon it, and you have taken them all from me," Farren yelled. "I do not fight for the land. I fight for the people. You can have the damn land."

Farren quickly swiped out with one of his swords and caught the Grand Master off guard. It grazed against the brown, scaled skin and left a slight cut. The Grand Master went into a rage, batted away the swords and reached through the bars to grab Farren by the neck. His grip was firm and the prince gasped for air. Farren's strength left him quickly and his other sword clattered to the floor. The Grand Master was finished fooling around. It would end now. He squeezed even tighter and Farren's vision started to blur.

"Where is your protector? Who will save you this time?" said the Grand Master.

In his waning seconds, Farren's life flashed before him, clear and vivid. He saw his mother and father sitting regally on their thrones. He saw Kara running happily through the open fields outside the city. Her hair was blowing in the wind and she was laughing. Then he saw his brother. Bishop stood above him, powerful and strong. He put his hand on Farren's head and mussed his hair, as he always did when he wanted to reassure him. Farren's heart quickened and tears started to stream down his cheeks. His mind returned to the real world and his vision was blurred again, but he saw in front of him his brother's face. It was not friendly, but stern and emotionless.

"Brother?" he said.

The Grand Master laughed. "Foolish child, your brother is dead. And soon you will be."

Farren's eyes widened. "Brother!" he forced through the Grand Master's firm grip.

The Grand Master stopped his laughing and turned, following the prince's astonished face. His gaze soon stopped when it was met by a pair of fiery red eyes. "Impossible," he whispered. Before he could react, a shocking force smashed into his face and, in a burst of flames, his body went crashing into the far wall. The whole room shook violently and it seemed as though the ceiling would come down around them. Farren's body fell limp to the floor and the cage around him burst into dust. Overwhelmed by pain, Farren fell unconscious.

A few moments later, the Grand Master pulled himself up from the rubble and looked back towards the middle of the room. His body was battered, bloodied and bruised, and a scorch mark ran across his temple, but his anger was overcoming his pain. In the low light he could see the form of a man.

"Who are you?!" the Grand Master screamed.

62

nearly everything in the room had gone dark, except the few glow lights along the wall. The throne room was never used at night, so there was no need for light. Despite the lack of light, the shadowed figure that stood above Farren's limp form seemed to have a glow about it. Even though the figure stared right back at him, the Grand Master could not make out who it was. It was a man, that was certain, but the face he saw just moments earlier could not be true. It was only for a second and the light was poor. At least, that is what he told himself.

He shouted, "Who dares strike the Grand Master? Show yourself, or die where you stand."

The figure slowly started to move towards him, but he never made a sound. It was as if they floated across the ground. A chill ran up the Grand Master's spine, but he masked his fear. The man's face soon came into the light and the Grand Master roared in fury. "It is not possible. You are dead. I killed you myself."

The man's hair was long and the color of rich amber. It was pulled back in a loose tie. His face was covered with a rough beard, as if he had been in the wild for ages. In contrast to his haggard appearance, he wore a striking black cloak with a grey leather tunic that spoke of immense nobility. Despite all of this, the Grand Master only saw his face. Even through the thick beard he recognized it. It was a face he had seen in the mirror for months, but now it again stood in front of him as a face that was not his own; a face that he had stolen. It was the face of Bishop Kaiser.

The Grand Master continued his rampage. "You are dead at the bottom of a ravine. I watched you fall from the cliff with a poisoned needle in your chest. No human could survive such a height. My men said they saw your body. It cannot be. Who are you?" The man said nothing. He just stood with a cold stare. "Answer me!" the Grand Master bellowed.

In the blink of an eye, the man launched himself forward at an inhuman speed. In three powerful bounds he was at the Tellurian and, with one punch, the Grand Master was doubled over, coughing and vomiting on the floor. It was like a giant had struck a hammer into his stomach. He could hear the man's silent breathing above him, but the Tellurian could not move. Before the man could make another attack, spikes shot up from the ground under his feet, forcing him to retreat back.

The Grand Master calmed his breathing and forced himself back up. The man was just calmly standing a short distance away, staring back at him.

"Now, I know for sure," said the Grand Master. "You cannot be Bishop. No human has this kind of power. Those eyes; they are filled with fire. I have not seen the likes of them for six hundred years. You are Ignati." The man still stayed silent. "You do not need to say it. I know it is true. Those same eyes have haunted me since I last saw them. You look so much like the human, it is uncanny. You surprised me at first, but that will not happen twice. I will not allow your kind to stand in our way again."

In that moment, they heard the shouts of Coal come from down the hall. The fierce attacks from the mysterious man had shaken the entire palace and the Commander had raced back to see what was the commotion.

As he entered the room, his voice was clear. "Farren!" He feared for the worst and, when he saw the prince's body on the floor, his shouts became hysterical once again. He ran over and grabbed the boy. "Farren, are you alright? Wake up." A few moments later, Farren's eyes opened. His head ached and his vision was still blurred, but Coal's face was distinguishable.

"Coal?" he groaned.

"Yes, it is me. Are you alright? What happened?"

"My brother; he came to save us."

Coal did not know what to say. "Farren, Bishop is dead. He is not here."

"No, he is here." Farren sat up slowly. "Look," he said, pointing towards the middle of the room.

The mysterious man's back was turned, but there was something about him that seemed familiar. His hair was different, his build was stronger and his clothes were dark, but there was an aura about him that Coal had seen before. "Bishop? Is that really you?"

The man's head turned slightly. Coal caught a fleeting glimpse of his lifelong friend. Coal's astonishment was cut short, when the floor erupted around the man. Hundreds of vines exploded from the ground and grabbed hold of him. For some reason, the man did not fight back. It took only seconds before the man disappeared below a mountain of vines; his face as calm and impassive as it had been when he entered the room. When the vines had stopped growing, it looked as if an Everwood had grown in the middle of the room. There was no sign of the mysterious man.

"No!" screamed Farren, as he leaped to his feet and ran over to the mound of vines. He pounded against the wood. "Brother, can you hear me?"

The Grand Master laughed at the boy. "Thank you, child. Both of you, thank you. Because of you, I have, once and for all, slain the dreaded Ignati. Your final hope is gone. There will be no more surprise interruptions."

Farren's head lay rested in the bed of vines and tears were racing down his face. It was one thing to take away his brother, but quite another to do it again. He could take it no longer. He wanted it to be over. Just before he collapsed to the floor in defeat, his hand felt warmth. The vines were beginning to heat up. He backed away quickly. Then there was a deep rumble in the floor.

The Grand Master's cackling quickly stopped. Each one of them stood confused and in awe. The mountain of vines started to glow red and smoke rose out of cracks in the foliage. Retreating back and muttering under his breath, the Grand Master could not believe what was happening. The wood started to catch fire and burn away. The leaves burst into ash. Soon, there was just an intense ball of flame circling in the room. No matter how far back they stood, the blaze was too intense. Just before the heat seemed like it would seer off their flesh, the inferno disappeared, like a candle blowing out in the wind. At the center stood the man; seemingly unharmed. Not even his clothes showed signs of damage.

"But why!?" the Grand Master bellowed. "Why must you always get in our way?" The Tellurian could not control himself. He had retreated back up the stairs towards the throne. His sanity had reached its limit. The man started to walk towards the Grand Master, which provoked even more shouting and madness from the Tellurian. "Stay away from me, demon. Do not come any closer."

At the top step, the Grand Master stumbled. Before he could even regain his footing, the man had a grip around his neck. The strength of the man was incredible as he lifted him from the ground. The Grand Master could barely breathe and, even then, it seemed as if the man was holding back. He gazed into the Grand Master's fearful eyes and spoke. It was the first time that he had even made a sound, and his voice was eerily familiar.

"In the name of Kep, the left hand of the Almighty and King of Aliis, I condemn you to suffer pain, as you have made others suffer it." His hand glowed red and the body of the Grand Master squirmed in pain. The fire quickly ceased, but the Grand Master continued to struggle to free himself. "Experience fear, as did your enemies." The man drew a shining blade from his sheath. Seeing it, the Grand Master's eyes widened, but his struggles meant nothing. "And feel death, as your victims felt it." Farren and Coal could hear the Grand Master's gurgling cries of fear, but could make out none of the words. For a brief second, Coal felt a bit of pity for him, but it disappeared quickly. With one swift motion of the sword, the Grand Master fell limp in the man's grip.

He was cast aside, like trash at the foot of the throne. The room went silent. All that could be heard was the buffeting of the wind against the stained glass windows. Farren and Coal stood in amazement. They were not sure if they should cheer, or run. This new stranger had dealt with a creature that nearly killed them both, as if it was an ant. Their awe was mixed with fear. They did not know what to think.

Farren crept his way forward and said, "Brother, is that you?"

The man used the edge of his cloak to wipe the blood from his blade and then returned it to his sheath. He silently walked down the steps and towards the two men. Farren and Coal looked at him intensely, trying to find any sign of the man they once knew, but he gave them none. The man stayed silent and avoided their suspicious gazes. He passed by them both, without acknowledging Farren's words. There stood a man that the boy knew in his heart was his brother, but he acted a stranger. The Prince was stunned silent and could not react.

Coal, though, did not hold in his emotions. "Answer your brother!" he yelled. The man stopped, but did not turn.

"I know it is you Bishop," Coal persisted. "Your voice is unmistakable, even if everything else has changed. I do not know what has happened to you, where you have been, or even what you have become, but the Bishop I know would not let his brother suffer like this. The Bishop I knew loved his brother."

For seconds there was silence. The room seemed to darken even more as they all just stood there. Then the man hung his head and continued to walk away.

Coal raced forward and said, sternly, "He killed her. He killed Kara, your wife. She is gone, Bishop."

Again the man stopped. The words hung in the air. This time he turned his head slightly. "I know," he responded.

"If you were here, you could have saved her. You could have saved everyone."

After a long pause, the man responded. "And where were you?"

The words struck Coal so hard he lost his breath. His strength drained from him and he dropped to his knees. It was the finishing blow. To know it himself was one thing, but to hear someone else tell him how he had failed, especially his lifelong friend, was more than he could handle. His weakness had killed his sister. It was like a knife to his heart.

During Coal's silence, the man had walked to the door and Farren tried to chase after him.

"Please do not go, brother. I need you here. We all need you."

"Farren, stop," muttered Coal. "That is not your brother; at least not anymore. If there was any part of your brother in that man, it died long ago."

And with those words, the visage of Bishop Kaiser walked from view. The man had saved the kingdom, but there were no smiling faces following after him. This story would never be told at bedtimes. No one would ever know what had happened here and, the mysterious man would never be seen in Valoria ever again.

63

The sun had risen on a new day in the Waning Highlands. It was still early in the morning, but there was not a cloud in the sky and the rich glow warmed the bodies of every man still standing. The air was chill, but hearts were warm and light. The death toll was high, but these were Creed, not young boys. This was their life. They felt sadness for their lost comrades, but victory made the sacrifices worth cheering for, not wept for. Spirits were high and laughter had already returned to the men.

They had spent much of the night and the morning picking up the pieces of battle. With the scale of the carnage and the distance from the city, the normal customs of burial were not possible. Instead, each man was buried where he lay, with his weapon placed upon his chest. There were no markers for the graves or elaborate ceremonies. The victory in battle was worth more than solemn words said over a gravestone. The digging continued and probably would continue for some time. Shovels were sparse and bodies were plenty.

The few remaining Brivan and Davati soldiers were stripped of their weapons, but left unharmed. Their wounds were treated and they were fed well. Despite the nice treatment, there were still few words exchanged between soldiers of opposing sides. Free food and bandages did not cure decades of distrust and hatred, even if the feelings were not quite understood. The Brivans and Davati were allowed to bury their own dead as they pleased, as well. Their demeanor was not quite as cheerful, but the manual work, despite its purpose, did much to keep their minds off of the loss.

Minor Fanix and many of the surviving forces had escaped in the night and General Lockhardt had no interest in following. Without his ship, Fanix was of no concern and, if all went well, the Brivans would not be an enemy for much longer either. During the night, when the excitement of battle had started to fade, Weston's thoughts shifted to Coal and the fight he knew would be raging in Valoria. If Coal had failed, there may be another battle for them to fight soon. The thought did not soothe the General. Usually, the idea of the Commander losing a fight was absurd, but even the Creed needed divine help to find victory this time.

Did divine help come to Coal's aid as well? Weston had pondered.

Despite his weariness, these thoughts kept Weston up much of the night. Rather than lay in bed, he had joined some of his men in digging graves, which brought his mind a brief respite. Now, in the light of the morning, he was eating breakfast and talking with his captains. Sleep was a luxury as a soldier. He had learned to go without it long ago.

"Sir, we found the ship early this morning," Pion informed him. "It had drifted for nearly twenty miles before coming down gently in a forest just north of the Morian River."

"Did you encounter any resistance from the survivors?"

"At first, yes, but we took some Davati with us to ensure their cooperation. I left fifty of our men there to take care of the wounded and help them return to the camp."

Weston gulped down his cup of water and wiped his face clean. After putting his plate down he said, "How is the ship? Is she salvageable?"

"The Davati soldiers would not let us near her, Sir. Their only request, in return for their cooperation, was that we would leave the ship alone. Seeing as their numbers were far greater, we agreed to the request. From what I could see, though, she looked in fair condition, considering what had happened. There was considerable frame damage from the landing, put the engines looked intact, aside from the one that failed. I believe there is much to learn from it."

"Excellent," smiled Weston. "My father will be pleased. He has been obsessed with the technology for some time. When should we expect the remaining soldiers to return to camp?"

"If all goes smoothly, by sunset. Most of the survivor's injuries were psychological. It is not often you fall from the sky in an out of control city," Pion said with a smirk.

A Creed soldier walked up and saluted them both before speaking. "Sir, the Aerious has woken."

"Thank you, soldier," he smiled. The General slowly pushed himself up from his seat with a groan. The soldiers all moved to help him, but he waved them off. His side was bandaged where the knife had stabbed him, but the General had refused any special treatment, aside from that. "Return to your duties, men. Prepare for the arrival of the ship's soldiers. I want everyone with a place to sleep tonight."

With a quick salute, he walked off to find Kyte.

After the battle had abated the night before, the search for Kyte did not take long. He was found laying in the open field, with Drek standing watch over him. When the men approached, the giant eagle reacted with ferocity, and would not let anyone near. They finally had to bring Kaleb over to calm him. Kyte was then brought back to camp and put to rest in the General's tent. Physically he seemed to be fine, but there was something wrong with him that was beyond any of the Creed's understanding. His awakening was a joyful relief.

Upon entering the tent, Weston was greeted with a pleasant sight. Kyte was sitting up and eating normally, as if nothing had happened. The Aerious acknowledged him with a cheerful hello, then continued to eat.

"It is good to see you awake, friend," said the General.

"It is good to be awake," Kyte smiled. "I assume that victory has been had. The battle is over?"

"Thanks to you, yes. When the *Fionetta* started to fall from the sky, their retreat was immediate. It was as if they had seen a ghost," chuckled Weston. "How do you feel?"

"Better than ever. I think I just needed the rest. I have been on a long journey since this whole saga began. Now it is finally over."

As Weston sat down next to the Aerious, he suddenly realized that there was something different about him. He seemed paler, and his hair had lost some of its blue hue. Kyte noticed the General's stare and simply smiled.

"It is that obvious, is it? I was hoping that it would slip undetected, but alas, it was bound to happen eventually."

"What do you mean?"

Kyte got to his feet and started to pace the room. "Do you remember during the battle, there was a great gust of wind?"

"Yes, of course. It was right after that that the ship started to fall."

"Exactly. That gust of wind was from a surge of energy that exploded out of me. It took the form of wind because that is my power, but the energy itself came from the *Fionetta*. I do not know if you are aware, but the ship's engines are powered by natural energy."

"How is that possible?" Weston said with eyes widened. "To control energy is one thing, but to harness it is something far different."

"I do not know how they did it, but there was a large amount of energy captured in each engine. That is why I could not just simply destroy the ship. If the engines themselves were damaged and the energy released, it would have killed us all. Instead, I was forced to drain the energy from an engine and bring the ship down slowly."

"Incredible," Weston said in awe. "So, what happened then? The ship was brought down and you seemed unharmed, yet you were unconscious."

"The energy was more than I could handle. That gust of wind was the energy breaking containment. Luckily I had drained most of it, otherwise I would not be here. But...." He paused for a brief moment and seemed uncertain what to say. "The energy did not kill me, but it did leave its mark. As you have noticed, I have lost much of my luster," he said, flowing his fingers through his hair. "My link to the natural flow has been broken. I can no longer feel its presence."

Weston was astonished. "Are you saying you are incapable of using magic?" Kyte nodded. "Is it permanent? Will you be able to regain it?"

"It will take time, but yes, I will. Contrary to man's belief, Magi are not born with the ability to use magic. Magic is a learned art, just like anything else. It can fade and even disappear over time, but one can always relearn it."

"That is good news to hear. You have given up much for us and yet we barely know each other. I do not know if I would have done the same for a stranger. For a Magi to give up his magic must be a devastating sacrifice," said Weston.

"It is, yes. A Magi's worth has always been measured by his magic. A Magi without magic was not a Magi at all. But, that was then, this is now. Among humans I am the peculiarity. Not having magic will not ruin me. In fact, a life without magic for a while might be exactly what I need. It will be interesting to see how a human lives," chuckled Kyte.

"I am glad you think so," smiled Weston. "Do not get too comfortable. I hope that you recover it quickly. A strong hand such as yours is always needed in Paks. In return for your sacrifice, I can only extend to you my deepest gratitude. You are always welcome in Coroge, whenever you wish to visit."

"Thank you, Weston. I would like that very much. I think I have spent too much time hidden away in the Shroud. There is much of this world I have yet to see."

"You are a brave man, Kyte Valen. Even amongst Creed, you are a warrior beyond measure."

"Might I remind you," said Kyte. "That I am not a man." The Aerious smiled.

"Yes, you are right," said Weston. "But, you are more of a man than you might think for a while."

Their raucous laughter could be heard throughout the camp as soldiers toiled away to pick up the pieces of the largest battle of that age. That night, the men would sleep well. All the dead were buried and the next day the Davati soldiers would start their long and painful march home. The remaining Brivan soldiers would join with the Creed and march on Valoria. They were not sure what they would find when got there, but Creed did not leave a fight unfinished. Thus was the end of the Battle of Three Armies and the beginning of what became known as the Diamond Age.

64

For several days, the city of Valoria was silent; at least as silent as a city can be. The enormous battle in the square had left many of the towns' people wondering. Some had claimed they had seen a giant monster ripping down the buildings, other people said it was a tornado. Some even blamed the Creed and claimed that they had snuck into the city. All of this chatter ceased, when the rumor that the Supreme Regis had been assassinated came to light. There were murmurs and whispers about who the killer was, but none dared to cast blame on anyone for fear of retribution. The citizens were content to wait for the truth, something that Prince Farren had promised them.

It had taken time for Farren to recover from the past weeks. Physically, he had returned to his old self within a few days, but it took much longer before he was able to brush away the thoughts that circled in his mind. Even then, it was just temporary. There was no way that these feelings would ever pass for good. All he could do was move on and hope that his mind would fill with other things. Thankfully, the confusing dreams which had been haunting his nights had stopped, for now. He could never find a way to explain them, but he was certainly content with a few decent night's sleep.

The day after the fight with the Grand Master, they had received a message from Kyte that the battle against the Creed was over. They were victorious and Minor Fanix had slunk back to Fera. The Creed were marching to Valoria to bring aid, if it was needed. The news had lifted his spirits as he thought of how nice it would be to see Kyte and Kaleb once again. Although, this news also meant that he would need to speak to the citizens soon. If the Creed were seen marching on the city, the people would go into a panic. Coal had offered to make the proclamation, but Farren insisted that it be him. Besides, Coal was still a traitor in the minds of many of the Valorians.

Farren chose a sunny day. It was still late autumn, so it was cold, but none of the citizens seemed to mind. They all congregated at the base of the stairs leading to the palace grounds. Nearly the entire city came out that day to hear the young boy speak. A cloud of cold breaths hung over the mass of Valorians as they all whispered amongst themselves while waiting for the truth. When Farren finally took his place on the stage, the crowd went silent.

In the face of his apprehension, Farren spoke strongly and eloquently. He told them all the truth; at least all that was necessary. Since there were too many citizens that had witnessed the magical and unreal acts of the Tellurians, it was foolish to attempt to cover it up. He told them that all of the events of the past few weeks, starting with the attack on Bishop, were a part of a scheme devised by the late Councilman Datro. He had manipulated the Supreme Regis into releasing him and made him believe that it was the Creed who were responsible for his parents' death and the attack on him in the Shroud. The manipulating of Minor Fanix was also attributed to Datro. Nothing was spoken of the Grand Master and the plot that had occurred in the shadows.

The content of Farren's speech was planned out with council from Coal, Councilman Grey and Seno Pierson. Coal felt it necessary to have the political expertise of the Head Council in the discussion. Seno, upon hearing about the deaths of Syd and Kaine, had come to the palace of his own accord. It was Anton that recommended that he be a part of the discussion as well. His intimate knowledge of history and the Magi would be crucial. It took them days to come to an agreement on what was to be said and what was to be kept secret. To save Bishop's reputation and to prevent mass panic, his actions were deemed the consequence of Datro's manipulation, rather than that of a Tellurian imposter. In the end, Bishop was said to have been assassinated by Datro after discovering the plot. The Tellurians were not the masterminds of the scheme, but instead pawns of the scientist. Everything led back to Datro. The Davati, despite Minor Fanix's implicit role, were exonerated in order to prevent strife between the Sects.

To a politician, the contrived story was a work of art necessary to avoid panic and promote peace. To Farren, though, it was just a lie. He understood the reasons for it, but he was not pleased with brushing away the Grand Master's role in all of it. The creature was responsible for the death of many people that Farren loved, and it was as if he was going unpunished. Seno had told him that history was filled with evil doings that were disregarded for the benefit of the people. It was never the right thing to do, but it was necessary. It finally took Coal's comforting words to convince the young prince.

As Farren stood in front of the citizens and told his lie, he felt guilty, but also content. It was like he was bringing everything to a close. He was shutting the door on the evil that had enveloped his life for what seemed like ages. Even though he was erasing the acts of the Grand Master like they were just a nightmare, he would not allow those who had died to go unacknowledged. He took the time to speak emotionally about everyone who had sacrificed themselves. He spoke of Guy, Kaine, Syd, Kara and, of course, Bishop. He praised all of the soldiers, whether Brivan, Creed or Davati, who died in the battle that never should have occurred.

By the end of the speech, there was not a person in the crowd who did not have a tear running down their face. There were thousands who had lost a father, brother, or son. Everyone in Valoria had loved Bishop and the Lady Kara. Even as they cried and thought of their lost loved ones, the citizens of Valoria were in awe of the Prince's presence. He was no longer a naïve child. While they were burdened by past loss, the people's concern for the future was eased. This was a young man who could rule, just as his brother and father had. When Farren finally walked off the stage, he was followed by emotion-filled cheers.

The days following were better for the prince. A weight had been lifted from him. The energy of the people had returned. Even the palace was livelier. The servants, cooks and guards greeted Farren with smiles and laughs, instead of down-turned faces. He took time to walk through the grounds and even the bazaar; his old stomping ground. When the Creed arrived, Farren welcomed Weston with open arms. There was a small feast thrown in the General's honor and there was much merriment.

Only a few were invited, but it was a lively crowd. Coal was there, with Kaleb and Kyte. Anton and Seno arrived as well. Seno would never pass up an opportunity for free drinks. To Farren's surprise, Coal invited Reme and Dash, who were the cause of much of the raucousness. Weston arrived with his captains, Pion and Rouse. Even Ana, who brought with her Neesa and a handful of other girls from the tavern, was invited, much to the excitement of many of the men. At one point in the night, Farren looked around the room at the eclectic group of characters and thought to himself:

Would this sort of gathering be possible without the terrible events that had come before it? Does peace require war and death?

He brushed the thought aside. It did not matter. He was here now and, judging by the scene before him, the future looked bright. The gaiety lasted long into the night and, for a short moment, everyone seemed to forget their worries. It was a night that everyone needed and everyone enjoyed.

The only thing left to do to bring everything to a close was to crown the new Supreme Regis. The ceremony had been put on hold due to the unusual circumstances, but the citizens could not be kept waiting any longer. Preparations had started not long after Farren's speech and, only two days following Weston's feast, the event was held. Per tradition, it occurred in the palace throne room, which had taken weeks to return to its original glory. In preparation, palace servants spent days cleaning, decorating, and cooking. Rooms were prepared for all of the distinguished guests and the guards were quickly reminded of their responsibilities. Upon Farren's request, it would be the traditional ceremony with a small feast after.

For the first time in decades, the Minor of Coroge was in attendance. His arrival in Valoria was met with a mix of fanfare and contention. Many Valorians were happy to see a peace between the two sects, but others were not as forgiving.

The Minor himself could not have been more pleased to step into the capital city. He had spent much of his aging years regretting the relationship that had occurred because of his actions and hoping that he could see peace before his time on Paks was up. Farren was intrigued to meet the Minor, whom he had heard so much about. The night of Leo's arrival, he and Farren had spent hours just talking in Farren's chambers. Farren would later say that those few hours is where the foundation for his Regency was built. In those few hours, he had regained his strength again. What they talked about is anyone's guess.

The ceremony started in the early afternoon. The palace grounds were packed with people from all over Paks who had come to see the new Supreme Regis. Inside the throne room, the excitement was just as palpable. A select few dignitaries and friends were allowed to attend the ceremony. A long green runner was stretched on the ground that led from the door up to the throne. On either side, palace guards were stationed along its length and, behind the guards, stood the guests, who chattered anxiously among themselves. After a short time, a trumpet sounded and Farren entered.

The young prince was clad in the royal attire. A long green cloak trailed down his back, which covered the gray and green vest with the Kaiser crest embroidered on the chest. It was the same attire that Bishop had worn during his coronation, just tailored to the prince's size. He walked swiftly down the path towards the throne and stopped at the base of the stairs. Before him stood Anton, who smiled down at him.

"Welcome, Prince Farren. All those that stand before you are honored by your presence."

"And, I am honored by theirs," Farren said as he turned and smiled to everyone around him.

"This is a most joyous day for all of Paks. Although it represents the passing of a great man, it is also the beginning of something much greater," said Anton. "I have had the pleasure of seeing you grow up to be a fine man and I know that the kingdom will be in excellent hands. You are everything that your father and brother were, and more. Now, I know your distaste for ceremony, so I will make this brief."

Everyone in the room chuckled. Anton turned and received a sword from one of the guards. "Now, if you would please kneel," he said to Farren. He took the sword and pointed it at Farren's chest. "Do you, Farren Kaiser, swear upon your brother's sword that you will serve the kingdom with everything that you are?"

"I swear."

"Do you swear to protect all that dwell in its borders from harm?"

"I swear."

"Do you swear that if any of its citizens are in danger, you would give your life to keep them safe?"

"I swear," said Farren.

Then Anton took the sword and sliced it through the air just inches above Farren's head. "Remember this moment," Anton said. "Remember that the Supreme Regis is not above anyone. The Supreme Regis is just a man, as is everyone else. He only does what is best for them and does not reap anything for himself. The Supreme Regis is a servant and the people his master. Do you swear to serve the people in this manner?"

"I swear."

Anton sheathed the sword and lifted the royal crown up above Farren's head. "Then bow your head. With the power of the Head Council, I now decree you Supreme Regis of the Kingdom of Paks." He gently put the crown onto Farren's wavy locks. Farren rose to his feet. "Use this sword to protect the people as your brother did, and may your reign be long and recognized by a lasting peace."

With that, Anton got down onto one knee and bowed. Everyone else in the room followed. Farren unsheathed the sword and pointed it out into the room.

"Rise," said Farren. "Masters do not kneel before their servants. Neither do they kneel before their friends." Everyone in the room returned to their feet. "Many of you knew my father and all of you knew my brother. They were great men that can never be replaced. I cannot promise that I will be better than them, but I can promise that I will do everything in my power to try. We are long overdue for a true peace in Paks. I would like to make that happen, starting with the Creed." He looked over towards the Minor Leo and gave him a respectful nod. The aged Minor nodded back with a smile.

Farren sheathed his sword and walked up towards his throne. Behind the throne was a hallway that led out to the balcony and, at the door, stood Coal. He smiled as Farren approached.

"Excellent words," the Commander said.

"I was taught well," Farren responded.

The two men embraced as if brothers. They had been through much and it was all coming to a close. This was the start of a new story. Coal said to Farren, "Go say hello to your people, Your Highness. They are waiting for you."

"Stepping out onto the balcony, Farren was overwhelmed by the reaction. Cheers erupted from the thousands who swarmed down below him. There were so many, that he could not even see the grass under their feet. He waved his hand and they cheered even louder. The sound was almost deafening.

"You seem troubled," said Coal as he walked up behind Farren.

"Why would you say that?"

"I know you better than anyone, Farren. I know that you still dwell on the past. What has happened is a travesty, but nothing we do will undo it. We must stop looking back and start to look forward."

"They are all so happy," said Farren as he looked down at the crowd. "Yet they do not know the truth."

"Maybe that is why they are happy."

"Can you truly be happy in ignorance?"

"Everyone is ignorant of something, Farren. All that matters is that they are happy as they are now. Sometimes ignorance is better than truth, especially if the truth only leads to pain."

"But, what about brother and..."

"Bishop will be known for what he was," interrupted Coal. "He was a brave and loving man. That is how people will remember him. Kara, also, will be known for her kind heart and smiling face. Knowing how they died does not change that. Besides, *we* will know the truth. That should be enough."

The cheers from the crowd continued below, unabated. Despite its intensity, the noise was unheard by Farren as he thought of his brother. He thought of his parents and Kara, as well.

"I just wish they were here with us," he said.

"So do I," said Coal. "But, I know that they all would be proud of you, just as I am. You will be greater than all of them. I have faith."

Thus began the reign of Supreme Regis Farren Kaiser, 34th ruler of the Kingdom of Paks. His rule would be marked by a lasting peace between the four Sects of the Kingdom. He would be loved by many, hated by few. His adventures and gallantry would be known to all, from the far islands of Layalta to the deep jungles of Fera. The boy Regis would go down in history as more than just a fine ruler of men. But, that is another story, for another time. In this time, he is just a boy setting off on a new journey with a troubled mind, but an eager heart.

EPILOGUE

As he did more often than not, Seno Pierson was enjoying a nice drink; pintare on ice, his usual. This time, though, he was enjoying it in a different atmosphere. He sat back in his nice leather chair and picked up a book. Looking around at the hundreds of rows of shelves and texts, he smiled contently to himself.

Soon after Farren's coronation, Seno had been reinstated to his position as the head of the Valorian Historical Society. He was on the council again and was able to return to his office in the archives. He was so excited about the change, that he had not left the archives since his first day back, nearly one week ago. The mousy librarian, Poelis, had gladly greeted his return, as well. While sipping his drink comfortably, Seno was surprised by an unexpected visitor.

"I see you are enjoying reinstatement, Seno," said Farren, as he walked up behind the historian.

Seno nearly fell out of his chair in shock. It took him a moment to collect himself and get to his feet.

"Your Highness, it is not wise thing to come up behind a man while he is drinking. You might just make him waste some perfectly good pintare."

"I will keep that in mind for next time," said Farren with a smile.

"But, to answer your question, I am quite enjoying myself. I have you to thank for that enjoyment. No matter what I liked to tell myself, I truly missed this place."

"I loved to read as a child," said Farren. "Adventure stories were my favorite. They were always better when my father read them to me. They could take you away to such amazing, imaginary places."

"Some can take you to amazing places right here in Paks, from times long past. Books can do so many things. That is why I love them," said Seno. "If only there were more people who enjoy books as much as we do. They are an indispensable source of knowledge."

"I envy you, Seno. I wish that I could love my job as much as you."

And I wish that I could order around whoever I wanted, but alas I do not think that they will allow us to switch positions," chuckled Seno. "I do not think, though, that you just came down here to reminisce about old times, lad." He grimaced "I mean, Your Highness. Sorry, old habits die hard."

"You may call me whatever you please, Seno. I do not like the sound of Your Highness anyway. But, you are right, as always. As much as I would love to reminisce, I have other things to attend to. The life of the Supreme is not as glorious as people believe. I too wish I could switch positions sometimes," explained Farren. "You are correct, though. I came here to ask you about something."

"Something only a historian would know?"

"Something I hope a historian might know."

"Ah, excellent! Well, if there is a historian that might know it, I would be the historian to ask. Have a seat, Your Highness, and we can talk of history. Would you like a drink?"

"No thank you," said Farren. "I think it would be improper."

"But, you are the Supreme Regis, are you not? Nothing is improper for you," laughed Seno.

The boy could not help but smile as well. "Nonetheless, I think I will pass."

"Suit yourself. History is best heard and told with a drink in hand." He plopped himself down into his chair. "Now then, let me hear your question."

"I was wondering if you could tell me about a person named Kep. Are they an important human from history? I heard someone once call Kep the Left Hand of the Almighty. What does that mean?"

"Ahhh, you ask great questions, Your Highness. You also give me an opportunity to speak of older times, which I cherish doing. Kep was indeed an important figure in history, but he was no human. He was an Ignati; one of the first Ignati, according to our histories. You know of an Ignati, I assume?"

"Of course," said Farren. "They are the third, and said to be the strongest, of the Magi races."

"Quite right, Your Highness. Their magic consisted of flame. It was crude, but powerful. They were also immortal, unlike the Aerious and Tellurians, who just live extended lives."

"What is the Left Hand of the Almighty?"

"Interesting question. The Almighty, of course, is considered to be the god of Paks. He was the first of the Ignati and said to be the strongest. It was said that the Almighty gave life to the other Ignati. How he did, I do not know. The Almighty focused so much of his power on *giving* life, that his power to *take* it, eroded. He did not believe that magic was meant to harm but, of course, he needed to be able to keep the peace and enforce the law, so he created Kep. Kep is known as the Left Hand; The Destroyer. The Almighty was the Right Hand; The Creator. Together they ruled over Paks."

"Kyte told me once that The Almighty was killed by someone named Balin."

"Ah yes, Balin, the human Magi. It is a story told among the Magi. Some believe that Balin is now the god that looks over us, some do not. I myself do not put much merit in such a wild tale, but who am I to say what the truth is? The Magi have lived much longer than I and know much more."

"So, it is possible that this Kep could still be alive?"

"You are full of such interesting questions this evening, Your Highness," said Seno. "I suppose he could be. There are no records of his death, so it is possible. Judging by the events of late, I believe there are quite a few Magi still alive in this world. They just seem to want to go unnoticed."

"One final question and I will leave you to your work," said Farren "Kep is known as the King of Aliis. Is that a city of Paks I do not know of, or is it a place from the past? I have seen no mention of it on any maps."

"You will not find it on any maps, because it technically does not exist. Aliis, The Other World, The World Apart, The Kingdom of Ignati. Those are some of the names that it goes by. It is where the Almighty and all of the Ignati live. It is said that when Paks started to fill with all manner of creatures, the Almighty decided that there needed to be a separation between him and the rest of Paks. Therefore he put up a barrier; the strongest ever created. In essence it split Paks into two parts. Aliis is the land that he kept for himself and his Ignati. Paks he left for us."

"Can it be reached? Can you go there?"

Seno nearly spilled his drink he started laughing so hard. "Oh no, no, Your Highness. Aliis is not a place you can reach on your own. It is protected by powerful magic, unlike anything that still exists today. You cannot easily get through the door into Aliis."

"So, there is a door?"

"Actually two, I believe. But, they are not wood or metal doors. These are magic doors. They first must be found before you could ever think of opening them. They are invisible, just like the barriers you had to go through to enter the Forest of Rising Twilight. You cannot just knock and hope for an answer."

"But, if you could find a door, there is a chance that you could make it through?"

"You are an eager one, aren't you?" Seno chuckled. "I am not the one to ask about magic, lad. I only know what is told to me through books. If you truly want to know how to break through barriers, you might want to question your Aerious friend. But, do not get your hopes up. Aliis has been kept separate from Paks for a reason, lad. It is not a place for ordinary folk. We are meant to dwell there."

"But, what if you had to go? If there was no other way?" said Farren. His expression turned serious. "How would you get there? Do you know where one of the doors is?"

"I sense that I will not easily be able to dissuade you from your path, so I will not try. Coal told me you may come searching for information."

Farren stirred uncomfortably in his seat. He was about to say something when Seno interrupted him.

"Do not worry, though, I do not plan to get in your way. I just want to again warn you. You are a strong lad, but your experience with the Tellurians is nothing compared to what you would experience in Aliis. In Aliis you would only find pain. Ignati are far different creatures than what you have met. They have no remorse or emotion. They only do what they are ordered to do. It is not wise to meddle in their affairs." Seno shifted in his seat and took a sip from his drink. "That being said, I do not know where the doors are. Nobody does in this age. There are some that believe they do, but it has not been proven."

"Who?" urged Farren.

"The Gypsies of the Northern Sea, the Matroz. They have long believed that one of the doors lies on an island in the frozen wastelands far north of their domain in Layalta. In my opinion, they are crazed fools, but your quest is important to you, so I have told you all I know. I hope that helps."

"You have been more help than I could have asked for. Thank you, Seno, you are a good friend." Farren got up from his seat and brushed himself off. Seno rose to show him from the room. "I just have one final question," said the young Regis. "How do I get to Layalta?"

Edwards Brothers Malloy
Thorofare, NJ USA
April 13, 2015